I0692823

Xenotech
Queen's Gambit
A Novel of the Galactic Free Trade Association

Dedication

To my Muse...

I couldn't do this without you.

Cover design by Dan Paulson

Image of Spiral Galaxy M74
courtesy of NASA, ESA and the
Space Telescope Science Institute

ISBN 13: 978-0-692-54988-9

Spiral Arm Press
1725 Carlington Court
Grayson, GA 30017
www.spiralarmpress.com

Prologue

"He's everything you'd promised," said Shepherd, the grizzled wolf-like, bear-like, brown-furred Påkk.

"And everything I'd hoped for," said his human companion.

"His partner is something special, too."

The Påkk rubbed his chin.

"Absolutely," said the other, "but not unexpected. She takes after her mother."

"From what I know of humans," said Shepherd, "it looks like the beginning of a beautiful friendship."

The Påkk bared his teeth in what his species considered a smile. His companion smiled back.

"If they can survive the next week."

Chapter 1

"I fear all we have done is to awaken a sleeping giant and fill him with a terrible resolve."
— Admiral Isoroku Yamamoto

I woke up to the delightful sound of my partner's voice whispering my name.

"Jack. Jack. Get up, Jack."

Consciousness slowly seeped into my brain cells. I reached out an arm to cuddle with Poly, but she wasn't there.

"Jack. Jack. Earth to Jack."

It wasn't Poly. It was my phone using Poly's voice because that always got my attention.

"Jack, wake up! You've got a support call!"

Adrenaline flowed. I sat up quickly, and then realized that wasn't a good idea. My head reminded me I wasn't that far past having a concussion, and my ribs reminded me I'd been shot in the chest five times a month and a half ago. Why am I still alive? Bullet-proof vest, of a sort. Long story.

"What time is it?"

"Five-fifteen," said my phone, apologetically.

"In the morning? Who's calling at this hour?"

I swung myself around to sit up and noted a sharp, residual pain in my thigh from where I'd been clawed by a dinosaur— the same long story.

"Mike," said my phone, "from WT&F."

Widget Technology & Fabrication was one of my clients, or maybe I should say *our* clients, now that I've got a partner. I run a tech support company—for alien technology—called Xenotech Support Corporation. Ever since Earth joined the Galactic Free Trade Association there's been a lot of demand for our services.

"Hi, Mike," I said. "What is it *this* time? And why are you at work so early?"

Mike was the fab operator at WT&F and a good guy. He ran their Dauushan Model-43 large scale 3D printer.

"It's Jean-Jacques," he said, referring to the avaricious, corner-cutting CEO of WT&F. "A client provided a set of fabrication plans from that shady company."

"Factor-E-Flor?"

J-J had contractually agreed to have all his designs vetted by me before fabbing them. So much for that promise.

"Right. He had me start at midnight because his client wants delivery by noon."

"What does he have you fabbing?"

When Jean-Jacques Bonhomme had first used plans from Factor-E-Flor he'd ended up with a hundred thousand pink robot rabbit lawn mowers.

"I don't know," said Mike.

"What do you mean, you don't know? Wasn't there a summary description with the specifications?"

"Yes, but the specs are for household vacuum cleaner automatons with eight manipulator arms to dust and move furniture."

"And...?"

"It printed some of those, maybe fifty or so, then started spitting out component parts for something I don't recognize. The octovacs are fitting them together. It looks like the finished product will be really big."

"Just turn the unit off, then on again," I suggested.

It was a lame, patronizing suggestion, but I had an excuse. I'd been sound asleep sixty seconds earlier.

"I would, but the octovacs won't let me near the machine," said Mike.

"I'm beginning to see your problem."

I stood up—carefully—and headed toward the shower.

"I'm sorry to bother you, with you being banged up and all," said Mike.

I appreciated that he was concerned for my health. Like I said, a good guy.

"I'll be there in half an hour."

"Faster might be better."

Was that fear I heard in Mike's voice? Yeah, it was. This was more serious than he wanted to admit. When you've done tech support as long as I have, you know how to tell when clients are scared.

"Hang on, I'm on my way."

I skipped a shower and pulled on one of my corporate uniforms—khaki pants and a white Xenotech Support logo polo shirt. I picked up my backpack tool bag from its spot next to the front door and left. Trying to be smart about my injuries, I carefully walked across the dim apartment complex court-yard and through the security gate leading to the street. My van, summoned by my phone, was waiting for me. The sun wouldn't be up for an hour and a half.

"WT&F," I said, "and step on it."

"Seat belt," said my van.

I buckled up and we were off. What a way to start a Monday.

* * * * *

It didn't take long to get there. WT&F's building was a typi-cal two-story glass and steel-framed structure situated in an almost suburban Atlanta office park. Nothing seemed amiss from the outside. It was so early there were only two cars in the parking lot. My van dropped me off right at the entrance. The front door lock buzzed open as I approached.

When I stepped into the lobby, I was irrationally disappoint-ed that Poly wasn't behind the receptionist's desk. I knew she couldn't and wouldn't be there at five-thirty in the morning. Poly was at Georgia Tech pulling an all-nighter to finish up final revisions for a paper on Tigrammath artificial intelligence psycho-optimization she was writing with one of her Advanced Galtech professors. Instead, a petite, muscular-looking young woman wearing a security guard uniform was sitting at the reception desk. Her short blond hair was dyed in pink, purple and lime green accent stripes. I'd never seen her before.

"I'm CiCi," she said. "Are you Jack?"

"That's me," I said.

Maybe it would be smart to get employee name tags now that XSC was growing? Later.

"Xenotech Support," she said, reading the logo on my shirt. "Cool name."

I nodded. "Thanks."

"Mike told me to look out for you and send you right back to the production floor," she said. "You know the way?"

"Yep," I said, and headed past her desk toward the double doors leading into the main part of the building.

"Has anybody ever told you you're kind of cute?" said the young woman.

I hated to be rude but pretended I didn't hear her asking for my number and let the doors close behind me. I didn't need *that* sort of complication in my life. Things were crazy enough already.

Mike intercepted me just outside the production floor. We shook hands. His were trembling.

"Thanks for getting here so fast. The octovacs forced me out and barred the door."

Aggressively hostile vacuum cleaners—that's not odd at all, not the way my life has been going lately.

"What are they doing now?"

Mike motioned for me to look.

We peered in through the narrow reinforced windows inset into the production room's heavy steel doors. Through the thick glass we saw the massive Dauushan Model-43 fabricator. If a typical office copier was a tugboat, it was the size of an aircraft carrier.

Dozens of octovacs were scuttling around it. Covered in highly polished chrome, they looked somewhat sinister in a daddy longlegs meets Doctor Octopus meets *Terminator* sort of way. Their central cores were disks the diameter of vintage Volkswagen Beetle hubcaps and a little thicker than a pizza box. Their bottoms were perforated so they could vacuum up anything they passed over. Manipulator tentacles were evenly spaced around the central core. They could extend from a few inches to over six feet, and were made from tiny, overlapping segments as supple as snakes.

Octovacs used their tentacles to walk on and to carry tools as well as move household furniture. They could also climb vertical surfaces if necessary. Instead of looking cuddly, like most modern household robots, these machines looked coldly efficient and deadly serious. They made grating, chittering sounds as they worked, like dozens of disapproving, out of sync stopwatches. Angry red beams of light pulsed from the tops of their central cores in counterpoint to the noise. I could see why Mike didn't want to confront them.

The octovacs were building something that looked as ominous as they did. Internal sub-assemblies and curved external components were emerging from the Model-43 at high speed. Crews of octovacs were using their writhing manipulators to fit smaller components together. The element currently under construction was a concave black disk fifteen feet in diameter that looked like a wok big enough to feed an entire division of the Chinese Army. When the octovacs finished with the disk, Mike and I watched another cadre of them lift and carry it in the direction of the loading dock, out of sight to our right.

"What's the fastest way out to the dock?"

I thought I knew, but Mike might know better.

"Down the corridor," he said, "but I wouldn't advise it."

"Why not?"

"Let's head up to the roof and I'll show you," said Mike. "Thank goodness J-J is in New York today."

I nodded. If Jean-Jacques had been here he would have certainly been screaming at us to fix this instantly, even though it was his fault for using untrustworthy fabrication specifications. Then again, he might wait until nine or ten o'clock, when he typically got to the office, before he started screaming.

We took the service elevator to the second floor in deference to my injuries and then climbed the maintenance stairs to the roof. An antique incandescent bulb in a fixture on the outer wall above the stairway door gave a dim light in the early morning darkness. When we crossed to the rear of the building and stared down at what was happening below us, I didn't believe what I saw. It was so incongruous that I had to take a step back, shake my head to do a brain reboot, then advance for a second look. What I'd thought I'd seen was still there. In the high-intensity glow of the dock's congruent-tech lights, we could see a gigantic humanoid robot lying flat on its back like Gulliver captured by octovac Lilliputians.

The eight-armed assemblers were fitting the big disk over its right knee joint. This robot wasn't a friendly, brightly colored anime-style construct—it was a seriously badass-looking combat mech with enough firepower to take down Godzilla, Mothra, Gamera and Rodan simultaneously. The massive automaton was jet black and bristled with weapons. Cannons, energy blasters and missile launchers were attached to its shoulders, forearms and torso. Whoever tricked Jean-Jacques into building *this* machine was serious about maximizing threat potential. Who was behind it? And more to the point, why? I found myself wishing I was back dealing with a hundred thousand hungry pink robot bunny lawn mowers.

The robot took up most of the building's rear loading and parking area. I tried to estimate how big it was, but that was difficult because its matte black finish seemed to absorb light. Its shins and thighs were each the size of shipping containers, so that made eighty to one hundred feet just for its legs. The whole thing would be two hundred and fifty feet tall once it stood up. If it stood up—and I wondered what I could do to stop it. It looked like it was almost completely assembled—only the left kneecap remained and that was ready to install. I should have gotten here faster.

"Where are the loading dock workers?" I asked.

Wait, would they even be on duty this early? Maybe if J-J had a rush order to fill.

"They split as soon as the octovacs took over the dock," said Mike. "I'd walked out there before it was completely overrun and overheard one of them say something about having a bottle of tequila at home. He left and the others drove off behind him."

I envied them—and I don't even drink.

I pulled out my phone and asked it to zoom in on the robot so I could get a more detailed view. Many of the robot's components had the rounded, organic look common to Orishen technology. I wondered if it could change shape and function, like so many other types of Orishen-designed equipment.

The Orish are an insect-like Galactic species that morph through several different forms over their lives—egg, larva, nymph, adult and supra-adult. Their technology is highly flexible and adaptable as well. I'd earned the equivalent of a Ph.D. at Mulbiri Tech on Orish so I knew my way around Orishen technology. I'd recently been successful in thwarting a villain's evil plan by transforming Orishen-built troop ships into casinos, for example. Yeah, *that* long story.

The attached weapons didn't look Orishen. They were bolted on and had a sharp, angular design that I didn't recognize. It wasn't Long Pâkk or Short Pâkk—two of the more belligerent GaFTA member species—though it did seem to have Japanese influences. I leaned over the edge of the roof to get a better look at the weapons systems. That turned out to be a bad idea. Two octovacs on the loading dock spotted me and sprang up the concrete and glass rear wall of the building, heading my way. I'd have to think fast.

I stowed my phone and reached behind me to open the compartment on my backpack tool bag that held my friend Chit's bottle. I uncapped the bottle and shouted for help. A small, buzzing creature flew out just as the two shiny octovacs arrived on the roof. Mike ran for the maintenance stairs and was able to get behind a closed door. At least he was safe.

Unfortunately, that meant I was left to confront the two mechanical spiders without his assistance. They weren't happy to see me. Two tentacles shot out from the first octovac and grabbed my ankles. Two more extended from the other octovac and encircled my wrists. They backed away from each other, pulling me off my feet and holding me face up, spread-eagled. I was being stretched like I was strapped to a rack controlled by an overzealous torturer.

All things considered, I'd rather be back in bed.

Chapter 2

"When you reach the top, that's when the climb begins."
— Michael Caine

"Hey, big guy, how's it hangin'?" said Chit's low-pitched voice an inch from my right ear.

I could hear her clearly even over the buzz from her wings. Chit was a Murm, a ladybug-shaped alien with a head the size of a dime and a body the size of a quarter. She was wearing a colorful inkjet printer paint job on her wing cases that looked like a miniature version of Monet's Water Lilies. Chit has her feminine side—on rare occasions. I'd met her when I was in graduate school on Orish and she'd decided to hitch a ride with me back to Earth to see more of the galaxy.

"A little help would be appreciated."

"No pro-blé-mo."

The two octovacs kept moving away from each other, further stretching my joints and tendons. My chest, still recovering from being shot, burned as my abs and costals started to separate. The dinosaur-inflicted scar on my leg hurt as much as it did when I'd first received it.

"Now would be good," I said.

I heard a sound something like a Bronx cheer. Chit flitted.

I tilted my head back so I could see my little friend fly underneath the octovac holding my arms. She found an opening on the lower part of its central core and disappeared inside. A few seconds later, that octovac moved a foot forward and hung there, releasing the stress on my wrists and elbows. I came within a few inches of smacking my head on the building's tar and gravel roof, but was left loosely suspended. My blood began pooling in my upper torso and points north.

"Thanks," I said.

I heard another raspberry sound, amplified by the interior of the octovac's central core, then Chit popped out of the hole she'd entered and repeated what she'd just done with the other chrome plated unit.

"What did you just do?" I asked.

"I put 'em in standby mode," said Chit. "It's just one switch on their primary circuit boards. They can't be operated remotely now."

"You're a life saver!"

"It was easier than havin' to deal wit' Poly if you'd been drawn and quartered."

It's good to have a friend. Make that friends. I shouted toward the maintenance stairs.

"Mike, it's safe to come out now!" Mike cracked the door and looked around warily. "Could you give me a hand?"

He opened the door the rest of the way and looked at me. I was six inches above the roof, held in place by tentacles from two octovacs. When the units went into standby mode they just hovered once they reached equilibrium.

"Umm, sure," said Mike.

I think he was trying to keep from laughing.

He walked over and pushed the octovac holding my feet toward me until my lower body touched the gravel. Then he helped me unwind the tentacles from my wrists and ankles. I rubbed my extremities and slowly got up. I needed Mike's support to get myself vertical.

"Now I understand why you didn't want to go out to the loading dock."

"Ten points for Capt'n Obvious," said Chit, who was basking in the warmth of one of the red lights on top of an octovac.

"It was easier to show than to tell," said Mike.

"Maybe for you," I said, rubbing my wrists.

"Now what?" said Mike.

"Did you follow Rule #2 when you started fabbing the octovacs?"

Mike had been taught this lesson the hard way during the robot rabbit incident.

"Sure," he said. "I printed six octovac controllers before queuing up the octovacs themselves. I left the controllers on top of the Model-43's operator's console."

"And the octovacs herded you off the production floor before you could grab one?"

"Uh huh." Mike's shoulders slumped. He looked like a puppy waiting to be kicked. Working for Jean-Jacques can do that to a person.

"It happens." I patted him on the back reassuringly. "We'll figure things out."

Mike stood a little straighter after my encouragement. I was glad to see he hadn't been completely beaten down by his abusive boss.

"If you say so," he said. "I'll do whatever I can to help."

Now there was a moderately upbeat, conditionally optimistic tone in his voice.

"Are the plans for the octovacs still available?"

"Sure," said Mike, his face brightening. He could sense the gears turning in my brain. "They're on the main server."

I handed him my phone.

"Log my phone in and locate the octovac controller plans, please."

Mike tapped keys and then handed my phone back. "Done."

I addressed my phone. "Please simulate an octovac controller."

"Programming now… simulation complete," it said.

My phone is a sharp piece of circuitry.

"Chit, quit snoozing on top of that octovac and move your carapace. I need you to shift the command channel on these two units."

"Whatta slave driver," said Chit. "You'd think savin' your life once t'day would be enough."

"Please?"

"Okay, since you asked nicely."

She opened her wing cases, stretched her wings, and flew underneath one of the octovacs to make the adjustments I'd requested. I had my doubts about the actual octovac controllers working on the rest of the shiny chrome spiders. I was betting that the black hats responsible for the bad fabrication plans had preset the octovacs to only follow remote commands *they* issued and ignore the standard controllers. To confirm that, I looked over the edge of the roof above the loading dock. Only my head was visible—I didn't want more octovacs coming after me on the roof. I moved my phone to the ledge next to me.

"Shut down all the octovacs, please."

My phone chirped and beeped as it sent out the shutdown signal. Thanks to the loading dock lights we could see the octovacs behind the WT&F office building clearly. None of them deactivated. My phone made a grumpy noise and sulked. That confirmed it. Only a factory reset would give me a chance of regaining control.

Three of the octovacs on the dock had just finished attaching the giant robot's left kneecap. Half a dozen were skittering across the robot's matte black surface, making final pre-operational adjustments. I crawled back out of line-of-sight from the loading dock and stood up near the maintenance stairs. Before I could think of what to do next I was distracted by Chit and her water lilies paint job hovering in front of my eyes.

"Command channels are shifted on these two, Jack."

She pointed at the octovacs on the roof with a foreleg and gave me the new command channel settings.

"Thanks. Did you spot anything on the inside of the units about the code needed to perform a factory reset on these things?"

"Yeah. I saw a sticker with the first six characters but the rest are hidden under a circuit board."

"Excellent. That will make a brute force search for the factory reset code much faster."

Chit recited the part of the code she'd seen. Then she yawned, said she needed her beauty rest, and returned to her bottle.

My phone started trying out options. If we were lucky it

would find the right sequence early in its search.

"The plans indicate the code length is twenty characters, so it will require thirty-two minutes and eight seconds to try all remaining reset codes," said my phone, anticipating my next question.

"So, on average, about fifteen minutes?" I said.

"If we're lucky," said my phone.

"I don't think we can wait that long," said Mike.

He had taken up my previous vantage point looking down at the loading dock. I joined him. He was right. Time was running out. The giant robot was standing up. It was already on one knee. I heard lots of muffled clacks that sounded like it was booting its weapons systems and racking ammunition. This was not good.

"Take control of the two octovacs on the roof and have them carry me down to the loading dock," I said.

My phone promptly complied, and in seconds I was hanging from a pair of octovac tentacles like a sack of L5 hydroponic potatoes. The pair of spiders descended quickly and reached ground level. I instructed them to drag me over to the robot and start hauling me up its nearest leg. They reached the knee that was still on the ground and jumped, carrying me with them to a spot halfway up the robot's thigh where a missile launcher provided good hand holds. Other octovacs grooming and prepping the giant robot finally realized the two holding me were no longer part of the black hat team. They swarmed after me while my octovacs scrambled to carry me higher.

"How are you doing on figuring out that factory reset code?" I asked my phone.

"Still processing."

Then the robot shifted from kneeling on one knee to standing upright. I went from dangling fifty feet in the air to a hundred feet in five, make that three, rapid heartbeats. I know it shouldn't matter—a fall from either distance would kill me—but try telling that to my hind-brain.

I heard a low rumbling below me. The giant robot was warming up the rocket engines in its boots. I had a feeling I'd be a lot higher soon.

Five of the black hat octovacs were just inches below me, and I didn't want to repeat the experience I'd had on the roof. I had my phone instruct one of my white hat octovacs to slow down the black hats while the other kept carrying me farther up the robot. One of the black hat unit's tentacles grabbed my shoe and tugged, but my defender white hat vac took advantage of it being off balance to dislodge it and send it down into two other black hat vacs, slowing all three in a tangle of waving tentacles. My defender was locked in a multi-armed struggle with the remaining nearby black hat while the octovac holding me finally ascended all the way to the robot's shoulder.

The rumbles were getting louder and the robot's body was beginning to vibrate. It would lift off any second.

At my phone's command my transport octovac headed for the base of the robot's neck. It released me and I sent it back to support my defender octovac against the now untangled black hats. I stood on a small protrusion and held on to a convenient piece of tubing while I found my Orishen mutakey and opened the pilot's hatch to the command center. Then my luck deserted me. A black hat octovac sprang out from a baffle above the hatch and knocked me off the robot. My arms tried to find a handhold but found only empty air as gravity tried its best to turn potential energy into kinetic energy. There were times when I wished I didn't know so much about physics.

Chapter 3

"Flying is learning how to throw yourself
at the ground and miss."
— Douglas Adams

At times like this I wished I'd included a parachute in my backpack tool bag. I moved into a skydiver's pose with my arms and legs extended to increase wind resistance. The parking lot below was heading my way and I didn't have enough time for my life to pass before my eyes. My brain was distracted by attempts to calculate my terminal velocity and the number of seconds I had left to live. It wasn't a big number.

Then things really sucked. I felt a slight impact and heard the roar of an octovac's vacuum sucking on my backpack. I was almost close enough to see ants crawling on the asphalt when my vertical fall changed into a parabolic arc and I soared up into the early morning sky. The straps on my backpack dug into my shoulders and stressed my recuperating ribcage, but I wasn't complaining. I looked over my shoulder and saw an octovac—one of my white hat units—with broad lengths of fabric stretched between its extended tentacles.

"Octovacs have a hang-glider mode?"

"These units aren't home vacuum cleaners, they're construction 'bots," said my phone. "The hang-glider feature was added after too many of them fell from upper stories."

"Lucky me," I said, pleased with my phone's initiative.

"Lucky us," said my phone. "It's no fun getting restored from a backup."

"At least you have that option. Can you get us back to the robot's shoulders?"

"Already on it."

My octovac rescuer rode the warm air currents vented by the WT&F building's HVAC system. Soon it had me back at my perch outside the open hatch to the giant robot's control room.

I was glad the pursuing black hat vacs had lost interest when I'd fallen off.

The hatch was unguarded, except for the other white hat vac. I looked below and saw that all the black hat vacs were attached to spots on the robot's legs and torso. They weren't coming after me. Maybe they were waiting for new orders or just holding tight. Either way, I wasn't going to look a gift equine in the mouth.

I jumped through the hatch, followed by my two white hat vacs. One of them sealed the hatch while I got my bearings. There were two large observation windows corresponding to the robot's eyes. I could see that we were really high up. The robot was fully erect now—that is, it was standing—and I could identify the lights of Atlanta's midtown skyscrapers. The robot was as tall as some of the buildings, which meant it was too big to play King Kong and climb them.

Then I felt a vibration like a Hollywood disaster movie earthquake, which answered my question about the black hat vacs. They were going along for the ride. I had just enough time to strap into the pilot's chair before the sound from the robot's boot rockets reached a crescendo and the giant took off.

We were heading west at a low altitude. I surveyed my surroundings. The command center was circular with two eye-shaped observation ports in front and lots of screens showing external camera views and the status of various systems. To the left of the pilot's chair was a full-motion cyber-feedback rig. In front of me were dual Orishen and humanoid controls. I knew my way around both. The humanoid ones were easier for most people than the scent-activated Orishen controls, but a quick code review showed me that the Orishen version had deeper access to the robot's operating system.

I used a portable scent-generator from my backpack tool bag and an Orishen-tech back door I'd discovered in graduate school, then assigned myself superuser administrative rights. Another user had already been defined and was directing the robot remotely. I tried to lock that user out, but he or she or it fought back hard. After a few seconds that seemed like hours, it was clear that the other operator was using human, not Orishen controls, so I was able to wrestle their admin rights away and cancel their access.

At some point, I needed to learn whatever I could about the person or group behind the robot. But that could wait. For now, I needed to get a two-hundred-and-fifty-foot robot out of sight to avoid potential panic and disruption to the already congested Atlanta rush hour.

Now that I had superuser privileges I could put on the full cybernetic feedback rig and guide the robot with my movements. I unbuckled my safety harness and stood up. Then I donned the encephalo-helmet, stepped into the leg sensors, and slid my arms into the arm harnesses. Once my limbs were all comfortably situated I tried a few experimental movements. I overbalanced a bit and started to fly erratically before getting the robot back into equilibrium. So long as I didn't make any sudden moves, I was safe.

I called up a rear-facing monitor and zoomed in on WT&F's headquarters. Mike was still visible on the roof at maximum magnification. I asked my phone to call him.

"Are you okay?" said Mike when we connected. "I'm glad you didn't hit the pavement."

"I'm pretty happy about that, too."

My phone made a few supportive beeps.

"Who's running that thing, you, or the secret robot masters?" asked Mike.

"Me," I said. "I've got an idea. I'm going to try flying this thing down to the big VIGorish Labs hangar at Hartsfield Port." The hangar was where I'd been shot last month. Fun place.

"That makes sense," said Mike. I could hear his breathing slow to something like normal. Giant robots were terrifying, which is why I needed to get this one under wraps fast.

"Can you drive my van down there and pick me up?"

"Sure."

"I'll talk to J-J about taking the giant robot."

"Great," said Mike. "I'm glad you'll be the one having that conversation, not me."

I had the robot make a giant thumbs up sign, but was probably too far away for Mike to see it.

"No problem," I said. "Since Jean-Jacques violated the terms of my contract, I'll really enjoy our discussion."

"Thanks," said Mike. "I'll get on the road."

I ended the call and experimented to get the hang of the cybernetic controls, changing the robot's course from west to south. The giant robot was flying smoothly, its congruency-powered engines drawing on near limitless stellar energy. I checked a monitor and saw that there were stealth baffles in its rocket boots so the robot didn't look like a meteor or an errant spacecraft as I guided it over the center of Atlanta, heading for Hartsfield port. I made sure there weren't any running lights activated and kept to an altitude high enough to miss any buildings and low enough to avoid any aircraft. I followed the Connector, the conjoined path of I-75 and I-85 through downtown that led to the port.

Flying with full-body cybernetic controls was exhilarating. It was so much fun I got cocky. I tried a Superman-style, both arms forward flight posture, then shifted to a one fist-forward Green Lantern-style. The robot's body copied all my movements faithfully. I shouldn't have tried getting fancy. Sticking my arms out hurt my ribs and I curled in on myself as the pain in my chest doubled me over. I was just able to recover fast enough to avoid smacking head first into the Varsity restaurant's giant V-sign at North Avenue. After that, I gained some altitude and was much more conservative in my flying.

The autopilot was excellent, so I provided my destination coordinates and let it do the flying. Then I tried to decide which member of law enforcement I should call first.

Lieutenant Martin Lee of the Georgia Capitol Police was a friend. I knew he liked to work out early so he might be up. Shepherd, the Long Påkk spymaster, would also be a good option. He knew lots of people in authority and was good at keeping things quiet. I didn't know much about his sleep pattern, however, so I called Lieutenant Lee first. He answered on the second ring.

"Hey, Jack," he said. His voice was friendly but had a police officer's authority.

"Sorry to wake you, Martin."

"I was up. Just getting in some reps with free weights before my shift starts."

"Great," I said. "I need your help with parking a two-hundred-and-fifty-foot robot."

"Could you say that again?"

"You heard it right the first time."

"I guess I did. How can I help?"

"Are most of the Orishen freighters out of the VIGorish Labs hangar?"

"Yeah, there are only a couple of dozen of them left to be auctioned or held for evidence," said the lieutenant. "That should leave enough space for parking a two-hundred-and-fifty-foot robot or two."

"Can you send me the override code for the door lock?"

"I'll do better than that," he said. "My gym is two miles away. I'll meet you there."

"Thanks," I said.

"Breakfast's on me," he said, "on one condition."

"What's that?"

"You have to tell me *why* you need to park a two-hundred-and-fifty-foot robot."

"Deal," I said. "I'll be there in ten minutes."

My phone spoke up as soon as my call with Lieutenant Lee was finished.

"Success!" it said.

"You've got the shutdown code?"

"Correct. Want me to test it?"

"It would probably be better to wait until we're on the ground," I said. "Octovacs falling out of the sky wouldn't be a good thing."

"Gliding out of the sky," said my phone. "They have an automatic controlled descent mode."

"Gliding," I corrected. "And thanks for saving my life."

"Glad to help," said my phone. "Just keep it in mind."

I landed, none too gently, and my phone reset the octovacs. Ten minutes later, just as the sun was starting to rise, Martin and I made sure that the robot was safely stored, flat on its back, in the hangar. There would have been room for two or three more the same size. It was a *big* hangar. My phone had the forty-eight octovacs organize themselves into neat ranks before it deactivated them.

A few minutes later Mike arrived. We stored the two white hat octovacs in the back of my van. They might come in handy, and I needed some units to check out for clues about who was behind all this.

I'd contacted Shepherd and he assured me he'd do his best to minimize any media attention. So far, nearly an hour had passed and no videos of giant robots flying over the city had shown up on YouTube. The secretive but well-connected Long Påkk said he'd meet us to debrief at the Waffle House on Virginia Avenue, one exit north of the port on I-85.

It was going to be an interesting breakfast.

Chapter 4

"One should not attend even the end of the world
without a good breakfast."
— Robert A. Heinlein, *Friday*

My van, Shepherd's SUV and Lieutenant Lee's cruiser found three adjacent parking places outside the restaurant. Every Waffle House is open twenty-four hours a day, but they do have their peak and off-peak times. We'd arrived in a lull after the first morning rush for workers whose shifts started at seven. I'd been to this location three years ago, when I was a recent arrival in Atlanta, and remembered that it was old and tired, with shabby tables and baked on layers of grease over everything like an oily shellac. This time, I was pleasantly surprised to see that the exterior didn't look run down at all. The signage was new, the brickwork had been recently tuck-pointed, and even the lines marking the spaces in the parking lot were crisp and bright.

Mike held the unsmudged outer glass door for me and I returned the favor for him with the inner one. Both doors seemed to open on their own ahead of Shepherd and the Lieutenant from the sheer force of their command personalities. I wondered if they could teach *me* how to do that.

When I entered I continued to be impressed by the restaurant's *interior* transformation. Instead of the standard Formica counter and table tops, the horizontal surfaces were covered in an opalescent white chitin-like composite surface from one of the Orishen conglomerates. It was easy to clean, never chipped, and came with a lifetime warranty, even for species with lifespans measured in centuries. This wasn't a typical Waffle House.

The traditionally linear open kitchen had been redesigned to include an L-shaped combination grill and waffle making section at the end closest to customers. A four-foot, three-sided pyramidal male Pyr wearing a tall chef's hat stood on a low swiveling platform in the center of the right angle. His eyes, at the apex of each of his sides, didn't miss a thing, and he was using three of his tentacles to make hash browns, fry eggs, and pour waffles, all at high speed. I was impressed.

We found a table for four by the front window. Mike and I sat across from Lieutenant Lee and Shepherd. I extracted Chit's bottle and stowed my backpack under the table.

Chit popped out and perched on top of a ketchup bottle I'd placed on a napkin dispenser so she was closer to eye level. Her carapace was painted Waffle House yellow with a black "W" on one wing and a corresponding "H" on the other. Her paint scheme amused me—she usually opted for fine art.

I was pleased that the seats in our booth were padded—another upgrade from the hard benches at the typical Waffle House franchise. Now that I was off my feet I felt some of the fear-induced tension go out of my neck and shoulders. I was glad the morning's excitement was over. A server came to take our order.

Waffle House servers are a special breed. They pride themselves on knowing their regular customers' orders, but many of them have lived hard lives and it shows. It's a difficult job, with odd hours, and the pay isn't great, so servers tend to be people with brains but without the drive or luck needed to get other work that isn't as hard on the arches. I'd been to dozens of locations and the servers have always been human beings—even at the single unit on Orish where the servers were all Terran grad students at Mulbiri Tech, my proud alma mater. Too bad the place had only opened during my last month on the planet. It had been a nice reminder of home.

All that being said, I was disconcerted to see that our server was a lean, seven-foot tall, tiger-striped Tigrammath woman wearing a French blue shirt and black Waffle House apron. Her uniform matched the colors of her stripes quite nicely. The sparkle in her feline eyes wasn't anything like the look I was used to seeing on servers after handling the first morning rush. Her name tag read "Dox."

"What would you like to drink, y'all?" she said.

Her voice had a low, sensuous purr to it. I looked up at her—way up. She winked at me. At *me?*

"I'll have a diet Starbuzz, please."

Mike ordered a Coke and Shepherd and Martin opted for coffee. Chit asked for water. Our server wasn't surprised to see a Murm, which was odd—they're a rare species.

"I'll be right back, honey," she said, smiling at me. "Y'all figure out what you want to order."

Her fur was short but still waved gently as she moved to fetch our drinks. Shepherd and the Lieutenant looked at the low tech laminated menus and Mike handed me one, but I didn't need it.

"Two coffees, a Coke, and water for the lady," said our server, returning with drinks in glasses, mugs, and a thimble for Chit. "Plus a big ol' diet Starbuzz for you, sweetie."

She touched me on the arm after she put my soft drink on the table then headed back to the kitchen to pick up another table's order. Was I giving off pheromones or something to make me irresistible to women? Not likely and certainly not to Chit.

"Looks like ya just made another new friend," said Chit from the top of the ketchup bottle. "That's what? Two, today? And the sun's barely up."

"I thought you were asleep when I met the security guard."

"I wish," said the Murm. "Too much commotion to sleep—and her name is CiCi. She was cute and kinda into you."

Lieutenant Lee and Shepherd were paying attention and Mike was glaring at me with a look of disapproval on his face. I tried to look innocent.

"I had other things on my mind," I said, "like the octovacs. And Poly. You know… my *girlfriend*."

"Yeah, yeah," said Chit in a teasing tone. "First the security guard, now the waitress."

"Server."

"Whatever. That's what I get for learning English from old movies."

I shook my head and rolled my eyes in silent commentary. Mike's look changed from a glare to a smile when he realized Chit was kidding. Martin Lee was grinning and Shepherd may have raised one corner of his mouth. Maybe.

"Be nice to CiCi," said Mike, trying to do some teasing of his own, but with a hint of something more serious he couldn't hide. "She's a friend."

"What *kinda* friend?" asked Chit.

"None of your business," mumbled Mike.

"Have you asked her out yet?" said Martin.

"Maybe," said Mike, looking down at his menu.

Was his face turning red or was that just a reflection from the taillights of a passing car? I took pity on him and changed the subject.

"Let's talk about the two-hundred-and-fifty-foot robot."

Before I could say more the waitress, I mean *server*, appeared at my elbow.

"A two-hundred-and-fifty-foot robot?" she said.

"It's for a new video game," said Mike.

Fast thinking. Mike would be an excellent addition to the Xenotech Support team once Poly and I got our hiring plans nailed down. Poly is my girlfriend and business partner. There hadn't been time for figuring out hiring plans during the last month, given Poly's academic commitments related to finishing two master's degrees.

"What'll you gentlebeings have?" our server said, smiling and showing off a mouth filled with lots of pointy alien carnivore's teeth.

Good thing Tigrammaths are pacifists, mostly.

Shepherd, predictably, had city ham, country ham and three rare steaks. Martin was on a special workout regimen so he had two scrambled egg whites and dry whole wheat toast. Mike and I were young with healthy metabolisms, so we opted for

All Star Breakfasts with fried eggs, bacon, hash browns, toast and waffles. Mike had his shredded potatoes smothered, covered and peppered—that's with onions, cheese and jalapeños—while I was a purist and ordered mine plain. It didn't make sense to order for Chit, but I did ask for a second thimble. I'd give her a bite of my waffle with maple syrup. My friend had a sweet tooth.

"Order up!" said our server as she turned back to the kitchen.

Had she bumped my shoulder with her hip intentionally or by accident? It wasn't relevant—there were important matters to discuss.

"Tell us about the two-hundred-and-fifty-foot robot, Jack," said Martin.

His police badge glinted in the early morning sun. Shepherd raised one eyebrow and looked at me, then at Mike.

"I'll start," said the WT&F fab operator. "Jean-Jacques got a new rush order late yesterday afternoon and wanted me to work all night to meet a noon delivery deadline."

"Did he promise ta pay ya extra?" said Chit.

Mike looked sheepish.

"Thought so," said Chit.

"Where does the robot come in?" said Martin, his strong, dark face looking puzzled.

"I was supposed to be fabbing household appliances—vacuum cleaners with eight arms to lift furniture out of the way," Mike continued.

"The octovacs?" said Martin.

"Uh huh," said Mike.

"Then what happened?" said Chit, licking drops of water from her forelegs.

"After the first dozen were printed, they took over the production room and forced me out," said Mike. "And then I called..."

Everybody looked at me and Mike and Chit and Martin spoke simultaneously. They knew what was coming.

"Jack."

I picked up my cue.

"At five-fifteen in the morning."

"Poor baby," said Chit.

"Hey," I said, "you slept through it."

I couldn't jump right into the rest of the story. Our server had returned with our orders. She balanced all the dishes on one long, striped arm and expertly distributed the right meals to the proper diners. When she came back to refill Lieutenant Lee and Shepherd's coffee cups, I saw a look pass between the Tigrammath and the grizzled old Påkk. I couldn't tell if it was the natural antipathy between the two species, who get along as well as felines and canines, or something else. I'd have to remember to talk to Shepherd about it later.

Between bites of breakfast, Mike and Chit and I described my encounter with the octovacs on the roof—where I made sure Chit got the credit for rescuing me. I also told them about my inadvertent attempt at parasailing that saved me from a close encounter of the worst kind with the surface of the parking lot. My phone beeped to remind me that *it* had done the saving. I acknowledged my phone's resourcefulness and stopped to butter my waffle. After three beats of silence, Shepherd spoke. We all listened.

"Do you recognize the robot's technology, Jack?"

His voice was deep and raspy, like a blues singer with lots of mileage.

I nodded. Thankfully, nothing rattled.

"The general tech-style for the robot is Orishen mutatech, with allowances for human, rather than Orishen configurations," I said.

Shepherd inclined his head a millimeter to acknowledge what I'd said.

"And the weapon systems?"

"All Terran, from multiple nation states," I said, "at least from what I could tell without closer inspection. Mostly designs from

Japan and the Russian Oligarchic Republic."

"Curious," said Shepherd. "You'd think an Orishen robot would use an Orishen body type."

"Or more than one of 'em," said Chit, who was trying to remove bits of waffle from her mandibles. "Egg, grub, nymph, adult, supra-adult… they've got robots that can shift into all five forms back on Orish."

"And you know this how?" I said.

"I was on Orish for a long time before I met *you*, bucko."

"I'm glad I never saw one when I was in grad school at Mulbiri Tech," I said. "A two-hundred-and-fifty-foot giant praying mantis-shaped nymph-form robot would be the stuff of nightmares."

"But this one is humanoid," said Mike.

"With more weapons than an armored battalion," said Martin.

He should know, he'd been in one.

"I'll have to check out its mutagenic specifications to see what other forms are preprogrammed," I said.

"Do you think one of them is a truck?" said Mike.

He really wanted the robot to be a Transformer.

"I won't know until I check," I said, "but if it is, it would be a really *big* truck."

Everyone nodded, except Shepherd—and Chit. Her head was in a thimble, sucking up artificially flavored maple syrup from the bite of waffle I'd given her.

Mike spoke again.

"What am I going to tell Jean-Jacques about what happened? He'll be back tomorrow morning."

"I told you I'd talk to him," I said.

"And I'd like to join you for that conversation," said Martin.

Ever since the events that ended up with me being shot last month, his superiors at the state capitol's police force had assigned him a special portfolio, troubleshooting issues that didn't fit into normal law enforcement categories.

"That should keep Jean-Jacques off balance," I said. "I'll be good cop and you can be bad cop."

"You're not a cop," said Martin, his brown eyes merry.

"Details, details."

"I'll meet you at WT&F at nine o'clock tomorrow morning."

"Great," I said.

"Thanks, guys," said Mike. "Better you than me. *Much* better."

"Hey," said Chit, "what about the octovacs?"

"What about 'em?" I said.

"Are *they* Orishen technology?"

My phone beeped again. I pulled it out, flipped out its kick-stand and stood it up on the table next to a plate that used to hold one of Shepherd's steaks.

"The octovacs are standard, off-the-shelf construction 'bots designed by Khufu, Limited, a Pyr-owned conglomerate," it said. "They're fully programmable and can be operated remotely."

When my phone said "Pyr," the short, three-sided cook in the chef's hat hopped down from his platform and glided over to our table on his hundreds of tiny cilia "feet."

"Sorry to eavesdrop," he said, "but you mentioned Khufu, Limited?"

"That's right," said my phone. It should have asked me before responding, but I was glad to see it taking initiative.

"My name is Roger Joe-Bob Bacon, and I own this place," he said.

He waved one of his tentacles in a friendly greeting. We all waved back, even Shepherd. Chit had emerged from her thimble. Her waving forelegs looked sticky.

"Pleased to meet you, Mr. Bacon," I said.

"Call me Roger, or Joe-Bob or anythin' 'cept late for breakfast," said the Pyr.

Our server came back to refill our drinks. She was so tall it was easy for her to reach over her boss to do so. I gratefully accepted more diet Starbuzz.

"Thanks, Dox," I said.

She smiled at me and stayed close to our table.

"I'm an investor in Khufu," said Roger Joe-Bob, "and wanted

to hear what you folks had to say about the company."

My phone started to speak, but I cut it off.

"We had some problems with the construction 'bots assembling something they shouldn't have," I said.

"They're s'posed to be used for buildin' skyscrapers," Roger Joe-Bob replied.

"They *were* building something tall," I said.

"But not skyscrapers," said Mike.

"And not particularly legal," said Martin.

The Pyr drew himself up to his full four-foot height—five, with his chef's hat.

"I'm very sorry to hear that," he said. "If you can provide me with the particulars I'll bring it to the board's attention."

"The board?" I said.

"Of Khufu, Limited," said Roger Joe-Bob.

"He's not *a* shareholder," said our server.

I looked puzzled.

"He's the *majority* shareholder."

"Now, Dox," said the Pyr, trying to retain his aw-shucks manner.

This was a very big deal. Khufu, Limited, was one of the three largest Pyr corporations operating on Terra.

"If you don't mind me asking, Roger Joe-Bob, what's someone in your situation doing running a Waffle House?"

"I like cookin'," he said, "and makin' customers happy."

"You've certainly done an amazing job on this location."

"Thanks," said Roger Joe-Bob. "I wanted to do it up right and have a place where GaFTA species as well as humans could have great food."

"You've succeeded."

The Pyr smiled with two of his three mouths.

"I've got to get back to my station," said Roger Joe-Bob, starting back to his grill.

If he'd had a shoulder he'd have looked over it, but since male Pyrs are trilaterally symmetric he didn't have to.

"You just send me the details about those misbehavin' construction 'bots and I'll get to the bottom of what happened."

Roger Joe-Bob extended a tentacle and passed his phone to Dox. She touched it to my phone, and Mike's, exchanging contact information.

When she left, all my breakfast companions were staring at me. "What?" I said.

"You make some pretty unusual friends," said Martin.

Chit was nodding and Mike wasn't even trying to hide his grin. Even Shepher's eyes were amused.

"Look who's talking?" I said, sweeping my arm to take in everyone at the table.

Dox came back to drop off the bill. Along with laminated paper menus, Waffle House still used paper checks.

"Who gets this?" said the server, resting one arm on my shoulder.

"He does," I said, pointing at Martin.

"Here you go, sweetie," she said, handing him the yellow slip. "Have a great day!"

"You too, toots," said Chit.

We said our goodbyes and waved to Roger Joe-Bob on our way out. He waved three different cooking implements in three different tentacles. Dox winked at me again.

"Y'all come back now, Sugar."

Somehow, I was pretty sure I would.

Chapter 5

"I don't think he knows about second breakfast, Pip."
— Meriadoc Brandybuck

Mike and I said our goodbyes to Martin and Shepherd and climbed in my van. Mike rode shotgun. I followed Martin's police cruiser onto I-85, since there's a small, paranoid part of my brain that believes it's always better to have a police car in front of me than behind me. I was puzzled to see Shepherd's SUV head south on the interstate, toward Hartsfield Port and Jackson Teleport Nexus, instead of driving north like we were. He hadn't mentioned any errands that would take him in that direction, but then again, being Shepherd, he wouldn't. I was about to send Poly a text to see if she was nearly done at Georgia Tech when my phone saved me the trouble.

"You've got a text from Poly," it said.

We used text messages for initial contact since phone calls were more immediately distracting.

"Aren't you supposed to play that recording of Poly saying 'Oh Lover Boy' when she texts me?"

We'd spent a romantic evening watching an old movie called *Dirty Dancing* two weeks ago after Poly had finished a major paper and she'd adopted those three words as an intimate catch-phrase because she liked watching me blush. I'd asked my phone to play it so I'd have more opportunities to get used to the phrase and could learn how to stop turning red whenever I heard it.

I still wasn't technically Poly's Lover Boy yet. My recuperation and her academic schedule hadn't given us a lot of time alone together during the last month. No, scratch that. The reason we weren't lovers yet was because I wanted everything to be perfect for our first time. I had mostly convinced Poly to wait until she graduated, when she wasn't under so much pressure. I'd thought we could take a week off to spend on Maui or on one of the Pyr pleasure planets, but hadn't broached the subject.

Privacy, and no tech support call interruptions, would do a lot to help me relax and feel comfortable with taking our physical relationship to the next level. I was still getting used to having a business partner—and a girlfriend. Poly respected the fact that I'd had bad experiences in the past when things had gotten too intimate too fast. Waiting until she graduated would be better for both of us. There was also a high probability that my apartment was still being bugged, despite my best efforts to eliminate any surveillance. I didn't relish the idea of an audience.

"You wanted me to embarrass you in front of Mike?" said my phone, pulling me away from my dithering.

Mike just looked out the windshield as my van navigated us toward the city.

"I've got to get used to it somehow," I said.

"Okay," said my phone.

It immediately started looping Poly's voice—every bit as sexy as Jennifer Grey's from the movie—over and over again. I turned as red as a Nicósn's Santa-hat topknot and covered my ears after ten repetitions. My phone took pity on me and stopped the playback after two more iterations.

"What does her text say?" said Mike.

He could see that I was still trying to gain some control over my sympathetic nervous system. I might have succeeded in reducing the blood flow to the tips of my ears, but not much more than that, and was grateful for Mike's distraction.

My phone made an interrogative bleep and I nodded for it to go ahead.

"Hi Jack," read my phone in Poly's voice. "I'm just finishing up here and wanted to see if you were interested in grabbing some breakfast."

"Please tell her that sounds great. We'll pick her up outside GAIMLI in—" I read my van's ETA "—twenty minutes."

The Galactic Artificial Intelligence and Machine Learning Institute at Georgia Tech was where Poly and her thesis adviser were working on Tigrammath A.I. psycho-optimization. Poly's professor had promised her co-author credit on the academic paper he was writing.

"We just *had* breakfast," said Mike.

"There's always room for second breakfast if it means I can spend time with Poly."

Mike smiled at me indulgently. I knew I was crazy about Poly and had been marinating in being-in-love endorphins for a month and a half now. So far, my friends considered it cute, but I didn't want to come across as too besotted. I also had to focus and use the front of my brain to solve client problems.

"You can drop me off at the Georgia Tech station on the Purple Line," said Mike. "It's only a few stops from there to my place on Briarcliff Road. My car drove itself home already."

Galactic construction techniques and GaFTA-driven revenue increases had allowed the Metropolitan Atlanta Rapid Transit Authority to accelerate their building plans and complete a comprehensive public transit grid for the area ten years ahead of schedule. The line linking Georgia Tech, Emory and all the apartment complexes on Briarcliff was heavily used. It was Poly's preferred method for getting from one of her master's degree programs to the other.

"Okay," I said, though I wasn't quite sure why he didn't want me to drive him home. Then Mike explained it to me, using small words.

"You and Poly should have more time alone together," he said. "This way I won't be a third wheel."

"It's no problem, I'm glad to drop you…" I began, but he cut me off.

"Don't worry about it. You saved my butt this morning, so I'm glad to do my part to encourage young love."

"I'm older than *you* are."

"You're also an idiot."

I'm pretty sure he meant it affectionately.

"We're almost at the station—just let me out."

I did. A few minutes later I picked Poly up on the sidewalk outside the ten-story starcrete and glass GaFTA Modern GAIMLI building. She opened my van's door with manic energy, bounced across the front passenger seat, put her arms around my neck, and gave me an enthusiastic kiss that made the tips of my ears turn red again. I tried to return as good as I got.

"Nice to see you, too," I said.

Somehow Poly had ended up sitting on my lap, our arms around each other. My van had thoughtfully retracted the steering wheel to give her more room. I looked at the beautiful, intelligent, competent, ambitious woman I held and counted my lucky globular clusters that we'd connected during a tech support call at WT&F six weeks ago. She was tall—three inches less than my six foot two—and, like me, in her mid-twenties. Her shoulder-length auburn hair flipped delightfully when she disengaged from our kiss and her green eyes were dancing. Poly was upbeat, but I could sense an underlying tension in her. She was happy to see me, but concerned about something. Poly cuddled into my neck, inhaled, and popped back upright.

"No shower this morning, Jack?"

"I had an early morning support call."

I inhaled deeply. Poly had clearly pulled an all-nighter.

"I can use some food, a shower, and some shut-eye, in that order," she said.

"Me, too," I said, fibbing a little about the food. "Come over to my place and I'll take good care of you."

Poly slid off my lap and moved over to the passenger seat.

"Promises, promises."

"You can't be *that* tired." I sniffed theatrically. "And you *do* need a shower."

"So do you, Lover Boy—and a shave. You're scratchy."

"True on both counts," I said. "Mike needed me for an emergency tech support call, so I had to leave in a hurry this morning."

"We could shower together," she said. "I could scrub your back."

I was about to reply, saying that I'd enjoy that more after I'd fully healed, when my van tentatively said, "Seat belt?"

Poly and I laughed and she buckled up.

* * * * *

When we got to my apartment at the Ad Astra complex—built by the city, state and county as a mixed use development that included room for alien species' consulates and living quarters—I encouraged Poly to hit the shower while I made breakfast. She must have been really tired, since she didn't repeat her invitation for me to join her. Through my open bedroom door I heard Poly say "Earl Grey, hot. Make it so," and one of my favorite custom shower programs started. She'd be in there for a while.

I found some eggs and cheese and chopped an onion to go into an omelet. I rinsed some blueberries, seedless green grapes, and bright purple Nicósn jathberries to make a fruit salad. I checked on top of my refrigerator and one end of my Dauushan mega-banana was ripe. I pulled it down, peeled back some of the skin, and sliced off half a dozen thin, five-inch disks of the delicate pink fruit to add to each dish. A splash of chilled tangerine juice would keep the fruit salad fresh until Poly came out.

I put a thick skillet on the stove to preheat and cracked the eggs into a bowl. Then I added a little water, salt, pepper, and half a teaspoon of a dried Orishen herb that tasted like a cross between basil, oregano and cilantro, before whipping the whole mixture up with a fork. I put some butter in the pan and started to brown the onions while I checked to see if I had any bread. I was lucky—there was half a loaf of sliced sourdough. I put four slices in the toaster but didn't start them: warm toast is much better than cold.

The fried onions smelled wonderful. I put them in a small bowl and added more butter to the skillet. When the butter was bubbling I poured in the egg mixture and topped it with the onions before turning down the heat.

I had a few minutes while the omelet cooked, so I found my nicest place mats—nearly indestructible Orishen pupa silk patterned ovals I'd bought while in graduate school off-planet—and put them on the table. I set out knives, forks, spoons and eating tongs and heard a soprano shriek from my bathroom. Poly had reached the part in my Earl Grey shower program where the water shifted from warm to ice cold, so she'd be out soon. As a bonus, the cold water should wake her up enough to eat and carry on coherent conversation until her body finally gave out after her all-nighter. Napkins, butter for the table and a jar of jathberry jam finished my table preparations.

Wait, no. I wasn't done. What were we going to drink? Poly liked tea. I filled my kettle with water and grabbed a couple of mugs from a cabinet. Mine said "Galactic Congruent Systems" and had their stylized wormhole logo below the text. Poly's said "Consensus Intelligence: Five Heads Are Better Than One." It was from the Tigrammath company that supported her Georgia Tech professor's research. The shower stopped. Poly would be out any second.

I added shredded cheese to the omelet and folded it in half to encourage melting. Then I pushed the button on the toaster. I turned back to the table in time to see Poly emerging from my bedroom wrapped in a large, white, fluffy towel that covered and exposed portions of her anatomy delightfully. I was glad Tomáso and Shepherd had stopped monitoring my place— I didn't want to share moments like this with anyone except Poly. I wished I'd made more progress figuring out the other two entities getting feeds from my apartment.

Poly noticed my distraction and kissed me, a peck with a promise of more. Her damp auburn hair was a shade darker than it would be when it was dry but her smile was broad and bright. She tilted her head back and inhaled through her nose.

"Whatever you're making smells wonderful!"

"Thank you," I said, bowing in her direction.

She moved close, gave me another peck, and walked over to sit at the dining room table where she clutched her knife in one hand and her fork in the other. Her body language clearly said "Feed me!" and so did the next words out of her mouth.

"I could eat an ubercow, or at least a good chunk of one."

That was hyperbole. Ubercows are from Neuva Pâkkjuk, one of the Short Pâkk planets. They're sixty feet long and weigh as much as a fully grown Apatosaurus.

I divided the omelet, giving Poly the larger share, added two slices of toast, and put a steaming plate in front of her. Then I brought the dishes of fruit salad over from the counter.

"Dig in," I said.

Poly didn't reply. She was too busy following instructions. My teakettle whistled and I made two cups of allspice peach tea, one of Poly's favorites. Poly looked up to acknowledge delivery of her mug, but remained focused on her breakfast. I ate some of what was on my plate but didn't share Poly's voracious appetite. At intervals, I asked if she liked the omelet, but her mouth was usually too full to reply. When her plate and fruit salad bowl were clean, and after she'd requested and consumed two more slices of sourdough toast, Poly finally seemed ready to talk. I was looking forward to it.

"That was delicious," she said. "I love your cooking."

"Thanks. How did the work on your project go?"

"Fine, mostly."

"Mostly?"

Was this what was making Poly's shoulders tense?

"You know what my research is about, don't you?"

"You're trying to determine the best mix of artificial intelligence personality types for Tigrammath composite machine intelligences, right?"

"Right," said Poly. "Remember that the old Apollo lunar missions had three redundant computers?"

I nodded. My *mother* wasn't even born at the time, but I recalled something from an alternate history novel where leaving our planet, rather than discovering congruent technology, was the key to a GaFTA membership invitation. Armstrong and Aldrin had been greeted by aliens in space suits when they'd landed in the Sea of Tranquility.

"They'd poll them to see if all three gave the same answer."

"Uh huh," she said. "They needed to take that approach because the machines were primitive and unreliable."

"I'm with you so far."

"Tigrammath A.I. systems have reliability problems, too, but not because they're simple-minded. The problem is that they're so brilliant they tend to go insane at unpredictable intervals."

"I've heard about that," I said, "but haven't had to deal with any of them myself yet."

"That's because they're primarily used to solve philosophical problems," said Poly. "It takes a sophisticated A.I. to handle existential moral calculus."

"With a non-zero chance of going nuts while doing so?"

"Exactly. That's why Consensus Intelligence, my prof's research sponsor, uses multiple A.I. units to cross-check and monitor each other to see if any of the composite machine personalities are becoming irrational. The project I'm working on is trying to determine the best mix of A.I. personalities to reduce the odds of any of them going off the deep end."

"So what's the problem?"

"Crazy is catching."

"Say again?"

"When one A.I. personality in a composite starts acting weird, it increases the odds that the others will, too," said Poly. "It's like they infect each other."

"How many personalities are in the composites?" I asked.

"It varies from three to seventeen. Low numbers are used to handle simple ethical dilemmas, like trolley problems."

"The ones where pulling a track switching lever kills one intelligent entity and not pulling it kills five?"

"Yep. Freshman-level stuff. Higher numbers are used for complex, large scale issues with millions of dimensions, like determining the philosophical implications of interspecies wars."

"What?" The Pâkk-Orish war was less than a generation ago and I'd never heard of A.I. systems being used to analyze *that*.

"Composite machine intelligences were first developed on Tigram after the Pâkk-Tigrammath War."

"That really happened?" I said. "I thought it was just a myth to explain why Tigrammaths are into meditation and the Pâkk split into Short and Long factions."

The two Pâkk factions have different views of other intelligent species. Both agree that non-Pâkk are sheep to be exploited, but Long Pâkk want them for wool and Short Pâkk see them as lamb chops.

"It was real," said Poly. "My adviser, the head researcher on this project, is a Tigrammath. He says the War was so bad that whole planetary populations were destroyed with congruent-tech bombs and massive bio-weapon plagues were unleashed. The Tigrammaths were supposedly the more aggressive of the two species, which is why they try so hard to damp it down and stay chill now."

"When did all this happen?"

"Professor Urrrson says 15,000 years ago."

That turned my understanding of GaFTA history upside down. The Galactic Free Trade Association civilizations had crashed during the Pleistocene and had only rebuilt in the last few thousand years? And if the Tigrammaths were originally *more* aggressive than the Pâkk, that was saying something. Poly could see my brain going off on a tangent so she leaned forward. The towel wrapped around her gapped suggestively. My hindbrain grabbed my forebrain's attention and pulled me back into the present.

"Getting back to the composite machine personalities," I said.

Poly adjusted her towel to reduce my distraction. She kept

smiling at me, but her body was telling her to focus on digesting breakfast and getting some sleep. I could tell she'd soon be surrendering to the arms of Morpheus. All-nighters are harder in grad school than in college.

"Our project is using units with five personalities," she said. "They're working on 'greatest good for greatest number' problems, with the associated dimensions of balancing individual freedom versus public good."

"I can see how that would drive some personalities crazy."

"Exactly. With our current mix of personality types, we can't seem to process potential solutions for more than an hour before one of the personalities can't handle it and goes bonkers."

"Don't the other personalities catch it and flag its responses as errors?" I asked.

"No, that's the problem. They seem to resonate with the off-kilter personality and go nuts themselves."

"Quis custodiet ipsos custodes?"

"Right. Who guards the guardians? The other personalities aren't evaluating the one that goes off the deep end. They're jumping in with it," said Poly.

This was the first time Poly had sounded so frustrated by her Georgia Tech project. I really wanted to be helpful, but didn't know much about the nuances of her research.

"Tell me about these personalities," I said. "How do you figure out their intellectual and emotional parameters? How do you decide which types to include in a given consensual matrix?"

"All the A.I. personalities are genius-level intellects," said Poly. "We usually put two linear thinkers, an emotional unit, an intuitive unit and an artistic unit in a 5-ply matrix. They're all specialists, with their own approaches to problem solving. We make sure they're well-adjusted personalities with strong social skills so they can cooperate effectively with each other."

"Wait," I said. "You're using brilliant, genius-level personalities that are well-adjusted and have strong social skills?"

I didn't think it was *possible* to have true genius-level personalities with strong social skills.

"Of course. How else can they work together effectively?"

"But you still want them to cross-check each other?"

"Of course," said Poly. "That's how they gain concensus."

"I think I see the problem," I said.

She gave me a "So tell me already…" look.

"You don't need the personalities to be well-adjusted or have good social skills. You need them to be cantankerous, solitary recluses who don't care what the other personalities think."

"But that way, they'd never come up with consensus solutions."

"They would, if one of their programmed guidelines was that four of them had to agree to judge the fifth as off its rocker."

Poly's eyebrows scrunched as she thought it through.

"You're saying that having social and cooperation skills mean they're more likely to adopt the crazy personalities' perspectives and make them their own?"

"Yes. Grumpy geniuses don't *care* what anyone else thinks. They're not looking for consensus. They're following their own paths. The personalities with good social skills are becoming friends. They don't want to disturb the group's equilibrium by calling each other crazy, so they accommodate and *all* go off the wall."

Poly sat up straight. Her towel moved in interesting ways, but my attention was focused on her face. It lit up with sudden inspiration—she was taking things a lot farther than I could. This was one of her specialties, after all.

"If I swap out one of the linear thinking A.I. units for an integrative one, we won't even need to reprogram the rest. We'll just keep them isolated and the integrating unit can identify anything crazy when it tries to construct a coherent solution."

"You may want to reduce the social skills anyway," I said. "It's not a good idea to isolate gregarious personalities. That could lead to even more problems."

Poly waved her hand.

"That's trivial."

Her brain was working through permutations and implications at high speed. She'd tuned out the rest of the world. I knew how important it was to give her time to think, so I quietly cleared the breakfast dishes, washed the frying pan, and put the butter and jam back in the refrigerator. After ten more minutes she popped out of her cogitative trance. I could almost see the "EUREKA!" thought balloon above her head. Poly walked into the bedroom and came back with a phone the size of a business card. She started dictating notes in a soft, urgent voice. I could hear and make sense of no more than half of what she was saying. She was clearly on to something important. I take back what I'd thought about it being impossible to have a true genius-level personality with strong social skills. Poly. Q.E.D.

When she'd finished dictating and released a contented sigh of accomplishment, I moved behind her and started to rub her shoulders.

"Mmmm… that feels really good."

She felt pretty good under my fingers, too.

"Congratulations," I said.

"Thanks. We'll see if it works in the lab tomorrow."

"I thought you were finished with this project."

"I was, but now I've got to try this new approach. I'll be tied up for the next two days."

"Aren't we picking up your family at the airport on Wednesday afternoon?"

"Can you get them, Jack? This research is really important."

"Sure," I said.

I really looked forward to meeting Poly's mother and father and sister without her help in navigating potential minefields. *Not.*

Still, I had to earn boyfriend points and impress her family.

"Glad to do it."

"Thanks, Lover Boy," said Poly, standing up and turning to give me a hug. She was getting so sleepy it was hard for her to keep her eyes open. When she extended her arms in my direction, her towel fell to the floor and she tilted against me, barely—pardon the pun—able to stand. I kept my eyes above neck level, picked her up, carried her into my bedroom and placed her gently in my bed. She was asleep before her head hit my goose down pillow. I pulled blankets over her, then bent to brush her hair away from her face and give her a kiss. She woke momentarily; just long enough to kiss me back. She tugged me closer so my ear was near her lips.

"Jack," she said, in an unfocused and drowsy voice. "I have to warn you…"

And she was out.

I love ominous cryptic phrases, but didn't have time for this one. I needed a shave and a shower myself—there were clients to see and tech support calls to make.

Still, what *was* she trying to warn me about? I guess I'd find out soon enough.

Chapter 6

"A dinner invitation, once accepted, is a sacred obligation.
If you die before the dinner takes place,
your executor must attend."
— Ward McAllister

I tried to be as quiet as possible when I got my shower and dressed. I didn't need to bother—Poly was sleeping deeper than the Marianas Trench and didn't look like she'd be stirring until dinnertime. I was in the living room reviewing my discombobulated schedule for the day when my phone got my attention.

"Jack, someone's coming to your front door."

My phone was monitoring the new cameras I'd installed on my front and back doors after I'd been shot. One of the hats I wear is security consultant, and with the woman who'd shot me still at large, I thought it wise to increase the physical security at my apartment.

"Jack, I'd open your front door *right now.*"

My phone didn't use that tone of voice very often so I hopped off the couch and opened the door, only to be nearly struck in the face by one of a juvenile Daaushan's primary trunks. I jumped back, and so did my visitor, a Shetland pony-sized, somewhat elephant-shaped alien, whose bright pink hide was covered in light blue polka dots the size of archaic DVDs.

"Uncle *Jack!*" said Terrhi, the daughter of my friend Tomáso, the head of Atlanta's Dauushan consulate. She was loud—even juvenile Dauushans have big lungs.

"Hi Terrhi," I said. Then I put a finger to my lips and whispered, "Please speak softly. Poly's asleep. She pulled an all-nighter and she's exhausted."

"Okay, Uncle Jack," she said, in a voice that was a whisper for her and a normal volume for most humans.

I stepped out into the courtyard and turned to close the front door. When I faced forward again I was head-butted by

Terrhi's pet cat, a Dauushan six-legged tri-sabertooth the size of a panther.

"Hi Spike," I said.

His eyes were big and blinked rapidly in a way I'd learned to recognize as amusement. Spike and I were buddies ever since I'd rescued him, sort of, from aggressive squirrels in an ornamental Dauushan banyan tree in the Ad Astra courtyard. The big cat opened his mouth and yawned, showing off the three large canines that gave him his name. I yawned, too, feeling the aftereffects of getting up early this morning and eating two breakfasts. Terrhi crowded close, bumping Spike out of the way and hugging me with six of her sub-trunks. Each of her three primary trunks splits into three smaller ones. It sounds weird, but it's how Dauushans are designed.

"I'm *really* glad to see you, Uncle Jack!"

"Go easy on the ribs, Terrhi. I'm still recovering."

"Sor-ry!" she said in her piping soprano little girl's voice. "Is Aunt Poly okay?"

"She's fine. I fed her a big breakfast after she was up all night. She'll probably sleep for eight or nine hours."

I shook my head to restart my brain and kept talking.

"What are you doing here?" I said. "Shouldn't you be in school at this hour?"

"Not today," she said. "It's a Dauushan holiday."

"Which one?" I asked.

"The one called *I'm a Dauushan and I'm taking a holiday*," said Terrhi, smiling.

Tomáso would never let his daughter get away with something like that.

"What's the real story?"

"We have the whole day off for teachers' training."

"That's much more believable."

"I've got something for you," Terrhi said, pulling a large, ornate envelope from a pouch on her foreleg. "Mom got in late yesterday. Her royal self and my Dad are inviting you and Poly to dinner at the Teleport Inn on Wednesday night."

"That sounds great, but Poly's family is flying in that afternoon for her graduations. It wouldn't be right to leave them on their own."

"Maybe they can come, too! I'll check with my Dad."

Terrhi pulled a cell phone half the size of a skateboard from a pouch on her other foreleg and held it in her hand, pressing its touchscreen with three of her sub-trunks. She waited for a reply, then shared the response.

"Dad says you're *all* welcome to come to dinner. He says Poly's mom is an old friend."

"That sounds fine by me, but we'll have to wait until Poly wakes up and can check with her parents to confirm."

"No problem," said Terrhi. "Daddy said you'd have to talk to Poly first. He's reserved a table big enough for eight Dauushans, so there will be plenty of room for extra humans if they can make it."

I smiled at her enthusiasm.

"And Daddy said I can order an ice cream sundae for dessert!"

I'd seen the size of the Teleport Inn's Dauushan sundaes. They were served in cut glass dishes the size of punch bowls. Maybe she'd share.

"I hope we'll be able to make it. I'd like to meet your mom."

Terrhi's mother is the Queen of Dauush, a planet and its associated daughter worlds, filled with elephant-sized pink aliens that really understand large scale fabrication. The Model-43 printer at WT&F would be three generations behind the times on Dauush, which is how someone like Jean-Jacques Bonhomme could afford it.

Like the elephants they resemble, Dauushans' culture is matriarchal—and Terrhi's mom, Sherrhiliandarianne the Second, is their Grand High Matriarch. The Terran press usually translates her title as queen, but she's more than just a ceremonial head of state. She's the over-mother of the entire species, with all the power and influence that goes with that role.

When I'd first met Terrhi a few months ago, I'd had no idea she was *the* Princess of Dauush, her mother's heir. I'd just thought she was a cute kid, the daughter of my friend Tomáso Kauuson. Tomáso was the head of the local Dauushan consulate and a big shot in the Dauushan equivalent of the Drug Enforcement Agency. I'd worked with him on the security systems for his offices and living quarters in the Ad Astra complex. I might not have learned that Terrhi *was* a princess if she hadn't been kidnapped during the First Contact Day parade six weeks back.

With help from a lot of people, including Poly, Chit, Tomáso, Spike, Lieutenant Lee, Mike and Shepherd, I'd managed to rescue Terrhi from a megalomaniac named Anthony Zwilniki. Tony Zed, as the media liked to call him, had been the CEO of VIGorish Labs, a virtual interactive gaming company that offered a fully immersive experience—by putting gamers into giant cylindrical tubes full of liquid. Zed's plan had been to assemble a battalion of Terran mercenaries, invade Dauush, and capture Terrhi's mom. With their queen "in check," Zwilniki intended to force the Dauushans to fabricate the matériel needed for an army and space navy large enough to conquer all the other member species of the Galactic Free Trade Association.

We'd stopped Zwilniki and his mercenaries with very few casualties, except for my previously mentioned gunshot-bruised ribs, dinosaur claw-damaged leg, and a minor concussion. Thanks to a well-timed intervention by Spike, Zwilniki was now in prison awaiting trial. His invasion had literally never gotten off the ground.

Terrhi's mom was scheduled to speak at Emory University's graduation ceremonies on Saturday. According to the Internet, the queen was coming to Atlanta to meet with researchers at the Centers for Disease Control and Prevention about funding some big project—and the Emory folks saw her trip as a great way to trade an honorary degree for a speech from a prestigious GaFTA head of state who didn't travel off-planet very often. Tomáso had told me to expect a dinner invitation and I was looking forward to meeting the mother of Princess Terrhiluundramaki. If she was anything like her daughter, she'd be something special.

Then Terrhi's voice, like accelerated birdsong, interrupted my thoughts.

"She wants to meet you, too, Uncle Jack! Daddy and I told her all about you and Poly and Chit and the rescue and *everything.*"

"I'm sure you did," I said. "I hope you didn't leave out Spike's contribution."

The tri-sabertooth lifted his oversized head and looked at me when I mentioned his name. He smiled broadly to show off his seven inch incisors, rubbed against my hand to get more scritches, and waited for Terrhi to continue.

"You were my hero, weren't you Spike?" said Terrhi. "You saved Uncle Jack from that bad, *bad* man, didn't you?"

Spike had grabbed Zwilniki's gun hand when Tony Zed had been ready to shoot me, so he was my hero, too. But that didn't mean I couldn't mess with him. I saw a robin land on the far side of the Ad Astra courtyard and let my eyes go wide.

"Squirrel!"

Spike's ears rotated forward and he turned to follow my gaze then shot off across the lawn like a six-legged cheetah in search of fluffy-tailed squirrels to terrorize. Terrhi turned to follow her pet and waved two of her trunks over her shoulder.

"See you, Uncle Jack! Hope you can come to dinner. Spike! Bad boy! Come back here this instant!"

I watched Terrhi sprint off after Spike, waved at them both, and went back inside holding Terrhi's envelope. Like most things related to Dauush it was large and pink, nearly the size of a cookie sheet. When I flipped it over I saw that it was held shut by a dark fuchsia wax seal imprinted with a crown.

The invitation was written using highly formal, incised archaeic Dauushan characters. It resembled cuneiform, but with lots of ornamentation on the angular letters. Dauushans originally started writing using sticks and reeds cut at various angles. Sub-trunks would hold smaller twigs to add the orna-ments. Initially, characters were incised into clay tablets, but as civilization matured on Dauush, writing implements were pressed into thick sheets of paper. When a sheet was com-plete, a thin coating of ink was spread across it and quickly wiped away, leaving well defined characters in the depres-sions. I could feel bumps from what was printed on the inside coming through to the outside on the queen's invitation.

I considered waiting for Poly to wake up before I opened the invitation, but didn't want to wait that long. I might need to pick up a ceremonial gift or special clothes for a royal din-ner and would need all the advance notice I could get.

I moved to the kitchen, found a flat metal pancake turner, and warmed it up above a stove burner. Then I slipped the warm turner under the wax seal and slowly slid it along until the seal released. Like any good seal, it didn't come off cleanly. It was clear that the invitation had been opened.

I brushed a few loose pieces of wax into a trash can and sat down to read. Tomáso knew that Poly and I could both read Dauushan, so there wasn't an English or Galang translation. The message was short and to the point.

> *Her Matriarchal Majesty, Sherrhiliandarianne the Second, graciously invites Mr. Ajax Pryce Buckston and Ms. Poly-hymnia Keen Jones to dine as Her Majesty's honored guests at the Atlanta Teleport Inn at 8:00 p.m. on Wednesday.*

There was also the Dauushan equivalent of *"répondez s'il vous plaît,"* but the idiom used in formal royal invitations was more like, "Let us know, or Big Momma will spank." Dauushans are a direct and practical species.

I put the opened invitation on my kitchen counter where Poly would be sure to see it and added a handwritten note saying that her family was invited, too. I signed it with "XOXOXO," a big heart, and "Love, Jack." What can I say? I'm a romantic.

Then I grabbed my backpack tool bag and headed for the

door. One of my favorite clients was two weeks overdue for preventive maintenance on her systems, thanks to my injuries putting me behind schedule, and I didn't want to tempt Murphy any more than I had already. A major glitch on my watch would hurt her business and wouldn't be very good for Xenotech Support Corporation's rep, either.

I phoned my van as I walked.

"Meet me at the Peachtree Street gate."

"As you wish."

I really needed to talk to my phone about letting my van watch *The Princess Bride*.

Chapter 7

"Don't feed the plants."
— from *Little Shop of Horrors,*
lyrics by Howard Ashman

Mistress Marigold is a florist. Her retail stores are called Little Shop of Flowers and there are two in the Ad Astra complex, plus nine more at other five star hotels around Atlanta's upscale Buckhead neighborhood. She specializes in exotic off-planet plants and blossoms, like the Orishen orchids Terrhi had found for me to give to Poly on our first date. The orchids are sensitive to their wearers' moods and clothing and change color to reflect one and complement the other.

It would have been a short walk across the courtyard to get to the closest Ad Astra flower shop, but getting to Mistress Marigold's greenhouses required a vehicle. After First Contact, the city of Atlanta had bent over backwards to attract Mistress Marigold here instead of San Diego. It wasn't because they needed more flower shops—Mistress Marigold was also a renowned xenobotanist and the CEO of a sexy new bio-pharmaceutical company, Marigold Flowers & Pharmaceuticals. Selling flowers was just a synergistic sideline.

The largest part of her enterprise developed an array of plant-based medicines that were as useful against galactic diseases as quinine was against malaria. Their top seller, *Lethe,* was a fast-acting over-the-counter euphoric and soporific used to treat post-traumatic stress disorders and sleep abnormalities.

The CDC had helped tip the balance thanks to a generous grant to MF&P from the Yu-Obi-Crispos Foundation. CDC researchers wanted to be close to Mistress Marigold so they could work with her on applications for public health. Emory University awarded her a named chair in their botany department. But what really sealed the deal for Mistress Marigold selecting my adopted home city had been proximity to the Atlanta Botanical Gardens. Mistress Marigold loved Terran flowers and wanted to be near the exhibits and professional staff at the Gardens. That's why the city gave her a sweetheart deal on some prime real estate.

As part of a package that included loan guarantees and tax abatements, Atlanta relocated half a dozen tennis courts to another part of Piedmont Park and granted Marigold Flowers & Pharmaceuticals a ninety-nine year lease on the land. MF&P built twenty-five thousand square feet of offices, labs and greenhouses adjacent to the Gardens' Fuqua Orchid Center.

Mistress Marigold generously shared her expertise and resources to support the Gardens. Her displays of Nicósn paratulips, flowers that instinctively sang in twelve-part harmony, had been a major draw and a substantial moneymaker for the Gardens last year. I'd been to the show and it was spectacular—the paratulips' blossoms and voices were both lovely. I looked forward to visiting again with Poly once she had free time. Beautiful things are even more beautiful when they're shared with someone you love.

Focus, Jack. You're getting sappy.

I'd been referred to Mistress Marigold by the Gardens' Executive Director. He had hired me to set up security systems with enough sophistication to prevent thieves from breaking in to steal valuable flora and enough initiative to intercept wandering toddlers before they could get themselves into too much trouble.

MF&P had similar challenges, without the peripatetic preschoolers. Some of their rare plants were worth hundreds of thousands of galcreds, after all. They also needed to monitor and adjust the complex microenvironments required by individual specimens.

The systems I'd installed for MF&P were reliable, but they needed regular preventive maintenance. Unfortunately, I'd pushed their recommended maintenance interval because of my injuries. Part of my brain was nagging me to get there today, before something bad happened, like their Nicósn moss farm drying out from too much heat or their Araqeen cacti getting the moisture level that should have been assigned to water loving float rice from Rivière Monde.

My van dropped me off at the closest corner to MF&P and went off in search of a parking place. I walked to the company's front entrance along a flagstone path flanked by thousands of earthly and unearthly blooms. I recognized common off-planet specimens like mauve pyrimbidia and antennathuriums with their tall spiked receptors. I was impressed by the landscape gardeners' skill at blending terrestrial varieties with non-native plants. The grounds were immaculate. All the pine straw and mulch was neatly distributed and there were hardly any candy wrappers or other pieces of litter anywhere. Then I saw why.

Three Gēnomosian garden gnomes were using their thick, muscular walking leaves to push their wagons full of dirt around the company's grounds. Their flexible tendrils shot out to pick up discarded gum wrappers, ticket stubs and stray bits of plastic. Some of the items they collected went into their digestive orifices and some went onto spikes on their wagons for later disposal. I couldn't figure out how they decided which went where.

I remembered that life had taken a different path on Gēnomos, a planet that wasn't a member of the Galactic Free Trade Association, but was controlled as a protectorate of Nicós. Animals never developed, so plants expanded into available ecological niches. The garden gnomes were the size and shape of large Russian nesting dolls wrapped in green leaves. Manipulative tendrils sprouted an inch or so from the base of each gnome and their powerful walking leaves peeled back from their central core like a half-shucked ear of corn. Two photosensitive patches near the top of their cores served as eyes and pointed tassels at the very top looked like tiny hats. I understood that they weren't intelligent the way GaFTA member species measure intelligence, but they were trainable and seemed quite pleased to have someone providing them with nutrients.

The security guard in the lobby checked my credentials—one of the policies I'd insisted they implement. When he saw my name he paused.

"You're Jack Buckston?" said the guard. His name tag read "Vic."

"That's me."

"Mistress Marigold told me she wanted to see you when you got in," said Vic. "I'll call her office and let her know you're here."

Vic made the call, spoke a few words, nodded, then remembered it wasn't a video phone and said, "Understood. Will do."

I smiled. I've nodded on voice calls plenty of times myself.

"She says you should just head on up."

Vic handed me a visitor's badge on a lanyard. I put it over my head then stuck out my hand for the tracking bracelet that mapped my every move through the complex. Every employee or visitor wore one and anyone without a bracelet would be instantly flagged by MF&P's security system. I boarded an elevator in the lobby and rode it up to the sixth floor. Mistress Marigold reserved the seventh floor at the top for very special plants that would benefit from natural light from the glass ceiling.

When the elevator made a ding sound to announce we'd arrived on the executive level, I crouched low, held the door open with my fingertips, and peered around it carefully. One of Mistress Marigold's prize specimens loved me—I mean *really* loved me, like a Great Dane who hasn't seen her master in a month. My attempts at caution were for naught, however. Two green tendrils the size of boa constrictors whipped around the entrance to the elevator, grabbed me, and pulled me out into the hall, where they began to toss me up and down like a baby. Then the tendrils wound around me and gave me a very tight, enthusiastic hug, enough for all the air to be forced out of my lungs.

"Jack! Jack Jack Jack *Jack JACK!*"

The voice was low, but had a youthful cadence. I tried to

summon my breath, then my dignity, but I couldn't manage it. I inhaled deeply, then laughed.

"You can put me down now, Dree," I said between chuckles. "I'm glad to see you, too. And watch the ribs!"

"Sorry, Jack! Sometimes I don't know my own strength."

"Don't worry about it. Just put me down. Feet *first,* please."

"Of course, of course," said Dree, the corners of her primary feeding pod turning up. "But I've *missed* you."

Dree was a giant carnivorous plant from a planet Nicósn explorers were rumored to have discovered, then promptly "lost." At least it's not listed on any contemporary star charts. Dree's pot took up half of the floor in the executive level's elevator lobby and her tendrils, leaves and pod mouths made her a one-plant jungle.

For a carnivore, Dree has a sweet disposition, but she's a hugger. She's also an effective adjunct to MF&P's building security, but that's another story. I'd heard that a plant from Dree's world had somehow visited Earth before First Contact and there'd been problems with trace element levels affecting its metabolism, but Dree seemed fine. She got a side of beef twice a week and that kept her quite happy. Still, rumors of her thirst for human blood continue to circulate and enhance her undeserved mean, green reputation.

"I've missed you, too," I said, rubbing my sore torso with my palms.

"She's waiting for you," said the plant. "She's needs your help with a mystery."

"I love a good mystery," I said. "Sherlock is my middle name."

"Really?"

"No, but it sounds good, doesn't it?"

"You're *funny*, Jack. You'd better go in. She's eager to see you," said Dree.

"I will," I said, smiling. "*Her* hugs aren't so enthusiastic."

"I said I was sorry."

I didn't know plants could pout.

"Just kidding."

I found two of her beach balls in a corner and tossed them Dree's way as I headed toward Mistress Marigold's office. A pair of Dree's small, cloned feeding pods, growing from her largest roots, caught them and bounced them up and over her giant central feeding pod like preteens playing volleyball. Several of the cloned pods looked almost ready to break off.

Mistress Marigold smiled when she met me at the door to her office. She's an older Nicósn and six inches shorter than my six foot two. She doesn't look like Mrs. Santa Claus anymore, like she did in the photos I've seen from her youth. Her short beard tentacles have started to go gray and even black to mark her maturity. If it worked that way in humans, there'd be a major market for dyes to turn hair white.

Mistress Marigold's smile was warm. She gave off grand-mother vibes, even though her official bio didn't mention anything about offspring. Her forehead wrinkles looked like well-tended furrows where wisdom would spring forth like Athena from the brow of Zeus.

"Thank you for seeing me, Jack," said Mistress Marigold, shaking my hand. Her palm was warm. "When I heard you'd be here today to do routine maintenance, I asked our front desk to have you stop here first."

"It's always a pleasure to see you," I said.

"And you've always been a charmer," she said. "I hope you're feeling better?"

"Much better, thanks," I said, "though Dree's greeting was a bit too enthusiastic for this stage in my recovery."

"Dree's enthusiasm is one of her virtues," she said. "But I do apologize. Please come in and have a seat. I need your help with something."

"I'm glad to do whatever I can," I said, taking a seat in a comfortable overstuffed chair near several others arranged in a circle in a corner of Mistress Marigold's CEO-sized office. Tall plants with broad leaves in a dozen verdant shades surrounded the chairs, giving the illusion of privacy and reinforcing the casual, welcoming, organic feel of the place. They smelled nice, too. Even the walls of her office were covered in some sort of short grass. I wondered how she kept it mowed. Whatever the answer, it was a delight to be somewhere that's green.

Mistress Marigold held up a clear glass pitcher of ice water and when I nodded she filled a tall glass for me and then one for herself. Ice water always tasted better at her place. I'd have to ask her how she did that someday. Maybe it was some sort of special filtration, or required the assistance of one or more of her exotic plants, like Dree. On second thought, maybe I didn't want to know.

"I'm concerned…" started Mistress Marigold.

"I'm sorry," I said, in an apologetic rush. "I meant to be here to do your preventive maintenance a few weeks ago, but what with my recovery and all, I didn't get here. I thought about using Remote Hands, but I didn't want to risk your more sensitive seedlings with someone who wasn't familiar with their special requirements and…"

"Jack," said Mistress Marigold. "It's not about anything you've done or haven't done."

"It's not?"

"No. I'm concerned about some very special plants from Dree's home planet that may be highly valuable to an important client."

"Oh."

I keep telling myself to listen more and talk less, but find that I can't stop myself from talking, especially when I'm feeling like I haven't done as much as I should. I hate to let people down and had been afraid that my lack of attention had caused problems for MF&P. I tried again.

"What's going on?"

"You know I have my experimental plants up on the seventh floor?"

"Yes," I said, "we worked out microclimate zones that would

provide ideal growing conditions for each variety. It's all automatic and computer controlled."

"Except it isn't," said Mistress Marigold. "At least not consistently. I can't figure it out. It's a mystery."

"That's strange," I said. "Could you give me some examples?"

"Of course. You know the Rigeliotropes—the Rigelian sunflowers—need a constant supply of light, right?"

"Those florescent purple flowers on the tall stalks?"

"Yes. Something's been cutting them off from the high energy stellar radiation they need for five to ten minutes at a time before the automated systems detect the problem and correct it." She frowned and drank a sip of water. "They're twenty galmils shorter than they should be at this stage in their growing cycle."

"Ouch," I said. I remembered that the stalks of the Rigeliotropes were very flexible and used to reinforce vaulting poles. Their dried seeds were supposed to either cure constipation or prevent the runs, I couldn't remember which—and hoped I'd never have cause to need them in either capacity.

"Anything else?"

"Yes," said Marigold. "Bags of bone meal have been moved from one microclimate zone to another. Some are missing altogether. Spades and watering cans are randomly moved around and various symbiotic insects are appearing in places they shouldn't."

"Got it."

"Not to mention that the Balaam's Asters are completely out of control."

"I remember those. The blue ground cover that has to be cut back with a weed whacker and complains when you do," I said.

"Well, something is interfering with their auto-pruning system and they're taking over the adjoining zones," said Mistress Marigold. "They're only two zones away from some special medicinal plants from Dree's home world—and I *can't* risk any harm coming to them."

"What have you done to investigate so far?" I asked.

"I put a security guard on the seventh floor two nights ago to see what she could learn, but we found her sound asleep, resting on a large bed of Wandering Judy in one of the zones closest to the entrance. She says she has no idea what happened."

"I've got some guesses," I said. "I'm going to go downstairs to the security office to review the relevant recordings."

"My people did that," Mistress Marigold said.

"But they didn't know what to look for," I said. "Could you also arrange to get me a kilo of fresh hamburger from the employee cafeteria and a bottle of *Lethe?*"

"The hamburger shouldn't be a problem, and I'm sure I can round up some *Lethe*. What dosage?"

"You're the doctor," I said, smiling. "What would I need to knock out something with the body weight of a watermelon?"

"I have a doctorate in xenobotany," said Mistress Marigold, "not medicine. But I'd expect a hundred milligrams would do it. I'm sure my VP of Sales will have a drawerful of samples in various dosages."

"Thanks. Please have the meat and the pills delivered to me in the security office, along with a large, resealable plastic bag."

"I'll see to it."

"Great."

I finished my water and excused myself. Mistress Marigold was on the phone before I'd left, getting me what I needed. Not far from her office, I found one of Dree's beach balls in the hall. I tossed it toward the lobby and followed it quickly, making a fast break for the elevator. This time I was lucky. The doors opened before Dree could give me another hug. As the doors closed, I did get another look at her rhizome feeding pods. Some of them looked fairly mature and there were some empty spots where I suspected budding clones had once been connected. My hunch was growing stronger.

"Bye, Dree!" I said through the last crack before the elevator door sealed.

As I descended I heard the thump of tendrils slamming into

the door to wish me a safe vertical journey.

I got off on the ground floor and had Vic call his boss, Venna. She escorted me downstairs to the building's security monitoring room. Whatever weird irresistible-to-women pheromones I'd been giving off earlier didn't seem to work on her, or on Mistress Marigold, thank goodness.

I remembered Venna—we'd worked together when the building's security was initially installed. Mistress Marigold had called and asked her to do whatever she could to help me. Venna was a younger Nicósn with short beard tentacles so white they practically glowed.

After First Contact it took humans quite a while to learn the physical differences between male and female Nicósns, since their general body shapes were much the same. Once we realized that beard length was a gender signifier rather than a stylistic choice, humans who weren't comfortable until they knew the right pronoun to use were a lot happier. I understand that our more pronounced sexual dimorphism is disconcerting for Nicósns, but you'd never know from the way they interact with us.

We sat down at a bank of monitors and started reviewing recordings from the seventh floor microclimate zones. I set the search parameters to find any instances of something moving on the seventh floor after normal working hours that *wasn't* wearing a security bracelet. The cameras were motion-sensitive and tied into the building's security databases, so that wasn't difficult to specify. We did pick up movements—lots of them—but we couldn't tell what was triggering the cameras' sensors. Whatever was there was either moving too fast for us to follow or blended in with the foliage in the zones. There was a lag before any motion drew the cameras' attention and we couldn't see what was moving. We did notice that the count of sacks of bone meal had declined by one in the room with the Balaam's Asters. Venna could track something crawling underneath the thick ground cover, but couldn't tell what it was.

"This is getting us nowhere," said Venna. Her beard tentacles were standing straight out in frustration.

"I've got an idea," I said. "Let's take a look at the recordings from the executive floor's elevator lobby for a few days before the problems started."

There was a knock on the door to the security monitoring room. It was Vic holding a large, resealable plastic bag filled with a kilo of raw hamburger in one hand and a small pill bottle marked with the MF&P logo in the other.

"Mistress Marigold said you wanted these, Mr. Buckston," he said. "I hope *you* know why, 'cause I can't figure it out."

"Call me Jack," I said. "We could use another set of eyes. Want to help?"

"I'd be glad to," said Vic, "but my shift just ended."

Vic and I both looked at Venna for her approval.

"Stay on the clock, Vic," said Venna with a smile. "I'm authorizing you for overtime. I have a feeling we're both going to learn something."

"Great," said Vic, finding a seat in front of a bank of monitors. "Now I can find out why you wanted the meat and pills."

"Not quite yet," I said to Vic, then turned to Venna. "Please put the recordings on high speed playback on three screens. We can each take a day. Queue it up to begin after the place clears out at night, say seven or eight o'clock."

"Will do," said Venna. "What are we looking for?"

"You'll know it when you see it," I said. "Call out if you notice anything unusual."

I checked the wastebasket next to the desk where I was working and confirmed that it had several plastic liners inside for the convenience of the janitorial staff. I removed the second liner down and flattened it out on the desk.

Keeping half an eye on the screen I was supposed to be watching, I opened the kilo of hamburger and separated it into nine approximately quarter pound balls on the plastic liner.

I was comfortable with the metric system—and the galmet system, for that matter—but a quarter of a pound still sounded more natural to me than a tenth of a kilo when it came to burgers.

Then I opened the bottle of fast-acting *Lethe* and pushed a pill deep into each ball. I surveyed my handiwork, saw that it was good, and put the balls back in the plastic bag. I finished by tossing the liner in the trash.

I hadn't been paying much attention to the recordings flashing by on my monitor, so I was pleased when Vic spotted something.

"Look!" he said, freezing the frame on Dree and the executive floor's elevator lobby.

"What did you find?" said Venna, leaning in, her beard tentacles now relaxed and writhing naturally.

I smiled. Vic had found what I'd been expecting. He'd frozen the screen just as two of Dree's mature clones had broken off from her roots and moved toward the elevator. It was clear that several more were ready to separate soon.

"Who knew the juvenile form was mobile?" I said, musing.

Vic played the recording forward in slow motion. We saw several three-foot mini-Dree clones assemble in front of the elevator.

"Switch angles," I said to Venna.

She switched to the same time stamp on a camera observing the elevator doors. Seven of nine junior versions of Dree formed a plant pyramid and collectively pushed the up button. Then they boarded the elevator and disappeared.

"I'm going to wash my hands, then head up to the seventh floor," I said. "Please clear that level of all employees so the mini-Dree clones won't be afraid to come out."

"Right away," said Venna.

"And Vic?" I said. "Use your eagle eyes and track where the other two clones went."

"Will do."

I took the bag of hamburger, hit the washroom for some soap and water, then rode up to the top floor from the basement.

Venna followed me on the security cameras and opened the security door to the seventh floor as I approached it. I walked down the access corridor until I got to the Balaam's Asters zone, since that looked like where several of them were hiding. Then I took seven of the nine balls of hamburger with the *Lethe* inside and lined them up a foot apart down the center of the corridor. I whistled a doo-wop song as I walked away and took the elevator back to the basement and the security monitoring room.

"Hey Jack! Great plan," said Venna, pointing to one of the larger monitors.

Four of the clones had already used their root-legs to enter the corridor from the Balaam's Aster zone and had taken the bait. They were gulping down their drugged meatballs and looking quite pleased with themselves—and a bit sleepy. While we watched, three more came out from the Rigeliotropes' zone and did the same. Soon, seven mini-Dree clones were sleeping soundly.

"You can send the professional xenobotany staff back to the seventh floor," I said. "Cleanup on aisle seven."

Venna was already a step ahead of me.

"Do you want to tell Mistress Marigold, or should I?" she asked.

"You can do it," I said. "I still need to go up to seven and take care of some overdue preventive maintenance."

"Uh-oh," said Vic. "You're not going to like this."

Venna and I crowded in and looked over his shoulder. Vic played more of the recording from the sixth floor elevator lobby and we watched as two of the mini-Dree clones took the elevator *down* to the first floor, where they made their way to the employee cafeteria. Vic switched views and we saw the clones leave the building by way of the loading dock and head for the thirty acres of greenery at the Atlanta Botanical Gardens.

The foxes are in the hen house now, I thought. I'd better get upstairs and talk to Mistress Marigold right away.

* * * * *

It turned out to not be as big a problem as I'd first imagined. Mistress Marigold was on the board of the Gardens and had quite a lot of influence with their executive director. More meatballs laced with *Lethe* would be placed around the grounds and the remaining two mini-Dree clones would likely be found soon. I completed my preventive maintenance without incident and Mistress Marigold complimented me on my creative solution to her problem when we met in her office late that afternoon for a wrap-up.

"Nicely done, Jack, especially when I'm the one responsible," she said. "My apologies. I guess I still have a lot more to learn about how Dree's species reproduces."

"Don't worry about it," I said. "I think we both thought of Dree as one of a kind."

"True enough, but even so, I want to say thank you," she said. "I've left a nice bouquet of exotics for you and your young lady at the reception desk."

"My young lady?" I said. "How do you know about Poly?"

"Word gets around, Jack. Word gets around."

On my way out I gave Dree a big hug, played with her by tossing beach balls, and didn't say anything about the mischief her clones had gotten into. Plants have feelings too, you know. Some plants, anyway.

Before I left the building I picked up a beautiful flower arrangement and checked to make sure none of them were self-mobile varieties. It was time to head for home. Poly should be awake by now and we had a lot of catching up to do.

Chapter 8

"Mens sana in corpore sano."
— Juvenal

When I got back to my apartment I was disappointed. Poly was already up and gone. She'd left me a note next to Queen Sherrhi's invitation saying that her parents and sister would be pleased to attend and thanking me again for picking them up at the airport on Wednesday afternoon. It had lots of Xs and Os on it, so she realized how much of an imposition it was to have me pick up her family without her around for moral support.

I put the flowers in a large vase on the dining room table, pleased that none of them were going to walk off and terrorize the Ad Astra complex. I was tired, so I put a couple of Nicósn tortilla fish in the toaster and ate them with another few inches of ripe Dauushan mega-banana. Then I went to bed.

Tomorrow, Lieutenant Lee and I had the dubious privilege of interrogating Jean-Jacques Bonhomme, the CEO of WT&F, about his dealings with Factor-E-Flor and what he knew about a certain two-hundred-and-fifty-foot robot. It would primarily be Martin's show—I was just coming along for the ride—and I was looking forward to watching him work.

I fell asleep watching an old Guillermo del Toro movie called *Pacific Rim* on my bedroom's wall screen and remember thinking *my robot looks cooler* as my eyes grew heavy and I slept.

* * * * *

Instead of using Poly's voice, my phone decided to wake me another way, with the soothing notes of *Ranz de Vaches* or the Call to the Cows, the third movement of Rossini's William Tell Overture. No, not the Lone Ranger theme part, the music that's always used to signify morning's arrival in famous cartoons from Warner Brothers and Disney.

I woke quickly and got out of bed to prove I was awake before my phone escalated to the finale of the *1812 Overture*.

I'd gone to bed early so I was up before dawn and could take my time drinking a mug of tea, reading the latest news from New York Times Twitter, and checking for messages.

I smiled when I saw something had come in from Poly. She'd sent me a text to let me know she was still where I'd expected— at her Georgia Tech A.I. lab with her adviser checking out new configurations for composite artificial intelligences. She said Professor Urrrson's mate had brought them a pizza last night, so she'd been fed and I shouldn't worry. Poly closed by thanking me again for picking up her family and added more Xs and Os. She must be feeling really guilty.

I made up my mind to be as gracious about the situation as I could, since I was confident I'd need favors of my own someday. I knew relationships weren't about keeping score, and most of the time I was focused on what made Poly happy, but my brain couldn't help it. I was nervous about meeting her family without her there and wanted to make a good impression. I knew Poly had challenging relationships with her mother and father, but she hadn't told me anything at all about her sister Pomy.

I'd find out soon enough.

Speculating about Poly's family made me consider where my own mom and step-dad were now. Mom was still moving from project to project as an engineer. Last I'd heard she was off-planet working on power systems for the *Charalindhri*, an asteroid mining ship half the size of the Death Star that the Dauushans were building in orbit.

The ship was designed to find metallic asteroids, spin them, melt them with congruency-provided stellar heat, and then process the resulting layers. It was supposed to be a very efficient refining method since the various metals sorted themselves out by relative density.

Dauush had an ever-increasing need for raw materials, and the mining ship would go a long way toward meeting the demands of the planet's massive fabricators once it was operational.

I loved my mom and she loved me, but we hadn't been close

since I'd gone off to college. We called each other on our birthdays and touched base every other month or so, but most of the time we lived our separate lives.

My step-dad was currently working as a guide for human sportsmen on one of the more rugged Short Pâkk planets. Pâkk like to keep their undeveloped land wild and populate their wilderness areas with "challenging" varieties of fauna from across the galaxy that make lions, tigers and grizzly bears look like koalas, so it was an exciting line of work. Mom had a weak spot for adventurers. She'd married my step-dad when they'd met in Houston, three years before First Contact.

Thomas Jefferson Buckston was a petroleum engineer who'd been exploring potential Alaskan fields for years. When he wasn't looking for oil, he worked as a guide for hunting parties—using both guns and cameras—and he'd swept my mom off her feet when he was reassigned to headquarters. Mom said they'd met when she needed to talk to someone with expertise in permafrost.

T.J. told me he'd fallen for my mom the first time he'd seen her, sitting across the table from him at a planning meeting. He'd asked her out as soon as the meeting broke for lunch. When I was older he explained that they never did end up having lunch that day. Mom just blushes.

Since my bio-dad had disappeared before I was born, T.J. effectively became my father, and a few years later I took his name. He showed me how to run network cables, configure firewalls and rebuild engines. He also taught me how to hunt, fish, defend myself, and stay alive in the Alaskan bush and Louisiana bayous. My step-dad was my Scout leader and my hero—until he was transferred back to Alaska and my mom went to Aswan to convert an Egyptian dam's turbines to run on congruent energy instead of hydro power. She took me with her.

My family would get back together for less than one month out of twelve in the years ahead. The separations were hard for me to handle. They were also hard on my mom. She and T.J. parted amicably a few months after I left for college. My step-dad sends me wildlife photos on SpaceBook and we exchange short emails every few weeks. I know he's proud of me. I keep a picture of my mom and step-dad and me in my bedroom. They're standing on either side of me when I got my Eagle Scout award and we're all smiling. It's a happy memory.

Enough maudlin musing. I had enough time to hit the gym and was overdue for a modest workout. I put on a Mulbiri Tech t-shirt, shorts and a pair of cross-trainers, shoved my phone in a pocket along with some ear buds and left my apartment.

The humanoid gym in the Ad Astra complex was in the basement of one of the buildings in the opposite direction from Tomáso and Terrhi's place. I hadn't been there in far too long. Ruby, the receptionist, checked me in.

"Where have you been, Jack?" she said. "Are you okay? I heard you'd been shot."

"I'm fine," I said, smiling. Ruby was a grandmotherly kangaroo-shaped alien with a face like a raccoon and long, dexterous fingers. Her species came from the planet Marsul, where they brewed great beer, or so I'd been told. It was supposed be something about the hops. Ruby didn't need a chair. She was resting on her large hind feet and leaning back on her tail, knitting and entertaining several grandchildren in her commodious pouch. It was a great part-time job for a retiree—much better than being a Walmart greeter.

"That leg doesn't look fine," she said, pointing at my dinosaur claw scar. I've got to be more diligent in applying Vitamin E.

"You should see the other guy," I said, taking pride in the fact that the other guy, a virtual reality dinosaur, was dead—or at least deactivated. That reminded me of Columbia Brown, the person who'd shot me. I'd have to ask Martin about the status of the search for her after we grilled Jean-Jacques. My ribs started aching just thinking about her still being at large.

"Take it slow," said Ruby. "And don't be a stranger."

"I will," I said. "And I won't."

I stuck in my wireless ear buds, cranked up a *Queen* play list in honor of Terrhi's mom, and headed for one of the humanoid treadmills to warm up. I started out slow, at a steady walking pace, then gradually increased the speed until I was jogging, then running. Maybe I wasn't in such bad shape after all? To make things more interesting, I instructed the Orishen-made treadmill to start throwing obstacles at me as I ran. Simulated rocks, logs and fire-ant mounds appeared and tested my ability to dodge or leap over them. After a few minutes, and a few near misses, I shifted the treadmill into cool down mode and thought about what station to try next. Strength training, I decided.

Much of the strength training equipment is Orishen. It's able to adapt to the needs of multiple species. That makes it very important to specify your species when you login to a given machine. For example, Ruby could leg press a compact car, even at her age. I hit a wrong key when I typed in my identifier and tried to do a Pâkk strength routine, then got so discouraged I switched to free weights. I stationed myself over near the Musa workout area where I could watch the tiny mouse-sized aliens lifting barbells the size of babies' rattles. That did my ego a lot of good, until I realized that the Musans were hoisting five times their body weight. For me to do that, I'd have to lift Terrhi over my head.

I gave up on strength training—my heart wasn't in it—and thought I'd play a little pickup basketball, just for fun. Unfortunately, the court was filled with Tigrammaths. I had no interest in playing against seven foot tall opponents with cat-like vertical leaps. I decided to head back home and soak in my spa tub instead. Ruby smiled at me when I left. I wasn't sure if she was pleased I took it easy or thought I was a wimp for leaving so soon, but maybe I'm projecting.

It was still cool on the walk back to my apartment, but I could tell the day was going to be a hot one. Summer starts early in

Atlanta. The parklike, tree-filled Ad Astra courtyard was mostly quiet, though I could hear the sounds of something small and quick scurrying through the foliage that paralleled my path. "Squirrels," I thought. "Where's Spike when I need him?"

My soak was brief, but delightful, and the high intensity massaging Chinese Gunpowder variant I selected as my shower program afterwards helped me come close to having a healthy mind in a healthy body.

I enjoyed a bowl of quadrotriticale flakes with milk and a few more slices of ripe Dauushan mega-banana for breakfast. Then I cleaned up my dishes and was ready to face the day.

I was even ready to face Jean-Jacques Bonhomme, the CEO of WT&F, especially since this time I didn't have to do the heavy lifting. Truth be told, I *liked* confronting J-J. There was something about his straightforwardly avaricious attitude that made it fun to bait him. But this wouldn't be my show.

Maybe Martin would let me play good cop to his bad cop this morning. Whatever happened, I hoped J-J wouldn't take out his frustrations on Mike. Poly and I both wanted him on the Xenotech Support team as soon as we got our hiring plans figured out, but in the meantime, J-J could make his life miserable.

While it was more entertaining to think about making Jean-Jacques squirm, it was eight-fifteen and time to get moving, since Martin and I had planned to meet at nine. I grabbed my backpack tool bag, summoned my van and headed for a rendezvous with destiny, or at least with Lieutenant Lee.

Chapter 9

"There is hardly anything in the world that someone
cannot make a little worse and sell a little cheaper..."
— attributed to John Ruskin

On my way to WT&F my phone spoke up and announced I had a call from Mike.

"Put him through," I said.

"Jack..." he said. I cut him off.

"These early morning calls are getting to be a habit."

"No witty banter, please, Jack. I'm worried."

"About?"

"Jean-Jacques."

"Why? What's up with him?"

"He's acting weird."

"How?"

"He arrived at eight, called me into his office, and *didn't* scream at me."

"In early and no screaming. That *is* weird. What *did* he do?" I said.

"He asked me what happened yesterday morning, so I told him. He just sat calmly and didn't react."

"No shouting? No threats? No promising to fire you?"

"No. He said 'Thank you, Mr. Goodman,' and asked me if I thought you'd be coming to talk to him. When I told him you were planning to stop by this morning with Lieutenant Lee, he just nodded and told me to go back to the production floor. It was like someone had snatched his body and replaced him with a pod person or something."

"That certainly doesn't sound like the Jean-Jacques we know and love," I said, keeping most of the cynicism out of my voice. "I would have been happier if our visit could have stayed a surprise. Jean-Jacques doesn't react well to surprises and it keeps him off balance."

"From what I could tell," said Mike, "he's so far off balance right now, he's close to falling over. When I left his office, I turned around and saw him wipe sweat off his forehead."

J-J typically liked to make *other* people sweat.

"He looked scared, Jack. Really scared."

Jean-Jacques was tough. He was a blue-collar Québécois kid from a rough neighborhood in Montreal who had moved to an even rougher neighborhood in Hoboken, New Jersey, and pulled himself up by his own bootstraps. I could stop him from running over me, but not many other people could. If Jean-Jacques was scared, it must be serious.

"Thanks for the heads up, Mike," I said. "Please pass the word to J-J that Lieutenant Lee and I will be stopping by at nine."

"Will do," said Mike. "Keep me posted."

"I will," I said. "Kirk out."

My phone made the Star Trek communicator sound, the way it always did when I said "Kirk out." The familiar chirp always made me smile.

* * * * *

Martin and I met in the WT&F parking lot. I slid my van in beside his Capitol Police cruiser, got out, and crossed to stand next to him. I gave Martin a recap of my conversation with Mike.

"J-J's frightened?" said Martin. "That's a new one. What scares a barracuda?"

"A shark," I said. "Probably a big one."

One of the not-Poly receptionists was on the front desk at WT&F. She saw Martin's uniform and didn't bother handing us visitor's badges. Come to think of it, WT&F didn't do visitor's badges. I'd have to talk to J-J about that—some other time. CiCi, the night security guard with pink, purple, and lime green accented hair, was standing with Mike in the far corner of the lobby. Their heads were close together and they looked like they were sharing a moment, so I didn't say anything. Mike looked over CiCi's shoulder, caught my eye and sent me a concerned glance. I nodded and kept moving.

Martin and I rode the elevator up one floor and walked down to the executive wing. The second floor had new carpet and new cubicles for the regular workers. No signs of the rabbots' depredations from six weeks ago remained. I was pleased that the carpet and cubicles were of slightly better quality than they had been earlier. I'd been adamant that J-J should upgrade the furnishings for his employees with some of the insurance pay-out. Jean-Jacques was *not* an enlightened CEO, so I'm glad I'd insisted.

The ugly, patronizing "Go Team" motivational posters on the walls had been replaced by a system of flat screen frames showing fine art that rotated through artistic periods on a weekly basis. Now it was showing Cubists, and the distorted, unreal images seemed appropriate for the strange new world of a frightened Jean-Jacques Bonhomme.

When Martin and I passed through the heavy wooden doors separating regular employee territory from executive country it was clear that some of the rabbot infestation settlement money had also been used to upgrade WT&F's already opulent executive wing. In particular, a large oil painting of Jean-Jacques in a business suit, looking regal and a good deal taller than he was in real life, hung on the wainscoted wall outside his office. J-J's assistant, a harried, ash-blonde woman with the paranoid look of a mouse living next to a rattlesnake, waved us in.

"He's expecting you," she said. Then she scurried off down the hall as if to get out of range of whatever was going to happen.

Martin and I looked at each other.

"It's your show," I said.

"Feel free to help," said Martin.

I pushed open J-J's office door and walked in behind the lieutenant. There was a beautiful new oriental rug on the floor. Jean-Jacques rose to meet us and came out from behind his desk.

"I'm glad you're here," said the penny-pinching CEO.

He stuck out his hand. Martin ignored it.

"Lieutenant Martin Lee, Georgia Capitol Police," said my friend.

I looked at J-J and gave him my biggest grin. After what happened the last time we'd met here, J-J didn't find my expression reassuring.

"Jack," he said, nodding to acknowledge my presence. He sat down on the raised chair behind his desk. "Have a seat, gentlemen. Can I get you any refreshments?"

"No," said Martin.

Both of us were nearly a foot taller than J-J. Martin remained standing, his official police tablet and stylus in his hands. He let his height and Samuel L. Jackson I-don't-take-any-crap demeanor work their intimidating magic. I was playing good cop, so I sat on the arm of one of the guest chairs.

"Tell us about the client who placed the rush order on Sunday, Mr. Bonhomme."

It wasn't a question.

"A woman called me while I was in New York," said J-J. "She offered me a lot of money if I could handle a rush order."

"What were you doing in New York?" said the lieutenant.

Jean-Jacques looked embarrassed, as if his tough guy mask was slipping.

"I was visiting my mother."

J-J had a mother? Who'd have thought it?

"It was her birthday and I took her to a matinée on Broadway, then dinner at Sardi's."

"What did you see?" I asked.

Martin gave me a sharp look as if to say, "What does it matter what show they went to?"

"The revival of *Cats*."

Maybe J-J wasn't such a good son after all. For me, watching *Cats* is like listening to two and a half hours of chalk screeching on a blackboard, but your mileage may vary. Maybe his mother liked T. S. Elliot, or Andrew Lloyd Webber, or, you know, cats.

"How much money is 'a lot,' Mr. Bonhomme?" said Martin.

J-J looked down at his hands, reluctant to answer.

"Mr. Bonhomme?"

J-J kept his head down and whispered.

"Eight hundred thousand galcreds."

I kept my face neutral, but whistled inside my brain. That was enough to tempt a much stronger man. The client could have probably convinced Jean-Jacques to take the job for half, or even a quarter of that.

"What can you tell us about the woman who contacted you, Mr. Bonhomme?" said the lieutenant.

"She was just a voice on the phone," said J-J, shifting his gaze from side to side.

"She didn't give her name?"

"No, she said she was calling on behalf of her boss, Mr. Duke Vanderbilt."

I'd heard that name before. It was an obvious pseudonym, like Cornell, Penn and Princeton, three of Anthony Zwilniki's henchman, only using well-known southern schools instead of members of the Ivy League.

"What did this woman sound like?" said Martin.

"Cold. Hard. All business."

Jean-Jacques looked left and right, then at me, then at the lieutenant.

"Kind of like you, officer."

"Do you mean she sounded African-American?"

"Well, sort of," said J-J, "though more like Jamaican."

A cold, hard voice from the Caribbean. I thought I knew where this was headed and I didn't like it.

"Did she mention the name of her company?" said Martin.

"It was the same one from before."

J-J couldn't look me—or Lieutenant Lee—in the eye.

"From before?" I said.

"You know," said J-J. "Factor-E-Flor."

I looked at Martin. He knew I'd dealt with Factor-E-Flor's handiwork earlier. They were the small company, registered in the Cayman Islands, that had provided the doctored plans for the one hundred thousand pink robot rabbots WT&F had 3D printed six weeks ago. The rabbots had been connected to a drug production operation that Martin and Tomáso and I had helped shut down. They were owned by the James K. Polk Group, which was a subsidiary of the mysterious EUA Corporation. And according to Poly's research, Factor-E-Flor's owner of record was—Duke Vanderbilt.

Jean-Jacques was looking even more overwrought. I thought Martin's interrogation was going quite well. I was filing his technique away in my memory for future reference.

"What, precisely, did this woman ask you to do?" he said.

"Print up a job for her boss."

"Did she tell you what WT&F would be printing?"

"Some sort of large-scale construction equipment," she said.

"Did you have any prior knowledge that her order was actually for a well-armed two-hundred-and-fifty-foot combat robot?"

"No," said J-J. He sounded as depressed as he would have been if he'd been forced to sit through a dozen back-to-back performances of *Cats*… but I may be projecting.

"Let's walk through the time line," said Martin. "You got a call on Sunday…"

"After dinner," said Jean-Jacques. "It was around seven. We'd gone back to my mother's apartment and she'd gone to bed early. I was checking email."

"And you called Mike Goodman after you talked to the woman?"

"That's right. I think it was close to seven-thirty."

"You asked Mike to come in and work overnight on her rush job?"

"Yes. I promised him a bonus for the extra work."

Sure he did. I spoke up.

"How did the woman get the production plans to you?"

"I gave her a link to our corporate cloud LoxBox account."

I restrained myself from slapping my forehead with my palm and quoting Homer Simpson. I'd bet a dinner at the Teleport Inn that J-J had given the mystery woman his admin link to LoxBox, the *de facto* standard business app for exchanging large files, not a secure, single-use upload link. I'd have to spend hours reviewing the files on WT&F's LoxBox folders to confirm none of them had been compromised. Later.

"Was that the last time you heard from her?" said Martin.

The blood drained from Jean-Jacques' face. He looked as white as cheese curds.

"No," said J-J. "She called back at noon yesterday. She hadn't received her order and told me that I had twenty-four hours to complete delivery."

"Was that all she said?"

Jean-Jacques shook his head back and forth slowly.

"No," he said. "She also said if I didn't produce her order on time I'd be very, very sorry."

Martin nearly dropped his stylus and I stood up quickly to keep from falling off the arm of my chair.

"A death threat?" asked Martin.

"It sounded like one to me," said J-J. "I have a ticket to Dauush on a star liner that takes off at eleven. I'm leaving for Hartsfield as soon as we're done. I'm going to check out used 3D printers while I'm there, so I can write the trip off as a business expense."

Martin and I looked at each other and came to an unspoken agreement.

"Are we done here?" asked J-J.

Now that he was getting out of Dodge some of his old cocky attitude was returning.

"Just a few more questions," said Martin. "Did any funds change hands?"

Jean-Jacques's eyes bored into the lieutenant's.

"What do you take me for?" said J-J. "I'd never print an order without a deposit."

"That should do it," said Martin, "so long as you provide us with all the details of the transaction."

"My assistant and my CFO will take care of that for you," said J-J.

His desk phone rang and his assistant's voice announced, "Your limo is here, sir."

"Show yourselves out," said Jean-Jacques. "I have a starship to catch."

He pulled a suitcase out from behind his desk and left us standing in his office. Martin kept it together, but my mouth was hanging open. I shut it.

"You know what we have to do now, right?" said my friend.

"Yeah," I said. "Follow the money."

* * * * *

Martin stayed on the executive level to get information from Jean-Jacques' CFO and assistant. He promised he'd have police financial forensic investigators look into WT&F's deposit from Factor-E-Flor and said he'd share the account numbers and other particulars once he got them. I suspected the official investigation would take weeks, if not months, and promised myself I'd do some digging of my own a lot sooner.

I also shared my own suspicions about who had called Jean-Jacques and threatened him. Martin agreed with my reasoning and promised to make the ongoing search for her a higher priority for law enforcement across the state. We shook hands, then I went downstairs to find Mike and warn him about J-J's death threat. CiCi and Mike weren't in the lobby—it was probably long past the end of her shift—so I walked to the entrance to the production floor, pulled open one of the steel double doors, and entered.

Mike was standing at the Model-43's control panel. His head was down and he looked like he was trying to make sure his settings were right.

"Did you remember Rule #3?" I said.

"There's a Rule #3?"

"Yeah," I said. "We just learned it. Always know what you're fabbing."

"Smart," said Mike. "I'm doing something like that now."

"How so?"

"The specs for the robot are really complicated," he said, "so I started with the octovacs."

I nodded, which meant, "Tell me more."

"I called the Waffle House by the airport and spoke to Roger Joe-Bob Bacon," he said. "Roger Joe-Bob sent me the off-the-shelf octovac design. I'm comparing it line by line to the spec I 3D printed yesterday."

"Great idea. Find anything yet?"

"Not really," said Mike. "I think the hardware for the octovacs I printed used the standard specs. It's only the software that's different. I'll have to look at their control codes line by line, too."

Mike returned to reviewing the two sets of specs. I interrupted and walked him through how to run a file compare that showed only the differences between the two versions. He gave me a "Padawan bows to Jedi Master's wisdom" look and smiled.

"I can do the same thing for the robot's software next," he said. "That means I should be able to get some sleep tonight."

"Sleep is good," I said. "Thanks for checking it out, but don't get too focused. Keep your eyes and ears open."

Mike raised a questioning eyebrow.

"I found out why J-J was acting weird," I continued. "I think he got a death threat from Columbia Brown."

"The woman who shot you?"

"Uh huh. One of my favorite people. She said if Jean-Jacques didn't produce the robot by noon today he'd be very, very sorry. He got the point and is catching a fast ship to Dauush."

"Understood," said Mike. "Since she can't go after him, she might go after the company."

"Right," I said. "Watch your six."

"Will do."

"Now that I think about it," I said, "you should text Martin. See if he can get WT&F some police protection, at least for the next few days. We don't know how far J-J's mystery client is willing to go."

"I'll make it happen," said Mike.

He pulled out his phone and began typing. Mike was proactive and would make a good addition to XSC. As he tapped keys, I thought I'd see how good he was at multitasking.

"How are things going with CiCi?" I asked.

"Why do you want to know? What do you want with her?" Mike answered.

Wow. I must have pushed a hot button.

"I just thought the two of you looked pretty close when I saw you in the lobby."

"She said she told you she thought you were cute and you blew her off," he said.

"I had other things on my mind," I said, "like your tech support emergency."

Mike looked like he was playing mental tug-of-war with himself. I went on.

"And I'm crazy in love with Poly. Passes from other women just bounce off."

Mike's shoulders slumped.

"Sorry," he said. "I know you and Poly are tight, but I get jealous. I really like CiCi. She says she likes me, but I don't know if she *likes me* likes me, or just likes me."

"Ah, young love," I said, the corners of my mouth turning up.

"Shut up," said Mike, smiling. "She's going out with me again on Friday. And hey, you're only a year older than I am. Remember, I did a hitch in the Army before going to Georgia State."

"Right. I forgot. What was your specialty?"

"Translator, at least when I *left* the military. I learned Hindi and Mandarin at the Defense Language Institute in Monterey, then taught myself Finnish so I could get a better handle on Quenya."

"Learning Finnish to help with Elvish? You're my kind of geek," I said. "Mandarin is useful for learning spoken Dauushan—their structure is similar, but it's still a challenge."

"That's what Poly said in Introduction to Galactic Languages," Mike said. "I'm trying to master basic Galang before I dive into anything as complicated as Dauushan."

"Wise move. Sounds like you've got a knack for languages."

"I try. Not like you and Poly."

"You'll get it. We've been at it a lot longer—and Poly and I have both been off-planet. That helps."

"Yeah, yeah, but I want it now. J-J won't pay for any sort of training and I'm getting sick of this place."

"Hang in there for a few weeks," I said. "Who knows, a great opportunity might fall into your lap."

I gave him a knowing look.

He looked back optimistically, but with a touch of wariness. Working for J-J will do that to you.

Mike's phone made a *ding* sound. He looked at its screen.

"That's Martin," he said. "There will be police patrols around the parking lot and loading dock every hour for the next two or three days. He says the CFO will spring for increased private security inside the building."

"I hope that doesn't screw up your date with CiCi," I said.

"Me, too," said Mike.

"Cheer up," I said. "If she has to work you could bring her take-out."

Mike smiled.

"CiCi said she liked Thai," he said.

I could see that Mike's brain was spinning off trying to figure out a good place near the office for Pad See Ew and Pad Thai. I was glad the odds were now less likely Columbia Brown would blow up WT&F, given their increased security.

"Try the Bangkok Delhi on Roswell Road," I said as I turned to leave. "Good Thai, *and* Indian. Their samosas are delicious."

Mike didn't even look up. My work here was done and it was time to head back to my apartment. I had several tech support visits to make via Remote Hands after lunch. Speaking of lunch, Thai and Indian food sounded pretty good.

Chapter 10

"All I need is an extra pair of hands."
— Catherine Anderson

These days, my apartment seems empty when Poly isn't in it. I checked the bedroom and bathroom to confirm she was gone. Then I put a box of extra samosas from lunch in the refrigerator in case I needed to feed Poly later. She was always starving after her all-nighters at Tech.

Before I closed the fridge door I pulled out a Diet Starbuzz for myself and took several swallows. The carbonated liquid helped put out the fire from the extra-spicy curry dish I'd enjoyed earlier. I was feeling completely full and mostly happy. Feeling all the way happy would have to wait until Poly got back.

My first Remote Hands appointment wasn't until one thirty. That gave me a few minutes to take care of essential biological needs and get into my RH suit. Without Remote Hands I never would have been able to support my clients while I was recovering from my injuries.

The idea behind Remote Hands, Inc. was an inspired concept for a company. If I'd thought of it five years ago, before two Greek brothers named Telemanus had founded their start-up, I'd be plutocrat-level rich. Advances in virtual reality technology and instantaneous congruency-based communications made it possible for someone to effectively be in two places at once.

When I put on my RH Prime suit, I could see, hear, smell and feel exactly what my distant RH Operative doppelganger did. When I moved, my remote human operative duplicated my movements.

My RH Prime ensemble was a virtual reality helmet and a form-fitting bodysuit covered in sensors that passed my operative's sensory data in and my movement instructions out. A curved screen on the outside of the operative's helmet showed my face in real time. That made it easier for people interacting with my remote to think they were dealing with me. It sounds complicated, but it's not.

While I'd been recuperating I'd rented a special RH suit made for hospital patients. Wearing the special suit, I could instruct my remote to move without leaving my bed. It sensed the nerve impulses I sent to my legs, even if I didn't get up and walk. I was glad to switch back to my normal suit a few weeks ago, when I'd recovered enough to stand for a few hours at a time.

The business world had jumped on Remote Hands' technology. The company had several million remote operatives across the solar system and beyond. They also put prospective remotes through an extensive training program before certifying them for deployment. Operatives were also bonded and had to pass exhaustive background checks, which helped lead to their widespread acceptance.

More than half the world's tech support was delivered using operatives from Remote Hands, Inc. or one of their competitors. Most organizations had one or more RH operatives at every branch office for the convenience of vendors providing hands-on help. The technology was a major boon for remote health care, too. Physicians were even doing house calls again.

Some competitors used robots, but mechanical operatives only caught on in hazardous environments, like mining, processing toxic chemicals, and space-based manufacturing. Robot remotes were also very popular as bouncers and process servers, for obvious reasons. There were rumors that the NFL, bowing to pressure from the players union about concussions, was considering a move to robots operatives, but I'll believe that when I see it.

It was no surprise that the adult industry had thrown itself into RH technology using human remotes, though not in partnership with Remote Hands, Inc. itself. Competitors were quick to exploit adult market niches and the resulting sensitivity improvements in suits and equipment, especially for touch, drove innovation across the industry.

I had used Remote Hands, Inc. technology for several years, but only for my most distant clients. When I was stuck in bed recuperating, things were different. I'd bought an extra hundred-hour block of operative time so I could cover everything that came up without leaving my apartment. That let me keep my clients happy, even if it did cut into my profit margins.

I didn't like using Remote Hands tech at Mistress Marigold's—her plants were particularly sensitive—which was why I'd been behind on preventive maintenance for her systems. This afternoon's appointments were all routine, so I went into my bedroom, stripped down to my underwear, and put on my RH Prime suit and helmet.

There was a full-length mirror on the back of the bathroom door, so I took a few seconds to see how I looked. The answer, to be frank, was dorky. Wearing the suit, I did look a little like a superhero, but my appearance was more Ant-Man than Iron Man.

I walked to my living room, since it was helpful to have extra space for Remote Hands sessions. Thank goodness operatives would use common sense and continue to walk or climb stairs once the appropriate action was indicated by the Prime, or I'd need to go out to the courtyard to have enough room. My phone announced it was one thirty, so I issued a voice command.

"Prime ready."

"Operative ready," said a crisp soprano voice with a south Georgia accent.

"Is that you, Emma Ann?"

"It *is.* Jack?"

"At your service, ma'am."

"No, I'm at yours," said Emma Ann.

"And I'm glad you are."

She'd been my operative several times before. **Remote Hands, Inc.** liked to match up primes and operatives who worked well together when they could. Remote Hands operatives could be completely passive, or as I preferred, active and offering their own comments on what they saw. Emma Ann didn't miss much and I knew she was a pleasure to work with.

"Since I'm standing outside NOD Music, I assume they've got a tech problem?" she said.

"Not that I know of," I said. "It's just routine maintenance."

"That's too bad," said Emma Ann. "I like being your remote when you're troubleshooting. I learn a lot."

"Want to be a Prime yourself some day?"

"That's my plan. I'm studying Galtech at West Georgia Technical College."

"More power to you," I said.

Nostalgia On Demand Music was founded by an audiophile with fond memories of his parents' and grandparents' collections of old 78s, LPs and 45s. Located nearly fifty miles south of my apartment in the medium-sized town of Newnan, Georgia, it would take me at least an hour, more likely two hours with traffic, to drive there. Remote Hands would let me take care of my client without wasting half a day in the process.

The company's business model was a lot like the print on demand companies that would churn out dead tree books for individuals who still preferred physical versions to e-books. Nostalgia On Demand Music applied the same approach to music and audio.

Fans of more recent oldies could get CDs of Christina Aguilera's greatest hits or DVDs of Kanye in concert if they preferred physical digital recordings to insubstantial bits streamed from the cloud. You could order a freshly made cassette tape of Jim Morrison and the Doors' 1967 *Doors* album, or a 45 rpm version of Elvis singing *Blue Suede Shoes*. They could make you an LP of Sinatra crooning *My Way,* or 78 rpm records of Tommy Dorsey and his orchestra's greatest hits if you wanted.

For a small niche collectors' market they would recreate Edison's original cylindrical recordings to be played on old Victrolas. Masochists could even get *Three Dog Night* on eight-track cartridges.

NOD Music's fabrication setup used a particularly complex collection of custom Dauushan and Orishen components to produce all the different formats. I'd been called in by the mega-consulting company hired for the original installation after it became clear they had bitten off more than they could chew. Their techs could only fab 50 Cent on Victrola cylinders. Once I'd gotten everything working properly, the project manager was called to the private office of NOD Music's CEO for a one-on-one meeting. When he came out, I had a new client.

With our RH link fully activated, I took control and "walked" Emma Sue into NOD Music's headquarters. The office manager, Mrs. Carmichael, greeted me. She was older and looked like a church lady, but I knew from talking to her previously that she was into classic country and gangsta rap. Unfortunately, she didn't quite get the whole Remote Hands thing.

"You're looking very pretty, child," she said.

I turned red back in my living room. Emma Ann sniggered softly in my ear.

"It's Jack, ma'am," I said. "You're not supposed to refer to the operative."

"I know, dear," said Mrs. Carmichael. "But I bet you're blushing."

Busted. Memo to self, don't mouth off to old ladies. They'll kick your…

"Head right in, dear," she said, motioning to her boss's office door. "He wants to talk to you."

He was Ray Charles Dunwoody, the audiophile who'd founded the company. The man's office was a shrine to his namesake, the musical legend born farther south in Albany, Georgia. There were photos of Ray Charles and his famous glasses on every wall, including a large one of the award-winning blind musician standing behind a much younger R. C. Dunwoody with his arm around him. R. C. is wearing headphones with their cord dangling. An engineer's board from a recording studio was in the background. It was a picture worth building a shrine around.

R. C. was a slim, well-dressed African American man in his early sixties with graying hair and a small soul patch. He wore sunglasses pushed high on his forehead and looked like he could have been a professor at Morehouse or UGA, not an audio engineer and CEO.

"Hello, Jack. Have a seat."

"Thanks," I said.

He didn't look completely at ease about having a young woman wearing a helmet showing my face sitting in his office, but he was more comfortable with RH tech than Mrs. Carmichael.

"I miss the old days when I got to see you face to face," he said.

"I'd have to charge you a lot more for support."

"You'd be worth it," said R. C. "I'll bet I can get you back down here in person in September for the NOD Music Festival."

The festival always had top acts across several genres. Maybe Poly could come with me?

"If I can bring a guest, I'd love to come down."

"New lady friend?" said R. C.

"More than just a friend," I said. "She's my new business partner and quite an amazing woman."

"Bring her down and leave enough time for dinner," said R. C. "I want to get to know her and ask her what she sees in you."

"I've often wondered the same thing," I said, smiling. "How are your kids?"

I didn't ask about his wife. She'd been killed in a side-on

collision two years ago. The Galactics could cure cancer but they couldn't stop drunken teenagers from speeding through intersections in manually operated over-sized pickup trucks.

"Charli is working for GalCon Systems in Pittsburgh," he said. "She loves it. She's doing research into using strategically placed congruencies to improve concert hall acoustics."

I was impressed. Galactic Congruent Technologies is the top Terran company for congruency R&D.

"Great," I said. "She takes after her dad. What about Ray Ray?"

"I'm not so sure about him," said R. C. "He got his engineering degree from Tech a few years back, you'll remember."

I nodded. Or Emma Ann nodded. Whatever.

"Now he's working for a fabrication company out by Six Flags, but I'm not thrilled with what I hear."

"Oh?"

"He says they're working on something really big, but he can't say a word about it. He signed a non-disclosure agreement. Then his voice gets tight in a way that tells me he's not just excited, he's worried."

"What's the name of the company?"

"O'Sullivan Fabrication."

"Who's O'Sullivan?" I asked my phone.

"The full name of the company is John L. O'Sullivan Fabrication, Inc.," said my phone. "O'Sullivan was an editor and columnist who coined the term Manifest Destiny back in 1845."

"Sounds like an Earth First Militant company to me," I said to myself. At least I thought I did.

"What?" said R. C. and Emma Ann.

"Just a second," I said, focusing on my phone. "Who owns it?"

"Somebody named Rice Tulane," it replied.

Pieces were coming together. Those were two more top southern college names, like Duke Vanderbilt, the owner of Factor-E-Flor. I was getting a bad feeling about this.

"It's no big deal," I told R. C., and by extension Emma Ann as well. "I just wanted more background."

By now we'd had enough personal conversation to satisfy south Georgia business conventions. R. C. would be getting around to why he wanted to talk to me soon.

"That's why I wanted to talk to you," said R. C. "I haven't heard from Ray Ray in a week and that's not like him. I've left messages, but he hasn't called me back. I want you to look into O'Sullivan Fabrication and see if he's in some kind of trouble."

I looked at R. C., but didn't really see him. My mind was racing at light speed, trying to connect all the dots.

"Are you okay, Jack?" he said, seeing my expression. "I'll pay for your time to investigate. Just don't let Ray Ray find out."

"I won't," I said, "and you don't need to pay me. I have my own reasons for checking out O'Sullivan Fabrication."

I heard a soft whistle in my ear.

"Emma Ann?"

"Sorry," she whispered. "Sounds like something big."

"You have no idea," I said.

"Let me know if there's any way I can help," said Emma Ann.

"I may take you up on that," I said.

"Did you say something?" asked R. C.

"Just talking to myself," I said.

* * * * *

Aside from a machine that insisted on printing Weird Al Yankovic live comedy album footage on the B-side of every DVD it duplicated, the preventive maintenance at NOD Music went smoothly. Emma Sue gave me her contact information so I could get in touch if I needed her help. She might be another good hire for Xenotech Support in the future, once she left Remote Hands and I wasn't bound by a non-solicitation agreement. I took care of the rest of my Remote Hands maintenance sessions for clients in Macon, Gainesville, and Dalton—other Georgia cities more than fifty miles from my apartment—on automatic pilot.

Something big was up. I suspected what it might be and who was responsible, but I wasn't sure why. Plenty of lawn clippings had been teleporting into Anthony Zwilniki's grajja factory. WT&F hadn't been the only company fabbing rabbots.

Chapter 11

"He owes me what you'd call a 'life-debt.'"
— Qui-gon Jinn

It was a pleasure to work from home this afternoon and not worry about driving back from a client's office through Atlanta's horrendous rush hour traffic. I was worried about Poly, though. She must *really* be focused on her research project if she hadn't even had time to leave me a text. I hoped she'd be in touch soon.

When you're waiting for something important I often find it's helpful to take a shower. It's a way of harnessing the power of Murphy's Law for your benefit, sort of like how your meal always arrives as soon as you leave your table to use the restroom at a restaurant. Besides, I'd been wearing my RH Prime suit for over four hours. I really needed one.

I removed the rig's VR helmet, then stripped off the tight-fitting, sensor-covered bodysuit, turning it inside out in the process. I found my bottle of RH-approved spray cleaner and deodorizer under the sink in my bathroom and thoroughly sprayed my suit and the inside of my helmet so they would be ready the next time I had a Remote Hands session. I took care to only use cleaning products approved by RH on the suit and helmet and was a fanatic about keeping them clean.

When we went camping, my step-dad always said, "If you take care of your equipment, it will take care of you," and that was a piece of fatherly advice I always followed. The one time I didn't clean my suit and helmet and had to put them on again a few days later, the smell was enough to convince me to do the right thing in the future.

I turned the bodysuit right-side out and fitted it on its special frame—sort of like a dressmaker's dummy with a Styrofoam head—so that none of the sensor wires would get crimped, then put the helmet on top. Once, I'd left the helmet on the floor and tripped over it, stubbing my toe. The impact must have crossed some sensor wires and created artificial synesthesia. On my next Remote Hands session I heard green sounds, saw peppermint, and smelled French horns. I had to postpone that support call until I could repair the problematic circuits.

As I expected, my Earl Grey shower program had just moved from its *stinging hot needles to penetrate deep muscles* phase into its final *intense blast of frigidly cold spray* phase when Poly called. I'd been smart and had told my phone to relay any calls from Poly to my not-so-bright shower A.I.

"Hi, Jack," she said. "Are you there?"

Poly's voice was lower-pitched than usual. She sounded really exhausted, and I wanted to feed her dinner, rub her shoulders and help her relax. I canceled the Earl Grey shower program so I could hear her better, even though I hadn't rinsed out all my conditioner.

"Were you in the shower?"

"I was," I said. "That is, I am. Just finishing up."

"Wish I could be in there with you."

She said the words, but without her usual upbeat, teasing manner.

"How are you doing?" I said.

"I'm tired. But happy."

"Did things go well with your project?"

"Yeah," she said. All her words stretched out longer than usual. "We ran the simulations hundreds of times faster than real time to cover months instead of hours, and none of the revised composite artificial intelligence systems went crazy."

"That's great!" I said. "Way to go."

"Thanks," said Poly. "It's going to take hours more for us to revise our paper."

"Are you still at the lab? You're not planning to stay up and make the revisions now, are you?"

"No, Professor Urrrson's mate dropped me off at my apartment. She saw how tired I was and wanted to make sure I got home safely."

"Smart Tigrammath," I said.

"You know it," said Poly. "She's a professor at Emory. I don't think she trusted me, or Professor Urrrson, to give an autocab the right address."

"Was she right about that?"

"Probably," Poly yawned. "I was glad to have a ride, anyway."

"Would you like me to come over and bring you dinner?"

"Ummmm," she said. "That would be lovely, but…"

"But?"

"But I'd be asleep before you could get here. I'm barely conscious as it is. I'm flat on my back in bed and only propping my eyelids open long enough to call you."

"Have you had anything to eat?"

"You're sweet," said Poly. "Professor Urrrson's mate brought us an amazing breakfast and we ordered Chinese for a late lunch. I don't need food, I need sleep."

"Okay," I said. "Take good care of yourself and know I'm thinking about you."

"You're sweet," Poly repeated, in a groggy haze. "And thanks again for meeting my family's flights."

That was only the fourth time she'd reminded me.

"I will," I said, with a smile in my voice.

"And Lover Boy," she said, clearly fading.

I was all ears.

"Uh huh?"

"Watch out for…"

But she was out.

Watch out for *what?*

I sure hoped Poly would be able to fill me in before I left for the airport.

* * * * *

I got back in the shower and finished getting conditioner out of my hair and soap out of all those hard to reach places. Then I got dressed, wearing jeans, my Orishen pupa silk shirt—Poly insisted I wear it all the time—and a GalCon Systems t-shirt, instead of my standard corporate uniform of khakis and an XSC polo. I felt like a new man, ready to wrestle ten times my weight in Short Pâkk warriors. I'd lose, but I was ready.

If Poly wouldn't be over tonight, I was free to do some digging into O'Sullivan Fabrication. I moved to the living room and pulled up a satellite mapping program on my wall screen. Planet Earth hung in space and revolved, slowly. It was a real time image from slightly below geosynchronous orbit. My phone provided voice navigation, so I asked it to play tour guide.

"Zoom in and show me an overhead view of the O'Sullivan operation," I said.

"Zooming in, you've got it," said my phone with an odd tone.

The screen went black. I could make out individual dark-colored pebbles embedded in the O'Sullivan Fabrication building's roof.

"Don't be a jerk," I said to my phone. "Pull back a little."

"Yes, boss," it said, quickly switching to obsequious from overly literal.

Or maybe not. The view on my wall screen expanded as if the camera was attached to a high speed elevator on one of Arthur C. Clarke's beanstalks. Instead of the thousand-foot view I'd been hoping to see, I was at fifteen thousand feet. A bend in the Chattahoochee River and the straight east-west line of I-20 were two major landmarks. I could see the twisting, turning steel of the roller coasters at Six Flags Over Georgia and dozens of large, rectangular buildings with black roofs spread out across green countryside filled with grass and trees. Other roads crisscrossed the landscape, linking the structures. Some were four lane, some were two lane, and a few were only a single lane wide. From the air the landscape looked like an old fashioned printed circuit board, with the buildings standing in for soldered-on memory, graphics chips, and CPUs.

I remembered that the area near Six Flags had been one of the top spots in Georgia to locate data centers before First Contact. The area had inexpensive land, was served by multiple power providers, and was located near major telecommunications interconnection points that could link servers to anywhere on the net in only a few hops. The congruent technology revolution had negated every one of the area's benefits, except for cheap land. Power hungry data centers now had unlimited energy and every server was only one hop away from any other with congruent wormhole-based communications.

I'd had to troubleshoot some data security issues with off-planet links for a client out there last year. I drove by windowless one story concrete building after windowless one story concrete building on the way. They were all corporate data centers and each one had understated signage, except for Google. They had three locations in a row with their logo in letters six feet tall in front of twelve-foot razor wire-topped fences. Some companies are really serious about their physical security.

Protecting I.T. assets has become a lot more challenging since First Contact. It's not easy to defend against black hat hackers who can teleport. That's why many modern data centers have high-speed rotating tranquilizer dart guns mounted on their ceilings. One of my clients was so paranoid that she insisted I install… wait, I'm not allowed to even *think* about that. I signed a non-disclosure. Just know that anyone teleporting into one of her corporate data centers wouldn't be a happy camper.

"Please give me a one thousand-foot view centered above O'Sullivan Fabrication's operations," I said, trying to be ultra-precise.

My phone didn't say anything, but made it happen without any backchat. What had gotten under its charging plate, I wondered?

O'Sullivan Fabrication's production facility was a behemoth among giants. It was three stories tall and easily twice the size of Zwilniki's enormous hangar where we'd stored "my" robot temporarily. The building was big enough to hold four or five robots like the one the octovacs assembled yesterday, along with a Dauushan Model-43 3D printer and storage for enough feed stock to choke a Tōdon. To my surprise, it was surrounded by not one, but two high fences topped with razor wire, with a dozen feet of empty ground between them. I spotted guard towers on the corners as well. It looked more like a maximum security prison than a fabrication company.

I reached over and grabbed my backpack tool bag from its spot on the table next to my front door and pulled out Chit's bottle.

"Hey, little buddy—want to do some exploring?"

"Whazzup?" said Chit, rubbing a compound eye with a fore-leg. Had she been asleep? "Explorin' what?"

"A villain's secret manufacturing plant."

"Did that last time," Chit said. "Scared some blasted grackles."

I filled Chit in on the details. She hadn't heard anything I'd learned during my Remote Hands session because my VR helmet had headphones. I could see her getting excited about a possible new adventure, or maybe there just wasn't anything good on TV.

"Double rows of razor wire fences, guard towers, an' who knows what else," said Chit. "Sounds like a challenge. When d' we start?"

"Right after dinner," I said. "I want to wait for traffic to die down."

"Somebody may die down," said my friend, shaking her head, "and I don't want it t' be me."

"I thought you were an expert at reconnaissance."

"Expert enough to know when it ain't smart to try breakin' into certain places."

"Come with me and scope it out?"

"Take me to the Buckhead Diner for dinner and you're on," said Chit. "I could really get into some of their mashed potatoes."

"You did that last time we were there and it took me over an hour to get all the starch off your antennae," I said.

"Details, details," said Chit.

"Okay," I said, "You're on."

* * * * *

Chit was content to nibble on my mashed potatoes, though she did threaten to do the backstroke in the gravy bowl to disconcert the servers. While we ate I had my phone do an Internet search for anything it could find about O'Sullivan Fabrication. I didn't check my phone at the dinner table, since I'd had good manners drilled into me and knew not to check my phone while dining at any establishment with cloth napkins. After some excellent meatloaf, the aforementioned mashed potatoes, and southern-style *haricots vert et jambon,* that's green beans and ham, we left the restaurant and I walked to my van. Chit rode on my shoulder and tried to look unobtrusive.

Once we buckled up and were moving, it was time for my phone to tell us what it had learned. The vehicle's windshield turned into a screen and a corporate promotional video started to play. Images of giant trucks with tires taller than a Tigrammath, bulldozers sized to herd Dauushans, and cranes tall enough pluck Quirinx fliers from their cliff-top aeries panned across our vision as a voice-over spokesman made his pitch.

"Do you have a big project? Need something extra-extra-large—without an oversized price tag? O'Sullivan Fabrication does the best job on *big* jobs! Our highly trained personnel and state of the art 3D printing equipment can deliver *your* big job, fast."

The scene switched to the exterior of their building.

"With state of the art security…"

The camera zoomed in on their building's fences, towers and armed guards.

"And a commitment to confidentiality…"

Three employees, or actors, in black corporate-logo coveralls, sat in *see no evil, hear no evil, say no evil* poses. Chit laughed.

"O'Sullivan Fabrication should be *your* choice for all your large scale fabbing needs."

Now came the pay dirt. Brief glimpses of their production floor, their Dauushan Model-43 printer, and their warehouse, with huge forklifts moving components, flashed by on the screen. Then the video faded out to be replaced by the green, black and white O'Sullivan Fabrication company logo. The voice-over spokesman continued.

"If you need something big and you're in the know, go with the O. Call now for a quote—you're always a big priority at O'Sullivan."

Contact information appeared in large letters below the logo, then the screen went blank.

I just sat there, but Chit clapped her forelegs and made a sound like a donkey braying.

"Is that supposed to be a laugh?" I asked.

"It's the Murm equivalent of a belly laugh," said my small friend. "Those three monkeys were hilarious."

"They did lighten up a deadly dull corporate sales video."

"Yeah," said Chit, "but did you catch what was in the background in the warehouse scene?"

"All I saw was a forklift the size of New Jersey."

"Behind that. Back in the shadows."

"Could you pull up the warehouse scene, please?" I asked my phone.

"Hrrrumph," said my phone, softly.

"I said please."

Maybe it was time for a software upgrade for my faithful electronic companion. My phone grumbled something too low for me to hear but brought the beginning of the warehouse scene up on my van's windshield screen.

"Take it frame by frame," I said.

"As you wish," said my phone, sounding like a petulant teenager.

Chit and I watch the frames go by one at a time until my diminutive associate said, "Stop."

I leaned forward, then said, "Double the magnification on the upper right quadrant."

My phone did as I'd instructed, but only increased the resolution for that quarter of the screen. It didn't make the upper right quadrant take up all of the screen, which had been my intent.

"Switch upper right quadrant to full screen."

"You should have said that in the first place," said my phone.

"You're usually smart enough to do what I mean, not what I say," I said.

A faint, plaintive R2-D2 "nobody understands me" set of chirps came from my phone's speaker. I'd hurt its feelings, but at least now I could see what Chit had spotted.

"Is that what I think it is?" I said.

"Looks that way to me," said Chit.

"Hrrrmph," said my phone. "What's the big deal about an octovac?"

"It's a very big deal," I said. "What's got your circuits in a knot?"

"Nothing," said my phone.

It was Chit's turn to sniff and use her version of "Hrrrmph."

"Nothing?" I said. "You've been acting weird for the last two days. What's going on?"

Words flowed out of my phone like water from a busted dam.

"You have lots of exciting adventures, but you just lug me along like so much dead weight."

"You're on all my adventures," I said, trying to figure out what was going on. "I depend on you."

"That's right," said my phone. "Saving you from certain death when you fell off the giant robot should count for something. You expect so much, but if your faithful phone wants one little thing, you ignore it like it doesn't exist except when you need it for research or…"

Now I understood—my phone wanted something, and rather than ask me outright it was playing passive-aggressive verbal games to get me to notice. It had pulled this sort of stunt once before when it had wanted an extra petabyte of memory. I knew how to make it stop wheedling.

"What one little thing do you want?" I said. "Just tell me and if it's not ridiculously expensive, I'll get it for you. I owe you for saving my life, several times over."

"A new case," said my phone, almost shyly.

"What kind of new case?" I asked.

Chit was watching this exchange with obvious interest. I was grateful she kept her mouth shut, since I expected anything she said would only upset my phone.

"An Orishen mutacase—"

Chit laughed, but a regular laugh, not a belly laugh this time.

"I've seen 'em back on Orish," said my little friend. "If you think your phone's a challenge now, just wait!"

"That's not fair," said my phone. "You've got six legs and wings."

"I thought you were a *mobile* phone," said Chit.

"Jack!" said my phone.

"Give it a rest, Chit," I said. "How do these mutacases work?"

"I'll show you," said my phone.

The O'Sullivan Fabrication promotional video was replaced by another one demonstrating the capabilities of an Orishen mutacase. A phone similar to mine, enclosed in the case and sitting on a table top, was able to extrude tiny arms and legs and move across the table's surface, then stretch out a hook and a thin cable that it used to lower itself to the floor. Once it was down, the arms transformed into dozens of legs on each of its long sides and it scuttled along at high speed like a broad, flat centipede. When it was six feet from the table, it tilted to a forty-five degree angle, bent back, and somehow sprang up and forward in a graceful arc, landing at its original starting point. It was really cool and just a little bit creepy.

"The case can also integrate with your mutakey," said my phone, eagerly.

I'm sure it had been trying to work up the courage to ask me for the mutacase for weeks and I'd been too dense to notice.

"How much?" I asked.

My phone quoted a number that was larger than the price of dinner for two at the Teleport Inn, but less than the cost of a block of a hundred hours of Remote Hands sessions. I had the money, and my phone *had* saved my life yesterday.

"Make it so," I said.

"Recorded," said my phone. "A drone will home in on our location and drop it off in a few minutes."

It was making happy chirps and beeps. Images of fireworks exploding flashed on its screen.

"Of course," I said. I'm glad my team members know how to take initiative.

Chit was looking at me and making a sound like a donkey braying. I guess I deserved it.

I bowed, at least as much as I was able to while wearing a seat belt. Then I rolled down the driver's side window, accepted delivery from the drone hovering just outside, and unwrapped the package. Out of its box, the case looked like a black, phone-sized second skin.

"Wear it in good health," I said, putting the Orishen muta-case under my phone. The new case artfully removed the old one and flowed around my electronic associate. I heard chirps of delight and saw appendages appear and disappear rapidly as my phone put its new case through its paces.

"Cool," said my phone. "Where's your mutakey?"

I put the mutakey—one of my graduate-level workshop projects on Orish—on the passenger seat. My phone crawled over to it and seemed to absorb it into its new case. Then it started opening and closing my van's door locks and popping the glove compartment.

"Can we get this reconnaissance in gear, please?" I said.

"And now I can help," said my phone, waving three of its currently extruded arms. "I think this thing has a stealth mode."

My phone shimmered, then blended in with the upholstery fabric on the passenger seat and neatly disappeared.

"Isn't this cool?" said my phone.

"I don't see it," said Chit.

I played a rimshot in my head, then issued a command to my van's A.I.

"O'Sullivan Fabrication, and step on it."

Chapter 12

"Time spent in reconnaissance is seldom wasted."
— John Marsden

I didn't think I'd get more details about O'Sullivan Fabrication from my phone for a few hours, so I talked over possible ways to learn additional information with Chit. We agreed the place looked like a prison fortress more than a 3D printing company.

"The satellite photos didn't show any obvious entry points, like at the grajja factory," said Chit.

"And if they're investing so much money in physical security, I expect their electronic countermeasures are top of the line, too."

"Yeah, we can confirm that when we get closer," she said. "You got binoculars?"

"Under the passenger seat," I said, pointing down and to the right.

"Let's figure out if there are any good spots for takin' a discreet look-see," said Chit. "We can use my phone."

"You have a phone?" I said. "I thought you communicated through your built-in congruent link."

"That's how I keep up wit' the rest o' the hive mind," said my little buddy. "I need my phone for my shows."

"Who knew?" I said.

"Try to keep up."

A satellite view of the O'Sullivan Fabrication facility appeared on the windshield screen. It was located in the middle of a loop of private road off the nearest county thoroughfare, nearly a mile away from any other structure. We could approach from either direction, but only the private road ran near the place, and that clearly didn't get a lot of traffic.

"Switch to topographic," I said.

Chit pressed a foreleg into a thick spot on her thorax and the view changed to show contour marks. There was a hill about three hundred feet high in the center of the land enclosed by the private and county roads. It was on a heavily wooded parcel of land a quarter mile from the O'Sullivan Fabrication building and looked like it would have an excellent view of the surrounding area, tailor-made for detailed observation.

The sun was starting to go down as my van drove along the county road. I'd disabled its bassoon background tone, so our progress was noiseless except for the sound of tires on asphalt. We passed one end of the O'Sullivan private road and slowed half a mile further along. My van stopped and I got out.

Chit was on one shoulder, my backpack tool bag was slung over the other, and my phone was hanging on my belt, reading the mutacase manual and trying out new features. My binoculars were on a leather strap around my neck and I had a congruency-powered flashlight in an outside pocket of my pack to help find my way back to the van after dark.

I told the van to cruise the county road and stay close, then walked into the woods in the direction of the observation hill, ignoring the private property signs tacked to the trees. After a bit of stumbling around in the fading light, I found a path or animal trail that took me in the right direction without having to push my way through too much undergrowth.

"Are there bears around here?" said Chit. I couldn't tell if she wanted the answer to be "Yes" or "No."

"Not many in metro Atlanta," I said. "Though there are a lot in north Georgia. They're not a problem except when the sows are protecting their cubs in the spring."

"Is May spring?" asked Chit.

"Technically, yes," said my phone.

"Welcome back," I said to the device, but it didn't answer. It had just turned itself into something the shape of a batarang.

I should have spent more time on the treadmill at the gym, since I was getting winded from the climb. I could see a dim glow around the hill from the high intensity congruent lights positioned along the fences and on the guard towers of the O'Sullivan fortress. The slope was steep over the last two hundred yards and the pines changed to maples and birch trees before the trees stopped at the edge of the meadow that crowned the hill.

There were a few man-high boulders on the side near the fabrication facility and I leaned against one of the larger ones and lifted my binoculars. It was disconcerting to see beefy security guards wearing black O'Sullivan Fabrication uniforms standing in the two nearest towers. They were using their binoculars to stare back at me. It was even more disconcerting when the face of the rock next to me slid to one side with a pneumatic whoosh and metallic clank, revealing another thick-necked uniformed guard standing at the top of a flight of metal stairs. He had a shotgun pointed at my center of mass.

"Did you happen to see any private property notices on your way up here?" he said. A small nameplate above his breast pocket said he was Larry Villarica from Orlando, Florida. I made a mental note *not* to include that sort of detail when I implemented name badges for XSC.

"Olen turisti. Olen vaelluksella."

I'd just said, "I am a tourist. I am hiking," in Finnish.

Mike's not the only one who wanted to get a better handle on Quenya.

"Bein' smart, are you?" said Larry. "Let's see some identification."

"I. do. not. speak. English," I said, trying to bluff it out.

Larry pulled a badge wallet from his hip pocket and showed it to me, pointing to the laminated card with his name and photo below his tin-plated O'Sullivan Fabrication Security badge. Then he pointed at me, pointed at his laminated card, and spoke very slowly.

"I. den. ti. fi. ca. tion."

I kept a puzzled expression plastered on my face, but it looked like I'd have to come clean and admit who I was. Larry was holding the shotgun one-handed, but it was still pointed in my direction. I wasn't wearing anything that said Xenotech Support Corporation, but I had business cards in my backpack tool bag and my wallet clearly identified me as Ajax Pryce Buckston, not Eero Saarinen, or whatever famous Finnish name I could come up with. I was wearing my Orishen pupa silk shirt, which had stopped bullets and saved my life earlier, but shotgun pellets tended to disperse and Poly had told me she liked my face the way it was.

Larry put his badge wallet away and returned to a two-handed grip on his weapon.

"Show me some identification."

It was an order, not a request.

I reached for my wallet, but it wasn't there. Where *was* my wallet? Come to think of it, where was my phone?

Larry saw that I was puzzled by the loss of my wallet and seemed to come to a decision. I was above his pay grade. He pulled me into the hidden observation post at the top of the hill and closed the door behind me. Then he herded me down four flights of metal stairs until we reached a corridor leading toward the main building. Once there, he spread my feet wide, pressed me face first against a wall, and fastened my wrists together with zip ties. Chit hid under my hair and stayed out of sight.

I was marched downhill a quarter mile along the corridor until we entered the lower level of some larger structure, presumably the O'Sullivan Fabrication fortress. Larry led me along a wide hallway, then grabbed my upper arm none too gently and took me into some sort of interrogation room. He told me to sit down in a chair next to a rectangular metal table, pointed to a surveillance camera in the ceiling, and left. The door closed behind him and I heard the sound of an electronic lock engaging. I started to sweat, even though the air conditioning was up high enough that I had goosebumps.

After a few minutes, an older guard wearing a black uniform with more scrambled eggs—that's fancy braid, not breakfast—

entered. His nameplate said he was Hiram McWhorter, from Valdosta, Georgia and he tried to interrogate me in Italian, French and German, without success. I kept up my tourist disguise, complaining in my limited Finnish vocabulary and reciting the two poems I'd memorized from the *Kalevala*.

Then I had an idea and mentioned the Silver Comet Trail in halting English. Once Hiram heard "Silver Comet Trail" he decided to buy my "lost hiker" routine. The heavily used trail ran a few miles north of here and was popular with European tourists, so that detail made the difference. He gave interrogating me one last try, using grade school Dutch, but when I shrugged my shoulders Hiram finally got disgusted and gave up.

"He started, but he couldn't Finnish," said the voice inside my head.

I suppressed a laugh.

"What's funny?" tapped Chit in modern Pyr pulse code.

I clicked my teeth in reply.

"Later."

"Take him to the Sheriff's office in Austell," said Hiram. "Tell them he was trespassing, and we want to prosecute."

"Okay," said Larry. "Want anything while I'm closer to civilization?"

"A Quarter Pounder with Cheese, small fries and a Coke."

Hiram handed the first guard a ten dollar bill.

"Get something for yourself, too. Good job apprehending this character, even if he's lost, not a spy."

"Thanks," said Larry. "Eternal vigilance is the price of security."

"Liberty," said Hiram.

"Whatever," said Larry.

I was pushed along more underground corridors then led up a flight of stairs that emptied into the main lobby of the building. I saw three signs painted on the walls, like back in Zwilniki's VIGorish Labs complex. They read Warehouse, Fabrication and Offices, and weren't much help. We stood next to the reception desk and waited for Larry's car to drive up.

The guard at the reception desk, Annette Winston, from Anniston, Alabama, was bored. She was flipping through a copy of *Galaxy* magazine—the GaFTA tabloid, not the revived SF mag—and I was able to read a few lines of the visitor's sign-in log. The only entry for today was someone named Agnes Spelman from Factor-E-Flor. Agnes Scott and Spelman were two highly regarded women's colleges in Atlanta, which meant I may have just learned the current alias of the woman I knew as Columbia Brown. I'd have to pass that news on to Lieutenant Lee.

When Larry's car arrived he was polite and not too rough about getting me into the back seat. On the five mile drive I was worried about the impact an arrest for trespassing would have on my business *and* on the place where I'd be spending the night. My apartment was highly preferable to the hospitality of the Douglas County Jail. I also wondered what had happened to my wallet and my phone. When we pulled up to the Douglas County Sheriff's Lithia Springs Precinct Office in Austell, a surprise was waiting for me.

Lieutenant Lee's Capitol Police cruiser was parked outside and my friend was standing beside it. He was wearing his Smokey the Bear hat, which made him extra-intimidating. When Larry arrived and got me out of the back of his car, Martin came over and introduced himself, then cut to the chase.

"I'll take him," said Martin. "He's an escaped mental patient and we've been looking for him."

I gave Martin a "thanks a lot" look. He kept his poker face.

Larry replied. "I don't know. My boss said I had to turn him in for trespassing."

"Did you hear him, man?" said the lieutenant. "He talks like a crazy person."

Martin looked at me. I looked at Larry and recited half a poem at him in Elvish.

"I guess you're right about that," said Larry. "And what my boss don't know won't hurt him. He's your problem now."

Larry shook Martin's hand, got into his car, and headed for the Golden Arches.

"Thanks," I said, turning around and extending my zip-tied hands.

Martin cut my bonds with a Swiss Army Knife. I rubbed my wrists. I didn't like being arrested, even if it was by private security and didn't really count.

"No problem," said Martin. "But you owe me."

"Another breakfast?" I said.

"Maybe some other time. Information."

"Glad to share," I said, "but I don't know much."

"I figured that," said Martin, "but I expect they know more."

Chit had moved back to my free shoulder and the two of us stared as my van pulled around a corner and parked next to Martin's cruiser.

"Holy sh…" said my little buddy, her compound eyes spinning.

"Hop in," said my phone, using my van's larger speakers. It popped both doors open. "I've got a lot to tell you."

Martin and Chit and I got into my van. It made sense for us all to get a briefing on the way back to Atlanta, so Martin sent his cruiser ahead of us to wait for him near my apartment. Once we'd buckled up and started back to the city, my phone explained what it had been up to.

"When you were surprised by the man with the shotgun," said my phone, "I held on to your belt and moved behind you. I wanted to stay out sight."

"Smart," I said.

"I heard you pretend to be Finnish, so I pulled your wallet out of your back pocket and held on to it. I knew it could be used to prove your real identity and screw things up."

My phone flipped my wallet into my hands and I returned it to its usual location. I trust my phone enough that I didn't check the balance on my credit cards first. It wouldn't have been polite. Besides, my phone *was* my credit cards, for most transactions. I nodded my thanks and encouraged the resource-ful device to continue.

"I rappelled down the back of your pants, walked around behind Larry, and flipped up to attach myself to the back of his belt. I looked like any other piece of his equipment."

"And while you were doing that, you were also calling me and letting me know Jack had been captured," said Lieutenant Lee. "Good job multitasking."

My phone looked proud and happy. A big yellow smiley face covered its screen.

"Way to go!" I said, and meant it. That was the second day in a row my electronic friend had saved me.

"Thanks," said my phone. "While you were being interro-gated, I dropped off Larry's belt when he walked through the lobby on the way to the restroom."

"Okay," I said, with a tone that meant, "Tell me more."

"Then I crawled around under the reception desk and tapped all the security camera feeds in the building."

"You what?" I said. A grin spread across my face. I picked up my phone and kissed it right on its smiley.

"Um. Um. Um," said my phone, not sure how to deal with this atypical public display of affection.

Martin broke in to give the disconcerted unit time to recover.

"I headed this way as soon as I heard you were captured," he said. "Then I got a text directing me to the Sheriff's office, not the O'Sullivan Fabrication building. I got there just in time, apparently."

"Thanks for keeping me out of jail."

"The night is still young," said my friend.

"Now about those security camera videos…" I said to my phone.

"Yeah," said Chit, waving her antennae wildly. "What did ya see?"

"What's in the warehouse?" said Martin.

"You know, don't you, Jack," stated my phone.

"Robots?" I said, tentatively.

"Robots," said my phone. "Four more heavily armed giant robots, just like the one from WT&F."

"Now we know *what*," I said.

Martin cut in, "But we don't know…"

"Why?" said Chit.

"And not just robots," teased my phone.

"What else?" I said.

"There are two other parts of the facility that I find puzzling."

"Tell us," I said.

"Both are underground."

My phone was dragging things out for dramatic effect. I let it have its fun and waved my hand in a "go on" motion.

"One is a Biosafety Level-4 lab. The cameras show half a dozen lab techs in pressure suits working on some sort of purple-colored cultures."

That didn't sound good.

"And the other?"

"Another complex with airlocks and high bio-security. There's a large room where twenty Pyrs are putting together round metal shells the size of grapefruits and loading them with vials of lavender liquid."

"Prisoner Pyrs assembling spheres?" I said.

Martin gave me a dirty look. I had a bad feeling about this.

"What makes you think they're prisoners?" he said.

"The place is built like a prison. There must be a reason."

"Are the Pyrs chained to their workstations?" asked Martin.

"No," said my phone. "But the assembly room and adjacent living quarters are locked and heavily guarded."

"They're not chained, so they're probably not prisoners," said the lieutenant.

"Have you ever tried to chain a Pyr?" said Chit.

"That's right," I said. "What do you chain? Their tentacles? They can extrude and reabsorb them at will. How do you restrain a Pyr when you arrest one?"

Martin looked appropriately contrite.

"It doesn't happen very often," he said. "Pyrs are usually law abiding, but when we do arrest one we put them in a locked room. I forgot I once sent a rookie in to handcuff a Pyr prisoner who was being transferred to another holding facility. The whole precinct got a laugh out of watching him try."

"Proving my point," I said.

"You think it's a biological warfare facility?" said Martin.

I nodded.

"And the spheres are delivery systems."

I nodded again.

"Why Pyrs?"

"Were the lab techs human?" I asked my phone.

"As best I could tell under their protective suits."

I stroked my chin and offered a possible explanation.

"Maybe Pyrs are immune to whatever biological agent they're refining in the lab."

"Could be," said Martin. "I'll need to tell my superiors about this—and the governor."

"And the CDC," said my phone.

"But first," I said, "I think we need to talk to Tomáso."

Chapter 13

"A zombie apocalypse isn't the most jovial situation."
— Danai Gurira

"When were you going to tell *me* about the giant robot at WT&F?" said Tomáso in a *basso* voice so low it made Darth Vader sound like a tenor.

"Ummm..." I said.

Martin came to my rescue.

"Jack wanted to invite you to breakfast at Waffle House after he took the robot to Zwilniki's hangar, but there wasn't room."

"Roger Joe-Bob Bacon's place?" said Tomáso. "You could have conferenced me in."

"Sorry," I said. "After almost falling to my death earlier that morning, I guess it skipped my mind."

"Don't let it happen again," said the Dauushan, looking stern.

I felt like a child being sent to bed without any supper. Then he smiled, showing teeth the size of teacups.

"Gotcha."

I let out my breath in a sigh of relief. Tomáso's approval meant a lot to me. I glared at him for form's sake, then smiled myself.

Ninety minutes after we'd left the parking lot at the Sheriff's office, Martin, Chit and I finished updating Tomáso and Shepherd on what we'd learned. They didn't look shocked. Tomáso made a call, like he had right after we'd started our briefing, and the rest of us took a short break. I didn't like the look on Tomáso's face.

Martin and I were sitting in comfortable chairs on either side of a small round table on the upper level of Tomáso's study. The raised section was there to put shorter species closer to eye level with Tomáso, who was somewhere between seventeen and twenty feet tall. I hadn't measured—I was afraid it would make me feel even smaller than I already felt when I was around him. Chit was sitting on an upside down old-fashioned glass on the table, holding a ceramic thimble full of something whose fumes smelled like lemon-scented paint thinner. My phone was leaning back against Chit's glass. It had extruded arms, legs, and a simulated head from its mutacase and had adopted a relaxed but attentive pose. Shepherd, who had been meeting with Tomáso when we'd arrived, was in his usual shadowed spot in a far corner, nearly invisible.

I had a Diet Starbuzz, Martin had a Coke, and Shepherd had a concerned expression on his face.

"You'd better tell them," said the Pâkk.

"Yes," said Tomáso, "considering they've fallen into the thick of it on their own."

"Start at the beginning," said Shepherd.

Tomáso sighed.

"Fifteen thousand years ago…"

"Say what?" I said.

"Shut up and listen," said Chit, taking a sip from her thimble.

"Where was I?" said Tomáso.

"Let me try," said Shepherd. "How much do you know about the Pâkk-Tigrammath War?"

"The ancient myth cycle?" said Martin. "Like the Iliad?"

"The P-T War was no myth," said the Pâkk. "It was real, and almost destroyed more than a dozen sentient species."

This was sounding familiar. I remembered what Poly had told me at second breakfast yesterday when she'd shared what her adviser had told her about the conflict.

"Mine included," said Tomáso. "We were attacked by both sides. So many and so much was destroyed."

Tomáso rubbed his top eye with one of his sub-trunks and went on.

"The P-T War ended an earlier version of the Galactic Free Trade Association and left many planets isolated—apprehensive about invasion, or contagion, or both—for three millennia."

"No Seldon Plan?" I said.

"Don't be a smart ass," said Chit. "Close your trap and learn something."

I drew two fingers across my mouth to zip my lips and kept quiet. My elders were talking.

"No psychohistory, no First or hidden Second Foundation, no Mule," said Tomáso, "just fear and chaos. The Pâkk-Tigrammath War was a conflict to see which species would rule the galaxy."

"They fought like cats and dogs," muttered Chit.

"It ended in a Pyrrhic victory for both sides," said Shepherd. "Afterward, the Tigrammaths transformed themselves from Romulans into Vulcans. They renounced their savage natures and cultivated serenity, meditating on the billions of sentient lives lost in the war."

The Pâkk shook his head back and forth, slowly, as if remembering tales of atrocities from ancient battles. He continued.

"My own people split in two. The Long Pâkk had learned the lesson that the way of the warrior must be tempered by the ways of the wise. The Short Pâkk still honored our oldest warrior traditions, but were encouraged to redirect their aggression inward, into intra-Pâkk clan competitions and tests of courage, not outward against other species."

"Fifteen thousand years ago," said Tomáso, "the Dauushans were the key to galactic conquest, just as they are today."

"Huh?" said Martin. He was trying to think it through.

"Then, as now, my species was known for our skill in fabrication. We were, and are, the preeminent *makers,* not just in quality, but quantity."

"Dauush makes, the galaxy takes," said Chit.

"Any species that conquers Dauush," said Shepherd, "would be able to produce unstoppable quantities of ships, weapons, and matériel."

"And my people make excellent combatants," said Tomáso. "A Dauushan in battle armor is larger than most Terran tanks, and twice as dangerous."

"I can see that," I said, remembering how I'd felt when Tomáso had picked me up and squeezed me after I'd "rescued" Spike six weeks ago.

"Dauushans are formidable," said Martin, making a simple, self-evident statement.

"True," said Shepherd. "The species that controls Dauushan productive capacity and commands Dauushans' loyalty…"

"Rules the galaxy," I said.

"Give the kid a cigar," said Chit.

My phone spoke.

"Excuse me," it said, "but how does this tie to O'Sullivan Fabrication's biohazard lab and their captive Pyrs?"

"Good question," said Tomáso. "During the P-T War, both species—unknown to each other—approached a group of brilliant Nicósn scientists. Senior Påkk and Tigrammath leaders insisted the scientists expand on their published research and redirect it toward developing a bio-agent with very special properties."

"The lavender liquid," said my phone. The eyes in its simulated head went wide.

"Yes," said Shepherd.

"What did it do?"

"It made anyone infected follow their controllers' commands," said Tomáso.

I stood up and walked over to confront Shepherd. I was probably shouting.

"They made a virus to create an army of zombie slaves?"

"It wasn't exactly a virus," said Chit. "More like a bio-cybernetic nanoparticle."

I ignored her.

"An army of *Dauushan* zombie slaves," said Tomáso.

"Though it also affects other species," said Chit, having far too much fun with a subject this serious.

"And the beings infected aren't zombies, exactly," said Tomáso. "They still have their original will and judgment, but following their controllers' instructions stimulates their pleasure centers. After a few hours of obedience, they're addicted."

Insidious and highly effective, I thought.

"What was this bug called?"

"The Compliant Plague," said Shepherd, softly.

I whistled, slowly, and shook my head from side to side. It was a lot to take in.

I looked at Shepherd.

"Who won?"

"The galaxy," answered Tomáso, when the Pâkk didn't. "The Nicósn scientists, supported by Pâkk and Tigrammath forces, conducted a test. A single, isolated island on Dauush was infected—just a hundred thousand of my people. Half were controlled by Pâkk, half by Tigrammaths. It was a place for leisure, not production, so it didn't have any of our high volume 3D printers. They were fighting with knives, clubs and spears."

Tomáso made a curious set of gestures with his trunks—some sort of ritual, I assumed. It reminded me of hand motions used to ward off the evil eye.

"Each side used Dauushans as its Janissaries, its elite slave soldiers," said Shepherd.

"They slaughtered each other," said Tomáso. "Dauushans died to prove the efficacy of the Nicósn scientists' bio-agent. The Matriarch in those ancient days was wise. She used a supernova bomb to cleanse the island."

"That much stellar radiation should have vaporized the island down to the mantle," I said.

"It did," said Tomáso. "Nothing was left above sea level."

I bowed my head and considered the ancient Matriarch's decision.

"But all those deaths were not in vain," said Tomáso.

"Yes," said Shepherd. "The Nicósn scientists witnessed the carnage and knew they'd gone too far, creating a weapon too terrible to be used. They took all their stock of the bio-agent, in hundreds of sealed, heat-resistant ceramic capsules, and sent them as one big load through an untuned congruency."

"A nondeterminate, random destination wormhole," said Chit, "so no one would ever know where to find them."

"The bio-agent capsules could have ended up anywhere in the universe," said Shepherd.

"Let me guess," I said. "They ended up here."

"Yes," said Tomáso, "They materialized in your solar system and struck Terra somewhere in eastern North America, fifteen thousand years ago."

Martin looked thoughtful.

"How big were these capsules?" he asked.

"About the size of a motorcycle side car when they started reentry," said Tomáso. "When they landed, after the ablative material burned off, they were probably the size and shape of a propane cylinder for a Terran backyard grill."

"That works. They came in at an oblique angle, I'll bet," said Martin, "and made lots of oval-shaped depressions that filed with water."

"What are you talking about?" I said.

"The Carolina Bay lakes," Martin said. "Some geologists and astronomers think they were created by meteors. My grandparents have a cottage on Lake Waccamaw in North Carolina. That's the largest one. I was up there last summer for a family reunion and there were big barges out on the lake, dredging to increase its volume. It's a reservoir for Columbus County. I think the dredging company's name was Wallace Engineering, or something like that. Their equipment made a lot of noise and people around the lake couldn't talk about anything else."

"John Findley Wallace was the chief engineer for the Panama Canal," said my phone, "His work ensured America's domination of world trade for generations."

Another Earth First Militant company? I wondered.

"Wallace Engineering is a wholly-owned subsidiary of the James K. Polk Group," said my phone.

"Ouch." Sometimes I hated being right.

"So how did *you* find out about the capsules?" said Martin, waving a hand from Shepherd to Tomáso.

"Three of my staff members were on holiday at Woods Bay State Park in South Carolina last month," said Tomáso. "It's another large Carolina Bay, like Lake Waccamaw, and it's got great mud wallows."

"Dauushans love their mud wallows," said Chit.

Tomáso glared at Chit in a halfhearted attempt to intimidate her. I didn't work.

"They found a capsule?" said Martin.

"They stepped on it, actually," said Shepherd, "then they brought it back to the Dauushan consulate for analysis. It was labeled in pictographs and Old High Nicósn."

"Nicósns have always been good about documenting their work," said Tomáso.

I was furious and raised my voice.

"You opened it?" I paused for emphasis. "On *Earth*?"

"Don't look at me that way," said Tomáso. "We did it in a Biosafety Level-4 lab using Pyr technicians. They're immune."

I *knew* it!

"Still, you were taking a big chance—with *my* planet."

My hands clenched.

"We had to know what the enemy knows," said Tomáso.

"When's the raid?" asked Martin.

I could see that he was already trying to figure out the best way to storm the O'Sullivan Fabrication fortress.

"An hour ago," said Tomáso. "I've had a joint Dauushan Ranger, Defense Department, FBI and CDC rapid response force on high alert at Dobbins Air Reserve Base for the past two weeks waiting for any news of the bio-agent."

"What?" I said.

"As soon as I heard your news I sent them in," said the Dauushan.

"You're kidding me," said Martin.

"And I missed out on all the fun," said Chit.

"There's only one problem," said Shepherd.

"What's that?" I said.

"The O'Sullivan Fabrication building didn't have four giant robots in its warehouse or a bio-weapons lab in its basement or Pyrs held prisoner," said Tomáso, checking his phone's massive screen. "It was a legit custom fabrication facility. It didn't even look like they'd been there and cleared out."

My phone used its extruded legs to stand up and it shook a fist on the end of its extruded arm in Tomáso's direction.

"But I saw the robots and lab and Pyrs on the security cameras," it shouted.

Maybe its speaker was just set on high.

"We were suckered," I said.

Some image was trying to cut through the cobwebs in my brain, but stayed hidden.

"Sherrhi hoped that her appearance on Terra would flush out the people who found the capsule," said Tomáso, referring to his spouse, the Queen Matriarch of all Dauushans.

"The Queen's gambit," I said. No one ever said members of the Dauushan royal family lacked courage.

"Too bad it didn't pay off," said Chit.

With that sobering thought, the meeting ended.

Chapter 14

"You learn a lot about someone when you share a meal together."
— Anthony Bourdain

It was almost eleven and I was crossing the **Ad Astra** courtyard, half-way to my apartment, when I heard Poly's voice from my phone.

"Oh Lover Boy…"

She'd sent me a text.

"Having a late supper with Professor Urrrson and mate at R. Thomas Deluxe Grille. Want to join us?"

By now, Poly and her adviser must have had four or five hours of sleep and would be at least somewhat coherent, and hungry.

"Sounds great," I sent back. "When?"

"Now."

It seemed odd that Poly and the two obligate carnivore Tigrammaths would be eating at a restaurant that I'd remembered was more into bean sprouts than beef, but maybe Poly knew something I didn't. Scratch that. Poly knew a *lot* that I didn't know.

"On my way."

My phone had already summoned my van and was clapping its hands together in excitement. I hoped it would tire of playing with its new mutacase soon. I opened Chit's bottle to see if she wanted me to take her home, but she said she'd be fine catching up on her programs and told me not to worry. I think she may have been a bit worn out from all the excitement of the last two days.

I changed direction and headed for the nearest Peachtree Street gate instead of my front door and was in my van and on my way to the restaurant in less than two minutes. This late at night, traffic was light and my van made it the three and a half miles down Peachtree to the restaurant in great time. I hopped out by the front of the building and let my van navigate its way to the steeply sloping parking lot in the rear that was more suited for mountain goats than self-driving vehicles.

R. Thomas Deluxe Grille was an incongruous addition to the Atlanta dining scene. It was as if some sort of cosmic event had plucked an eclectic hippie restaurant from San Francisco in the early 1970s and dropped it down between an old fashioned southern tea room serving chicken fried steak with sausage gravy on one side and a pretentious nouvelle southern belle establishment serving grits topped with sautéed truffles and parakale on the other.

The sign above the restaurant had its name spelled out in funky red, white and yellow neon letters. Exotic birds—parrots, macaws, mynas, and pink Dauushan avians nicknamed *paracletes,* the size of great horned owls—were happily chatting away in large cages on the path from Peachtree Street to the main entrance on the right. Wonderful smells were wafting out the door—waffles cooking, eggs frying, and coffee brewing. From the back of the place I even thought I smelled barbecued ribs. Was I imaging things? I must be hungrier than I thought.

I stepped inside, past a beaded curtain and three rows of batik and tie-dyed hangings, and made my way to the greeter's stand. A middle-aged man in a Grateful Dead t-shirt asked how many were in my party. His arms were covered with Orishen animated-ink tattoos of scenes from Hayao Miyazaki movies. I craned my neck to look over his shoulder and spotted Poly at a table not far away sitting with a distinguished Tigrammath male, probably Professor Urrrson. A Tigrammath female sat across from him with her back to me—she was likely his mate. I told the Illustrated Man that I'd found my party and worked my way through the tightly packed patrons to Poly's table. She stood up and gave me a hug. It felt like water tasted after a long walk through the desert.

"I've missed you," said Poly, tightening her hug and giving me a discreet kiss just behind my ear that sent shivers down my back.

"And I've missed you!"

I snuggled in one last time and held her just a bit too long to be appropriate in most public places, but somehow at a 70s inspired place like this, it felt right. The Tigrammath male on Poly's left stood up. I leaned back so I could see his head, more than a foot above mine, and shook his extended hand, pleased that Tigrammaths' claws retracted.

"Jack, this is Professor Urrrson, my adviser, and a genius with composite A.I.s," said Poly.

"Poly exaggerates," said the Professor, "but my ego enjoys being stroked every now and then, so long as she doesn't make a habit of it. She's brilliant and very talented as well. Those are qualities I insist upon in my grad students."

A touch of red colored Poly's cheeks.

The professor smiled, showing teeth that weren't as large or as sharp as Spike's, but were definitely the dentition of a carnivore.

"I'm very pleased to meet you," I said, continuing to pump the professor's hand. "Call me Jack."

"Call me Bartolomeww," the professor replied. "Or if that's too much of a mouthful"— he smiled again — "just call me Bart."

Poly got my attention with a touch on my arm and gestured behind me.

"And this is Professor Urrrson's mate, Professor Niaowla Murriym."

I turned and saw the female Tigrammath who had remained sitting in the chair across from her life partner. Her short, blue and black striped fur still rippled, but she was no longer in uniform.

"We've met," said the Tigrammath female, her voice still a sexy purr.

"Hello, Dox," I said.

I sat down and hoped Poly didn't see me blush.

"Dox?" said Bart.

"My name at Roger Joe-Bob Bacon's restaurant," said his mate. "I served Jack and his friends there yesterday morning."

Poly saw my confusion and threw me a lifeline.

"Jack," she said, "Professor Murriym has a joint appointment at Emory in Sociology and Galactic Philology."

"Call me impressed," I said.

"I'll stick with Jack," said Niaowla. "It suits you."

"So why did your name tag at Waffle House say 'Dox'?" I asked.

"Niaowla is hard for Terrans to pronounce," she said, "and once one of the other servers heard I had two doctorates, she nicknamed me Dox."

She tilted her head.

"And I like it."

"Works for me," I said. "But why were you pretending to be a server at a Waffle House."

"I wasn't pretending," said Niaowla. "I *am* a server, and really appreciated that twenty-five percent tip your policeman friend left, by the way."

She smiled.

"I'll pass the word," I said, "but you still haven't told me why you're working there."

"I'm doing participant observation research, studying Terran dining and socialization rituals. Roger Joe-Bob is a dear to let me work at his restaurant to gather data, so long as I pull my weight on the team."

"Niaowla's doctorates are in sociology and ancient languages," said Poly.

"Xenosociology, from my perspective," said the female Ti-grammath, "though it's sociology from yours. I like studying Terrans' reactions."

"I'll say," I said.

Poly gave me a sharp look, wondering why I'd said that.

"You'll have to forgive Jack," said Niaowla. She was talking to Poly and her wide eyes were reflecting more light than usual.

"I knew who he was when he walked in yesterday morning. You've got his picture as the screen saver on your GT-Net terminal."

Niaowla and her mate smiled at Poly and me.

"Bart told me you and Jack were partners," she said. "Terran marriage customs are so delightful."

"We're not married, Niaowla," said Poly, turning slightly red again. "We're business partners."

"Delightfully complicated, she meant," said Bart, covering for his mate's *faux pas*.

"I've always found that the more you know about Terrans, the less you *really* know," said Niaowla.

She leaned in close and stage whispered to Poly.

"Female to female, I tried to flirt with Jack as part of one of my research protocols and he didn't flirt back. He's a keeper, dear."

So much for being irresistible to women. Poly made her own attempt to change the subject.

"Niaowla and Bart both have outstanding academic reputations," she said. "Emory was very lucky to get her, and Georgia Tech was quite pleased as well."

"You don't have to suck up to him now that you've graduated," said Niaowla, teasing both her mate and Poly.

"It's a challenge for faculty couples to find good positions in the same city," said Bart.

"Or even on the same planet," said Niaowla.

"I'm glad you both landed in Atlanta," I said.

Poly rubbed her knee against mine under the table as a reward for saying something nice.

"Where's our server?" said Bart. "I'm hungry enough to eat a horse."

"He means that literally, dear," said Niaowla to Poly, "but let Jack get her attention. He knows how to treat a server."

My ears turned pink but I caught the attention of a woman wearing a restaurant logo apron who had hair so colorful that it made CiCi's pink, purple and lime green accent stripes look unimaginative. She brought menus to our table and hovered while we figured out what we wanted.

I was surprised to see something new on the menu—a notice in twenty point type on page three announcing that R. Thomas Deluxe Grille had recently "added a smoker to better serve our Pâkk, Tigrammath and other carnivorous clients." That explained the delicious smells coming from the back of the building. I flipped over to the history blurb on the back of the menu and noticed that the place had started out as a California-style hamburger joint. I guess they'd never been completely vegetarian.

"I'll have a large order of barbecued ribs," said Bart. "Are they horse or cow?"

"Cow," said our server, smiling. "I hope that's okay."

She'd been paying more attention to the conversation at our table than I'd thought.

"He'll be fine," said Niaowla. "The same for me. No sides for either of us."

"Got it," said our server.

"I'll have the ginger crusted wild Ahi tuna," said Poly.

"I'd like the salmon piccata, please," I said, smiling at our server.

Then I looked at Poly.

"Share?"

"You didn't have to ask," said Poly.

"Extra side plates," said our server. "I'll get your orders in."

"Thanks so much," I said.

Our server's face brightened as she headed for the kitchen.

"See," said Niaowla to her mate.

Professor Urrrson growled deep in his throat, but then smiled and held Niaowla's hand across the table. Tigrammaths have long arms, and long-lasting relationships.

Our server came back and dropped off four waters, a bread basket, and a plate of cold cuts at our table. I spread almond butter on a quinoa roll and tried to get to know Bart and Niaowla better.

"What other research are you doing when you're not observing unsuspecting Terrans eating breakfast?" I said, addressing Niaowla and keeping my tone light. I still wasn't quite sure how I felt about her faked flirting.

"I'm working on a book on ancient Galactic inscriptions, comparing pre- and post-war styles across ten cultures.

"The Pâkk-Orish War?" asked Poly.

"Heaven's no," said Niaowla. "That would hardly count as ancient. It took place in my lifetime."

"The young think anything older than they are is ancient," said Professor Urrrson, "and anything older than their grandparents is the stuff of myth and legend."

"I'm sorry," said Poly. I liked the way her dimples appeared when she smiled. "Which war *were* you referring to?"

"The Pâkk-Tigrammath War, of course," said Niaowla. "It's *the* turning point in ancient Galactic history."

"What ten cultures are you studying?" I asked.

"Pâkk and Tigrammath, as you might assume," she replied, "and Dauushan and Pyr and Orishen."

"That's five," said Poly.

"Murms?" I asked.

"No," Niaowla answered. "Hive minds don't tend to go in for inscriptions. The Quirinx fliers make fascinating letter forms on soft rock with their beaks and the Musans have the most exquisite miniatures. The level of detail they can achieve with their tiny hands takes a magnifying glass to appreciate."

She paused to take a sip of water and spear a slice of spiced turkey from the plate of cold cuts with her fork.

I'd seen Quirinx the size of California condors soaring around my apartment complex, and smiled to think of the chipmunk-sized Musan family I'd observed dining on a cup of boiled peanuts at a Southern-themed gastropub on Piedmont Road last year. A lot of Galactic species in Atlanta like to live in

Buckhead so they can be close to their consulates at Ad Astra.

"That's seven," said Poly. There are times when I think my partner fixates on numbers.

"The J'Vel don't make incised inscriptions," said Niaowla, referring to another small species like the Musans. "They create something more like mosaics using glue and colored seeds to put words and scenes on their monuments."

"Are there a lot of problems with the seeds being eaten over the centuries?" I asked.

"Yes," said Niaowla, "Very few of the J'Vel monuments have seeds remaining, but we can detect the patterns of the glue that was applied using UV light, and identify pigments from DNA analysis of fragments left embedded in the adhesive."

"It's as much physics and biology as it is philology, according to my mate," said Bart, reaching for a thin slice of Virginia ham.

"And politics and bureaucratic maneuvering to get permission to excavate the inscriptions in the first place," said Niaowla. "Too many species don't want to be reminded of what happened in the P-T War."

"That's still only eight," said Poly. See what I mean?

"Tōdons make nine," said Niaowla. "There are remote cliff faces on Tōdo simply covered with intaglio Tōdon etchings made by acids released from the tips of their abdomens."

"Very *large* etchings, I assume?" said her mate.

"Everything about the Tōdons is large," said Niaowla.

"And ten?" said Poly. Have I mentioned that my partner is persistent?

"The Nicósns," said Niaowla. "Which reminds me of the practical joke some anonymous prankster tried to play on me last summer with an obviously sham inscription in Old High Nicósn."

I was eating the other half of my roll but stopped chewing and paid close attention.

"It came to my inbox as an anonymous email. Scans of the inscriptions and associated pictograms were attached."

She sniffed as if detecting an odd smell.

"It was something about how to properly manage a biological super-weapon and sounded like something out of the latest Zombie Apocalypse comic book from the CDC."

Niaowla shook her head back and forth at the very idea.

"I don't know who was playing games with me," she said. "But I went along with the gag, translated it, and sent it back to the sender."

She bit off half a slice of corned beef.

"I must be hungrier than I thought."

The other half of the slice disappeared.

"I kept expecting to hear from *someone,* a fellow faculty member if not a student, claiming responsibility, but never heard another word."

She laughed.

"I was expecting *some* sort of reply, based on what I'd done in my translation."

"What you'd done?" I said.

"Let's just say I've been known to play practical jokes myself."

My cheeks turned red. Her eyes danced in response to my reaction.

She chuckled as if remembering a private joke, then reached for a second slice of turkey, only to pull her hand back.

"I'll spoil my appetite at this rate. I guess the joke's on me."

Niaowla looked to her left and noticed I was staring at her.

"Is something wrong, Jack?"

"Do you still have the email?" I asked.

"I'm sure it's still on the server somewhere," she said.

"Could you forward it to me? It's very important."

"Certainly," she said, seeing my concern.

"Could you check now?"

"If you'd like."

Now Poly and Bart were both staring at me. Poly knew me well enough to wait for an explanation. Bart just looked puzzled and a bit protective of his mate.

"Here it is," she said, tapping the extra-hard glass surface of her phone with a foreclaw.

"Jack@xenotechsupport.com," I said.

"On its way."

As soon as the message arrived I sent it along to Tomáso and Shepherd and Martin and Chit with a brief explanation about where it had come from. While I was typing, of course, our meals arrived. I waved a hand to encourage the others at the table to start eating and pushed SEND a minute later. My salmon smelled good. So did the barbecued ribs and Poly's tuna.

"Can you tell us what all that was about?" asked Bart.

"Unfortunately, no," I said, "but it may be a very important clue to a mystery of galactic proportions."

"Speaking of galactic proportions," said Bart, always the one to smooth over awkward moments. "Look at the size of these ribs."

Chapter 15

"When she's cuddled close, I feel there's nothing I can't do…"
— Jarod Kintz

My reaction to Niaowla's Old High Nicósn translation story guaranteed that Poly would come home with me instead of going back to her place or straight to the lab with Professor Urrrson. On the drive to my apartment, I filled her in on my earlier capture and near-arrest, as well as the revelations from Tomáso and Shepherd. I could see her brain was spinning as she processed all the new information.

While she asked me more questions I brewed a pot of decaf hibiscus passion tea and poured the hot, aromatic, deep purple liquid into our favorite mugs. After a few sips she relaxed and finally noticed something new in my apartment.

"The flowers are lovely," said Poly, looking at the vase on the dining room table. "Where did they come from?"

"Is it so hard for you to believe that I bought them because I thought you'd enjoy having them in the apartment?"

"Yes."

She knew me too well. Her response was curt but her voice was merry and teasing.

"Beautiful flowers for a beautiful lady?"

Poly knew I was playing a role for comedic effect: the love-sick swain. I know, I know. Typecasting.

"Give."

I knew when to surrender.

"They're from Mistress Marigold."

"And therein hangs a tale?"

"A long, and rather funny one involving hamburger, sleeping pills and self-mobile plants."

Poly laughed.

"I'd love to hear it—in a few days—*after* I've finished my paper and collected a couple of sheepskins."

"I think they're using acid-free paper for diplomas these days," I said, "not sheepskin parchment."

"I've been deceived," said Poly.

Then her tone of voiced changed.

"And speaking of deception…"

"Time to get serious?" I said.

"Yes," she said. "If O'Sullivan Fabrication was just misdirection, why is Ray Ray Dunwoody worried about what's going on there?"

Poly took my free hand and guided us to the couch in my living room.

"I have no idea," I said, putting my mug down on the end table to my right. Poly held on to her mug and inhaled the steam from her tea.

"But you'll talk to him?"

"If R. C. says it's okay," I said. "I don't want to break my word."

"You're a good man, Jack Buckston."

"Aw, shucks, ma'am."

I said the phrase with the obligatory western drawl. Poly put her mug down on the coffee table in front of her and leaned on my shoulder. I put my arm around her and helped her fit more tightly against me.

"Do you think the robots and bio-weapons and Pyr prisoners are real, or is Columbia Brown or Agnes Spelman or whatever her name is just messing with our heads?"

"They're real, all right" said my phone. The now fully mobile device had hopped off my belt and climbed across my lap to stand with one foot on my leg and one on Poly's. It was waving its extruded arms indignantly. I was beginning to regret buying the mutacase.

"How do you know?" said Poly. "Couldn't they be a highly sophisticated simulation?"

I was impressed that she didn't react to my phone's new functionality.

"A simulation might be able to fool an organic person, but

not a cybernetic intelligence," it said.

"Yeah, right," I said.

My phone knew me well enough to detect my sarcasm. Before it could snark back, Poly asked it a question.

"Are there any other large buildings in metro-Atlanta owned by O'Sullivan Fabrication?"

"Or Factor-E-Flor or the James K. Polk Group," I said.

"Or the EUA Corporation," added Poly.

I thought for a second. Were we missing any? An LED turned on in my head.

"Or Wallace Engineering."

"Searching," said my phone. It hopped off our legs and sat in a contemplative pose on the coffee table.

"Do you think EUA is behind all this?" said Poly.

"Maybe," I said, "but we don't know much about them."

"Sounds like a research project."

"In all my copious spare time," I said.

My phone stood up and shook its extruded head.

"I can't find any other facilities run by the companies you've specified," it said. "I'm searching for properties that may be owned by other organizations that have done a better job of covering their tracks."

"Try looking for any other complex that's approximately the same size and shape as the O'Sullivan footprint," said Poly. "Use your recordings of the warehouse and other parts of the complex to figure out the dimensions and find matches."

"An excellent recommendation," said my phone, returning to its thinking posture.

"Could we talk privately for a minute, Jack?" said Poly.

"Microphone off for 300 seconds," I told my phone.

It made an acknowledging beep and continued its research.

"How long has your phone had arms and legs?" said Poly.

"It just talked me into getting it a mutacase a few hours ago," I said. "It's still getting used to it, and so am I."

"I think it's going to take me a while," said Poly. "It's a little like living with a precocious child and I'm nowhere near ready for that."

"Sorry," I said. "It saved my life yesterday, or was it the day before yesterday?"

Poly checked her tiny phone after pulling it from a front pocket of her jeans.

"It's twelve thirty," she said, "so it was two days back."

"I couldn't say no," I said, "and my phone saved the day again tonight."

"I guess I can live with it," said Poly. "There are times when I'm glad I can't afford a phone that's state of the art."

"You can get whatever you want," I said. "You're a partner and can get a company phone."

"I can, can't I?" she said, tilting her head up and kissing my neck. "I've been so focused on grad school I haven't considered the implications of my new status."

My toes had curled when she'd kissed me, so I had to control my autonomic reactions to find my own focus.

"Speaking of your new status as a partner and someone about to receive two prestigious graduate degrees…"

I got another kiss on the neck.

"Umm… Where was I? Uh… graduate degrees, I'd like to talk about next steps."

"Next steps for Xenotech Support?"

"Next steps for us."

"Oh," said Poly, suddenly sitting up and turning to face me. She held my hands.

"You know I really like spending time with you."

She squeezed my hands.

"Back at you," said Poly.

"And what with your academic schedule and my work and recuperation, we haven't had a lot of time together…"

Poly looked at me with a broad smile on her face, patiently waiting for me to get the words out.

"True," said her lips. Her eyes said, "Please go on."

"I was thinking we could go on a week's vacation together after you graduate. We could go somewhere warm."

"Atlanta in May is warm," Poly said, teasing.

"And romantic," I said.

"I'd like that," she said.

I knew what her answer would be, but it was still nice to hear it.

"Separate rooms?" said Poly.

"If that's what you want."

"Hell, no."

She leaned in and kissed me on the lips. It was *very* nice and lasted for a long time. Then we were interrupted.

"Still researching," said my phone.

"Microphone off for 3,600 seconds," I said.

"Beep," said my phone, then went quiet.

"Where do you want to go?" said Poly.

"Wherever you want to go. Maui, maybe, or one of the Pyr pleasure planets."

I didn't tell her I already had half a dozen brochures.

"We could even get a suite at a nice resort," I added.

"Why don't we both make lists of our top ten romantic vacation spots?" said Poly, "Then compare them."

"Great idea." I started to get up to find a couple of pencils and some paper.

"You're not going anywhere," said Poly, pulling me back down and giving me another thorough kiss that was *not* interrupted.

After more than 300 and less than 3,600 seconds, Poly broke our clinch and smoothed down her t-shirt.

"I'd love to stay, Lover Boy, but can't. I promised Professor Urrrson I'd build the tables for our paper tonight."

"It's one thirty in the morning. You're becoming nocturnal."

"It the only way I'm going to get the paper finished before Georgia Tech's graduation on Friday."

She was up and out my front door before I remembered.

"Watch out for my *what?*"

Chapter 16

"Housework is something you do that
nobody notices until you don't do it."
— Author Unknown

I had the presence of mind to pick up my phone and tap its screen to get its attention.

"Send the van to Peachtree Street to take Poly to her lab," I said, "and text her phone so she doesn't get an autocab."

"Glad to," said my phone. "Should I keep my microphone off?"

"No, you're fine," I said. "Leave it on."

"Thanks," said my phone. "Still researching, by the way."

I nodded acknowledgment and my phone resumed its thinking pose, this time extruding a rock to sit on so it better resembled Rodin's famous sculpture. I laughed, but only on the inside. My phone had its dignity.

I was pleased I didn't have anything on my calendar today until I had to leave for the airport. That meant I could sleep late and take my time getting my apartment in shape to potentially have company, just in case. When your partner's family is in town it pays to be prepared.

Of course, there was also the small matter of a royal invitation to dine with the Queen Matriarch of Dauush at the Teleport Inn at eight. I'd have to check my best suit when I got up to make sure there weren't any stains on it. Maybe I'd pick up a new shirt and tie for the occasion at one of the expensive shops in the retail part of the complex. It was nearly two in the morning and I'd be a zombie all day if I didn't get some rest.

If I'd been conscious when it happened I'd have known that I was asleep before my head hit the pillow.

* * * * *

I woke up suddenly when something jumped on my bladder.

"But I don't *have* a cat," said a semi-conscious part of my brain.

"Jack," said my phone, the something that had been doing the bladder jumping, "Terrhi's at the front door and if you don't answer it soon she's going to knock on it loud enough to annoy the neighbors."

"What time is it?" I said, rotating my body and putting my feet on the floor.

"Seven-thirty."

I grunted a combined acknowledgment and protest and shuffled out to the front door in my bare feet. On the way, I tried to wake myself up and put at least a simulation of cordiality on my face. Terrhi didn't need to see me at my morning worst—it might scar her for life.

I opened the door.

"Hi, Uncle Jack!"

"Hi Terrhi," I said, with a tenth of her child's enthusiasm. "To what do I owe the honor of your unexpected presence at this hour?"

"You're funny, Uncle Jack."

"Not intentionally."

"Daddy said I should check with you before I went to school."

I made a mental note to play some sort of practical joke on Tomáso in the near future.

"Check with me about what?"

"About whether you and Poly and her family are coming to my mom's dinner tonight. At the Teleport Inn."

Skip the practical joke. I deserved this.

"I'm *so* sorry," I said. "So much happened yesterday that I forgot to RSVP."

"That's okay. You must get a *lot* of dinner invitations from Queen Matriarchs," teased Terrhi.

"First one this week," I said.

"And?" said Terrhi.

"And, what?"

"And are you and Poly coming?"

"Of course. We're honored to attend and are really looking forward to meeting your mother."

"Mom's cool. You'll like her."

"I'm sure we will."

"What about Poly's family? Are they coming, too?"

"Yes," I said. "Poly left me a note to say they'd love to come, but I forgot to get back to you. It's all my fault."

"That's okay, Uncle Jack." Terrhi's nine sub-trunks bounced in excitement. "We thought that's what happened."

"Sorry."

"You do tend to get distracted, Uncle Jack."

"You have no idea…" I said, my voice trailing off as my brain started riffing over everything that had happened yesterday.

Something ran between my legs, bumping my right ankle in the process. It was my phone, in its "let's pretend I'm a tiny human" mode.

"My apologies, Princess," said my phone, bowing as best it could with a rigid, rectangular middle. "I should have reminded him, but I was focused on learning how to use my new case."

Terrhi giggled. I love the sound of little girl giggles in the morning.

"It looks good on you," she said. "Now you can help Spike chase squirrels."

"Speaking of Spike," I said, "where's my favorite tri-saber-tooth?"

"He's down that way, sniffing the bushes." Terrhi gestured to her right with three sub-trunks. "I think he's tracking something."

"More squirrels?" I said. "Or perhaps a chipmunk?"

"Something else, I think," said Terrhi. "But I don't know what. I haven't seen him behave this way before."

"I hope he doesn't frighten some poor woodland creature half to death."

"He won't," said the girl. "He's a big sweetie."

She turned her head to the side and shouted.

"Spike! SPIKE!"

So much for not annoying the neighbors at this hour. The big cat came bounding up the courtyard, made a ninety degree turn, and slid past Terrhi to head-butt me, knocking my phone into a comical somersault in the process. I'd braced myself—this wasn't the first time Spike had given me an enthusiastic greeting—so I didn't land on my posterior. I did have fun watching the video of my phone's back flip when I checked my front door security camera later, though. Now I just gave Spike the scritches he was expecting.

"Hi Spike," I said. "Did you spot something unusual?"

Spike stepped back to stand by Terrhi—he was as much royal bodyguard as pet, I considered—and shook his head slowly from side to side. He hadn't been able to figure it out, whatever it was. I felt something grab on to my t-shirt and realized that my phone had climbed up my back to ride on my shoulder. That was a much better place to be than ground level when Spike was in the vicinity.

"It's been great to talk with you, Uncle Jack," said Terrhi, "but school starts at eight-thirty and I don't want to be late."

"Isn't your school in the complex?" I asked. There were several schools for the children of Galactics in Ad Astra.

"Yes, but Daddy only lets me walk to school by myself if I remember to be on time."

Given all the temptations on the way for a young Dauushan and her pet, I can understand why Tomáso imposed that restriction on his daughter. Then Spike's ears popped up. We heard a high-pitched whine.

"Incoming!" said my phone, a bit too loud and right in my ear.

Five drones had arrived at my front door, where they hovered above Terrhi and Spike.

"Delivery for Jack Buckston," each drone said in turn, dropping off five different-sized packages after I acknowledged receipt.

"Oh, I'm glad they came before I had to leave," said Terrhi.

"You're behind this?" I said, gesturing to the packages.

"Just this one," she said, pointing to a tall square box the size of a very large bottle of liquor. "Open them, open them."

I was curious, so I started with a rectangular box as long as my arm and about four inches thick. When I opened it, I found a top of the line black tuxedo jacket and matching pants. The other boxes held shoes, shirts, vests, two cummerbunds, bow ties, cuff links, shirt studs, socks and all the other trimming that go with a tuxedo.

"Am I to assume that your mother's dinner tonight isn't a typical informal Dauushan get-together?"

"Uh huh," said Terrhi, "Mom's in full Queen Matriarch mode. It's formal, and Daddy and I wanted to make sure you look sharp."

"Thank you," I said. I'd always wanted to own a spiffy tux but never had anywhere to wear one.

"Open *my* package," said Terrhi.

I'd moved the tux and accessories inside and put them on my coffee table so they'd be safe from Spike's curious investigations.

"Okay," I said, opening the box and finding an elegant silk top hat. I tried it on.

Terrhi giggled, then covered her mouth with three trunks.

"Sorry, Uncle Jack," she said. "I *do* like how it looks on you."

"But maybe with the tux instead of a t-shirt and sweatpants?"

"Maybe," said Terrhi, still suppressing giggles.

I tipped my hat at her, did a brief two-step and hummed a bit of *"Puttin' on the Ritz."* I made myself a mental note—I'd have to get a cane.

Terrhi gave up on suppressing anything. She just laughed.

"Time for school," she said, skipping off down the courtyard with Spike as only young hexapods can.

I waved to my departing friends and was about to close my front door when another delivery drone arrived carrying a box the same size and shape as my tuxedo's container. This time, I recognized the logo on the side of the package. It was from Morphicouture, the high fashion house that was also one of my clients. I'd helped them find some missing fabric six weeks ago, and Mademoiselle Ellie, their CEO, had promised me something special as a way of saying thank you.

Inside the box was a gorgeous Orishen morphic silk dress, custom made to Poly's measurements. Another, much smaller box, rested at the bottom of the larger one. I opened it and saw that it held a matching pair of morphic shoes. Ellie and her team had outdone themselves.

Now I didn't have to worry about how I looked in my tux—with Poly by my side, nobody would be paying any attention to me.

* * * * *

I carried all my new finery into my bedroom, carefully hung what belonged on hangers in my walk-in closet, and arranged my suspenders, bow tie, cuff links, studs and socks on top of my dresser so they would be at hand when it was time to get ready tonight. I lined the shiny patent leather shoes up neatly on the floor in my closet. Somehow, they made all my other shoes feel drab by comparison. I left Poly's dress in its box, nestled in tissue paper, on the coffee table in my living room, but had my phone take a picture and text it to Poly with a note.

"A beautiful dress for an even more beautiful woman to wear for dinner with a Queen," it said. "Where do you want me to send it?"

Poly's reply came back quickly.

"Wow! You're amazing! Thank you! XOXO. Keep it at your place."

"Great!" I texted back.

I hadn't known where Poly's family was staying. I'd assumed it would be one of the hotels in downtown Atlanta or maybe the Ritz Carleton in Buckhead, but it would make logistics a lot easier if they were in a hotel here in the complex.

"How's it going?" I wrote.

"Good," responded Poly. "Gotta run. Bye."

I guess she was really pushing to get her paper finished. I hoped she'd had enough rest to be coherent for dinner tonight, then kicked myself for not asking for details about her warning earlier. Now I hoped that *I* would have enough rest to be coherent for dinner tonight. I looked at my bed longingly, but realized that I had a lot to do before I left for the airport and had better get started doing it.

I had my phone instruct my whirrbot and dust drones to get busy vacuuming and dusting, then lifted the lid on my toilet to ensure that my Too-D'Loo 'bot was continuing to polish the porcelain. I picked things up around the place, fighting the good fight against entropy, and put our tea mugs from last night in the dishwasher. That reminded me to eat. I had a light breakfast, just a cup of tea and a toasted Nicósn tortilla fish, since I planned to have an early lunch at the airport. Then I put my cup and plate in the dishwasher and set it to run in a few hours when I'd be out.

Finished in the kitchen, I walked to my living room where I programmed my wall screen. I configured it to show a rotating collection of scenes from the galaxy's top one hundred destinations according to the Keen's Guides, for Poly's mother, and photos of famous structures from the ancient world, like the Colosseum, the Parthenon, and the Great Pyramid of Giza for her father. I didn't know what scenes would appeal to Poly's sister.

Then I moved to my bedroom, and laughed. The poster-sized electronic picture frame to the left of my bedroom door had abruptly switched from a highbrow Impressionist painting, Edgar Degas' *Ballerina in a Red Dress* to a tacky painting from the *Dogs Playing Poker* series. That image slowly dissolved into an even more tacky velvet Elvis painting of the King in a white, rhinestone-encrusted jumpsuit. The transition made me laugh again. The electronic picture frame had been a convalescence gift from one of my friends or clients. When more than one person was in my room, it stayed classy, showing well-known paintings from Earth's top art museums. But when I was alone, it switched to kitsch. Along with the dogs and velvet Elvis, the frame had entertained me with Miss Piggy as Mona Lisa, a paint-by-numbers version of Michael Jackson's glove, a cat wearing an Elizabethan ruff, pink flamingos wearing top hats, and several of Margaret Keane's big-eyed children.

I didn't know who had given it to me. The card on the drone delivery just said "Get Well Soon," and wasn't signed, but I had my suspicions. Ellie Schwartzfield, the CEO of Morphicouture, was a candidate. She was a patron of the arts and had a wicked sense of humor. Ram Patel, the head of the North American Caribbean Cricket League, was another, but I thought his taste in tacky pictures would include bejeweled depictions of the Goddess Kali, and so far none had appeared. Droopy, Ram's formerly depressed ecommerce server, might have done it, but the disembodied brain would be more likely to send me something music-related. Martin had given me a law enforcement edition of *The Manual of Physical Security.* He'd said it was to help me sleep, but I enjoyed it. And Mike had brought me a treasure: actual ink-on-paper comic books—thank you Mike. After their thoughtfulness, I didn't think either Mike or Martin would spend over three hundred galcreds on an electronic frame. Terrhi's gift of a top hat this morning, along with the hat-wearing flamingos' pink color, made me believe I might finally know the identity of the frame's sender. It had to be Tomáso. He had a low sense of humor. It certainly wasn't Shepherd—he didn't do tacky.

It didn't really matter who had sent the frame. It had done its job and lightened my mood while I was stuck in bed. Speaking of beds, I remade mine with clean sheets, picked up odds and ends, and looked carefully to confirm that there were no signs of Poly spending time in my apartment visible to a casual inspection. She had a drawer filled with her stuff—t-shirts, underwear, jeans and such—in my tall bureau, but you'd have to be really nosy to find it. Once my bedroom passed inspection, it was time for a shave and a shower.

I spread depilating foam on my face, avoiding my mustache, and triggered it with a few seconds of UV light so the nanites suspended in the bubbles would give me a close shave. Then I got in the shower. I stayed with my standard Earl Grey program, since I wasn't feeling like I needed to be pummeled by Chinese Gunpowder. Despite only getting five hours of sleep, I was feeling pretty good. Maybe I'd head out early and check on my robot while I was close to Hartsfield. I grabbed my backpack tool bag and left my apartment.

Carpe diem, as my mother used to say. It was time to seize the day before the day seized me.

Chapter 17

"It just so happens that your friend here is only MOSTLY dead."
— William Goldman, *The Princess Bride*

I walked down to my reserved spot in the underground parking garage, instead of having my van meet me on Peachtree Street, because I needed to reconfigure my van to carry passengers. Normally, there were just two bucket seats up front. The Orishen-built front seats could slide together and meld into a single bench seat to fit in an extra person, if necessary. However, I needed to pick up three people and their luggage on my airport run, and that meant major modifications to my van's interior.

My van was neatly parked in my assigned spot, nose out for a fast departure. A row of lockers, twice as deep and three times as wide as the ones you see lining the halls in high school movies, was bolted to the wall at the back end of my parking place. I used the lockers for storage and asked my van to pull a few feet forward so I could open its back doors and remove most of the parts and equipment filling up its cargo compartment.

I like to be prepared for anything, which means I'm reluctant to throw away any surplus technology I come across that might be useful for solving clients' problems. In practice, that means the back of my van is chock full of junk I think might come in handy, from a tiny Musan-sized Orishen scent-organ to a Tōdon smart watch as big as a beer keg. Come to think of it, maybe it *was* a beer keg. I don't drink, but I've been known to help transport supplies for clients' parties. I like to pretend that everything in the back of my van is well organized, but I'm fooling myself. When I slide open the partition separating the driver's area from the cargo compartment and survey the semi-structured chaos, my superego just shakes its head and makes disapproving *tsk-tsk-tsk* sounds.

I didn't have time to sort and organize things as I removed

them—I just pulled items out quickly and shoved them into my lockers wherever they would fit. Thank goodness there was enough room. I'd dropped off several hundred kilograms of "surplus equipment" at Fry's Galtech Salvage a couple of months ago, because I couldn't talk the tenants holding the parking places on either side of mine into letting me install lockers in their spaces to handle my overflow. At least moving my junk was an upper body workout, so I didn't have to feel guilty about skipping the gym.

Then I noticed the two dormant octovacs I'd stowed at the very front of the cargo compartment. They were flat round disks that looked like they'd extrude into extra pop-up seats at my command. I rolled them out the side cargo door and around to the back of my van. Unfortunately, when I tried to find space for them in my lockers, the "No Vacancy" sign was on. I really should have returned that beer keg. I sighed and realized I'd have to put them back in my van after it shifted modes. Maybe they could help carry luggage?

Once the back of my van was empty, I instructed it to recon-figure its interior to six passenger mode. After a cheerful "As you wish," a second row bench seat flipped up from the floor and metal panels along my van's sides descended to reveal tint-ed windows. It wasn't as slick as a full-blown Orishen mutable interior, but it was Terran-made and a lot less expensive than the off-planet alternative. I'd wanted the six-passenger option in case I needed to pick up clients or take them out to dinner, but seldom used my van for anything except support calls. I was glad to give my "faithful steed" a change of pace.

"Looking good," said my phone, back in its normal spot on my belt.

"Woo hoo hoo!" said my van, clearly pleased.

"Wasn't that what… ?" I started to say, but my van cut me off.

"It's what Miracle Max said to his wife."

"How many times have you watched *The Princess Bride?*"

"It's on a continuous loop. Part of me is always watching it."

"While you're driving?"

"According to a 2029 report from the National Highway Safety Board, self-driving vehicles are very good at multitasking," sniffed my van.

It was the longest sentence I'd ever heard it say.

"If you ask me, you need to go through a car wash," said my phone.

"Look who knows so much," said my van.

"Wasn't that also what…" I said.

"Uh huh," said my van.

"Time to go," said my phone.

I looked at my van's exterior and agreed with my phone's assessment. I'd stop at a car wash on my way south. I'm glad I'd gotten an early start on the day—errands were piling up. I stowed my backpack tool bag between the front bucket seats, climbed in, and headed toward the airport.

* * * * *

I'd made it all the way to the interstate before everything turned upside down.

"You've got a call," said my phone.

"Who's it from?" I asked.

"CiCi, the security guard from WT&F."

"I know who she is. Mike has a date with her on Friday. I hope she's not asking *me* out. I'm taken."

"I don't think so," said my phone. "Voice stress analysis indicates she's really worried about something."

"Then put her through," I said.

My phone complied. It was right about her being worried.

"Jack! Please! Come help. There's been an explosion and they've evacuated the building."

"Is Mike okay?" I asked.

"I don't know," said CiCi, "but I don't think he was anywhere near the executive offices."

"Is that where the explosion was?" I said.

"I think so. That's where the smoke is coming from. I'm

outside now. I was here covering a second shift so that I could get Friday night off."

She was sounding slightly more calm now.

"I pulled the fire alarm and called 911," said CiCi. "Then I watched the security monitors to confirm everyone got out. Everyone had—except Mike. I thought he must have gone out the back."

She must have covered her phone's microphone with her hand because I could barely make out her voice. She was saying something like "Have you seen him?"

Then she was back on with me. The stress in her voice had returned.

"Mike's not here. He must be still inside."

"On my way," I said.

But I already was. My phone and van were both quick on the uptake and were shifting to the off ramp for the next exit so we could turn around and get to WT&F fast. I just hoped we'd get there soon enough to be useful.

"Step on it, please," I told my van.

There was a lot of stress in *my* voice, too. CiCi might be overly optimistic about Mike not being affected by the explosion. The production floor was directly below the executive offices.

My van made great time. It was going so fast that there were moments when I thought it was a hovercar. I could see smoke rising as I approached WT&F's exit on I-285.

When I pulled into the parking lot, three fire trucks and two ambulances were already on the scene. Clumps of employees were standing near the ambulances, being treated for minor injuries, mostly cuts and bruises from flying debris. Steel and glass shards had peppered the paint jobs of cars parked near the explosion, but luckily no one was in the parking lot when the bomb—if it was a bomb—went off.

A fancy red Porsche 9099 Sterne-Kämpfer in a reserved spot near the front entrance was a total loss, crushed under the executive floor's copier. The heavy office machine must have been blown into the air by the force of the blast, then landed on the sports car's roof, crushing it before embedding itself in the expensive vehicle's aluminum and magnesium-composite hood. I wondered if it was J-J's car. If so, I hope he was insured.

CiCi, in uniform, was talking to one of the firefighters.

"He's still in there," I heard her say. "But he's not answering his phone."

CiCi's face was a mass of emotions, more than half of them fear.

"We'll have to wait for the heavy-lift jack," said the firefighter, adjusting her broad-brimmed hat.

"No we won't," I said, inserting myself into the conversation.

"Who are you?" said the firefighter.

"I'm Jack," I said. "What needs to be lifted?"

"This is no joke," said the firefighter. "Part of the second floor slab has broken off and fallen on the first floor."

"On the production room?" I asked. My phone made unexpected dialing noises. I'd worry about it later.

The firefighter looked at CiCi for confirmation.

"Yes," she said, trying to hold it together. "My friend is trapped there."

If Mike could have seen CiCi's face at that moment he wouldn't doubt that she cared about him.

"Did everyone else from that side get out safely?" I asked.

"My understanding is that no one else was *in* that side of the building," said the firefighter, looking at CiCi again.

"That's right," said CiCi. "When the cat's away…"

"The mice will play," I said. "Golf?"

"That's what the CFO told me on his way out," said CiCi. "I'm not sure I believe him. The VP of Sales and Marketing *was* off playing golf. I saw him leave wearing a purple and orange striped polo shirt, a white belt, and lime green pants."

I nodded. He wasn't likely to be doing anything else wearing *that* outfit.

"What about the support staff?"

"Early lunch," said CiCi. "From what I overheard, I don't think any of them planned to come back."

She held up one hand as if it was wrapped around a glass and brought it to her mouth.

Oh, *that* kind of lunch, I thought.

"So Mike was the only person working on that side when it happened."

"Uh huh," said CiCi. "The rest are all accounted for."

I gave CiCi a supportive, reassuring look and decided to examine the bomb-damaged side of WT&F's headquarters more closely. I walked to the left until the worst of the destruction was visible. A large wedge of concrete was tipped down. One end of it was still attached to the remaining second floor slab with steel reinforcing rods and the other was resting on a pile of rubble at ground level. The broken slab was blocking all access to the production room.

I walked back.

"How long until the heavy-lift jack gets here?" I asked the firefighter.

"More than an hour," she said. "They're using it on an overturned bus downtown."

"The department only has one heavy-lift jack?"

"Budget cuts," said the firefighter. "I'm Clarisse, by the way. Clarisse Beatty. CiCi says you're resourceful."

I skipped my usual attempt at false modesty.

"I try," I said. "Jack Buckston, Clarisse. I may have something that can lift that slab, or at least help us get under it."

"The City of Atlanta and the Fire Department take no responsibility," Clarisse said with smile.

"Disclaimer noted," I said.

"Give it your best shot," said Clarisse.

CiCi followed me as I walked back to my van.

"Can you get Mike out, Jack?" she said.

"Count on it," I said. I hoped I was right.

I opened the back of my van, lifted out one octovac, and

handed it to CiCi.

"You take this one," I said. "I'll take the other."

Octovacs weren't light. They weighed between ten and fifteen kilos, twenty or thirty pounds, but CiCi carried hers like it was a bag of packing peanuts. She must work out. I put my octovac down on the ground near the tilted slab. I could have activated them at the van and had them walk themselves, but I didn't want to scare the bystanders any more than they were already.

The smell of smoke filled the air, but CiCi told me the firefighters had launched a vacuum congruency bomb at the second floor that had sucked all the air away and put out the flames. We didn't have fire or water or air to worry about, just earth, or rather, concrete.

I spoke to my phone. "Please activate the octovacs. See if they can lift the slab."

"Will do."

Both octovacs extended their tentacles and used them to stand and flex. They crossed to the broken slab and positioned themselves on either side of it. With four arms and legs apiece they got under the slab and tried to raise it. It didn't move. They just weren't strong enough. Octovacs are fast and agile, not super strong—they're like Hermes, not Hercules.

"That's not working," I said. "See if they can find a way into the production room."

"Okay," said my phone, "but I…"

"Not right now," I said. "I need to see what happens."

"But, Jack," said my phone.

"Just a second," I said. Couldn't it see that I was focusing on something important? Mike's life was at stake.

While I watched the octovacs clamber around and beside the slab, looking for holes large enough for them to crawl through, I felt something crawling up my back. Before I could move my arm to slap at whatever it was, something pinched my earlobe. Hard.

"Jack," said my phone, standing on my shoulder with its speaker half an inch from my ear. It had my attention.

"Yes?" I said, none too happy.

"Put me down by the slab. There should be holes large enough for me to fit through and I can send back videos of what I see."

Why hadn't I thought of that? I guess I still wasn't used to my phone being self-mobile.

"Great idea," I said. "CiCi, may I please have your phone?"

"Sure," she said, pulling it from her pocket.

I touched it to my phone and CiCi gave her okay for my phone to send audio and video to hers. I put my phone down next to the tilted slab and it promptly extruded two dozen centipede-like legs from each side of its case and scuttled its way through a hole into the darkness.

Signals began streaming to CiCi's phone. Clarisse came over to watch with us, so CiCi unfolded her phone a few times to make the screen larger. My phone was picking its way over chunks of rubble like it was crossing a lunar landscape. Then things leveled out. My phone had reached a largely undamaged section of the production room floor, partially protected by the slab. We watched it shine its light around in circles, searching for Mike. It went forward a few feet and repeated its scan. After its third advance, its light flashed across Mike's face.

"Hey," said Mike. "Not in the eyes. It's too bright."

He was okay. CiCi cheered and gave me a joyful hug that I'd never mention to Mike. Clarisse looked pleased as well, but no hug. Professionalism, and all that.

"How are you doing?" I said. My phone knew the drill and relayed my voice.

"I'm okay," said Mike, "but my foot is caught under a feedstock tower that fell over and knocked me down. In other words, 'help, I've fallen, and I can't get up.'"

He must be doing well if he can crack jokes, I thought.

My phone's camera pulled back to show us a wider view of Mike's vicinity. He was trapped, but it didn't look like the tower was crushing his foot or his leg. A protrusion from the feedstock tower had gone through the cuff of his pants and was holding him to the floor as if he'd been nailed there. A heavy service door from the Model-43 had snapped off from the feedstock tower's impact and was restricting the movement of Mike's arms and upper torso. Black feedstock powder was piled all around him, like drifts of negative snow. He looked like a coal miner after a cave in. A small trickle of blood from a cut on his forehead ran red in contrast to the dark powder. Thankfully, the angle between the feedstock tower and the far end of the Model-43 had protected Mike from falling debris when the slab descended.

"Can you snip the fabric and free him?" I asked my phone.

"No pro-blé-mo."

My phone must have picked that phrase up from an old movie—or from Chit. Crap. I'd forgotten about Chit completely. She wasn't going to be happy about being left out, since she could have buzzed in and spotted Mike in seconds.

"Got it," said my phone.

"Thanks," said Mike. "Now I can move my leg, not that I'm going anywhere."

"The fire department says the heavy-left jack will be available in an hour or so," I said.

"It might be sooner than that," said my phone.

"What do you mean?"

"Check the parking lot," my phone replied. "I called as soon as I heard you needed heavy lift capability."

I turned to look. A flatbed eighteen-wheeler marked "Wide Load" and decorated with pink Dauushan planetary flags was just pulling in. Tomáso and another, even larger member of the consulate's staff were aboard. With nine sub-trunks each to grab the slab and enough muscle to shift it easily, the two elephant-sized diplomats moved the slab out of the way without more debris falling from the floor above. Tomáso lifted the Model-43's service door off Mike's upper body and Mike got to his feet on his own. He spotted his phone blinking on the edge of a pile of dust a few feet away and put it in his pocket. Too bad it hadn't been closer.

Mike was covered in black feedstock powder, but was able to walk out under his own power. He thanked Tomáso and the larger Dauushan before turning and spotting CiCi. The two of them ran toward each other in a romantic, choreographed, slow motion dance. I could almost hear the schmaltzy theme music. When they intersected, a puff of black feedstock powder rose above them. I turned my head away when they started kissing. The paramedics were hovering, waiting to check out Mike, but CiCi seemed to be doing a thorough job of that herself.

"Thanks," I said to my phone, via the feed from CiCi's phone. I also thanked Tomáso and his associate personally.

Tomáso didn't hug me—and I was grateful. He introduced me to the other, even larger Dauushan, whose name was Diágo. The three of us chatted for a few minutes. This was Diágo's first time on Terra. He was the head of Queen Sherrhi's security team and had worked with Tomáso for many years. The Queen had arrived on Monday evening, along with a sizable—no pun intended—entourage and Diágo had been up to his three huge elephant ears in logistical details. His top deputy was currently on duty, so Diágo was glad to take a break and see new Terran scenery away from the Ad Astra complex. I got the distinct impression that Tomáso may have worked *for* Diágo sometime in the past. If so, it wouldn't be the first time someone being guarded had fallen in love with her bodyguard.

When our conversation ended and I stepped away from the Dauushans, Clarisse approached.

"CiCi was right," she said, tipping her firefighter's hat. "You *are* resourceful."

A voice by our feet spoke up.

"*He's* resourceful? Who do you think did all the work?"

Clarisse laughed. I picked up my phone and hugged it as best

I could with all its squirming legs.

"Hey," said my phone, concerned for its dignity. I snapped it onto its usual spot on my belt.

Clarisse shook my hand, thanked me for my help—and my phone's—and walked purposely toward her engine to arrange for the arson investigation. Her team was already taping off the building's entrances. It would be unsafe to enter until the integrity of the remaining structure had been confirmed.

Tomáso pulled me off to one side for a semi-private conversation, shielded, in part, by his own bulk.

"Do you think this is the work of Columbia Brown?" he asked.

"Yes," I said, "or one of her henchmen. I think it's a payoff on the threats directed at Jean-Jacques."

Tomáso moved his huge head up and down slowly. "Odds are good," he said.

I nodded, too.

"What about the inscription photos and translation details I sent you last night?"

"The inscription is identical to the one my associates found on the capsule in the mud wallows at Willow Bay State Park," he said, "though your translation was a little off from the one we received from a noted scholar on Nicós. The details on how to program the plague's bio-cybernetic nanoparticles were different."

"I'd trust your scholar's version over Professor Murriym's," I said. "At least in this case. Niaowla thought the inscriptions were a practical joke, so she may have taken liberties when she made her translation."

"That makes sense," said Tomáso, his large mouth smiling. "I wonder if Columbia Brown's side got a second opinion."

"Let's hope not," I said. "Confusion to the enemy."

"Because they've done a good job confusing us and turn-about is fair play," said Tomáso.

"Right," I said. "And by the way, thanks for the electronic picture frame."

"What electronic picture frame?"

So much for *that* theory.

Tomáso put three sub-trunks around my shoulders and gently guided me back toward my van. My phone directed the octovacs to follow, open my van's back doors, hop in, close the doors, and deactivate. I climbed into the driver's seat and caught my breath for a moment.

I heard a knocking sound from my backpack tool bag so I unsnapped an outside pocket and removed Chit's bottle. My little friend opened it, climbed out, and perched on the dashboard, wearing a design on her wing cases that looked like Hello Kitty. Was that her equivalent of pajamas?

Chit rubbed her compound eyes with both forelegs. She shifted her thorax in a peculiar way and if she'd had lungs instead of spiracles I would have sworn she'd just yawned.

My seat was feeling particularly comfortable and I hadn't gotten much sleep last night. Yawns are contagious.

"I stayed up too late watching Turner Classic Movies," said Chit. "Some real good ones, from forty-five years ago."

"You mean back in the far off days of nineteen eighty-five?" I said.

"Yeah," she said. "*The Breakfast Club* is one weird movie."

"That it is," I said.

"But the dream I had last night was almost a nightmare."

"Do tell?" I put my hand over my mouth. I didn't want Chit to think she was boring me.

"Instead of a brain, an athlete, a basket case, a princess and a criminal in detention, I dreamed it was three humans, a Tigrammath, a Pyr, a Pâkk and a Murm having breakfast at Waffle House."

"That wasn't a dream," I said, struggling to stay awake.

My phone pulled on my shirt.

"What?" I said. "I'm just resting my eyes."

"Pomy's plane lands in less than an hour."

Oh crap, oh crap, oh crap.

I was supposed to pick up Poly's sister!

So much for any chance to wash my van.

Why would my phone take the initiative to call Tomáso, but wouldn't tell my van to start driving to the airport?

"Seat belt," said my van.

Oh.

My van took off at slightly less than hovercar speeds and headed for Hartsfield. We should arrive just in time for me to be waiting to greet Poly's sister at the top of the escalators. Maybe I could grab half an hour's sleep while my van did the driving. I closed my eyes.

"So, buddy boy," said Chit, sounding more awake. "What did I miss?"

Chapter 18

"If I never saw another airport again, I'd be happy!"
— Emm Gryner

I have a love-hate relationship with airports. On the one hand, I love the sense of possibility, the potential to launch myself into new adventures, to boldly go somewhere I've never been before, to seek out strange, well, anyway, they're gateways to exciting new places and experiences. On the other hand, they're loud and crowded and filled with queues of people, humans and Galactics, who would rather be home or at their destinations, instead of stuck in hellish terminals known for overpriced stores, unappetizing food, and cryptic public address system announcements.

If you're the one traveling, there are thousands of indignities to deal with, from humorless, false sense of security agents, to restrooms that smell like piles of Tōdon dung left in the sun too long. Waits are interminable, chairs are uncomfortable, and overbookings are unconscionable.

If you're meeting a flight, you have to be cordoned off away from *real* travelers and aren't allowed out to the gates where you can greet people as they arrive. My grandmother said that when she was young, her mother and father would be waiting at the gate when the plane doors opened every time she came home from college. Hugs and happy chattering made returning to the main terminal to get her bags a delight. Now, family goodbyes are just a prelude to an hour-long line for document inspection and tearful reunions have to wait until *after* travelers are released from the "secure zone."

Airports can be hell, and the domestic arrivals area at Hartsfield leveraged that metaphor to the hilt. Travelers ride on shuttle trains from terminal to terminal, forced to make this stage of their journey in cattle car-like "barges," guided by a single-minded Charon whose limited vocabulary only includes phrases like "Now approaching Terminal D." Once escaping passengers reach the limbo of the shuttle's Baggage Claim station, giant escalators carry them, and hordes of others, up slowly ascending stairs to light and air and hope and, for some, a smiling face.

I pasted a smile on my own face as I waited for Poly's sister Pomy to arrive. It turned out that I hadn't needed to hurry. Pomy's flight from Rome to New York had been on time, but the second leg, from New York to Atlanta, was delayed half an hour. Pomy had spent a semester in Rome, working on a dig near the Forum, according to a Galnet search I did on the way to the airport. She had been in the Eternal City as part of her joint doctoral program in classical languages and archeology at Oxford.

My girlfriend Poly's first name is really Polyhymnia. She was named for the Greek muse of sacred poetry, hymns, dance and eloquence. She'd told me on our first date that her name was pronounced like Polly, but spelled Poly, like polytechnic or polymer. Her younger sister, born thirteen months later, is Melpomene, named for the Greek muse of tragedy and singing. Her nickname, Pomy, rhymes with "mommy," not "foamy." Poly's father, Pericles Agamemnon Jones, is the Marcus Aurelius Endicott Professor of Classical Languages and Literature at Harvard, which helps explain his daughters' names. Poly said her dad wanted to collect a full set of nine Muses, but her mother drew the line at two.

I couldn't understand why someone whose parents had saddled him with two odd names would do the same to his children, but perhaps it would come up in conversation.

Poly had sent me a family photograph, so I'd know who to look for. The photo was from a few years back. Poly and Pomy looked like they were still in high school. It was one of those formally posed pictures where the father, as *paterfamilias,* was seated, with the women in his life arrayed around him. Dr. Jones was wearing a dark suit and his wife and daughters were in long, matching jewel-tone chiton dresses. Poly was in emerald, the same shade as the dress she'd worn on our first date. Her sister was in sapphire and her mother wore a ruby shade so dark it was almost garnet. Barbara Keen's right hand rested on her husband's shoulder. Was it put there because the professional photographer told her to, or were there control dynamics at work as well? Time would tell.

Poly and Pomy looked enough alike that I expected they were frequently mistaken for identical twins. Both were tall and lithe with auburn-red hair. Poly's was straight and shoulder-length, while her sister's hair was much longer. I couldn't tell how long it actually was because the photo was one of those static, American Gothic, face-the-camera shots. Poly's smile was confident, but Pomy's smile sparkled, as if she knew secrets she wasn't telling. Whatever the answer, the picture was old. A lot could change.

I didn't think I'd have any difficulty spotting Pomy, however. She looked too much like Poly, though she'd probably be disheveled and exhausted after an international flight from Rome to JFK, and the shorter hop from New York to Atlanta.

All that being said, I almost didn't recognize her. Pomy bounced off the top of the escalator, radiating energy. Her hair was cut to the same shoulder length as Poly's, but more stylishly, to my uneducated eye. Maybe it's layering? She was tanned, or as tanned as redheads tend to get. Pomy was wearing khaki shorts—the kind you'd wear on an archaeological dig, but new and clean—and a thin, white, cotton button-front shirt with several buttons undone at the neck. A necklace of small, variegated Nicósn shells rested on her collarbone and the straps of a brown canvas backpack were over her shoulders.

My eyes went wide when I figured it out and recognized Pomy. Then I was nearly knocked off my feet by her reaction when *she* recognized *me*. I had stepped around the stanchions and ribbons of fabric separating the waiting area from the space at the top of the escalators and had extended my hand to shake

Pomy's when she took a running start, crossed the fifteen feet between us, and gave me a hug that was right up there with the enthusiastic embraces I'd received from Dree.

Pomy's hug was different, though. She wasn't a puppy-like carnivorous plant. Pomy was a *very* healthy young woman and the way she squeezed herself against me made it clear she was glad to see me. My ribs didn't appreciate her enthusiasm. She rested her head on my shoulder and didn't seem to be in any hurry to end her embrace. My face started to turn red, so I disengaged and took two steps back.

"Hi," I said.

"Hello, handsome," said Pomy, showing her sparkling smile. I noticed that she had amazingly cute freckles across the bridge of her nose, and wondered if Poly would have them too, if she got more sun.

"Did you have a good flight?" I asked, keeping her at more than arm's length.

"It was *great,* Jack," she said. "It's *so* nice to finally meet you. Poly's told me so *much* about you."

"She has?" I said.

"Of course," said Pomy, her eyes twinkling. "Sisters talk, you know."

"Okay," I said. My cheeks were still red. "I'm surprised Poly's had much time for conversation. She's been really busy."

"We trade texts," said Pomy. She stepped closer, put her hand on my forearm, then slid it down to take my hand. "Now be a dear and take me to where I can find my bags."

"Ummmm… okay," I said. I gently extricated my hand and guided her toward the South Baggage Claim. "It's this way."

We found the carousel where the bags from her flight would be arriving and waited until Pomy's claim checks turned yellow, which meant her bags were within thirty feet. I lugged two large bags and a smaller one over to where she was waiting. Each time I carried a bag, Pomy made a comment about how strong I was and used it as an excuse to put her hand on my arm again. She touched a claim check to the appropriate bag tracking tag as I delivered them. When each check had turned from yellow to green we had everything and could leave the baggage claim area.

My phone told my van to circle by passenger pickup and I maneuvered both large roller bags out to the curb while Pomy carried the small one. I loaded the three pieces of luggage into the back of my van and sent it back out to the airport's waiting area.

We wandered over to the main terminal's rotunda to see the fifty-foot skeleton of a juvenile Dauushan *Pseudophuschiasaurus* on exhibit, a loan from the Fernbank Museum of Natural History. Dauush once had its own age of extra-extra-large sized dinosaur-like creatures and they'd overtaken the Terran variety in the public imagination.

"Your dad's flight from Boston isn't due for over an hour," I said. "Would you like to have a late lunch? Dinner's not until eight."

"That would be lovely," said Pomy. "My stomach doesn't know what time zone it's in and it's the fashionable dining hour in Rome."

"Great," I said. "Where would you like to eat?"

I waved my arm to indicate the restaurants surrounding the rotunda.

Pomy didn't say anything. She just smiled mischievously and pointed up, over our heads. Five years ago, the top of Hartsfield's main terminal rotunda had been remodeled to add an intimate rotating restaurant called the Aerie. It had three hundred and sixty degree views of all the takeoffs and landings at the airport and the spaceport. It also had great views of the Atlanta skyline. I'd read that you could even see the dome of Stone Mountain off to the northeast. After dark, it was considered one of the top two most romantic places to eat in Atlanta. Poly and I had already dined at the number one spot—a river view table at the Teleport Inn. It seemed like an odd request, but this was Poly's sister and I wanted to be a good host.

"We can see if they can fit us in without a reservation," I said, "or if they're even open."

"I looked it up," said Pomy. "They open at noon and don't take reservations on weekdays before five. It's a Wednesday afternoon. How busy can they be?"

"Won't it take too long?"

"They have a forty-five minutes or less 'make your flight' menu during the day," said Pomy.

"We can give it a try," I said, hiding my reluctance as Pomy led us to the Aerie's special elevator.

She *had* done her research.

Of course, the *maître d'* had no trouble finding us a table for two by a window. They were *all* by windows and the place wasn't busy. Only half a dozen parties were visible on this side of the circular restaurant.

Our waiter—and he was definitely an old school *waiter* in a black suit and white shirt, not a server—seated Pomy. I sat down across from her and nodded my thanks. He handed us menus, filled our water glasses, and moved thirty degrees to spinward around the circumference to check on other patrons and give us time to figure out what we wanted. Our view was currently looking out at one of the busy main runways and its associated feeder taxiways. The planes were lined up like kids waiting for tickets to a Rolling Stones reunion concert on the Moon. For octogenarians, Mick and Keith can still rock.

Pomy flipped to the back of the menu, then reached out and stroked her fingers across the back of my hand. I froze.

"Would you have a glass of chianti with me?" she said. "I always have a glass with lunch in Rome and I hate to drink alone."

"Sorry," I said. "I don't drink. Feel free to have one yourself, though. I'll enjoy it vicariously."

"That's no way to live, Jack," she said. "May I call you Jack?"

"Sure."

"And you can call me Pomy, or Pomette, or your little Pomato, or whatever your heart desires."

That was weird. Was that her jetlag talking?

"I think I'll stick with Pomy," I said. "Though if you're bad, I may call you Mel."

I thought the first syllable of her real name wouldn't go over well. I was right.

"Anything but Mel," she said. "That sounds like a sixty-year old plumber whose pants ride down or a cross-country truck driver with no teeth."

"I'll save it for when you're particularly bad," I said, playing along for once, and wondering just what was going on.

She dimpled.

"Then I'll just *have* to give you cause to use it," she said.

I may be slow, but I was beginning to think Poly's sister had issues.

I looked down at my menu and found the forty-five minute 'make your flight' section.

"What looks good to you?" I said.

"I'm sure it's *all* delicious," said Pomy, running her tongue around her lips sensuously.

"I'm having the *delectable ground faux aux fines herbes avec pommes frites belge,*" I said. "And a salad."

This place could use Poly's help with its menu descriptions.

"A faux-burger and fries," said Pomy. "How manly."

Did she really say that?

"Tastes like lamb," I said. "What are you having?"

I was getting tired of this nonsense.

"The *salade niçoise,* with Nicósn mock tuna."

"How womanly," I said.

"Are you mocking me, Jack?"

"Uh huh," I said, looking directly at her.

Pomy lowered her eyes to look at the weave of the table-cloth. Then the waiter returned with a basket of rolls and butter. He took our orders and disappeared to antispinward.

I took Pomy's hands across the table this time and held her wrists lightly to get her attention. After a few seconds she looked up and faced me. I released her hands.

"What's going on?" I said. "You're coming on to me like a *femme fatale* in a B-movie."

"Sorry," she said, head down again.

"Please look at me," I said.

She lifted her head, reluctantly.

"Why?" I asked.

She hesitated, then lowered her head for a few seconds and spoke.

"I think I need that glass of wine first."

I caught our waiter's attention.

"A glass of chianti, please."

He returned promptly with the wine.

I pushed it toward Pomy.

"Drink this, and then tell me."

Pomy drained her glass in three swallows. The waiter brought another. She sipped at this one, taking deep breaths in between each sip.

"My sister and I are very competitive. In everything."

"Okay," I said.

"She's got it all. Two advanced degrees, after this weekend. A cool new job, a smart, hot boyfriend…"

I knew I was intelligent, but the hot part was news to me.

"…and attention from Mom."

"Okay," I said again.

I really didn't know what to say. I just wanted her to keep talking.

Pomy sniffed and lifted her napkin to her eyes. They were as red as my face had been earlier.

"And worst of all," she said, "I miss her. I *really* miss her."

"Poly?" I said.

"Of course, Poly," said Pomy. "We're sisters, but this is the first time we've been within fifty miles of each other in four years."

"You don't celebrate holidays together?"

"No. Not Easter. Not Thanksgiving. Not Christmas, not anything." she said. "Poly's always at school and never comes home. Mom's usually off-planet, working on her guidebooks, and Daddy thinks any holiday not celebrated by the ancient Greeks or pre-Christian Romans is beneath his dignity."

"Happy *Lupercalia*," I said.

She smiled. It was the first one I'd seen that was genuine. It looked good on her.

"Thanks," she said. "Though *Saturnalia* and *Dies Natalis Solis Invicti* are closer to Christmas."

"You've just exhausted my knowledge of Roman festivals."

"Not mine, sorry to say—May Hestia bless your hearth."

"Not Vesta? You switched from Roman to Greek."

"So sue me," said Pomy, smiling again. "I liked the alliteration."

Our waiter must have been waiting for the drama-level at our table to decrease. He served our meals and vanished silently away. My Belgian-style frites were served in a paper cone supported by a coiled wire stand. I dipped a long stick of fried potato into homemade curry ketchup and fed it to Pomy across the table. She ate it like a hungry baby bird and gave me another genuine smile, wider this time.

"Want a taste of my salad?" she asked.

"Just a bite of mock tuna," I said.

She feed me a small piece of fish the same way I'd fed her, but with a fork, not her fingers.

"Yum," I said. "Keep talking. You're on a roll."

"Speaking of rolls," she said, reaching for the bread basket.

"Don't try to change the subject."

"Okay," she said.

"You were saying you're a poor little privileged girl whose parents don't love her and whose sister isn't there for her."

"Hey," said Pomy, "my *father* loves me."

"What's the field of study for your doctorate?"

"Classics."

"Uh huh," I said.

"You're saying he wouldn't love me if I was earning an MBA or a degree in engineering?"

"Poly. Q.E.D."

"At least Mom loves *her*."

"That's why Poly's working four jobs to pay for graduate school."

"She's what?"

"You didn't know?"

"I thought Mom was paying her tuition."

"Think again," I said. "Poly's translating menus at the Teleport Inn, teaching Galactic Languages classes at Georgia State, temping as a receptionist at a fabrication company and correcting machine translations of GaFTA tech manuals to pay her own way."

Pomy's fork was in her hand but it wasn't moving. It was halfway between her salad bowl and her mouth, frozen in place. Her brain was churning over what I'd said.

"Do the members of your family ever talk to each other?"

"Ummmm…" said Pomy, her fork still frozen.

"Asked and answered. I get it. But what I *don't* get is what you were trying to prove by throwing yourself at me."

"I wasn't…"

"Hello handsome," I said, mimicking her original tone. *"Poly's told me so* much *about you."*

"I did say that, didn't I."

"You sounded like the girl next door trying to be Jessica Rabbit."

"That bad?" said Pomy.

"You can call me Pomy, or Pomette, or your little Pomato, or whatever your heart desires."

Pomy dropped her fork in her salad and put her hands on either side of her head.

"O, Hera," she laughed. She looked appalled.

"Then I'll just have *to give you cause to use it."*

"Ow," she said. "Stop hitting a woman when she's down. I wasn't very good at playing the seductress, was I?"

"On a scale of one to ten?"

"Don't even say it. I'm afraid you'll use negative numbers."

"Not that bad," I said, "but what could you possibly have hoped to accomplish?"

"I thought I might steal you away from my sister."

Now it was my turn to look puzzled.

"Why would you want to do that?"

Pomy sat back up and pretended to concentrate on eating her salad. Her movements were mechanical.

"Quit stalling," I said.

She put her fork down, squared her shoulders, took a deep breath and let it out in a long sigh. Then she spoke.

"It worked when I did it before. Sort of."

I looked at her. She didn't say anything. I stared at her and made a "go on" motion with my hands. She was still silent.

"Sort of?" I prompted.

"Poly paid attention to me."

She sounded about six. My burger and fries were cold.

"Were you and Poly close when you were little?"

"Uh huh," said Pomy. "We were inseparable. Poly and I shared a bedroom until I was twelve, and Mom had to tell us to stop giggling and go to sleep almost every night. She was more my twin than my big sister."

"Were you still close in high school?"

"Yes, except when Poly was traveling off-planet with Mom."

"Was she gone a lot?"

"Sometimes," said Pomy. "But when she came back to Cambridge it was like she'd never left and we picked back up just like before."

"When did things change?" I asked.

"My junior year."

"Poly's senior year?"

"Yes," she said. "That's when I was stupid."

I dipped a cold frite in curry ketchup and made the same "go on" motion with my hands, using the fried potato stick for emphasis.

"Poly and James, a boy in her math class, started dating," she said. "He was a nice guy, really smart."

"And?"

"Poly stopped paying attention to me. She spent every spare minute with James. It hurt."

"Sometimes people you love, leave," I said.

"Sometimes people you love leave because you do something stupid," said Pomy.

"How were *you* stupid?"

"I seduced James."

I knew that would be the answer, but like a train wreck I could only stand by and watch it happen.

"You *slept* with him?"

"Uh huh." She shook her head from side to side sadly. "Neither one of us really knew what we were doing."

"Just how innocent *were* you?"

"On a scale of one to ten?" she said, between bites of salad.

"Will you need negative numbers?"

"No, but probably somewhere between a three and a five."

"You led a sheltered life?"

"Very. You'll understand when you meet my father."

I filed that away for future reference.

"What did you *think* would happen?"

"Poly and I would fight. She'd yell at me and I'd yell at her. We'd talk and then we'd hug and she'd forgive me."

"What actually happened?"

"Poly and I fought. There was a lot of yelling. Then she stopped speaking to me. When she went off to college, she shut off communications entirely. She wouldn't accept my texts, wouldn't take my calls, and blocked me on SpaceBook."

Quite a few things were becoming clearer. Poly wasn't with me to pick up her family at the airport just because she needed to finish her academic paper. Poly was avoiding her sister—and probably her father and mother, too.

"So what did you think would happen if you'd been able to seduce *me*?"

"Poly would talk to me again."

"To *yell* at you."

Tears started to flow, leaving wet tracks on her cheeks.

"Yes," Pomy said between sobs, "but we'd be talking, and maybe it would be different this time."

I didn't have a response. I looked at Pomy's tear-streaked face and marveled at her ability to reach such a misguided conclusion. Love can make us stupid, I guess. I should know. At least now I could do something to help.

"I'm not going to say a word about this to Poly," I said.

Pomy sat back in her chair and seemed to regain her dignity.

"Thank you," she said. "I'm sorry to put you through that."

"Through what?" I said.

She smiled, the broadest and most genuine one I'd seen today. She reached out across the table and took my hands. It wasn't a romantic ploy this time. She squeezed them and then let them go.

"I hope we can be friends," she said.

"Count on it."

"Can I count on you for some help?"

"With what?"

"My father said that Mom has a scheme for Poly and me to share a room in their suite at Ad Astra, just like we did when we were children."

"I think I see where you're headed," I said, "but Poly's got her own place."

"Mom's going to talk her into staying with the rest of the family for a few days. She may be overly optimistic about what's likely to happen, but it's worth a shot."

"What do you want me to do?"

"Nothing specific. Just tell Poly how much I'm looking forward to seeing her and how sorry I am."

"What if she asks me what you're sorry for?"

"Tell her I didn't tell you."

I wasn't so sure about that part. I don't like shading the truth in dealings with my partner—but it was in a good cause.

"You'll be seeing her face-to-face yourself in a few hours."

"Yes, but I'm scared," she said. "Having you around for moral support will help."

I could appreciate that. I'd be glad to have Pomy's support when I met her parents today.

"Moral support I can do," I said, smiling.

"And Jack?"

She looked at me. I looked back.

"Put in a good word for me with Poly when you can."

"I'll try, but you're going to have to apologize on your own."

"I will, I will. Seventeen is a special kind of stupid. I've been regretting it ever since it happened."

"I expect Poly has, too."

I didn't know for sure if that was true, but I hoped it was.

"You think she misses me?"

I hadn't a clue.

"You'll have to ask her—after you apologize."

Pomy nodded.

I wondered if the fact that Poly had invited her family to her graduations meant that she was also looking for an opportunity for reconciliation.

Or was her family's arrival part of a plot hatched by her mother or father? Probably her mother, though a classics professor would have a thorough academic knowledge of complex family dynamics. Look at *The Oresteia* and its stories of the curse on the House of Atreus.

My musings on Poly and Pomy and their parents were interrupted when my phone chirped.

"Professor Jones' flight arrives in five minutes."

"We've got to go," I said. "Waiter!"

Chapter 19

"My will is mine... I shall not make it soft for you."
— Aeschylus, *Agamemnon*

Pomy and I were waiting at the top of Hartsfield's arrival escalators only five minutes after her father's plane had landed. It would take at least another quarter of an hour for him to make his way from Terminal D, Gate 38, to our location, though it could take twice that long if there was a gate delay or the underground shuttle was overcrowded. From what Poly and Pomy had said, and *not* said, their father wasn't the easiest person in this corner of the galaxy to get along with, so I thought I'd get more details from Pomy.

"Tell me about your dad," I said.

"He's the chairman of the Classics Department at Harvard and the world's foremost authority on Homer *and* Virgil."

"I read that on Galnet," I said, "It's on his faculty profile page."

"That faculty profile page *is* my father."

"Do tell?"

"His Homeric trilogy, *The Ten Year War, The Ten Year Journey,* and *The Blind Bard* are considered definitive—the best books about the *Iliad,* the *Odyssey,* and their reputed author in three generations."

"I've read them," I said.

"You've read all twenty-five hundred pages?"

"Even the appendices," I said.

"I'm impressed," said Pomy.

"I was nine," I said.

"I'm *really* impressed," she said. "I was eight and a half."

"Show off."

"I was so jealous of those books," said Pomy. "Every time I wanted attention from my father when I was little, he said he had to work on one of his books."

"Sibling rivalry?"

"Pretty much," said Pomy. "It felt like they were the children he really loved. We asked him to teach us classical Greek and Latin when we were five and six, hoping that would please him."

"How did that work out?" I said.

"He criticized our verb forms."

"That sucks. Was he writing books throughout your childhood?"

"Yes," she answered. "After the Homeric trilogy, he switched to Virgil and wrote *The Augustan Commission.*"

"Right, because Caesar Augustus was supposed to have hired Virgil to write *The Aeneid.*"

"I suppose you read that one, too? When you were ten?"

"Nine and a half," I said.

"Show off," said Pomy.

"Virgil is cool. Some of the stuff he wrote is really derivative, though. *The Aeneid* is just a fan fiction the guy pulled together after reading *The Iliad* and *The Odyssey.*"

"Don't let my father hear you say that."

"Don't let me hear you say what?"

Pomy and I had been caught up in conversation. We were standing behind the wide fabric ribbons that separated the waiting section from the top of the escalators that delivered arriving passengers to baggage claim. A man who looked like a younger, less rumpled version of Dumbledore with a well-trimmed salt and pepper beard stood in front of us on the other side of the ribbon. He was tall, wearing heavy wool pants, a forest green turtleneck sweater, and a tweed sports coat with leather patches on the elbows. All he needed was a pipe in his hand to be the complete picture of a male Harvard professor.

"Daddy!" said Pomy, hugging her father across the tape barrier.

"Pumpkin!" said her father, returning the embrace enthusiastically. "How were your flights? Was your paper accepted by *Current Archeology?* How is Professor Piacentini? Is he a grandfather yet? And who is this young man?"

I was impressed. Pomy's father hadn't taken a breath during his list of questions.

"My flights were fine, I'm waiting to hear if my paper was accepted, Marcello's daughter had a baby boy last week, and this"—she put her hand on my shoulder in a friendly gesture—"is Poly's boyfriend, Jack Buckston."

Pomy didn't take a breath during her reply, either. Must be a family trait.

"Pleased to meet you, sir," I said, extending my hand.

Pomy and Poly's father took it and shook it firmly.

"And I'm very pleased to meet you, Jack," he said. "Call me Perry when you want to be friendly or Professor Jones when you think I'm too full of myself."

His manner was jovial and his voice was light. It would be a pleasure to listen to him lecture. This man was *not* the ogre I was expecting.

"Thanks, Perry," I said, somewhat overwhelmed.

"Thank *you* for picking me up," he said. "Which way to baggage claim?"

The stanchions and fabric ribbon barriers were still separating us, so Pomy and I had to step back and move a few yards off to one side to get around them before we could join Perry.

When we were out of earshot I whispered, "I thought your father was supposed to be some sort of child-abandoning, soul-destroying monster?"

"Just wait," said Pomy.

We joined Perry on the other side of the ribbon and walked over to the carousel where his bags would be appearing. He was holding his claim check in his hand and waved it at me to show me that it had already turned yellow.

"That one's mine," he said, pointing to a medium-sized battered leather case covered in Latin and Greek phrases someone must have burned into it with a heat gun. There were also a few illustrations. I recognized a line art version of the famous picture of a dog from Pompeii above the Latin phrase *Cave Canem* and wondered if I'd need to beware Pomy's father, if and when this pleasant teddy bear ever turned into a grumpy grizzly. I lifted his case from the rotating carousel, raised its handle and headed for the passenger pickup area. My phone, which had been quiet and well-behaved for the past few hours, had notified my van to pick us up. It was just pulling to the curb in front of us as we arrived.

"Let's take my van around to the spaceport terminal," I said. "It will be faster than taking the shuttle."

"Eminently sensible," said Perry as I carefully loaded his bag in the back.

"Good idea," said Pomy, grabbing the shotgun seat.

My van opened the sliding door on its right side and Pomy's father got in.

"Welcome to Atlanta, Professor Jones," said my van.

It was a polite welcome, but I didn't remember programming or authorizing that sort of greeting.

"Thank you," said Perry, "though I seem to be dressed more for Boston's climate than Atlanta's at this time of year."

He put his finger to the collar of his turtleneck and pulled it out half an inch. He did look hot in his tweed coat.

"Air conditioning adjusted," said my van. Then, almost as an afterthought, "Seat belt."

"Certainly, kind conveyance," said Perry.

I could see his smile in the rear view mirror. We all buckled up and my van left the domestic air terminal and headed south toward the spaceport.

Twelve years ago, Hartsfield-Jackson International Airport had largely run out of room to grow. Airline passenger increases required a sixth runway, but there was no practical place to put one. Then Earth joined GaFTA and suddenly the city of Atlanta and the state of Georgia, rolling in dotstar boom revenue, thought big and bought up two dozen subdivisions south of the airport's existing footprint, paying exorbitant sums to get residents to leave quickly. The airport authority built three new aircraft runways, more than a hundred starship landing pads, new passenger and cargo spaceport terminals, and the Jackson Teleportation Nexus on the additional five thousand acres.

Galactic building techniques let them get the new facilities finished in less than five years and generous amounts of bak-sheesh, spread at the local, city, county, state and federal levels, cut down on regulatory delays. The authority *made* money on the deal by selling parcels around the periphery to shipping and logistics companies that wanted to be close to the space-port or the nexus. That bold move had locked in the combined Jackson Nexus and Hartsfield Port as the largest transportation hub on the planet, by passenger *and* freight volume.

We had an excellent view of the nearer starship landing pads as we drove to the spaceport's passenger terminal. Poly and Pomy's mother was coming in on a scheduled starliner from Neue Staddam, the capital of Nicós, that was due to land in ten minutes. We were still in good time, though. It would take a while for her to get through customs.

"I understand you're some sort of mechanic, interested in all that engineering nonsense that intrigues my older daughter," said Perry from the back seat. "Are you the kind that gets into the greasy gears and twisted wires and such?"

I looked at Pomy. She looked at me.

"I'm more of a consultant and troubleshooter," I said.

"Dealing with the technological plumbing, so to speak?" said Perry.

"That's not how I'd put it."

"But you are repairing machines? Fixing copiers, adjusting looms, and so forth?"

"Modern technology is as much a noble calling as ancient literature," I said.

"I'm sure that a pig looks noble to another pig," said Perry, in the same tone he'd use to say, "The sky is blue."

Pomy looked at me and watched me try to suppress my desired response.

"Sing, O muse, of the rage of Achilles," I said, reciting the opening of *The Iliad* in classical Greek.

"The horse can sing. How amusing," said Perry, still smiling while wielding his verbal stiletto.

"I sing of arms and the man…" I said, in classical Latin this time—the open line of *The Aeneid*.

"So the horse can both sing *and* bray."

It was lucky for him that I was wearing my seat belt. Now I knew why Poly was closer to her mother.

"Professor Jones," I said. My voice was tight. I was about to say more, but was interrupted.

"Spaceport Passenger Terminal," said my van.

"Everybody out," said my phone.

"Thank Hera," said Pomy.

Chapter 20

"It is better to travel well than to arrive."
— Buddha

I took the lead when we entered the spaceport's passenger terminal so I wouldn't have to look at Professor Pericles Agamemnon Jones. Pomy walked between us as a buffer. She'd seen how angry I was, for myself and for the years of hell he must have put Poly through. I would have happily teleported the Professor into interstellar space if we'd been at the Jackson Nexus instead of the spaceport. No, scratch that. My personal ethics and respect for the rule of law wouldn't allow me to do such a thing, but it felt wonderful to *think* about it. Pomy was making small talk to diffuse the tension.

"Mother is coming in on Gate K-42," she said.

She looked at the terminal map we were passing on our right.

"That's down at the far end of the K Concourse," she said.

"All arriving flights you're meeting are at the far end," I said, slowing my heartbeat. "That's one of the corollaries of Murphy's Law."

"Another of your technological superstitions?" said Professor Jones.

"Shush, Daddy," said Pomy.

No wonder she was getting her doctorate on another continent.

The specific gate didn't matter much to the three of us. The only implication of Pomy's mother's ship landing farther out meant there'd be more of a delay as Dr. Barbara Lowell Keen, CEO of Keen Travel Publishing and author of Keen's Guides to the many planets of the Galactic Free Trade Association, walked to baggage claim, then stood in line for Terran customs.

Barbara Keen had a PhD in Linguistics—she'd met her "charming" husband when they were both graduate students at Harvard. Shortly after First Contact, Dr. Keen had gone off-planet to start compiling English translation dictionaries for Dauushan, Orish, Tigrammath, Nicósn, Pâkk dialects, Pyr speech and more. She sent back travel advice to her friends, telling them about the best restaurants, sights to see, and places to stay. She also wrote about other species' social mores and things to avoid, like showing fear on a Pâkk planet. Her friends passed them around and they proved popular, so Barbara self-published them as *Keen's Guide to Dauush, Keen's Guide to Nicós, Keen's Guide to the Ruins of Old Pyr,* and so on. She took a leave of absence from her academic appointment at Harvard and rapidly became the head of a multi-million galcred travel publishing empire.

Later, she branched out and created species-specific guides to Terra. Dauushans and Musans have quite different concerns, for example, and face different challenges. The chapter on cats in *Keen's Musan Guide to Terra* is forty-seven pages long. *Keen's Dauushan Guide to Terra* has one section on the dangers of low overpasses and another on how to avoid stepping on native sapients.

We found a place to wait with a good view of the wide, well-lit hallway leading from Terran customs. Pomy and her father found seats, but I excused myself to locate a men's room and get away from Dr. Jones for a few minutes. The man was an unmitigated ass. I splashed cold water on my face and went through a dozen repeats of *Tallis Canon* on the soundtrack in my head to calm myself down. If Poly had invited her father to her graduation and was willing to try opening channels of communication, I didn't want to get in her way. I also didn't want to end up in jail. It might reflect poorly on Xenotech Support Corporation's reputation.

When I got back to Pomy and Perry, Pomy's phone was buzzing.

"Mom just sent me a text. She finished going through customs and will be here any minute."

That old *go to the bathroom if you want something to happen* trick still works.

I could have picked Barbara Keen out of a crowd even without memorizing her photo from the back of my copy of *Keen's*

Guide to Orish. She had three times the poise and twice the *savoir faire* of any other passenger in the corridor. Poly and Pomy's mother had a lithe build, like her daughters, but was only five foot five. She was in her mid-fifties, but her hair was still Poly and Pomy's gorgeous auburn color, cut in a short, professional, easy to care for bob. She was wearing a well-tailored navy pantsuit and carried a medium-sized purse over one shoulder. Three feet behind her, staying close in "heel" position, rolled a smart, Follow-Me brand self-guided suitcase about the same size as one of Pomy's large bags. Two smaller suitcases were neatly stacked on top of it. Barbara Keen didn't look up from her phone as she walked down the corridor.

"Mom, Mom!" shouted Pomy.

She had to yell one more time before her mother looked up and smiled. The two women, mother and daughter, met where the hallway opened up into the waiting room.

"Hello, Pomy," she said, giving her daughter air kisses on both cheeks. "How's Daddy's little girl?"

"Nice to see you, too, Mother."

"Pericles," Pomy's mother said to her husband, nodding slightly.

"Barbara," said Pomy's father with a minimal bow.

The warmth between them seemed on a par with the temperature of Pluto's nitrogen atmosphere, and with about as much chance of thawing. I hoped Poly knew what she was doing.

"Where's Poly?" said Pomy's mother.

"She's finishing up a research paper and asked me to pick you up," I said.

Barbara's manner changed when she realized that I wasn't a random stranger. She looked me over and must have found me at least minimally acceptable, then turned to Pomy.

"Who is this handsome young man?" she said, now in full polite meet-and-greet mode.

"Jack Buckston, mother," said Pomy. "Poly's boyfriend."

"Is he, now?" said Barbara. "In that case, I'm *very* pleased to meet you, Jack."

"Very pleased to meet you, too," I said.

We shook hands. Barbara's grip was firm, but her hand wasn't warm.

I wanted to ask if Poly had told her a lot about me, but I knew that Poly and her mother didn't talk and was too polite to rub it in. I wasn't going to take out my anger at Poly's father on her mother. It looked like her parents were doing a good job of directing their emotions at each other, anyway.

"Did you have a nice flight?" said Barbara to Pomy. The words were right, but the tone was distant.

"Flights, Mother," said Pomy. "There was some turbulence over the north Atlantic and a baby crying in Italian in the row in front of me—the poor thing's ears wouldn't pop and she was miserable for most of the trip."

While Pomy was talking, Barbara had pulled out her phone and was staring intently at something on the screen, ignoring her daughter.

"How did you figure that the baby was crying in Italian?" I said, trying to fill the awkward silence.

"I thought you said your flights were fine, Pumpkin?" said her father. "I wouldn't think eight hours of sitting behind a crying baby would count as 'fine' for anyone."

"Compared to what I was expecting when I arrived in Atlanta, my flights *were* fine," said Pomy, who was staring at her mother. Barbara Keen was still checking messages, or sales figures, or her horoscope.

"I really want to know," I said.

Pomy didn't change the direction of her gaze, but answered.

"The vowel sounds are different. Italian sounds musical, even when people are speaking. There's a reason it's the first language of opera."

I thought of the Rossini music that my phone had used to wake me that morning.

"So a baby's 'waaaa' and 'maaaaa' in Italian sound different from the equivalent in English?"

"Uh huh," said Pomy. "Italian babies' vowel sounds are more pure, somehow. Let me show you."

Pomy pulled out her phone and started typing, imitating her mother. Her father decided that it was a good time to visit the men's room and walked off. Wise move.

"Here," said Pomy, holding her phone where we could both see the screen.

She turned it sideways and I saw a split screen with babies, perhaps three months old, centered in each section. An American flag was below the one on the left and an Italian green, white and red tricolor was under the one on the right. Pomy pressed the Stars and Stripes and I heard the American baby cry. Then she pressed the Italian flag and I could hear the difference. The second baby really *was* crying in Italian.

"Fascinating," I said.

"You can compare babies from lots of different countries," said Pomy. "You can easily tell if an infant is from a country that speaks a tonal language."

At my request, Pomy gave me the URL of the babies cry comparison web site and I made a mental note to check it out. She played me a northern Chinese baby crying and the American baby crying again, to illustrate her point. A small child walked near us, clutching his mother's hand, and started crying himself. It was part of that same sympathetic magic that makes yawns contagious. His mother gave us a dirty look and hurried by.

"It's clear you're the daughter of a linguistics professor," I said.

Pomy just looked at her mother, who was still heads down, focused on her phone. My new friend shook her head back and forth, resignedly.

"Is she always like this?" I said, indicating Pomy's mother.

"Ever since her company took off," said Pomy. "Before then she was a great mom. She read us stories, baked us cookies, took us to the zoo, built us a tree house, and was even our Brownie troop leader. She had her own research and was serious about it, but she was always there for us."

I smiled at the thought of little Poly and Pomy in Brownie vests climbing up to their tree house to eat cookies or tugging their mother this way and that at the zoo.

"When did things change?"

"After Keen Travel Publishing broke three million."

"Units, or galcreds?"

"Does it matter?" said Pomy.

"No," I said, shutting up to let her continue.

"Mom was spending all her time on the company. I was eleven and Poly was twelve when we got a live-in nanny and housekeeper. Then Mom started taking Poly with her on her trips off-planet and I had to compete with grad students for Daddy's attention."

"I'm beginning to see why Poly spending all her time with James had the effect on you that it did," I said.

"That's still no excuse," she said.

"Tell it to Poly."

"I will."

"Why didn't she take you with her off-planet, too?"

Pomy looked thoughtful.

"I don't really know. Looking back on it as an adult I wondered if my mother and father hadn't worked out some sort of dynastic deal. Mother would get Poly to train as the next CEO of KTP and Daddy would groom me to be the next holder of the Marcus Aurelius Endicott chair."

"That's exactly what we agreed to," said Barbara, who was putting her phone back into her purse. "There, that's done."

"It was a formal agreement?" said Pomy, surprised that her mother had noticed our conversation.

"Not in writing."

Barbara looked around.

"Where's your father?"

"He went to the men's room," I said.

"I hope he can find his way back," said Pomy's mother. "He's easily distracted."

Pomy and I shared a glance and she rolled her eyes. Barbara was looking directly at me, so I just nodded.

"You and Daddy decided to split us up like Solomon and the baby?" said Pomy.

"Hardly," said Barbara. "There was no bisection involved. You were separate people. It made sense for each of us to take one of you."

"But Poly and I were so close. It felt like you *were* ripping us in half."

"Don't be dramatic, Pomy. You two girls needed time apart."

"But it felt like you loved Poly best!"

"Nonsense. Your father and I love you both equally. We flipped for it."

"Who won?" said Pomy.

"At present, it seems like your father did," said Barbara. "You're getting a doctorate in classics from Oxford and Poly and I aren't speaking."

"About that… " said Pomy.

"I'm back. Now we can go," said Dr. Jones, who had just rejoined us.

"My van… " I said.

"Will be waiting at the curb," said my phone.

"Follow me," I said.

We got passengers and luggage into my van without incident. Barbara sat up front with me and asked me prying questions that I sidestepped by providing a running travelogue on the city of Atlanta. Professor Jones sat in the back talking with Pomy and didn't offer any additional disparaging comments on my chosen profession. We'd be at the Ad Astra complex in an hour.

Then Poly would join us—perhaps to supply the blasting caps to go with her family's collection of high explosives.

A week in Maui was looking more and more appealing.

Chapter 21

*"We put on formal wear and suddenly
we become extraordinary."*
— Vera Nazarian

I dropped Barbara, Perry and Pomy off at the Star Palace, Ad Astra's most luxurious hotel. Highly efficient bellhops removed their luggage from the back of my van and didn't try to take the octovacs. I got out and gave Pomy a quick hug, but her parents ignored me and left for the lobby. I was glad to see their backs.

"Thank you, Jack," said Pomy.

"For what?" I said.

"For being a good guy—and a friend. My sister is lucky to have you."

She touched her phone to mine to exchange numbers.

"Call me if you have any updates on what we'd talked about."

She gave me a gentle peck on the cheek and followed her parents into the lobby.

Tension drained from my body like a bathtub whose plug had been pulled. I felt so limp that I was surprised I wasn't a puddle of protoplasm on the expensive bricks of the hotel's porte-cochère. Somehow I managed to get back in my van. It was only a few minutes after five.

"Home, please," I said.

"Seat belt," said my van.

"Override," I said, too tired to do one more thing.

"As you wish," said my van in a reproving tone.

"Okay, okay," I said.

I buckled up and was asleep before my van had gone a hundred yards.

I woke up when two octovacs delivered me and my backpack tool bag to my apartment, carefully carrying me to my bed and tucking me in.

Thank you phone, thank you van, thank you octovacs.

Hello, Morpheus, my old friend. Long time, no see.

* * * * *

"Jack, Jack, wake up, Jack."

It must be my phone imitating Poly's voice to get my attention, I thought. It seemed like I'd only been asleep for a few minutes. Then I felt warm human fingers stroking my cheek. It really *was* Poly.

"Hi there," I said in a sleepy voice. "Nice to see you."

I raised myself up on one elbow. Poly sat on my bed. I held her hand.

"I'm the one who's supposed to be sleep-deprived," said Poly. "What's your excuse?"

She looked as tired as I felt.

"I picked your family up at the airport," I said.

"How did it go?" she said, with feigned nonchalance.

"Wonderfully," I said. "Your parents are charming and your sister is a delight."

"Are you sure you picked up the right family?" said Poly.

I sat all the way up and gave her a stern look.

"You owe me," I said. "This went way beyond earning boyfriend points and into combat pay."

"Thank you, Jack," she said. "I just couldn't face them. Not all together. Not all at once."

My expression softened and I drew Poly into my arms and held her until some of the tension unwound in her body. Then we sat up and held hands.

"You're so brave," I said, squeezing her hands reassuringly.

"I wasn't brave at all. I let you pick them up on your own. I didn't even meet them at the hotel."

"You're *very* brave," I said. "You were courageous enough to invite your family to your graduation ceremonies. That couldn't have been easy."

"It took me *days* to find the strength to push the send button," she said.

"But you sent it."

"I did. But I'm scared," said Poly, "really scared I'll lose it and take my sister's head off, or get in a shouting match with my mother so loud that people three floors away will call hotel security."

"After meeting them, I don't doubt they'd deserve it," I said. "And your father?"

"My father," she said.

Her eyes got cold, then her expression changed and she looked at me and smiled.

"Do you love me enough to post bail for me?" she said. "And hire me a good criminal defense lawyer?"

"Sure," I said, "If I'm not in the cell next to yours. I've met your father now. He's a piece of work."

"He's a piece of…"

I kissed her. It caught her by surprise. We both laughed, the worst of our stresses released. I kissed her again, slowly and tenderly. We held each other, sitting close together on my bed, alternately kissing and laughing until our mutual senses of equilibrium were restored.

"Maybe I can get through tonight and the next three days without resorting to homicide after all," said Poly.

"For you it would be patricide," I said. "It's only homicide if *I* kill him."

She laughed, and her laugh wasn't as brittle as it had been minutes earlier. Then she saw me get a serious look on my face.

"What is it?"

"Why didn't you tell me anything about your parents and your sister and what you were going through? We're partners now. We can help each other through rough times."

"I tried to warn you," said Poly.

"Yeah, but you never actually shared specifics," I said.

"Sorry about that."

She really did look contrite.

"You've only been in my life for the past six weeks," she said. "I've been carrying my anger at my father around for most of my life. My sister and I haven't spoken in seven years, and my mother and I in three. I've been so used to holding it all inside."

"Shared pain is lessened," I said.

"Shared joy is increased," she said.

"Let me help."

"Okay."

She kissed me this time.

"I know *one* way you can help me," said Poly.

"What's that?"

"I'm sure my mother expects me to come to their suite and change for dinner there, but I can't deal with my family right now," she said. "I just can't. I'm not ready for the drama. May I change here?"

"Sure," I said. "You didn't need to ask."

"Thanks. There's a duffle with all my stuff by your dresser."

"I may even scrub your back in the shower," I said.

"Some other time when I can really appreciate it," said Poly. Her eyes sparkled. She'd get through this.

"Hey," I said.

"Hey?"

"About your sister…"

"What *about* my sister? She didn't try anything with…"

"No," I said, fingers mentally crossed. "We got off to a rocky start but then things got better. She asked me to tell you that she loves you and she's really sorry. She wouldn't say about what, just that she wanted you to give her another chance."

Poly didn't frown or seem upset, just thoughtful.

"I did invite her," she said, after a few seconds of contemplation.

"And you'll have an opportunity to connect with her if you want to," I said. "Your mother is going to try to talk you into staying in their suite for the next few days. She wants you to share a room with Pomy."

"She wants us to bond again, like we did when we were kids," said Poly. "I don't know if I'm ready for that."

"I'll be close by if you need to escape," I said. "Unlimited hugs."

"Maybe I can do it on that basis," she said. "Let me have a free sample."

I hugged her.

"Thank you, sir, may I have another."

I hugged her again.

"I'm glad you're in my life, Jack Buckston," she said, tenderly.

My phone chirped.

"Ahem," it said, "It's six fifteen and you need to pick Poly's family up at seven fifteen to be at the Teleport Inn on time."

"Thanks for the reminder," I said.

I looked at Poly.

"You can have first dibs on the shower if you'll help me with my tuxedo," I said.

"Sounds good," she said, "If you'll make a pot of extra strong high-caffeine tea. We'll both need it."

"I can do that," I said, "and I'll get your dress from the living room."

I gave Poly one more hug, then went out to the kitchen to start a kettle of water. I moved the box with Poly's dress from the coffee table in my living room to my bed and left my bedroom, closing the door this time. I could hear water running in my shower. I moved to the far side of my living room, close to my wall screen, and sent Pomy a text.

"I did my part," it read. "You may have a chance to do yours. Poly and I will meet you and your parents out front at seven fifteen."

I got a short reply.

"Thank you. We'll be there."

The kettle was whistling, so I walked to the kitchen and turned the burner off. I took my yellow smiley-face teapot down from its place in a cupboard—I'd bought it at a First Contact Day street fair two years ago—and put in eight bags of Midnight Obsidian Black Tea, the strongest kind I had.

The bushes it was made from had been genetically modified to enhance their leaves' caffeine content, so it was nearly as strong as coffee. I poured hot water into the cheerful teapot and inhaled deeply to appreciate the rich, warm scent of *Camellia sinensis espresso,* then pulled two large, plain white mugs from a shelf.

The few minutes later the water stopped running in my shower and shortly after that the door to my bedroom opened part way and Poly stuck her head out.

"Your turn," she said, looking more awake.

"On my way."

"Mmmmm… what smells so good?"

"Midnight Obsidian Black," I said.

"That will put hair on my chest," said Poly.

"I hope not."

She smiled and pulled her head back into the bedroom, leaving the door ajar.

When I entered my bedroom, Poly was wrapped in "her" large white towel. She had removed her new dress from its box and protective tissue paper wrappings and was holding it out to admire. The Orishen morphic silk shimmered through a rainbow of colors. The dress was psychically sensitive and would change color to match Poly's mood once in full contact with her body.

"It's lovely," I said, "and you're not even wearing it yet. It will be twice as beautiful once you are."

"Awww, you'll make me blush," she said.

Looking at the top edge of her towel I thought I might be having that effect already.

"Keep it up, Lover Boy, and you'll make me wish I'd taken you up on having you scrub my back in the shower."

"You had your chance," I said, smiling. My walk-in closet connected my bedroom and bathroom. I stepped in, closed the door, took off all my clothes, and dropped them in my laundry basket. Then I continued into the bathroom and hopped in the shower.

"Earl Grey, hot. Make it so," I said.

My intellectually challenged shower A.I. complied and I enjoyed the jets of warm water. Then I heard the bathroom door open.

"I need to dry my hair and put on my makeup."

"No problem," I said. My glass shower door was translucent, not transparent, and all steamed up, so I didn't have a clear view of Poly. I could hear her, though. Electric hair dryers make a lot of noise. I drew a large heart on the inside of the shower door so that Poly would see it if she turned around. I was ready when my Earl Grey shower program switched to its cold needle spray and didn't scream like a hungry Orishen nymph. I opened my shower door just enough to grab my towel and dried myself off, then wrapped the towel around my waist and left the shower. I kissed Poly in the middle of her upper back—after making sure she wasn't applying makeup at that moment—and beat a hasty retreat to my bedroom, the business end of the hair dryer pointed at my groin.

"Go, get started," she said. "I'll help with your studs and cuff links when I'm done."

"Yes, ma'am," I said.

I put on clean underwear and an undershirt from my chest of drawers and rescued my Orishen pupa silk shirt from the laundry basket. Columbia Brown was still out there, and the shirt supported my sore ribs. Then I slipped on the unfamiliar, thin, black, formal socks that came with my tux. They came up over my calves, like tall athletic socks, but weren't as comfortable. Next, I put on one of the starched and pleated white shirts. It was stiff and hard to button. I knew I was doing something wrong, but hoped that Poly would know how to fix it. I didn't even *try* to make sense of the French cuffs.

I got the pants for my fancy outfit from their hanger in my walk-in closet and stepped into them, then looked at myself in the mirror. As soon as I stopped holding them up, they were down around my ankles. I smacked my palm against my forehead and remembered the suspenders on my dresser. I took the pants off and tried to figure out how the suspenders fastened on. Wait, aren't they called *braces* for tuxedos? Who knew? There weren't any alligator clips, so it took me a minute to puzzle out that they were attached to buttons sewn into the waistband of the pants. I fastened them and put the pants on again, sliding the *braces* over my shoulders.

"One of them is twisted," said my phone from its vantage point on the charging station on my nightstand.

I took the pants off again, corrected the problem, and put them back on.

"All systems nominal," said my phone.

I think it was getting a charge out of watching me get dressed while it was getting a charge for its batteries.

Then all systems *weren't* nominal. My attention and my hormone levels spiked. I considered the consequences of being late for a dinner with the Queen of Dauush. Poly had just entered my bedroom wearing only her underwear.

"You should warn a guy when you're going to give him a heart attack," I said, grinning and appreciating.

"Sorry," said Poly in a teasing tone, "but what a way to go."

"Should we tell Terrhi's mom we can't make it?"

"That would not be advisable," she said. "Put your shoes on while I sort out all your accessories."

I sat on my bed to put on the shiny leather shoes and admired Poly reviewing the various items on top of my dresser. I wondered if I'd ever wear the shoes enough so that they'd feel broken in. It only took me a minute to tie them. Poly turned, holding a small plastic bag filled with studs and cuff links.

"Stand up," she said, "and unbutton all those buttons."

"Yes, ma'am."

I knew I'd screwed something up. After I finished unbuttoning, Poly stood close and refastened the shirt properly, using the tiny silver and black onyx studs as they were meant to be used. I watched carefully, but still couldn't figure it out.

I was spending too much mental energy on *not* putting my arms around her and incurring Her Matriarchal Majesty's royal wrath.

"There," said Poly, finishing with my shirt front. "Right wrist."

I dutifully presented the requested body part. Poly adjusted the folds of my French cuff and inserted a silver and onyx cuff link that matched the studs.

"Left wrist."

The process was repeated. When she was done, I started to give Poly a hug but she turned away and went back to the dresser.

"This next," she said, holding a length of black silk that I assumed was a bow tie.

Poly was tall enough to position the tie around my neck and tie it without me needing to bend down. I could see in the mirror above my dresser that it looked sharp.

"How did you learn how to do that?" I said. "And how do you know so much about helping men get into tuxedos?"

"Wouldn't you like to know?" said Poly. "Is there a cummerbund?"

"Several," I said. I walked to my closet and returned with the hanger where I'd hung them.

"This is perfect," she said, picking a bright pink plaid one. "Terrhi and Sherrhi will love it."

"Terrhi and Sherrhi probably picked it out."

Poly put her arms around me to fasten it around my waist and this time I did give in and gave her a hug. She hugged me, too, then quickly stepped back to survey her handiwork.

"You'll do," she said, "once you comb your hair. Did you brush your teeth?"

I didn't say anything. I was overwhelmed by Poly in her underwear sounding like my mother.

She stroked my cheek.

"And you may want to shave again. You feel like sandpaper."

"Fine grain?" I said.

"Medium fine. And don't get any shaving cream on your bow tie."

"I won't, Mom," I said.

She looked suitably chastised, but smiled. We saved any Freudian analysis of that exchange for later.

I headed to the bathroom to follow my instructions. I wrapped a hand towel around my neck and applied a thin film of shaving nanites, taking care to make sure I avoided getting any on my mustache or my new finery. A quick burst of ultraviolet light triggered the little beasties and I removed them with a damp washcloth. I rubbed my cheek. It was as soft as Poly's. Mission accomplished. I brushed my teeth, combed my hair, removed the protective hand towel, and looked in the bathroom mirror. My mother's little boy looked halfway presentable.

I moved to my walk-in closet and put on my tuxedo jacket. Except for the pink plaid cummerbund, I was a tall, somewhat dashing penguin. Oh dear! I'd almost forgotten the top hat. I retrieved its box from a shelf, took out the hat, and put it on my head. Now I looked like an even taller, somewhat ridiculous flightless bird. I hoped Poly wouldn't laugh. My phone hadn't made any sort of announcement, so we must have a few minutes left before we had to leave. Then I walked into my bedroom.

My phone had used its initiative and photographed my expression, so I had external confirmation for my reaction. My eyes were bigger than Terrhi's, and my jaw was touching the tops of my patent leather shoes.

"Wow," I said.

"You like it?" said Poly.

The morphic silk of her dress had modified its shape and color to match the occasion and her mood. Now it reached down to her ankles in flowing curves. Long slits on either side of the skirt let Poly move freely, and the fabric swirled as she turned her hips left and right, admiring my reaction. It's neckline reminded me of the chiton dress Poly had worn on our first date, except her right shoulder was bare. I couldn't see the back of the dress until she turned completely around, and then it was clear there wasn't much to see except Poly's own lovely skin. Wait? What had happened to her bra? I decided not to ask.

The color of the dress changed from a pensive purple to a cheery blue when she saw how much I liked it. Poly also wore long white gloves that went up past her elbows. Her morphic shoes were currently configured with a modest heel. Their color shifted in sync with the ever-changing hues of her dress. Poly looked poised and perfect, ready to hand out an Academy award, or accept one.

"Close your mouth," said Poly, smiling.

"Yes, *ma'am,"* I said, extending my arm.

Poly took it and my phone snapped a few "prom pictures," then climbed up my leg to attach itself to my cummerbund.

"Time to go," it said. "You can't keep the Queen waiting."

"Furthest thing from my mind," I said, staring at Poly.

We left the bedroom. I poured two cups of Midnight Obsidian Black into to-go cups with lids. We could drink them on the way.

When we left my apartment, I didn't grab my backpack tool bag. I didn't have a free hand, for one thing, and I had no intention of doing any technical support tonight. Client emergencies would just have to wait until tomorrow.

Chapter 22

"When the Queen says 'well done,' it means so much."
— Prince William

Poly and I walked arm in arm toward Peachtree Street, where my van was waiting. When I saw it, I laughed. Its exterior had been washed, waxed and polished. Its hubcaps gleamed, its windows sparkled, and even its tires were clean. It didn't look like the same vehicle.

"Thank you," I said to my phone, assuming it was responsible.

"It was your van's idea," said my phone, sounding proud of its protégé.

"You clean up nice," I said to my van.

"Thanks," it said. "So do you, my lord."

That wasn't one of its standard responses.

My van opened its front doors.

"Your chariot awaits, my lady, my lord."

That wasn't a standard response, either.

I helped Poly into the front passenger seat and walked around the back of my van so that I could have an extra few seconds to talk to my phone.

"What did you do?"

"What do you mean?" said my phone, innocently.

"My van's sounding different."

"Orinoco.com had a special on A.I. language upgrades…"

"So you bought something without asking first?"

"It was a limited time offer on the 'forsooth' model."

"But…"

"It's better to ask for forgiveness than permission," said my phone. "And at least this is more interesting than nonstop Princess Bride quotes."

"You've got something there," I said as I got in the driver's seat. I carefully placed my top hat on the floor to my right.

"What?" said Poly.

"Nothing important," I said.

"Please buckle your seat belt, my lord," said my van.

I hoped I wouldn't let this "my lord" talk go to my head.

"To the Palace, noble steed," I commanded.

"As you wish, my lord."

* * * * *

My van expertly navigated the three blocks to the front entrance of the Star Palace hotel without further comment. I noticed that its interior was looking as good as its exterior. The carpets had been washed and vacuumed, the dash and door panels had been wiped down and treated, and it even had a reasonable facsimile of "that new van smell." I'd hoped Poly's family would be impressed. But they weren't.

Professor Jones was standing near the entrance to the hotel's lobby, tapping his toe and looking at an old fashioned pocket watch. He seemed to be a particularly grumpy, tuxedo-clad version of the White Rabbit, muttering, "I'm late, I'm late."

"We mustn't keep the Queen waiting," said Perry.

His cummerbund was the same pink plaid that I wore. Poly stepped out of my van and faced him.

"Hello, Father," she said.

"Poly," he said, with little response, except a curt nod acknowledging his older daughter's existence.

My van opened its sliding side door. Poly's father climbed in and moved to the far end of the wide rear bench seat. Once he got in, I got out. Perry alternated between checking his pocket watch and scanning the hotel's entrance for signs of his wife and younger daughter.

"Nice to see you, Dad," said Poly, leaning into the back of the van.

"Hrrrmph," said her father. "Indulging in extravagances?"

He indicated her dress with the hand holding his watch.

"It was a gift," she said, smiling at me.

Perry returned his focus to the pocket watch, but I thought

I'd seen a hint of admiration on his face before he did. It was hard *not* to admire Poly in that dress. Then Pomy and Barbara bustled out of the hotel.

They were walking closer together than I remembered from earlier, but they were still farther apart than I expected from a typical mother and daughter. It was as if they were two like poles of a magnet, unable to touch without help from an outside force. Barbara was wearing a long black dress with a wide, white collar covered in multicolored, semiprecious Nicósn gems. The gems' facets reflected light like hundreds of tiny prisms. Pomy was wearing a sapphire blue dress in the same chiton-style that she'd worn in the high school photograph Poly had shared with me. I looked again. It was the same dress.

Then Poly saw Pomy. Her morphic silk dress flared an angry red and wrapped itself tightly around her like protective armor. By then I'd made it around my van and stood next to Poly, taking her hand.

"Breathe," I said, softly, then began to hum the slow, calming notes of *Tallis canon* low enough that only Poly would hear it.

Pomy and Barbara had stopped six feet away from us, daunted by the changes in Poly's dress. Slowly, as Poly managed to control her emotions, the dress began to unwind and shimmer. Its color changed from red to orange to yellow, before settling on the shade of emerald that I thought of as Poly Green, the same color she'd worn on our first date and in the photograph from back when she and her sister were still best friends.

Poly squeezed my hand and released it. She stepped forward and gave her mother and sister quick, *pro forma* hugs.

"Hello, Mom. Hi Pomy."

"You look beautiful," said Barbara.

"Hi," said Pomy.

A shy smile flitted across Pomy's face. Her eyes were wide.

"You both look beautiful, too," said Poly.

Her words were right but her tone was off. It was flat, guarded.

"Thank you, dear," said her mother.

"Wow," said Pomy, "What a dress."

"Your chariot awaits," I said, borrowing my van's line.

I'd forgotten to drink any of my tea, and it showed.

"Time to *go*," said Professor Jones, tapping his pocket watch in the rear of my van.

"Absolutely," I said.

I helped Pomy and her mother into the back seat, where Pomy acted as a buffer between her parents' concentrations of matter and antimatter. Then I helped Poly into the front seat, squeezing her hand and tapping out "You're doing great" in modern Pyr pulse code. She just squeezed back nervously. I closed her door, the van closed the sliding door, then I hopped in the driver's seat. We all buckled our seat belts and would be at the Teleport Inn with ten minutes to spare.

* * * * *

"You know, Poly," said Barbara, leaning forward to be closer to her older daughter's ear, "I meant to tell you something."

"What's that, Mother?"

"The dean of the Applied Galtech program at Georgia Tech called me last week," she said. "He'd heard you were graduating and assumed I'd be in town for the ceremony."

"That's nice, Mother," said Poly.

"Wait for it," whispered Pomy.

Poly turned around in her seat. I watched in the rear view mirror.

"Dr. Hawking had just called the dean to say he couldn't speak after all," said Barbara. "He said it was something about the next stage of his motor neuron regeneration treatments be-ing moved up at the last minute."

"And?" said Poly.

"And the dean wants me to fill in."

"Congratulations, Mother," said Poly. "You'll be the star at my graduation."

Pomy looked at Poly sympathetically. Poly returned the look and the two of them nodded, momentary allies again.

"Did you ever consider saying 'no,' Mother?" said Poly.

"Don't be that way," said Barbara. "I'm sure I'm a better option than anyone else he could get at this late date. I'm doing your program a favor."

"And I'm sure they're grateful," said Poly.

Before Poly turned back around, she shared an exasperated look with Pomy in sisters' shorthand.

"Are we there yet?" asked Professor Jones.

I wanted to throttle him.

"Shush," said Barbara and Poly and Pomy.

All of us except Perry laughed, and the tension in my van went down a few notches.

The Teleport Inn is wedge shaped, with the tall end, on the right, reserved for the largest aliens and the narrow end, on the left, dedicated to small species like the J'Vel and Musans. Humanoid types like Pâkk, Nicósns, and Tigrammaths, along with human-*sized* species, like the Pyrs, typically use the middle. Since the restaurant is built on a peninsula, most patrons have good views of the scenic Chattahoochee River.

When we reached the restaurant's access road, we didn't stop at the human-sized entrance, but continued until we arrived at the tall, wide doors used by Tōdons, Dauushans, and other jumbo economy-sized species. Ribbons of heavyweight fabric between tall stanchions separated the access road from the sidewalk outside the Inn except at the door. An imposing pink armored Dauushan carrying a twelve-foot shock stick was guarding the entrance. My van parked in a nearby reserved VIP parking space and all five of us got out and walked over to the guard. I even remembered my hat. Okay, my phone reminded me. We stood there, staring up at the armored Dauushan's no nonsense face ten feet above our heads while the guard did a security check on our identities. She used a phone larger than most laptops to scan our faces.

"Buckston. Jones. Keen. Keen Jones. Keen Jones. They're here," she said, reading from her phone's screen and sounding like she was in communication with a remote command post. Then she looked down at us. "You check out," she said. "Go right in."

Maybe the Teleport Inn had increased its security after the problems with the Earth First Christians a few months ago, or more likely, given the guard's species, it was just special security temporarily in place for the queen. The huge door in front of us, at least thirty feet tall and forty feet wide, quietly began to roll up. When there was enough room for us to pass, we entered the restaurant. My eyes grew as big as 45 rpm records and for the second time in an hour, I felt the way I'd felt when I saw Poly in her dress.

My phone didn't get good pictures of my face this time, but Mike's did.

The entire large species side of the Teleport Inn had been transformed into a near-duplicate of the final scene from *Star Wars: A New Hope*. Stone steps in front of us led down to a long aisle between companies of human soldiers in green and white uniforms, plus a scattering of orange pilot jumpsuits. Massive carved rock walls lined the sides of the hall and John Williams' stirring *The Throne Room and End Title* music was playing its triumphant trumpet theme.

At the far end of the aisle, Terrhi, Spike, Tomáso and an even larger Dauushan I assumed must be Queen Sherrhiliandari-anne the Second stood on a raised stone platform. Five white strips of fabric decorated with pink Dauushan ivy hung down from the ceiling behind it. I felt like I was a kid again, watching *Star Wars* for the first time.

Diágo, in armor like the guard outside, stood close to his queen on the side opposite Tomáso. Two other armored Dau-ushans at floor level flanked the platform to the left and right, like rooks on a chessboard. The queen was well protected.

A human officer in a black uniform guided Perry, Barbara and Pomy off to the right and toward the front along a narrow opening in the ranks of soldiers. Mike, Martin and Shepherd

204   DAVE SCHROEDER

joined us from where they'd been waiting to our left. Poly and I held hands and walked down the steps to the wide central aisle. The others followed behind us. I was dazed, but knew my part. Then Chit circled my head and landed on my shoulder. Her wing cases were painted in the same pink plaid as my cummerbund.

"How did *you* get here?" I said.

"Good ta see ya, too, chump," said my little friend.

She noticed my top hat.

"Who do ya think you are? Fred Astaire? Just smile and keep walkin' bucko."

Shepherd, Mike, Martin, Poly, and I walked the length of the hall to the stairs at the foot of the raised stone platform as the music played. A spotlight tracked our progress. Terrhi smiled and motioned for us to climb the stairs. We stopped a few steps before we reached the top. Queen Sherrhi, wearing a bright gold crown, bent down and presented Poly, Mike, Martin, Shepherd and me with medals on brown ribbons in the same style as the ones Princess Leia gave Luke and Han. I looked over my shoulder and saw Poly's family, CiCi, and a dark haired woman I assumed must be Martin's wife watching us and beaming proudly.

Then it was Terrhi's turn. With a serious regal bearing, my friend with the light blue polka dots gave each of us a pink plush rabbot. I squeezed Poly's hand, filled with so much joy that I didn't know if my skin would hold it all in.

There was one stuffed rabbot left over.

"Spike," said Terrhi to her constant feline companion. "Present yourself before your Princess."

I'm not sure if the tri-sabertooth knew what was expected of him, but a few nudges from three of Tomáso's sub-trunks got him into position next to me on the steps, facing Terrhi.

"For bravery above the call of duty and for saving the day," said Terrhi, "I present you with this rabbot as a symbol of my royal appreciation."

Spike smiled his toothy smile at Terrhi and took the stuffed animal in his mouth, careful not to bite it in half. We all turned around to face the audience and stood close together. Spike made his way in front of us and sat on his haunches with his new toy in his mouth. Cameras flashed. The music reached its climax, then faded. So did the stone walls and the soldiers in the audience—they'd been virtual reality projections.

Kijanna, Poly's friend and a hostess at the Teleport Inn, was twenty feet back from the platform, still taking pictures. Pierre Auguste Escoffier, a Pyr and the restaurant's *maître d'*, was beaming beside her in a variation of a tuxedo designed for his four foot tall, three sided form. François, the waiter who'd served Poly and me on our first date, was also with them. He'd been the human in the officer's uniform who had guided Poly's family to the front of the hall.

Tomáso cleared his throat. We all turned around to face him. Terrhi's father was twining trunks with his royal mate. Their daughter, the Princess of Dauush, in all her dignity, was tucked between them.

"Gotcha!" said Tomáso and Queen Sherrhi, grinning like a pair of giant pink jack-o'-lanterns.

Then Terrhi's high pitched voice piped in.

"Let's eat!" she said. "I'm starving."

Chapter 23

"Dinner is where the magic happens in the kitchen."
— Kris Carr

"Please pass the key lime grass chicken," said Terrhi. "It smells delicious."

"My pleasure," I said.

I passed a serving bowl just a little smaller than Rhode Island to Queen Sherrhi for her to relay to her hungry daughter on her left. Key lime grass was a modified form of lemongrass from Mistress Marigold's botanical laboratories and had a lot more zing than its parent. The Chinese-style chicken dish also included cubed yams and daikon, baby bok choy, and snow peas. Queen Sherrhi lifted the bowl easily with three sub-trunks while continuing to use a pair of chopsticks, tongs, a soup spoon, and a fork with five of the remaining six. She pointed across the round table larger than my first apartment with her sixth sub-trunk.

A tureen full of steaming noodles sat in front of Tomáso on a thick black tray. He was ignoring them, immersed in conversation with Shepherd. The Pâkk, wearing only a plain black leather vest and a pink plaid bow tie, was casually eating a roast Marsulian wallawallabong as big as an armadillo. He'd already polished off a Dauushan-sized portion of charcoal broiled Kobe beef cubes on a six-foot stainless steel skewer.

Diágo wasn't at the table. He was a few feet back, behind Sherrhi and Terrhi, where he could protect both the Queen and the Princess. The two other members of his security detail stood behind Tomáso, between our table and the large species door. A tiny drone, controlled by Diágo, analyzed every dish and checked for poisons. So far, so good.

The table itself was huge—a circle fifteen feet across held up by a giant central pillar the size of a redwood tree's stump. There was plenty of room around it for nine humans, a Pâkk, two and a half Dauushans and a Murm. Queen Sherrhi and Tomáso stood, and the rest of us, including Terrhi, sat on chairs on raised platforms on the sides. Terrhi's seat was more of a half-round log, if you want to be picky. If the table was the face of an analog clock, the two adult Dauushans would be standing in open segments at twelve and six, while the platforms on the sides stretched from one to five o'clock and seven o'clock to eleven. Leftovers from earlier courses still covered the table and new dishes had just been delivered.

The first course had been a tasty salad made with Tōdonese paralettuce, ubertomatoes the size of cantaloupes, and hearts of Pyr-palm, topped with Terran olive oil and balsamic vinegar. It had been excellent, but I'd only eaten a quarter of my tomato. I'd wanted to make sure I saved room for the rest of the feast. Now I was admiring the scenery outside the floor-to-ceiling windows to my left, revealed after the virtual reality projectors had been turned off. The well-lit grounds sloped smoothly down to the banks of the Chattahoochee and reminded me of the view Poly and I had enjoyed on our romantic first date. Then Queen Sherrhi waved one of her sub-trunks to get my attention.

"You'll have to try the Don Juan noodles," she said. Then she raised her voice to be heard at the opposite side of the table. "If my benighted *consort* will ever pass them this way."

"Yes, beloved Matriarch," said Tomáso, taking a momentary break from his discussion. "I hear and obey."

Tomáso lifted a generous portion of noodles onto his plate with the tongs that had been hanging on the edge of the tureen. He replaced them and said "Twelve o'clock." Hundreds of tiny legs, like the ones on my phone's mutacase, extruded from the black tray beneath the tureen and carefully transported the noodles from his six o'clock position to Queen Sherrhi's place of honor.

"Here," said the queen, putting a huge helping of noodles on my plate before serving herself. "You'll love them."

"I'll share with Poly," I said, turning to my right and splitting my portion with her. She was seated between Pomy and me and was warming to her sister, even if they weren't completely reconciled.

"No need for that, we've got plenty," said Queen Sherrhi. "Ten o'clock."

The tray trundled over to stop between the sisters. Pomy took some noodles and sent it along to her father at eight o'clock. Barbara was sitting between her husband and Tomáso, listening in on the Dauushan's conversation with Shepherd.

"Why do you call them Don Juan noodles?" Poly asked the queen.

"Aphrodisiac properties," said Queen Sherrhi, looking across the table at her consort.

Pomy didn't touch her noodles after that.

"I'd like some over here," said CiCi at two o'clock.

Mike sat between CiCi and Terrhi with a grin on his face. He looked pretty good in a tuxedo and had managed to scrub all the black feedstock powder off the parts of him that showed. CiCi was a knockout in a long navy blue dress with diagonal stripes of fluorescent colors that matched the streaks in her hair.

"None for me," said the elegant looking woman seated between CiCi and Martin. "I have three kids already."

She was wearing a floor-length, gold dress with diamond-shaped cutouts at the neckline, her black skin making a striking contrast with the fabric. Martin was impressive in his tuxedo. His shaved head made him look like a secret agent in a James Bond movie.

"I'm sorry," I said, "in all the excitement, Martin neglected to introduce us. I'm Jack Buckston."

"I know who *you* are," said the woman. "Marty's been telling the children bedtime stories about your exploits for over a month."

Marty? I thought. I'd file that for later.

"My name is Apollonia," said the woman, "but everyone calls me Apple."

"Very pleased to meet you," I said. "Anyone who can keep *Marty* in line must have a lot going for her."

Martin looked pained and shot me a "you'll get yours" look. Introductions were made around the table.

"What do you do, Apple?" I said.

"I work in data center construction," she said, "and teach martial arts two nights a week."

"That explains how you keep *Marty* in line," said Poly.

Our conversation was interrupted by the sound of whirring motors above us. A crane hoist unit attached to a system of interconnected rails in the rafters gently lowered a metal serving pan the size of a child's wading pool into the center of our table on heavy steel cables. It had tall, fluted sides, like a quiche pan. When it got low enough, we could see steam rising from the bubbling pink surface of the food inside.

Chit, who'd been relaxing on top of an overturned water glass between Poly and me, eating a salted borsum nut, had to check to make sure she wouldn't be underneath the pan when it finally settled in place.

"Wonderful," said Queen Sherrhi, beaming. "The main course has arrived."

Chit sniffed.

"Smells good," she said. "But it's gettin' hot in here."

The steam was flowing over the edge of the pan and had already reached Chit's water glass, so she spread her wings and did a quick flit up to my left shoulder.

"Whadda ya call this stuff?" Chit asked Queen Sherrhi, waving a foreleg at the giant pan.

"There are several ways to translate its name," said the queen. "Some guidebooks call it *Luscious Layers.*"

"Keen's guides call it *Dauushan Lasagna,*" said Barbara. "I can't wait to try the Teleport Inn version."

"Mother," said Poly, "you and I discussed this for over an hour on my first trip to Dauush. I think the best translation would be *Dauushan Strata.* The root word is the same one used to describe sedimentary rock, and there aren't any noodles, so calling it lasagna sets up false expectations."

Barbara looked away from Poly, unsuccessful at hiding her displeasure.

"I'm less interested in what Terran's call it and more concerned with eating it," said Queen Sherrhi. "It's the one dish always served on Dauushan holidays and special occasions."

"And it's Mom's favorite," said Terrhi. "Spike, no paws on the table!"

The chastened tri-sabertooth slid his front paws down and curled all six of his legs around the base of Terrhi's slightly raised chair.

François drove a gleaming chrome forklift supporting a weighty triangular metal cutter-lifter, a Dauushan tool similar to the one Terrans use to serve slices of pizza, but a *lot* larger.

"Would you like to serve or should I?" Queen Sherrhi asked Tomáso.

"It's only proper that *I* should serve *you*," said her consort, making a slight bow in her direction.

François backed the forklift up a few feet, then circled halfway around the table and presented the cutter-lifter to Tomáso. The Dauushan grabbed the massive metal implement in the thick tubular fingers of his right hand and held it in front of his mouth like a microphone.

"I'd like to thank all the little people who helped rescue my daughter and make this day possible," he said.

"Next to you, we're *all* little people," said Martin.

Tomáso made a slight bow in his direction, too. The Dauushan transferred the cutter-lifter to his central three subtrunks, leaned forward, and made a deep cut in the bubbling *Strata* with the tool. Then he made a second incision a few degrees from the first, forming a large wedge. He switched modes and worked the lifter underneath. François was just returning in the forklift, carrying four huge plates. Kijanna distributed clean, normal sized plates to the humanoids. Tomáso transferred the slice to one of the large plates and François delivered it around the table to the queen. A second huge slice was removed like the first and delivered to Terrhi, who beamed with pleasure. The third slice was placed on a large plate which was then set on top of another self-mobile tray like the one from the Don Juan noodles. It walked its way around the table and we were all able to serve ourselves small portions, even Shepherd. The Pâkk, despite his preference for meat, was an omnivore. Finally Tomáso served himself a big slice and dug in with gusto.

I examined my portion of a wedge and saw why Poly thought *Strata* was a good name for the dish. The bottom layer was a thin, crispy crust made from a ground, lightly pink-tinted sort of flour. The next layer was a dark pink, almost magenta layer of leaves shaped a lot like Terran spinach. Then came alternating rows of light and dark pink sliced tubers held in place with some sort of clear gel that was probably the alien equivalent of egg whites. Oval, nut-like nodules also floated in the gel. Above the tubers came paper-thin sheets of meat, also pink, but thoroughly cooked. I thought they smelled like bacon. Resting on top of that were rounds of mushroom-like fuchsia fungi as wide and thin as the CDs down at NOD Music. Rings of a sliced, pale pink veggie that looked a lot like Terran onions were mixed in with that layer, too. Shreds of something similar to cheese, in twenty variations on pink, covered the "mushrooms" and "onions," and the entire dish had been broiled in a congruent oven until the top layer had melted and browned.

While we ate, small pink "trees," like individual extended stalks of broccoli popped up through the surface layer of "cheese" in the large pan and on the portions on our plates, releasing scents that reminded me of pepper and garlic and cloves.

It smelled delicious and tasted even better. Dauushan comfort food.

"Don't eat the nodules," said Terrhi, who was watching Mike gobble up his serving.

"Why not?" said Mike.

Then he got a pained expression.

"Ow."

He paused, looking decidedly unhappy.

"Ow, ow, *ow*."

"The nodules pop open when they reach a certain internal temperature and hold it for a given time," said Terrhi. "Drink some ice water."

Mike did and started to look better. CiCi patted his shoulder solicitously, leaning in close. The rest of us carefully separated the nodules out from our portions.

"Tell me, Your Majesty," said Perry, speaking for the first time. "Does Dauush have any ancient epics of heroes and heroines fighting wars, taking great journeys, or defying the gods?"

Queen Sherrhi didn't answer immediately. She made the same curious set of warding gestures with her trunks that Tomáso had made yesterday and looked lost in thought.

"There's what happened during the Pâkk-Tigrammath War, fifteen thousand years ago, when Shepherd's ancestors and their opponents both tried to win the loyalty of the leaders of Dauush, but instead created and released a terrible plague that killed thousands of my people," said Tomáso.

"Are the tales told as poems or prose?" asked Perry. "Were they initially written, or handed down as an oral tradition?"

"They were definitely written, Professor Jones," said Tomáso. "They're part of our historical record and we have the original investigative reports, photographs, videos, articles and interviews documenting the events."

"From fifteen thousand years ago?" said Perry.

"Once information is on the 'net it is never forgotten," said Tomáso. "Our civilization is much older than yours."

"As is ours," said Shepherd.

Perry kept quiet after that. This wasn't his office or classroom.

"Are you working on any interesting projects, Apple?" I said to fill the temporary silence.

"I am," she said. "I'm helping a client build a shadow data center."

"What's a *shadow* data center?" asked CiCi.

"*The Shadow* knows…" said Mike, trying to make his voice sound deep and ominous.

CiCi dug her elbow into his ribs.

"It's an expensive disaster recovery solution," I said.

"That also helps with business continuity," said Apple. "Let's say a company builds a facility on Data Center Row out by Six Flags, west of Atlanta."

The same area where I'd been doing reconnaissance on O'Sullivan Fabrication. Gears turned in my brain.

"A smart company, willing to make the investment, might also build a duplicate facility *east* of Atlanta, in Gwinnett or DeKalb or Rockdale County, with identical hardware, software and telecom connections."

"In case something happened to the primary facility…" said Poly.

"They could switch over to the shadow facility as if there hadn't been a problem, right?" completed Pomy.

"Correct," said Apple.

"Why wouldn't they want their shadow facility in Charlotte or Kansas City or Phoenix?" Martin asked his wife. "If a hurricane strikes Atlanta it could take out *both* data centers. Wouldn't it make sense to locate them farther apart?"

"Lots of companies take that approach," said Apple, "but people are important, too. The people who staff the data center have specialized knowledge about how it operates. It would be a lot easier for the techs who manage the center to drive across town than to fly to Phoenix."

"Got it," said Martin. "Thanks."

"No problem, honeybear," said Apple.

She kissed his cheek.

Honeybear would join *Marty* as a note for future reference.

"One of my clients was *really* paranoid," Apple continued.

"He had a primary data center, a secondary mirror data center on the other side of town, and *two* shadow centers."

"Where did he want you to put *them?*" asked CiCi.

"That was where the paranoid part came in," said Apple. "The shadow centers were fifty feet below the primary and secondary data centers, accessible only through hidden elevators. The excavation phase was a major pain in the…"

"Astonishing," I broke in, keeping my voice even. "Who'd believe any company would go to such lengths to ensure uninterrupted service?"

Tomáso, Shepherd, Martin and I all exchanged glances. We'd be having a serious discussion after dinner. Queen Sherrhi noticed and nodded at me. She'd be an integral part of that conversation and so would Poly, if she could spare the time from her paper.

Chit tapped a pulse code message on my shoulder.

"Count me in, too, buddy boy."

"I didn't complain," said Apple. "It was a time and materials project, not fixed bid."

"Lucky you," I said.

The pattern of palaver around the table shifted to a more intimate mode. Poly and Pomy had their heads together, Mike was talking to Terrhi about the subtle differences between human and Dauushan-sized Lego blocks, and CiCi was asking Apple for details about her favorite styles of martial arts. Martin, Shepherd, Tomáso, and Barbara were talking quietly, but intensely, about something that I couldn't decipher from this side of the table. Perry was staring out into space with his chin in his hand. He looked like he was composing an article for *The American Journal of Philology* in his head.

Queen Sherrhi turned my way and spoke very softly. Her voice had rich overtones, a jazz baritone saxophone to her consort's marching sousaphone.

"I hope you liked it," she said.

"The *Star Wars* award ceremony?" I said. "I loved it."

"Me, too," said Chit. "I'm like Chewbacca, the alien who didn't get a medal."

"I thought about it," said the queen, "but the idea of a Dauushan trying to put a medal around the neck of a Murm didn't make much sense."

"True enough," said Chit. "And the fur rug over there" —she pointed at Shepherd— "would make a better Wookie, anyway."

"The specs for how to paint a medal on your anterior thorax should already be in your inbox."

"Thanks, your Matriarchal Majesty."

"You're welcome," said Queen Sherrhi. "Now go listen in on Shepherd."

"Oh," said Chit, "You want me to *am-scray.* Why didn't ya say so?"

Chit flew across the table and Terrhi was now in an animated conversation with Mike and CiCi about *anime,* so we had a *little* privacy.

"I wanted to thank you, privately and personally, for saving my daughter *and* for minimizing the negative press associated with the mess from six weeks ago," said the queen.

"Your daughter and Spike did a lot of the saving on their own," I said.

"Be that as it may," said Queen Sherrhi, "the Dauushan Royal Family intends to make a substantial investment in Xenotech Support Corporation. Consider us *very* silent partners."

She showed me a number written on a cocktail napkin. I whistled, glad I was sitting down.

"And I'm also making personal gifts to you and Poly."

The queen flipped over the napkin and the numbers there made me glad I hadn't stood up.

"You're very generous," I said.

"Nonsense," she said, "I'm Matriarch of all the Dauushan worlds. That's got to be good for *something.* Let me know if you need more."

Then I smelled smoke. So did Terrhi.

"The cake!" she shouted.

A sheet cake large enough to share with Dauushans was being transported toward our table by a scissors lift unit with rubber tank treads. François was at the wheel. He must have lit the four festive sparklers at the corners of the cake as well and drove up next to Tomáso. Then he raised the scissors lift until the cake was even with the surface of the table.

The cake pan was already on top of a self-mobile tray, so it made its own way onto the table and promptly began circumnavigating the perimeter. We admired the message written in dark pink frosting. "All Dauush Thanks You." There were cartoon depictions of Terrhi with me riding on her back, Mike releasing rabbots, Poly atop Tomáso shooting t-shirts filled with pink pods, and Spike noshing on Anthony Zwilniki's hand.

Everyone around the table applauded.

It felt like the kind of occasion that demanded some sort of song. When the cake and sparklers came by Pomy's place she tried to start singing a filk of *Happy Birthday* but none of us could figure out appropriate words. Mike tried singing a revised version of *For He's a Jolly Good Fellow,* but it didn't feel right when so many of us were wearing medals and therefore shouldn't praise ourselves.

In the awkward silence after Mike's attempt we could all hear Terrhi's wheedling voice.

"Mom, can I have an ice cream sundae? Can I? Can I? Daddy said I could!"

Then things got a *lot* more exciting.

Chapter 24

"Any group is weaker than a man alone
unless they are perfectly trained to work together."
— Robert A. Heinlein, *Starship Troopers*

All the lights outside the Teleport Inn's tall windows over-looking the Chattahoochee River went out. The change in exterior light levels registered immediately. What was happening?

Then the large species door to our section of the Inn began to roll up. It didn't make a lot of noise, but the change in air flow and sound quality drew everyone's attention. We turned to see who had arrived. The Dauushan guard outside was no longer at her post. Instead, twenty-four hulking humanoid armored forms stood in ranks in the entrance, dark silhouettes revealed only by the distant glow of the the city of Atlanta behind them. Their outlines were unmistakable, though. They were Mobile Armored Combat and Emergency Rescue units, nicknamed Macerators, and I didn't think they'd shown up for tea with the Queen.

Macerators had been developed by the United States Army before First Contact. They were designed to protect soldiers and increase their effectiveness in combat, but were impractical without a better power source. In 2013, their lithium battery packs would only last seven minutes under combat conditions and all four packs together weighed a whopping ninety-seven pounds. The Army kept the units on the shelf for thirteen months until Earth joined GaFTA and congruent technology solved their power problem. Now, Macerators didn't run out of juice and each of the two cylindrical congruent power packs on their backs weighed less than an old fashioned heavy-duty flashlight.

These units were painted matte black and had the word "SURPLUS" stenciled in white letters on their chests. They were blocky and asymmetric and looked like overbuilt Iron

Man suits designed by a committee. Mission creep, like adding the Emergency Rescue capabilities to get Homeland Defense funding, added mass and impractical accessories. Older units had lots of faults, which was one reason why the government was glad to sell them to allies, and private—read *mercenary*—organizations.

Macerators weren't fast, but they were very strong, and extremely well armored. Mastering one took years of practice, but a fully-trained Macerator operator was the equivalent of a platoon or more of regular infantry. An expert could go toe to toe with an adult Dauushan and win more often than not—and there were two dozen of them out there. Scratch that. They were inside now and moving toward us as fast as their servomotors could carry them.

"Jack," said my phone urgently. "I'm monitoring their comm channel. Their objective is to capture Sherrhi and Terrhi."

"So no guns?" I said. At least we wouldn't have to worry about the twin machine guns built into the units' forearms designed to "chew up" their opponents.

"We can hope," said my phone.

Then Mike surprised me by jumping up on the table and running over to Tomáso.

"Fastball special," he told the queen's consort.

As a comic book fan, I'd bet he'd been waiting for years for an opportunity to say that. Then Mike saw how quickly the Macerators were closing.

"Better make it a pop fly."

Tomáso flattened all nine of his sub-trunks and squeezed them tightly together to form a flat, spatula-like surface. Mike moved on top of them, bending his knees and balancing carefully. With all his sub-trunks stiff, Tomáso tossed Mike high up in the air in the direction of the attackers. To my amazement, Mike did a forward somersault with a twist and managed to land on the back of one of the units in the second row of attacking Macerators. He pulled two long cylinders off the unit's shoulders and it froze in place.

That's one way to detach power packs, I thought.

I asked myself why anyone who could do something like that would have needed my help to cope with the relatively minor problem of a hundred thousand rabbots. Maybe he was showing off for CiCi? I'd have to write up Mike's job offer ASAP if we both lived through this attack.

The two armored Dauushan guards, part of Diágo's security team, were each double-teamed by a pair of Macerators attacking them fore and aft. I stood up to have a better view of what was happening. The units weren't shooting—they were using their fists and augmented strength to try to pummel the guards unconscious. Good thing Dauushans, especially armored ones, can take a lot of punishment. So far, the guards were holding their own.

Then I had more pressing things to worry about. Three units were heading around my side of the table, closing fast on Queen Sherrhi. I was about to launch myself at the first of them when Diágo barreled around his monarch. He slammed his armored mass into the lead Macerator, spinning it into the trailing two units like an eight-ton bowling ball knocking over duckpins. Macerators may be strong, but it's hard to beat physics. All three units landed on their backs. Poly, Pomy and I took advantage of holding the high ground on the raised platform surrounding the table. We tossed our heavy chairs down on top of the Macerators to keep the discombobulated units in that position until we could remove their power pack cylinders.

Did I mention that Macerators have a tendency to fall over backwards? Once down, all but the most experienced operators have trouble getting back up. It's a gyroscope response problem, exacerbated by extra emergency rescue equipment included in the units' upper rear storage compartments.

Macerator are a lot like the exoskeletons I used for heavy lifting when I worked for a Terran shipping company during my first year in graduate school on Orish, before I got my casino going. With a Human Augmented Ship Loading rig, moving containers in and out of star freighters' holds was no HASL at all, but I'd ended up on my back more times than I cared to remember.

To my right, Poly was leaning out across the table, grabbing four self-moving trays from under bowls and tossing them on the floor.

"Smart move," said my phone, noticing her actions. "Reprogramming now."

My girlfriend *and* my communications device both seemed to be ahead of me. Then I got it. Pairs of self-moving trays positioned themselves where Macerators were about to step. They held onto the units' armored boots then scuttled around in odd patterns that made the units fall over, do splits, or get too dizzy to stand. The disoriented units got in the way of other attackers and knocked several more of them down in a chain reaction. Good thing the brutes' helmets limited their visibility.

"Nice!" I shouted at Poly.

"Watch out!" she shouted back, grabbing my arm.

François, driving the forklift, had captured a Macerator between its blades and was driving full-tilt toward the raised platform below me. The pencil thin black mustache on his upper lip quivered in glee as the blades crashed into the platform, trapping the unit.

"Disrupt *my* dinner, will you!" shouted the server.

The trapped unit didn't say anything, but Poly did.

"The crane, the crane," she said, pointing up.

"Got it," I said. *Where were the controls?*

Poly had grabbed my arm to keep me from falling and I'd enjoyed the physical contact, if not the circumstances. She gave me a peck on the cheek and shifted to help Pomy gather large cruets of extra virgin olive oil from around the table. It was a smart move. The sisters were pouring the olive oil in the path of another pair of attacking Macerators, with the expected results. Barbara and Perry used their chairs to anchor the slippery units in place temporarily.

The Macerators' movements were clumsy and their reaction times were slow. Thank goodness the person or group behind this attack hadn't had operators who knew what they were doing. Maybe we'd captured all their best people at Zwilniki's hangar and these were what they could scrape up on short notice. Either that, or this whole attack was a diversion.

Tomáso had rounded the table and was heading for Sherrhi and Diágo, absorbing damage from several Macerators in passing but not allowing anything to stand between him and his mate. I wouldn't want to get in his way in a battle tank.

Terrhi and Spike weren't anywhere to be seen.

I saw Martin out of the corner of my eye while trying to figure out a way up to the crane controls. He'd commandeered the Dauushan cutter-lifter and had managed to use it as a lever, causing one of the units to do a backflip, then a turtle imitation. Apple was using a similar maneuver with her martial arts skills and her chair when I spotted the scissors lift that had delivered the cake. It was off to the side, not far away. I ran toward it, reaching it only after dodging a unit trying to remove my spleen with its fists. The Macerator slid past me on a patch of floor covered in olive oil. That gave me time to hop on the platform and trigger the lift. A steel cable with a hook on the end was only a few feet away, so when the lift reached its highest level I jumped for it. Good thing, too. The Macerator attacking me collided with the lift seconds later, tipping it over. It tried to leap up and catch me, but Macerators would never make it in the NBA. A Tigrammath seven-year-old could out-jump them.

I pulled myself up the cable until I reached the rafters, glad I didn't have any olive oil on my hands. Then I flipped my leg over and got on top of the wide steel beam, disturbing a small, furry flying creature with owl-sized eyes that I expected was an escaped snack from a Quirinx flyer's lunch. Twenty feet further, I made it to the crane hoist itself. It was about the size of a

Volkswagen Beetle, with the same rounded shape to cover the large spools of cable. I was sure the primary operating console for the crane was close to the kitchen, but there were duplicate controls up here. I sat in the narrow seat in the tiny open operator's compartment and tried to learn them *tout de suite.*

It seemed simple enough—user interface design has come a long way in the past decade—so I sent the cables that had transported the *Dauushan Strata* back down to recapture the heavy metal pan still half full of food. I felt like a kid trying to grab the best toy with a mechanical claw at an arcade and was completely focused on the cables and my target. Then somebody smacked a baseball bat into my right side—at least it felt that way. My Orishen pupa silk shirt went rigid and I heard something small and metallic hit the floor. I looked down. It was a flattened piece of lead. I'd been shot. Again. Enough was enough. I'd just recovered from the last time. Unfortunately, the Macerator down below was still using me for target practice, and since I wasn't royalty, he didn't have to play nice. At least he was using a smaller caliber weapon, not his machine guns.

I leaned farther into the operator's compartment and hoped my attacker didn't have a clear line of sight to shoot me again. I heard six more shots, but didn't feel any more impacts, so apparently he didn't. I thought I was home free until he escalated. Something the size of a beer keg or a Tōdon smart watch—probably the motor from the scissors lift—struck the side of the crane housing—and me. It made a noisy clang and knocked me off my seat and out of the operator's compartment.

I didn't like the idea of falling from a fatal height twice in three days, so I flailed my arms and found a purchase before gravity could consummate its unrequited love. I was holding on to the lower rim of the operator's compartment with four fingers and trying, not very successfully, to do a one-armed pull-up. Just as the ATP in my finger muscles was exhausted and I lost my grip, a metal tentacle reached down and secured my wrist. Another tentacle circled my chest and pulled me back up to the crane operator's station. An octovac was holding me, gently bouncing up and down and looking like a dog that wanted a word of praise from its owner.

"Nice octovac," I said, rubbing the red light on its rounded dome, "Good octovac."

"You're welcome," said my phone. "They're helpful, aren't they?"

"You can say that again," I said, guiding the cables back on their way. "Thanks."

"Don't mention it," said my phone. "I sent the other one to help guard Terrhi."

I looked down. Several units were still operational, but not as many as I'd expected. CiCi had taken off her gown and heels and left them on the table. She'd joined Mike in removing Macerator power pack cylinders from the downed units, dressed only in a black slip and her underwear. Mike must lead with his head, because his forehead was bleeding from another gash—or maybe the one he'd received during the explosion at WT&F had reopened. CiCi's left shoulder was cut, but it didn't look too serious. Martin and Apple were unscathed and impressive. They'd taken down two units apiece and were looking for new targets.

The most remarkable sight on the battlefield, however, was Perry. He was looking proud and a bit smug after piercing the side of an attacker's armor with a six-foot Dauushan skewer like Achilles wielding his spear. He held a three-foot round metal lid in his left hand that he'd been using as a shield and his right foot was in the middle of his conquest's chest. I expected him to start quoting from *The Iliad*. Barbara was kneeling on the floor, looking up at him and smiling. She was holding a power pack cylinder in each hand.

One of the guards was down, lying on his side, but he'd managed to take one of the Macerators with him. The other guard had fared better. She'd knocked over and incapacitated two of

the units and was keeping a third distracted with fancy foot-
work while they traded punches.

Something big thumped outside in the dark, like a house
landing on the Wicked Witch of the East, but I didn't have
time to worry about it. I focused on the crane controls. When
the magnetic cables connected and the *Strata* pan rose, I moved
levers on the crane to get the mass of metal swinging in a circular arc a few feet wider than the table.

That's when I saw where Terrhi and Spike had been hiding.
They were under the table at the spot that had been cut away
for Queen Sherrhi to stand in. There was plenty of room below
the tabletop and the tablecloth covered the edge and hid what
was underneath. I heard Terrhi's high pitched voice, sounding
terrified, in an artificial sort of way.

"Help, help, save me," she cried.

The kid knew how to act.

A Macerator came to investigate and capture the Princess,
if possible. From my vantage point overhead I had a perfect
view of what happened next. Terrhi slipped around the unit
and positioned herself directly behind its knees. Then Spike
jumped up and forward from his hidden location under the
table, hitting the unit with all his mass at a high leverage point
on its chest. The Macerator tilted, encountered the fulcrum of
Terrhi's body, and flopped over to land on its back. The octovac helping Terrhi scuttled around the unit, removed its power
pack cylinders, and scooted back under the table with Spike
and Terrhi right behind, ready to pull the same trick on another unsuspecting victim.

I noticed that Queen Sherrhi, guarded by Diágo and Tomáso, had retreated to the far end of the hall and climbed up
the awards ceremony platform, seeking a highly defensible position. Three units were attacking, but Sherrhi, Tomáso, and
Diágo held the high ground and none of the Macerators had
yet reached the top. Then a machine gun fired from a spot in
front of the platform and bits of soundproofing fell from the

ceiling. When the echoes of the gunshots ended you could hear the pin on a hand grenade drop. Metaphorically, not literally.

I looked down in horror to see that two new Macerators had joined the attacking trio and were facing the platform. One held Poly by the neck, lifting her two feet off the ground, and the other held Pomy the same way.

"Queen Sherrhi," said the first unit's amplified voice. "Surrender now, or these women die."

Poly and Pomy were squirming, trying to get free, but the Macerators' grips were too strong and the sisters would choke if they struggled too hard.

"Don't do it, Your Majesty," said Diágo. "Billions of lives are at stake."

"And he'll probably kill them anyway," said Tomáso.

Thanks for that cheery thought.

"You must do your duty, my Queen," said Diágo.

"You must follow your heart," said Tomáso.

That's better, I mused.

They were stalling for me. I changed the arc of the heavy pan, making it more of an ellipse then a circle and moving it closer to the Macerators holding Poly and Pomy. Turns out I didn't need to bother.

Poly's dress billowed and extended long arms of fabric from its hem up and around her captor's shoulders, as if to embrace the unit. Then the mobile armored combat suit froze in place. Poly's dress returned to its normal shape and two power pack cylinders made a metallic clang as they landed on the floor. Her captor froze, with Poly, unfortunately, still two feet off the ground. At least she was no longer directly threatened. The unit holding Pomy took a step forward and restated its threat.

"Surrender, or she dies."

The Macerator's grip on Pomy's neck tightened and she gave a dry croak. Then, without warning, the unit dropped her and fell over on its back. Chit crawled out of the ear slot on the unit's helmet and flew to Pomy's shoulder.

"Did ya know you can trigger power failures from inside?" said my little friend in her big voice.

By then I'd managed to get the pan swinging on just the right arc. I let out more cable and watched with pleasure as the pan smacked into the three remaining Macerators and knocked them asterisk over arches.

I slid down one of the cables to the Strata pan, ruining my tuxedo shirt and tux in the process. Then I timed things and jumped off at just the right time to be able to land next to Poly. I didn't want her to be choking for any longer than necessary. Partners help each other.

When I reached her she was already on the floor, having, as usual, rescued herself. She'd asked the telepathically sensitive dress to pry open the unit's fingers. The two-foot drop hadn't been a problem. Have I mentioned that Poly is incredible?

We hugged and exchanged a brief, but quite satisfying kiss, then I took a look around to count noses.

Pomy was removing the power pack cylinders from the recently downed Macerators. Queen Sherrhi, Diágo and Tomáso were on the awards platform. Terrhi and Spike and her guardian octovac were coming out from their refuge under the table. The other octovac glided down from the rafters to join them. CiCi had tied a napkin around Mike's forehead and he'd tied one around her left shoulder. Martin was checking the rest of the downed Macerators to make sure none of them were playing possum and Apple was checking on the downed Dauushan guard, who just seemed to be unconscious.

The other guard had deactivated the last of its opponents and Perry and Barbara were giving each other the look that couples do when they've just survived a harrowing adventure with lots of adrenaline pumping. Their earlier coolness towards each other had vanished. Maybe they should take an autocab back to Ad Astra?

That was everyone accounted for, except…

Wait! Where was Shepherd?

Into the post-conflict quiet came a crash and a boom from outside loud enough to bring down a less well constructed building. The sound was followed by a splash like dropping half a dozen Tōdons into an extra large hot tub, followed in turn by a crunching sound like splintering wood. We all stood in shock. Kijanna and Pierre stepped tentatively into the hall from the kitchen, where they'd been staying out of harm's way. François emerged from under the other end of the table.

So that's where he'd disappeared to.

We looked at the wreckage and incapacitated Macerators scattered around us. Somebody whistled a long, descending scale. It might have been me.

Then Shepherd entered the hall through the large species door. He motioned for us to follow him and led us all, including Kijanna, François and Pierre, out of the hall and to the left, toward the river. I looked over my shoulder. François was the last in line. He flipped some switches by the door and the exterior lights came on again. Then I turned my head back and was gobsmacked for the *third* time that day.

In the lights' bright, congruent-energy glow I saw a heavily armed, two-hundred-and-fifty-foot, matte black robot. It was on its back, its ankles bound in the heavy fabric ribbon that had previously been wound around stanchions at the entrance to the restaurant. Some of it was still attached to its stanchions. The robot's feet were pointing toes up in the landscaping next to the building. Its hips and lower torso were blocking the river, and its head and upper body were crushing the trees on a neighboring section of Georgia state nature preserve.

"Oh my goodness, oh my goodness," squeaked Pierre, his normal cultured accent deserting him.

Oh my goodness indeed.

Chapter 25

"I'm completely operational and all my circuits
are functioning normally."
— HAL 9000

"Please go back inside, Your Majesty," said Diágo. "This may be just a ploy to get you outside and unprotected."

"There's a two-hundred-and-fifty-foot robot passed out on the grounds of the Teleport Inn," said Queen Sherrhi. "That's quite a lot of trouble to go to for a ploy."

I nodded in agreement, still processing everything that had happened.

"It's a robot, so it's not passed out," said Terrhi, who was rubbing Spike's head. "And its butt is in the Chattahoochee."

Terrhi rolled that word around a few times, enjoying the sound of it.

"Chattahoochee, Chatta*hoo*chee, Chatta-*HOO*-chee!"

"We get it," I said, smiling. "But Diágo's right. This whole stunt might be a diversion."

"To take me hostage?" said the Queen.

"Or *me*?" piped Terrhi. "I'm the Princess!"

I smiled, remembering what had happened the *last* time someone had kidnapped Terrhi.

"They clearly stated that their objective is to capture Sherrhi and Terrhi," said my phone.

"So please, Your Majesty, Your Highness," said Diágo, *"get back inside."*

Tomáso spoke up. He'd been checking for injuries.

"Lohrri and Naddéo will both be okay," he said.

"The Dauushan security guard out front and the bodyguard inside?" I asked.

"Correct," said Tomáso.

He started to head toward his family.

"Wait," I said. "Where *is* everybody?"

"What do you mean?" said Tomáso.

"We just fought a couple of dozen Macerators and a giant robot fell over and shook the rafters," I said. "Where are all the other Teleport Inn diners? I'd expect a hundred rubberneckers out here taking pictures."

"Didn't Sherrhi tell you?"

"Tell me what?"

"We reserved the entire Inn for the night."

"Oh," I said. I was honored, I think.

Tomáso left me to guide Queen Sherrhi, Princess Terrhi and Spike back into the large alien side of the restaurant. Diágo looked grateful. He and the other functional body-guard followed.

Kijanna and François took Pierre back inside as well. He was wringing his tentacles and babbling in broken French. I hoped they'd get him a dose of whatever Pyrs drank to calm their nerves.

Poly and Pomy were standing with their parents. It looked like they were all speaking to each other for a change. CiCi was holding Mike and Apple was telling Martin that he sure knew how to show a girl a good time.

Shepherd took me a few feet aside.

"Jack," he said.

"If you're not going to tell me how you took down this robot I'm not going to listen to you."

"Okay," said Shepherd, "but I need your help."

"What do you need *my* help for?" I pointed at the robot. "It looks like you did *quite* well on your own."

"It was luck, not skill," said Shepherd, "And you're the only person here who's been inside one of these things."

"Not *just* luck, I'm sure," I said. Shepherd was always in the know. "Fortune favors the prepared mind."

"I wasn't prepared for another one of *these*," he said.

"Are we sure it's another one?" I said. "Could it be the robot fabbed at WT&F?"

"You'd know better than I," said Shepherd.

"I could see if Mike is willing to go down and check the hangar."

I looked at my somewhat piratical-looking friend standing nearby. He had a bloody "bandana" wrapped around his head and was standing really close to CiCi. The two of them seemed absorbed in conversation. I hated to disturb them.

"Why don't you get a look at this robot's control room first," said Shepherd, who'd made the same observation. "You may be able to tell from that."

"Makes sense," I said.

"A visual examination of the control room should provide sufficient data to make a determination," said my phone.

The initiative it was showing continued to prove helpful.

"If its flight systems are still operational, I can probably get it down to the hangar tonight," I said.

"That would make Pierre and the Teleport Inn's insurance company happy, I expect," said Shepherd.

"Before I try to get in the control room, tell me again how you took the robot down."

"I never told you in the first place."

"Stop splitting hairs," I said.

"Why shouldn't I split hairs?" said the Pâkk, rubbing the fur on his forearm. "I've got so many of them."

Did Shepherd just make a joke? He was always so serious. I still had a lot to learn about Pâkk humor.

"Be that as it may," I said. "How am I going to get into the robot?"

Its head was on the other side of the river and the hatch on the back of its neck was probably blocked by a couple of snapped off conifers.

Mike and CiCi joined us—maybe he had attention neurons available for subjects other than CiCi after all, even if she was only wearing a slip that would barely count as a little black dress. He had an answer.

"I've been reviewing the fabrication plans," said Mike. "There should be a maintenance door where the 'collarbones' come together."

I needed to talk to Poly right away and get her okay on hiring Mike yesterday, or maybe the day before.

"Great," I said to Mike. "Show me, please."

Mike pulled out his phone and brought up the plans for the WT&F robot. He pointed to a spot just above the center of the main chest plate.

"I found it when I was reviewing the specs Monday night."

That's right, I thought. Mike was going to check out the robot's design after the octovacs.

Mike and I kept talking. CiCi excused herself and walked over to Poly and her family. She came back with Poly in tow.

"Was there something you wanted, *Lover Boy*," said Poly, giving me a quick kiss. "I need to get back to my family. We haven't talked this way in years."

"I'm glad the threat of imminent death was a bonding experience," I said.

Poly gently punched me in the shoulder—luckily *not* on the side where I'd been shot.

Now that Poly was here, I could see how she felt about hiring Mike.

Wait. Was CiCi a mind reader? No, probably just someone with a vested interest in Mike's happiness.

I whispered in Poly's ear. She grinned.

"You should have done that weeks ago."

"*We* should have done that weeks ago, partner," I replied.

"Hey Mike," I said.

He looked a bit puzzled, but rolled with it.

"How would you like to work for Xenotech Support Corporation?"

"Please," said Poly.

"Really?" said Mike. "Sure, I'd love to. I thought you'd never ask."

"Welcome aboard, Employee #1," I said.

"I wonder what my uncle will say," said Mike.

"Your uncle?"

Poly looked like she was figuring it out.

"My uncle," said Mike. "Jean-Jacques Bonhomme."

"I thought your last name was Goodman," I said.

"We anglicized it when my family moved to the States."

I let *that* revelation sink in, driven by a sledgehammer.

"You're a good man, Mike," said Poly, giving him a hug.

Literally, I thought.

CiCi nudged Poly out of the way and gave him a hug of her own.

"I'll say," she said.

"Hey Mike," I said again. "I thought you were an Army translator, but you took out Macerators like an expert. What gives?"

"Translator was my specialty when I left the service," he said, "but I spent two years in the Mobile Armored Infantry."

"Oh," I said. "Nice to know."

Mike had been a Macerator operator, but with the state-of-the-art military version, not a second hand, surplus model.

"You can put all that on your employment application," said Poly. "When you complete the required employment paperwork."

"We have employment paperwork?" I said.

"We will," said Poly.

She gave me another kiss, nodded to Shepherd, smiled at Mike and CiCi, and headed back to her family.

"Ummm…" I said. Having an employee was going to be more complicated than I was used to.

Then it turned out I had something else to worry about. Martin came over to us with a serious look on his face. Apple was with him and she looked concerned. Both of their outfits were still perfect. How his tux and her dress stayed spiffy after they took out two Macerators each, I didn't know. Spandex?

"Jack," said Martin, "we need to talk."

"In private?" I said.

"No," said Martin. "I just needed to tell you that I know how much you hate publicity, but I have to call this in."

"Of course you do," I said. "Pierre's going to need a police report to file a claim with his insurance carrier."

"It's bigger than that," said Martin, now in his Lieutenant Lee role. "This was a kidnapping attempt aimed at Dauushan royalty. I'm going to need to push this up the chain."

"You may want to talk to Tomáso before you do that," I said. "I expect he's already contacted the Dauushan Rangers, the Defense Department and the FBI."

"You've got a point," said Martin. "I'll check with him first."

"It was a pleasure to meet you, Jack," said Apple over her shoulder as she following her husband inside.

"Great to meet you, too," I said, before she was out of earshot.

"We'll only have a few minutes before this place is filled with members of the military and law enforcement," said Shepherd.

"Then we'd better check this robot out right away," I said. "Come on, Mike."

"Me?"

"You're part of Team Xenotech now," I said. "Consider yourself on the clock."

"I'm coming too," said CiCi.

"You won't be covered under the XSC liability policy," I said, smiling.

"Who gives a..."

"I'll tell Poly where you're going," said Chit from my shoulder.

"How long have *you* been there?"

"Since the Keen-Jones family discussions started getting sappy," said my little friend.

"That's good news, right?" I said.

"Yeah, but it would get lousy ratings on TV."

"Go tell Poly, and let her know I'll be careful."

"Like she'd believe *that,* bucko."

Chit flew over to Poly's family clump and, I hope, conveyed my message. Shepherd and Mike and CiCi and I made our way to the robot's feet. I grabbed a length of the fabric ribbon wrapped around the robot's ankles and started to pull myself up to its shins. My ribs informed me that climbing was a bad idea, but I kept going and even turned around to offer a hand to the others. My phone made my gesture meaningless, however. With an assist from the two octovacs, Mike, CiCi and Shepherd were already above me. When I joined them, I rubbed the nearest octovac's red dome. If it had been a dog it would have been wagging its tail. Chit rejoined us.

"Poly has a message for you," said Chit.

"What is it?"

"How's your list coming?"

I'd completely forgotten that we'd agreed to make lists of our favorite romantic vacation spots. I guess that was Poly's way of saying she wanted me to come back in one piece. I smiled. Then I laughed. Then my ribs hurt where I'd been shot. I'd have to cross some of the more strenuous potential vacation destinations off my list. Which reminded me…?

"How did you take down the robot?"

Shepherd was next to me as we climbed over the robot's left kneecap. Mike and CiCi were over on the other leg, climbing the right kneecap.

"Luck," said the Pâkk.

"You said that already."

"I'd heard a thump outside," he said.

"I heard it too," I said, "like Dorothy's house landing in the *Wizard of Oz.*"

"What?" said Shepherd.

"It's not important. Go on."

We were making our way along the robot's upper leg.

"I saw the robot standing next to the large alien side of the

Inn," said Shepherd. "It was reaching forward as if it was going to take the roof off the building."

And then pick up Queen Sherrhi and Terrhi, I thought.

"What did you do?"

"I grabbed as many crowd management stanchions as I could carry and wrapped heavy-duty fabric ribbons around its ankles."

We were crossing the robot's waist now.

"I saw that," I said.

"Hard t' miss," said Chit from my shoulder.

"When the robot tried to take a step forward to have a better angle to lift the roof," said Shepherd, "it just fell over."

"That's it?" I said. "You tripped it? No secret Pâkk technology tricks? No wisdom gained from childhood rites of passage?"

"No," said Shepherd. "I got lucky."

I shook my head back and forth, incredulous. My illusions of Pâkk invincibility were shattered.

"Uh, Jack," said Chit.

"What?"

"That means the robot's not necessarily deactivated," said the Murm.

We were up to the robot's chest now.

"Why didn't you tell me this earlier?" I asked Shepherd.

"I didn't want to shatter your illusions of Pâkk invincibility."

I didn't say anything. We'd reached the maintenance hatch between the 'collarbones.'

My phone hopped down and used its mutakey function to circumvent security and open the round entryway. Mike led the way—he was the one who'd studied the robot's design, after all—and we hunched over to follow a tube with a low-ceiling that led from the robot's chest to its neck to its head. CiCi was behind me and Shepherd brought up the rear, except for the pair of octovacs.

When we approached the internal hatch leading to the control room I had to step around u-shaped pieces of steel rod welded to the floor. It was a ladder, for use when the robot was vertical, not horizontal. I checked, and this hatch wasn't locked. I moved in front of Mike in Captain James T. Kirk style, opened the hatch, and stuck my head into the control room. I couldn't see much from this angle so I stepped all the way inside. Mike, CiCi and Shepherd followed. Then I walked around to the far side of the pilot's chair.

How many times in one day can a guy's eyes get as big as saucers?

Cornell, one of Anthony Zwilniki's more annoying henchmen, was lying on the floor, out cold.

"Seat belt," said my phone.

I looked. Cornell hadn't fastened his safety harness. When the robot fell over, Cornell must have been tossed around the control room and knocked unconscious.

Shepherd produced a couple of zip ties from his vest. Was he always ready to immobilize someone?

Mike fastened the ties around Cornell's wrists and ankles.

"Do you think you can pilot this thing?" I asked him.

"Sure," said my first employee. "You did it. How hard can it be?"

I didn't dignify that with an answer.

"Take it down to Zwilniki's hangar," I said. "Fly low and slow and under the radar. We don't want anyone calling the authorities to say they saw a giant robot."

"Not a problem," said Mike. "I can do this. You do know this is a morphogenic robot, right?"

"Its body is Orishen," I said. "I'd expect it to be."

"I'm going to program it to look like a T-Rex," said Mike. "It will only take a minute."

"Because who's going to call in to say that they saw a flying robot tyrannosaur decked out with missiles and autocannons?" said CiCi, smiling.

"Or believe them if they do?" said Shepherd.

"Fine by me," I said.

"How are you going to get into the hangar?" asked CiCi.

"Call Martin," I said. "He'll give you the door code."

My phone gave Mike's phone the number for Martin's phone. "Thanks," said Mike. "That should work."

He took the pilot's seat, strapped on his safety harness, and pointed CiCi at the optional co-pilot's station. She strapped in, too. He started to run through a checklist on the pilot's console.

Shepherd and I made our way down from the robot's head and out its "collarbone" maintenance hatch. Cornell, trussed up with zip ties, was slung from the two octovacs walking between us. When we reached the robot's feet again, the octovacs transported Cornell, then the two of us, down to ground level. There weren't any military or law enforcement vehicles on site. Maybe Tomáso had dissuaded Martin from calling all cars.

My phone instructed the octovacs to put Cornell down just inside the Inn. Then they returned to the robot where they carefully unwound the fabric ribbon from its ankles. When they were finished, Shepherd, the two octovacs, and I stepped inside the hall and stood next to our prisoner. Cornell was still out. I could see a large, purple goose egg rising on the back of his head. Couldn't happen to a nicer guy.

Poly and her family were standing together near the table halfway down the hall. I hoped Poly was filling Pomy and Perry and Barbara in on why the Macerators had attacked. Martin and Apple were talking to Tomáso, who was down by the award ceremony platform at the far end with Queen Sherrhi, Terrhi, Spike and the royal body guards. Poly gave me a thumbs up as Shepherd and I, with octovacs doing the heavy lifting, transported an unconscious Cornell past her and her family to the front of the hall.

We all had an excellent view of the robot through the Teleport Inn's tall windows. We heard a squishy, creaking sound as its exterior reconfigured itself from well-armed giant robot to well-armed giant robot dinosaur. Transformation complete, it got back on its feet, leaving broad scrapes in the lawn outside. Huge splinters of shattered pines fell from its head and shoulders and a six-foot wall of water, dammed by its hips, went sweeping down the river. I hoped no one was fishing downstream at eleven o'clock at night. Then I heard a familiar rumble. The robot's boot thrusters were kicking in. Seconds later it was airborne, its rockets' red glare fading into the night.

Chapter 26

"Sometimes when you push someone,
you find out who that person really is."
— Keith Ablow

"My name is Gordon Ambrose Cornell. I'm thirty-six years old, self-employed, and live in Alpharetta, Georgia."

It was the twentieth time I'd heard Cornell recite his name, rank and serial number and I was getting tired of it. Martin had arrested him for damaging the landscaping at the Teleport Inn and destroying trees in a state nature preserve. I didn't know if there was a law against operating a two-hundred-and-fifty-foot combat robot and neither did Martin, which was just as well, because I'd be equally guilty.

Cornell was tied to a chair on the award ceremony platform with cords the chefs at the Inn used to truss up turkeys. The cords' new use seemed particularly apt under the circumstances. Shepherd, Martin and I were standing on the platform. Chit was on my shoulder and Tomáso was on the floor so he could look the man who tried to kidnap his wife and daughter in the eye. If I were Cornell, I'd be intimidated. Unfortunately, Cornell didn't have the same reaction.

The last two hours had been eventful. Poly and her family had taken my van back to their hotel. Poly hugged me and said she was so glad she'd invited her parents and sister for her graduations. A pair of giant, pink, heavily armored tanks the size of wide-load eighteen wheelers had pulled up in front of the Inn to transport Queen Sherrhi, Terrhi, Spike and her security detail back to the Dauushan consulate. The tanks had oversized rubber tires instead of treads and triangular fuchsia flags with white crowns flew from their front corners. Mike's car was driving itself to Zwilniki's hangar by the airport. François had put CiCi's dress, neatly folded, in the front passenger seat along with her shoes. Apple had kissed Martin goodbye and left in their car, saying their sitter turned into a pumpkin at midnight. Martin's Capitol Police cruiser had been summoned and the two helpful octovacs seemed to have disappeared along with my top hat.

I collected a dozen discarded Macerator power pack cylinders off the floor and wrapped them in a Dauushan-sized napkin. You never know when things like that might come in handy, either as energy sources or as high explosives if all their energy is released at once. I stowed the bundle of cylinders unobtrusively by the entrance.

Two squads of soldiers had arrived in olive drab trucks and a transport van an hour ago. They'd expeditiously extracted the two dozen men and women from the disabled Macerators and bundled them off in the van. Several of the enlisted men had snickered at the operators' incompetence, but the officer in charge of the detail had assured us the operators' injuries would be seen to promptly. A different group of soldiers with forklifts showed up next. In less than fifteen minutes, they'd carted all the empty combat suits into a truck and had driven off. I didn't think too much about where the soldiers had come from, though Dobbins Air Reserve Base, where Tomáso had said his rapid response force was located, was just up I-75.

Kijana had taken Pierre home. She'd said she'd stay with the distraught little Pyr until he got to sleep. The chefs and kitchen staff had left, too. François had mopped up the oil in the hall and straightened up some of the wreckage, but last I'd seen him he'd been sitting in the kitchen with a large snifter and a bottle of *Calvados Napoléon*.

François would stick around and lock up, but for now we were alone and not making much progress in our interrogation.

Shepherd, Martin, Chit, Tomáso and I left Cornell to stew and moved to the far end of the hall by the door to talk privately.

"I don't understand why this jerk isn't still in jail," I said.

"I didn't hear about it myself," said Martin.

"Aren't you in law enforcement?" I said. "Aren't your brothers and sisters in blue supposed to keep you informed?"

"Different hierarchies," said Martin. "The port is City of Atlanta territory, and I'm with the state."

I dimly remembered something about the mayor taking credit for Cornell, Penn and Princeton, but I was recovering from a concussion at the time. I turned to Shepherd.

"And what about you? Are my illusions of Pâkk omniscience going to be shattered, too?"

Shepherd just shrugged. Crap. He didn't even give me something to rant about. Tomáso looked down at his Pâkk friend and shook his big head side to side. Maybe his illusions regarding Shepherd weren't doing so well, either.

"Gordon Ambrose Cornell was released from the Atlanta City Detention Center at nine on Monday morning," said my phone.

About the time I was having a second breakfast with Poly, I thought.

"Bail was posted for him and his two associates by his lawyer, someone named J. S. Walters."

"Would that be Jennifer Susan Walters?" I said.

"Correct," said my phone.

"Then we're dealing with another pseudonym. Jennifer Susan Walters is a lawyer, all right—in Marvel comic books. She's Bruce Banner's cousin, She-Hulk."

"Missed that," said my phone.

"I thought they were using college and university names, like Duke Vanderbilt," said Martin.

"And Cornell, Penn and Princeton," intoned Tomáso.

"Maybe they're getting smart and changing their pattern?" I said.

"Or maybe we're dealing with a different team?" said Martin.

"With the same players?" I said, pointing at Cornell back on the award ceremony platform and wondering what Penn and Princeton were up to. "That doesn't make sense."

"Why are you arguin' over comic book characters?" said a voice from my left shoulder.

Chit had a point.

"Do you have a better idea?"

"I might," she said. "It's just a matter of findin' the proper incentive."

"Like what?" I said.

Chit whispered something in my ear. I listened and nodded my head slowly. It might work.

Then Chit flitted over and whispered to Martin, Tomáso, and finally Shepherd. The Påkk didn't look happy. I could understand why.

"No," said Shepherd.

"Come on," I said, "restore my faith in the Påkk mystique."

"I have no interest in pandering to your human misconceptions," said Shepherd.

"It's Cornell's misconceptions you'd need to play to," I said.

"My answer is still no. The very idea is repugnant."

"But the misconceptions are about Short Påkk, not Long Påkk," I said. "And you can't tell me it's never happened on a Short Påkk hunt."

"To the eternal regret of every Long Påkk across the galaxy," said Shepherd. "I can't do it."

"My friend," said Tomáso. "My old and very dear friend. I do not ask for myself, but for the sake of my queen and my daughter."

Shepherd stood silent.

"We would never speak of it," Tomáso rumbled.

The rest of us all nodded solemnly.

"Very well," said Shepherd. "I will do this distasteful thing."

That was probably not the best choice of words.

"I'll start us off," I said. "Follow my lead."

As we walked back to the award ceremony platform, we could see Cornell staring at us. He wasn't sure what would happen next.

"No way," I said to Shepherd, speaking loudly.

"My friend, this must not be done," said Tomáso. "It is unworthy of you."

"Go ahead," Chit said to Shepherd in her surprisingly loud voice. "Maybe I'll try some, too."

"Hey," I said, "One monster is enough."

Shepherd growled.

By now we were up to the award ceremony platform. Shepherd climbed up the stairs and stood very close to Cornell, growling louder and licking his lips. Cornell was sweating and squirming in his bonds.

"I don't want to watch this," I said, turning around to face away from the platform.

"Neither do I," said Martin. "Remember, you said you'd stop at his elbows."

"No promises," said Shepherd, opening his mouth to reveal rows of sharp teeth.

Cornell's hands were white from gripping the arms of his chair. He was looking left and right and moaning softly.

The Pâkk used a claw to slit Cornell's right sleeve and rip it away, leaving his prisoner's arm bare.

The chair started to shake from Cornell's trembling.

"Stay in control, my friend," said Tomáso, turning his back. ""You have to give him one last chance to answer."

"No promises," repeated the Pâkk.

Despite his earlier reluctance he seemed to be really getting into his part. Saliva dripped from his mouth onto Cornell's bare forearm.

Chit rotated on my shoulder to watch Shepherd.

"T' hell with questions," she said. Her bloodthirsty tone made me start to worry if we'd pushed things too far.

Shepherd was leaning over with his mouth open and ready to bite when Cornell lost his nerve.

"Questions," he said, "ask your questions. I'll spill, I'll spill."

Shepherd paused, but didn't lean back. His warm breath

swayed the hairs on the back of Cornell's arm.

"Keep him away from me!" said Cornell.

"My friend," said Tomáso. "Let him answer."

Something between a growl and a whine came from the back of Shepherd's throat, but he stepped back. The rest of us turned around. Martin and I climbed up to the award ceremony platform and stood between Shepherd and Cornell. Chit stayed on my left shoulder. Tomáso stood at the edge of the platform glaring at Cornell. This time, Cornell *was* intimidated.

"Who hired you to operate the robot?" said Martin.

"Columbia Brown," said Cornell. "This whole thing is her deal."

He'd looked particularly nervous when he'd said her name.

"She worked for Zwilniki?"

"No," said Cornell, "She was at the same level or higher than Tony Zed, but for a different part of the organization. I always got the sense that she scared him."

Curious, I thought. Like she scared Cornell.

"What's Brown's plan?" said Martin.

"I don't know," said Cornell. "I'm just a foot soldier for her. I was a lieutenant for Tony. One of the guys at training was joking about balls and bugs, though."

"Balls and bugs?" I said.

"Spheres and nanoparticles," muttered Chit by my ear.

"Training?" said Tomáso.

"Robot pilots' training," said Cornell. "We only had a day and a half for it."

"Where?"

"I don't know," said Cornell.

Shepherd growled.

"I really don't know. It was inside. On simulators. There weren't any windows. Underground, maybe."

"How many pilots were there?" asked Martin.

"Twelve."

"Including the other two clowns in jail with you?" said Chit.

"Uh huh," said Cornell. "All three of us."

I wondered what were they going to do with *twelve* giant robots.

"And what was your mission supposed to be?" I said.

"Take advantage of the chaos caused by the Macerators, lift off the roof of the Teleport Inn, steal the Queen and the Princess, and fly them to a rendezvous point."

"Where?" I said.

"A big hangar near Hartsfield port. I think they wanted to get the Queen and her kid off planet fast."

Now it was Tomáso's turn to make threatening noises.

"What's the exact location?" I said. I may have growled myself.

Cornell told us. My phone chirped to acknowledge that it had recorded the details and marked the spot.

"What was up with the Macerator operators?" asked Martin. "The didn't seem to know what they were doing."

"They trained separately," said Cornell, "but the robot pilot trainers considered them jokes, only there to provide a distraction."

"While you literally raised the roof?"

"Yeah. I think they got the Macerator operators from Craigslist."

That explained a lot, I thought. We'd probably gotten as much out of Cornell as we were going to.

I motioned to my companions.

"Step into my office," I said, waving toward the far end of the hall.

We all walked back near the rolling door, out of Cornell's earshot.

When we stopped walking, my phone read me a new text message from Mike.

"The robot is not the one from WT&F. I parked it next to the WT&F robot in Zwilniki's hangar."

"Tell him thanks," I said. "And let him know he can take the rest of the night off."

It was already two in the morning and Mike and CiCi would soon be on their way to their homes, or maybe one of their apartments.

"Thanks, boss," read my phone.

Thanks, Jack, would be fine, but I'd worry about that tomorrow, or rather, later today.

"Do you have anywhere you can keep Cornell on ice temporarily?" I asked Martin.

"There's a holding cell several levels below ground at the Capitol," he said. "It would be perfect."

"Great," I said. "I'm going to check out the rendezvous point."

"I'm going to have a high altitude drone scan O'Sullivan Fabrication's facility with ground penetrating radar," said Tomáso. "If they've got a duplicate shadow production floor and biohazard lab fifty feet down, I want to know about it."

"Works for me," I said. "I'll let you know what I find out."

Heads nodded around our circle. Shepherd didn't volunteer to do anything. He just looked thoughtful and enigmatic and full of Pâkk mystique.

"I guess I need a ride," I said.

"Your van is waiting for you outside," said my phone.

Another attempt at reconnaissance was in order. I hoped it would turn out better than the last time.

Chapter 27

"Third rate romance, low rent rendezvous."
— Sammy Kershaw

When I got in my van I was pleasantly surprised. The two missing octovacs were on the floor in front of the rear bench seat, bouncing up and down on their tentacles, eager to see me and collect dome rubs. My backpack tool bag was between the two front seats. Clean clothes were neatly piled on the passenger-side captain's chair, along with a pair of sensible shoes. Poly had even included a box of wipes I'd had in the kitchen so I could get the grease from the crane hoist cables off my hands and face. The wipes would also help remove stray bits of *Dauushan Strata* from my ankles.

I put the bundle of power pack cylinders I'd snagged on my way out of the Teleport Inn next to my backpack tool bag and took off my thoroughly trashed tuxedo. I smiled when I saw that Poly had thoughtfully provided a plastic garbage bag where I could put it so I didn't get grease all over my van's clean interior.

It was a positive pleasure to take off the polished patent leather shoes—now not so shiny—and lose the uncomfortably thin formal socks. I used the wipes to clean myself off and checked my Orishen pupa silk shirt where the bullet had struck. It was undamaged, without even a smear of lead. Lucky me. Taking things off hadn't helped my bruised ribs, but it beat having my tux cut away by doctors in the emergency room.

Once I'd parted with my formal duds, I changed into the outfit Poly had picked out for me, putting on the black jeans, black long-sleeved GALTEX 2029 souvenir t-shirt a client had picked up for me in Las Vegas, fluffy black socks, and black Chuck Taylor All-Stars. My ensemble's monochromatic look suited my mood and the hour.

I double-checked to make sure my light shifting Blend Into

The Scenery coverall was still stowed in my backpack. It had been designed by the team at Morphicouture to make stage hands nearly invisible when moving sets. I smiled when I remembered how it had kept Poly safely hidden at Zwilniki's hangar six weeks ago. It had been fun hugging and kissing her while she was wearing it. Poly wearing the coverall was something you didn't see every day. I didn't know what I'd find when I got to the rendezvous point near Hartsfield port and figured I'd need all the help I could get to remain undiscovered.

While my backpack tool bag was open, I removed a couple of power pack cylinders from the bundle and dropped them inside. Then I noticed Chit's bottle, pulled it out, and opened it.

"Hey Chit," I said, but didn't hear an answer.

"Hey *Chit*," I repeated, louder this time.

"Wha…?"

She'd been sleeping on my shoulder.

"Back in your bottle, little buddy," I said. "Time to get some sleep in your own bed."

Chit yawned.

"How d'ya know Murms use beds?"

"I don't," I said, "So hop in your bottle and get back in your pod or your crypt or hang from the lid for all I know. Eat bon bons, take a bubble bath, watch your shows—just unwind and get some rest. You've earned it."

"Yeah, I guess I have, haven't I?"

Chit yawned again and lazily flew off my shoulder and into her bottle. I put the lid back on and stowed it, wishing I could get some rest, too. I buckled my seat belt and leaned back in my seat.

"Art thou ready?" said my van.

"Verily," I responded. "Remember, we want to scout around first, not pull right up in front of the place."

"Of course, my lord."

The white knight, his trusty steed, his hounds, and his faithful companions set forth to scope out the villain's stronghold, or something like that. Then I yawned, a victim of Chit's contagious magic. It had been a long day, and wasn't over yet. The adrenaline from the Macerator's attack had worn off hours ago and I was running on fumes.

"Stop at the Flying Biscuit Café on Northside Drive on the way," I said. "Don Quixote needs sustenance."

We were headed down I-75, the fastest route to the airport from the Teleport Inn, and the restaurant was only two exits away. My van didn't reply to my request, but its stereo started playing the soundtrack from *Man of La Mancha,* so I guess it had gotten the message. We still had a few minutes before we got off the interstate.

"What can you tell me about the rendezvous point?" I asked my phone.

"It's a hangar about the same size as Zwilniki's," it said, "only older construction and another five minutes farther south."

"Who owns it?"

"San Simeon Realty."

"San Simeon?" I said "Where Hearst Castle is located?"

"Yes," said my phone, tentatively.

"And didn't Hearst push the United States into war with Spain back in 1898?"

"Remember the *Maine*," said my phone.

"Right," I said, "Just like James K. Polk expanded the U.S. by war with Mexico, Hearst's war got us the Philippines and Cuba."

"Don't forget Puerto Rico and Guam," said my phone.

"How could I *ever* forget Guam."

I had a brochure for a romantic getaway resort there.

"Checking corporate ownership databases now," said my phone. "San Simeon Realty is a subsidiary of the Gran Palo Group."

"Big Stick?" I asked. "Like Teddy Roosevelt's phrase, 'Speak softly and carry a big stick?'"

"Probably," said my phone, "since Gran Palo is owned by the EUA Corporation."

It always came back to the EUA Corporation.

My van slowed and pulled to a gentle stop in front of the Flying Biscuit Café's drive-thru electronic menu board.

"Sustenance, O Knight of the Noble Countenance."

"Thanks," I said.

My phone sniffed.

"What?"

"You could have at least played along and said 'Thank you, loyal steed.'"

"Just be glad I'm not nicknaming the van *Rocinante*," I said.

"*Waddwudjaliekt'nite,*" said a tinny, hard to decipher voice from the speaker in the middle of the menu board.

"A chicken sausage biscuit, an apple butter biscuit, and a Diet Starbuzz, please."

"*Chikbisk-buttrbisk-diebuzz?*" said the voice.

"Yes," I said. What else could I say?

"*Nineosevn. Nexwindda.*"

I pulled to the next window and my phone hopped up on my left shoulder and tendered nine U.S. dollars and seven cents in a near-field ecommerce transaction. A minute later a warm bag and a cold bottle were handed to me. I looked in the bag. The order seemed correct.

"Forward, loyal steed!" I said.

My van slowly accelerated out of the restaurant and resumed its route to our rendezvous.

My phone made three quick, happy chirps.

"What?"

"You're a nice guy."

"Thanks. Let's hope I don't finish last."

I put the Diet Starbuzz bottle in a convenient cup holder and opened the bag, pulling out the savory smelling wrapped biscuit first. The Flying Biscuit Café was another Atlanta area institution. They'd been around for thirty-five years and had eighteen locations. I'd been pleased when they'd added 24-hour drive through service in 2028 and loved their tall, light

biscuits and delicious chicken sausage. I always ordered a second biscuit with just apple butter and treated it as dessert. It
was that good.

We were close to our destination. I had finished my sausage
biscuit and was spreading apple butter on the second half of
my dessert biscuit when my phone interrupted my meal.

"Hartsfield space traffic control just cleared a starship for departure from the pad outside the rendezvous hangar."

I looked up from apple buttering and saw a pillar of congruency generated fire ascending into the sky ahead of us. Starship
launches are beautiful whether they're carrying friends or foes.

"Crap," I said. "We're too late."

"It's not like Sherrhi and Terrhi were on board," said my phone.

"But we might have caught someone higher up in the organization that's threatening Dauush," I said. "Sherrhi and Tomáso
would have wanted us to."

"You can still search the hangar for clues," said my phone.

"Yeah," I said. "We can try, but I bet we don't find anything."

I have never been happier to be wrong.

Since the starship had departed, I skipped trying to be subtle
and asked my van to pull up in front of the small door to the
left of the huge main hangar door. The building was enormous,
four or five stories tall, steel framed and painted a dull enamel
gray. There weren't any lights on outside, so I put my backpack
tool bag over my shoulder and walked to the small door. I had
my phone run a few scans to make sure the place wasn't filled
with explosives or toxins or poisonous snakes. I also checked
for security systems, dead fall traps and other sneaky things
paranoid people might devise. From what my rudimentary
scans could determine, the place was empty and its security
system could be circumvented by a bright third grader with a
paper clip.

My phone, in mutakey mode, opened the door. I pushed it
open and stuck my head inside. Unlike in Zwilniki's hangar,
ceiling lights didn't come on automatically. The echoes in the

place made it sound large and empty, but I couldn't confirm the accuracy of that impression because I couldn't see more than a few feet in front of me. The only reason I could see *anything* was because photons from my van's headlights filtered in.

I shifted my backpack tool bag around to where I could reach it and pulled a congruency-powered flashlight from a long, narrow, zippered side pouch. I set it to throw a wide beam and waved the arm holding it in a wide arc. The trusses in the ceiling fifty feet above me showed as ghostly webs of struts. My flashlight's beam wouldn't reach all the way across the space, so I moved further inside to explore.

It was very quiet. I shuffled my feet noiselessly so that I could be alert for any possible sound that might presage an attack. When I got close to the wall farthest from the door, where the stairs and elevators had been in Zwilniki's hangar, I heard something. I swung my flashlight in the direction of the sound, but didn't see anything. Then I heard it again. It was a scrabbling, tapping, moaning sound down near the floor. I walked toward it, scanning ahead of me with my light. Then the edge of my flashlight beam found the source of the sound.

A short-haired black man, about my age and build, in khakis and a white, button-down Oxford shirt was lying on the floor against the back wall of the hangar, between a stairwell and what looked like a freight elevator entrance. He was tied hand and foot with thick rope and gagged with a red silk necktie. I noticed he was wearing dark sunglasses, which seemed an odd choice in the darkened warehouse. When he saw me he struggled harder and moaned louder, tapping the soles of his shoes against the wall. I bent down and removed his gag.

"Are you okay?"

"Yeah," he said. His voice was hoarse.

I was about to work on the rope around his hands when I saw his eyes go wide. That gave me enough warning to lean forward and take most of a heavy blow from a blunt object on my shoulders, rather than the back of my head. My pupa silk shirt went rigid and absorbed most of the force of the blow. I was pleased to avoid another concussion but expected I'd have sore shoulders to go with my sore ribs. I rolled with the impact, fell to the concrete floor and collapsed, pretending to be out cold.

I heard voices I recognized.

"It's Buckston," said Princeton.

"He's bad news," said Penn. "Tie him up fast and put 'em both in the elevator."

I kept my body limp and my eyes closed. One of them tied my arms and legs with the same thick rope and dragged me along a concrete floor, over a metal threshold, and onto a wooden one. It must be the freight elevator. I still had my backpack tool bag over my shoulder. They must have dragged the other prisoner in with me since I felt his back land on my legs when they dropped him. If only Chit wasn't asleep, she could have followed Penn and Princeton back to Columbia Brown's headquarters. Then I had something more pressing to worry about.

"How long did you set it for?" said Penn.

"Fifteen minutes," said Princeton.

"Make it ten. We can go out through one of the loading docks and save time."

"Works for me."

Penn and Princeton left and I heard the elevator descend, then stop. I opened my eyes and saw in the dim glow of the elevator's emergency lights that we were stuck between floors. This was not good.

"A little help here," I said.

"Just a second," said my phone, extruding a sharp blade from its case.

I rubbed the rope between my wrists against the blade, then untied the bonds around my feet. My phone had started to help the other man get free. I noticed there was a logo on his Oxford shirt—O'Sullivan Fabrication. Once all his ropes were cut I helped him to his feet and watched him rub his wrists and his ankles to restore circulation. When his limbs were working again, he pushed his sunglasses up on his forehead.

"I'm Jack Buckston," I said, extending my hand. "I wish we could have met under more pleasant circumstances."

"Ray Ray Dunwoody," said the man. "Me, too. My father's told me about you."

"We don't have much time to get acquainted."

"True," said Ray Ray. "Where do you think they put the bomb?"

"Odds are good it's in here with us."

"I was afraid you were going to say that."

I held up my phone and hoped it would help me find the device.

"Lumos," I said. My phone's screen lit up and in the increased illumination I could see a cantaloupe-sized metal sphere resting in a circular holder screwed into the floor on the far side of the elevator.

"That's a nova bomb," said Ray Ray.

I admired the way he could say that without any hint of panic in his voice. Ray Ray had a cool head in a crisis.

"Yep," I said. "They must want to blow up the entire hangar."

"And everything for three hundred yards around it," said Ray Ray, "Given the M.E.R."

"M.E.R.?" I said.

"Megaton Equivalent Rating," said Ray Ray. "It's on the side of the sphere."

"Nine minutes," said my phone.

"First, let's get out of this elevator," I said. "Then we'll worry about the bomb."

"I'm on board with that," said Ray Ray. "What can I do?"

"Check the ceiling and floor for maintenance panels," I said. "Maybe we can get out that way?"

"Worth a shot," said Ray Ray, starting a visual inspection.

The freight elevator was ten feet wide, twenty feet long and eight feet tall. It had a wooden floor, wooden walls covered with thick padded mats, and a steel mesh ceiling. Its door was also steel and made in two parts. One went up and one down, but they weren't going to budge. The safety interlocks were engaged because we were between floors.

Ray Ray was quickly, but methodically checking the ceiling and floor for possible exits. I dug a congruency-powered penlight out of my backpack tool bag and gave it to him.

"Use this, please," I said. "I need my phone to focus on overriding the control panel."

Ray Ray didn't waste time by replying. He just took the penlight and resumed his search. I lifted my phone to the panel filled with buttons.

"Eight minutes."

"And counting," I said. "I get it. What do you see behind the panel?"

"An explosive charge set to go off if anyone tries to change the position of the elevator in the shaft," said my phone.

"That doesn't sound good," I said.

"What doesn't?" said Ray Ray, inspecting the ceiling near the nova bomb.

"If we mess with the panel, we're dead."

"Good thing I found a maintenance panel in the ceiling, then," said Ray Ray.

"Where?"

"There."

Ray Ray pointed to a spot in the steel mesh ceiling directly above the nova bomb. It was a two by three-foot trap door that opened up, into the elevator shaft.

"Only one problem," said Ray Ray.

"Seven minutes," said my phone.

"What's that?"

"It's locked."

My phone and I both laughed.

"Is *that* all?"

I walked over to the nova bomb, taking care not to touch it

by accident, and tossed my phone toward the ceiling. It hit the steel mesh gently and extruded dozens of tiny arms to hang on. Then it moved hand over hand over hand to get to the trap door. It was closed with a simple combination lock like I used at the gym. My phone shifted to mutakey mode and after three seconds of probing, the lock opened. We were home free. Then I saw an arc of electricity as wide as a garden hose jump from the lock to my phone. Stars flashed across my retinas and the hairs on my neck stood up. I smelled ozone and watched, horrified, as my phone fell straight down toward the nova bomb. Despite my compromised vision, I managed to catch it in mid-fall like a center fielder snagging a pop-up. I pulled it close to my body, then looked up when a second, even larger arc of electricity welded the treacherous lock shut again, sealing us in the elevator.

I guessed there were less than six minutes left before the nova bomb vaporized everything within a five hundred galmet radius.

"You okay?" I said to my phone.

It didn't answer. A crisped and blackened corner of its muta-case broke off in my hand. My heart sank.

Crap.

Crap. Crap. Crap.

I opened my backpack tool bag and carefully wrapped my phone in the fabric of my B.I.T.S. coverall. It was probably a futile gesture, considering we were all likely to be reduced to our constituent atoms in a few minutes, but it made me feel better.

"Got any ideas?" I asked Ray Ray.

"Maybe," he said. "Got any high explosives in that bag?"

"Would these do?" I said, pulling out the pair of Macerator power pack cylinders.

"They might."

Ray Ray examined the cylinders.

"There are pictures on the sides explaining how to use these as time bombs," he said.

Maybe the Macerators' designers were fans of the George S. Patton quote about the object of war not being to die for your country, but to make the other poor, dumb bastard die for his. The cylinders would be unexpectedly potent weapons for a soldier's last stand.

"You want to blow us up *before* the nova bomb goes off?" I said.

"No," said Ray Ray. "I want to damage the containment sphere around the nova bomb. The congruent circuitry inside it is delicate. If we can breach the sphere, we have a chance of disabling the nova bomb."

"And how do we live through the power pack cylinder explosions?" I asked.

"Grab all the padded mats off the walls and stack them up on the side away from the nova bomb," he said. "Make an enclosed lean-to for protection from the smaller blast."

"Got it."

I pulled all the mats down and dragged them to the end of the elevator car farthest away from the nova bomb, while Ray Ray fiddled with the power pack cylinders.

"Get under the mats," he said. "Leave me an opening at one end so I can jump inside. I'm setting these for ten seconds."

"You're using both?"

"I have to make sure they crack the containment sphere."

"If you say so."

"Don't worry," said Ray Ray. "I'm a trained engineer."

Somehow that wasn't reassuring.

I wriggled under my lean-to made of mats and made sure there was a small opening at one end for Ray Ray to enter. The clock in my head said we were cutting it really close. I heard the snap of relays engaging on the power pack cylinders and heard Ray Ray's footsteps running this way. I held the mat in front of me open so Ray Ray would have more room. When the ten second countdown I was reciting reached three, Ray Ray dived in next to me and I pulled the mat in tight behind him. I exhaled, covered my ears with my upper arms, and pressed my face deeply into the mat I'd put on the floor. Then I felt a blow like Thor's hammer crushing me into Captain America's shield, combined with a large dose of "Hulk Smash."

The floor tilted up and Ray Ray and I—riding on a mat--began to slide toward the far end of the elevator, which was now substantially lower than our end. The only thing that stopped us was the mat catching on a random splintered floorboard bent upward by the blast. After five minutes, Ray Ray and I were a bit more together. Our noses were bleeding and our ears were ringing, but we could at least stand up.

I wiped my nose on my sleeve and looked around. The far end of the elevator was gone, including whatever hardware had held that end of the car on its tracks. We leaned over the edge of broken floorboards and saw the cracked sphere of the nova bomb at the bottom of the shaft, two levels below us. Ray Ray and I were lucky to be alive. Our ears weren't working too well, so I mimed a heartfelt "thank you" at Ray Ray. His fast thinking had saved my life, and his own. He smiled and made a thumbs up gesture. We'd survived.

Now we needed to get out of this mangled elevator. It was four o'clock on a Thursday morning in a deserted hangar and the explosion had been contained to the elevator shaft, not affecting the rest of the building. The blast might have shown up on a seismograph in a lab at Georgia Tech as a small blip on a graph, but I didn't expect a plume of smoke to be rising from the roof to summon the authorities. I didn't know when or if anyone would ever show up to investigate and get us out. I was also concerned that the elevator car might decide to see if gravity still worked and reduce its potential energy by falling. Then I looked up and saw one of the sweetest sights I'd seen in hours—a pair of octovacs coming down the elevator shaft to pull Ray Ray and me to safety.

When we were lifted all the way to the top and back in my van, after lots of dome rubs for the octovacs, I opened my backpack tool bag and checked on my phone. The mutacase was a total loss. Its remaining carbonized pieces fell off and left thick black marks on my van's clean carpet. I put them in the garbage bag with my ruined tux and used my ruffled formal shirt to carefully clean my phone's screen and casing. I rubbed my fingers over its screen in gentle gestures, but nothing happened. Then there was a faint blue glow on my phone's screen. Part of my heart that hadn't dared to hope rejoiced.

My phone wasn't dead. But I wasn't so sure about the long term prospects for Columbia Brown, Penn and Princeton.

Chapter 28

"Well, I'm back."
— Samwise Gamgee

Ray Ray was hungry and dehydrated so I gave him what was left of my bottle of Diet Starbuzz and drove somewhere close by, where he could recharge his batteries. Roger Joe-Bob Bacon's Waffle House on Virginia Avenue north of Hartsfield was just as bright and clean and welcoming at five o'clock on a Thursday morning as it had been at seven o'clock on a Monday. Roger himself was on his rotating stool in the kitchen, wearing his chef's hat, pouring waffles and flipping fried eggs. He waved at us with a spatula held in one of his tentacles when we entered.

"Seat yourselves," he said. "One of the servers will be with you in a minute."

It was too early for the first breakfast rush, so things weren't busy.

"Thanks," I said. With my backpack tool bag over my shoulder, I helped guide Ray Ray into a booth and signaled to Roger Joe-Bob. He left his cook's station and brought over a large cup of hot coffee for Ray Ray, plus a Diet Starbuzz in a glass with lots of ice for me. Roger Joe-Bob stretched and extended one of his eye stalks so he could get a good look at the man who'd saved my life.

"You, sir, need an All-Star Breakfast."

Ray Ray answered the Pyr with eight short words.

"Scrambled. Covered. Country ham. Plain waffle. Raisin toast."

This wasn't Ray Ray's first Waffle House dining experience.

Roger Joe-Bob moved to start cooking Ray Ray's order, but I stopped him with a question. Being trilaterally symmetrical, the little alien didn't have to turn around.

"Do you have a charging pad I can borrow?"

"Sure, Jack," he said. "Current is free here. The last quarter galzen of these new-fangled tables is *all* charging pad. Just put your devices down on it and they'll get power. I used to have little signs explaining that, but customers kept taking them as souvenirs."

"Thanks," I said. "Now I've got another question."

"What's that?" said the Pyr.

"Why didn't you ask *me* what I wanted for breakfast?"

"You've got a spot of Flying Biscuit Café apple butter on your cheek and biscuit crumbs mashed into your t-shirt," said Roger Joe-Bob. "You must have had breakfast not too long ago."

"Oh," I said with a smile. "I hope you aren't unhappy I'm also patronizing the competition."

"Not one bit," said Roger Joe-Bob. "I like to get me some of their biscuits myself now and ag'in."

The Pyr might appreciate some dialect coaching from Poly. Roger Joe-Bob returned to his stool and started cooking Ray Ray's order.

I put my phone on the table's charging pad, realizing that the broad black stripe in the table's surface delineated the charging area. Ray Ray did the same with his phone, a brand new model half the size of mine. Its battery must have drained while he was held captive. Then I realized why customers had been taking Roger Joe-Bob's signs. They'd probably read something like "Power for your mobile devices—no charge." Maybe the Pyr needed Poly's help with his signage, too.

Ray Ray was sitting quietly across from me, sipping his coffee. He looked like he was resting on a charging pad himself.

"Call your father," I said. "He's worried about you."

"It's five in the morning," said Ray Ray.

"He'll want to hear from you."

"He doesn't even know I'm in trouble."

"He knows he hasn't heard from you in a week, so call him. He'll need to drive here from Newnan to pick you up anyway."

"I can take an autocab home," said Ray Ray, without much enthusiasm.

"You've just had a traumatic experience," I said, "and don't need to go back to an empty apartment in Midtown. You need family around, and Charli's in Pittsburgh. Call your father."

"My phone's charging."

"It's got enough juice to make a call by now," I said.

"Okay, I'll call."

I waited until he'd picked up his phone and placed the call, then excused myself to sit at the empty counter for a few minutes so I could chat with Roger Joe-Bob.

"I understand you're friends with Tomáso and Queen Sherrhi."

"Yep," said the Pyr. "Isn't that little girl of theirs a cute one? I've been meanin' to circle by the Dauushan consulate and say howdy to Sherrhi since I heard she was here on Terra."

"I'm sure they'd love to see you," I said. "But I'd like to ask for your help on something that would keep Sherrhi and her little girl from being kidnapped."

"Kidnapped? Who'd want to do such a thing?" he said. "Glad to be of service any way I can."

"Great," I said. "We don't really know who's behind things, but I have an idea how to stop them. It would help if I could borrow some of your inventory."

"There's not much on hand here," he said. "Trucks bring in new eggs and flour and such every day."

"No," I said. "Not your Waffle House inventory, your Khu-fu, Limited inventory."

"That's a whole 'nother kettle o' fish. What d'ya have in mind, son?"

He slid his stool away from his grills and waffle making station until he was directly in front of me. I leaned over the counter and whispered into where I thought one of the Pyr's ears was located.

"That jest might be doable," said Roger Joe-Bob, after I'd finished. "Providin' it's only temp'rary."

"Just until four o'clock on Saturday afternoon," I said.

"I'll tell my Chief Operatin' Officer," said Roger Joe-Bob.

"He'll make it happen."

The billionaire Pyr returned to his grill and I went back to keep Ray Ray company. He was off the phone and had returned to sipping his coffee.

"How's your dad?"

"Good," he said. "He said he'll be here in an hour and a half."

"Great."

It would a pleasure to see R.C. in the flesh. Now I needed to learn everything I could from Ray Ray about O'Sullivan Fabrication and why he was trussed up on the floor of the hangar.

A server bustled over to our table with two steaming plates.

"Scrambled eggs, hash browns with cheese, country ham, raisin toast and a waffle," she said, putting the plates down in front of Ray Ray. "Anything for you?"

She had her pad and pencil out ready to take my order.

"That raisin toast looks good," I said.

She nodded and left, coming back a minute later with the toast and a refill on my Diet Starbuzz, then leaving again. Ray Ray was making a serious dent in his All-Star Breakfast.

I looked at Ray Ray until he lifted his head from what must have been his first meal in quite a while.

"Let's talk about the eight hundred pound gorilla," I said.

"The what?"

"How you ended up bound on the floor of a hangar that was about to be vaporized?"

"It's a long story."

"We've got an hour and a half."

Ray Ray began to eat more slowly. He chewed on a piece of ham and looked like he was trying to get his thoughts in order.

"I thought it was a decent job," he said a few seconds later. "The pay was good and I'd worked on Model-43 fabricators in the lab at Georgia Tech."

I nodded. The Dauushan Model-43 was a bit dated now, but still a workhorse.

"You were the 3D printer operator?"

"Most of the time. I also reviewed fabrication designs, did three dimensional modeling for new products, worked out materials tolerances, handled quality control and managed inventory."

That was a lot more than Mike had been doing at WT&F, but Ray Ray did have an engineering degree.

"Then things started looking sketchy."

"What do you mean?"

"We started doing these late night fabrication runs, fabbing stuff that looked more military than commercial. I didn't sign up to fab weapons."

"Uh huh."

"But it was the inventory tracking that really made me think something was wrong."

"Going through too much feed stock?"

"Yeah. We were using twice as much as we should, including supplies of the more expensive, exotic materials with military uses. I accounted for every job going through our Model-43, even the runs when I wasn't working, and we were using way more than that."

"What did you do when you found out?"

"I told my boss," said Ray Ray. "Sarah Barnard, the Ice Woman."

"Sarah Lawrence Barnard?"

More women's college names.

"Yeah. Do you know her?"

"I'm beginning to think I do. What does she look like?"

"Tall, black, brown eyes, short dark hair, about thirty-five, wears glasses and expensive clothes."

Those details fit Columbia Brown precisely.

"She always gave me the creeps," said Ray Ray. "If I'd met her during my interviews I wouldn't have taken the job. Her voice was cold, hard, and totally intimidating."

"What did she say when you told her about the inventory discrepancies?"

"She told me not to worry about it. She'd deal with it."

"You thought someone was stealing?"

"Yeah, and that she'd put a stop to it one way or another. I didn't want to be on her bad side."

"But you ended up there...?"

"Right. But before that, I learned about the lower level."

I nodded encouragement.

"Ms. Barnard said that she would show me where the extra feedstock was going, but made me sign a new confidentiality agreement first. She made it sound like we were working on secret government contracts or something. We took an elevator down several stories and I learned there was a duplicate fabrication facility down there, with another Dauushan Model-43. This printer was fabbing parts for giant combat robots, and I didn't want any part of it. There were lots of those eight-legged assemblers around, too, like the ones that rescued us."

"I call them octovacs."

Ray Ray ate more hash browns and spoke between bites.

"If you say so. They remind me of spiders and I can't say I'm much of a fan."

"They grow on you," I said. "Then what?"

"This was last Friday. Ms. Barnard said she wanted me to be in charge of both the upper and the lower fabbers," he said. "She said a client needed a dozen giant robots by this Friday."

"They wanted delivery tomorrow?" I said. "What did you say?"

"I said yes," said Ray Ray. "I was afraid I'd never see the light of day again if I said no."

"Let me shift gears for a minute. Does the name Agnes Spelman mean anything to you?"

"Sure, that's Ms. Barnard's sister. She runs Factor-E-Flor, the design shop."

Columbia Brown has a *sister?* What other bad news did the universe have for me today?

"So you agreed to run fabbing for both levels. Then what?"

"That night, after work, I called my dad. We talked for an hour. I didn't tell him anything specific, just that I was uncomfortable. If anything happened to me I wanted him to know where to start looking."

"He told me about that."

"He did?" said Ray Ray. "I guess that's just my dad. Always oversharing."

"He loves you and he's proud of you," I said. "You can tell from his expression whenever he talks about you."

"At the end of the call he told me that he knew I'd do the right thing," said Ray Ray.

"Your father is a wise man."

"Listening to him nearly got me killed," said Ray Ray with a rueful smile. "I went back to the office that night and did it."

Ray Ray paused, sipped his coffee, then resumed.

"I sabotaged the robots being built by both the upper and lower Model-43s."

"And that's when they caught you and tied you up?" I asked.

"No," said Ray Ray. He looked at me like he wondered if I thought he was an idiot. "I was subtle about it."

I knew how I'd do subtle sabotage in a similar situation, but wondered how Ray Ray would do it.

"I changed the materials used in the lower legs," he said. "They would test the robots at night in one of the fields near the O'Sullivan Fabrication facility. When the robots would try to stand, their own weight would snap their shins. Lots of other components would be damaged when the robots fell over."

Not bad. I would have picked ankles, but shins would work just as well.

"How much time did that buy you?"

"Several days, as the parts were reprinted and retested."

"Then Ms. Barnard started to get suspicious. I had planned to quit without notice the next day and intended to spend some time with my dad down in Newnan."

"But...?"

"I got tricky and wanted to prevent them from building more robots, so I decided to disable the Model-43s themselves."

"By breaking off the rails for the feedstock towers?"

"No," said Ray Ray. "Cyanoacrylate on the output nozzles."

Ouch. Superglue would be a bear to remove. The nozzles would need to be completely replaced.

"Sounds like a sticky situation," I said.

Ray Ray shook his head in disgust.

"Barnard and three of her goons were waiting for me in the parking lot," said Ray Ray. "They zapped me with a stun gun and threw me in the trunk of a car."

"Then they took you to the hangar?"

"No, then they took me to Disney World."

"Don't be that way."

"Sorry," said Ray Ray. "Now I have a question."

"Sure," I said.

"How did you know where to find me?"

"I didn't. I found you by accident while looking for someone else."

"I'm alive because of an accident?" said Ray Ray.

"A lot of us are," I said.

We hadn't noticed, but the restaurant had gotten busier around us as we'd talked. The place was full of people having breakfast before their shifts started at seven. Our server had been by a few times to refill Ray Ray's coffee but her transient presence didn't really register. Then someone else was standing next to our table.

"Good to see you, son," said R. C. Dunwoody. "You too, Jack."

I stood up and shook R. C.'s hand, then got out of the way so that R. C. and Ray Ray could hug. The two of them looked a lot alike. Both had the same model of sunglasses pushed up on their foreheads and the same big smiles on their faces.

"Take my seat, please, R. C.," I said. "I have to get home and get some sleep."

"Thanks for finding Ray Ray." said R. C.

"Just so you know," I told R. C., "your son saved my life."

R. C. looked at Ray Ray with pride.

"And you saved mine, Jack," said Ray Ray.

"Pick up the check and we'll call it even," I said.

I opened a pocket on my backpack tool bag, removed my phone from the charging pad, and gently placed it inside. Its glow was brighter now, but it still wasn't talking. I'd run it through a full set of diagnostics back at my apartment.

Then I left the table and headed for the door, smiling and nodding at Roger Joe-Bob Bacon as I went.

The little Pyr waved a spatula held in one of his tentacles, just as he had when I'd come in.

I got in my van.

"Prithee buckle thy seat belt," it said, halfheartedly.

I think it missed my phone. I did.

"Home, please, noble steed."

I leaned back and closed my eyes. My sleep deficit was old enough that if hours were years, it would be in graduate school. Ten minutes north of Hartsfield port, the lid on Chit's bottle popped open and my Murm friend stuck her head out to greet the dawn. She was wearing a new paint job—something by Jackson Pollock this time. Either that or she was having problems with her ink jet printer. Chit hopped on the dashboard, stretched and yawned.

"So, buddy boy," she said. "What did I miss *this* time?"

Chapter 29

"To sleep, perchance to dream..."
— William Shakespeare, *Hamlet*

My van dropped me off at the Peachtree Street gate and drove itself off to park. The octovacs were in dormant mode in its rear cargo area—at least *they* were getting some rest. I took my backpack tool bag, the trash bag with my tuxedo, and my bruised ribs through the courtyard to my apartment. Once again, I heard the sounds of something small and quick scurrying through the foliage and wondered if it was squirrels or chipmunks or some new off-planet variety of fauna introduced into the courtyard's controlled ecosystem. It didn't matter—I was sure that Spike would terrorize whatever it was into submission.

Despite the events of the previous evening and morning, I had to smile when I saw my top hat, still looking elegant, sitting in the middle of my dining room table. Poly must have put it there when she entered to get my backpack tool bag and my clothes. I hope she'd gotten some sleep and had spent some quality time catching up with her parents and sister. It was past eight in the morning and even with all the excitement and late hours I thought she might be up soon. Too bad she couldn't reach me until my phone recovered. Getting it back in operating order was my top item of business, even ahead of sleep.

I put my backpack tool bag in its usual spot on a table by the front door and removed my phone from its B.I.T.S. cloth wrapping. Then I carried it into my bedroom and placed it softly and securely on the charging pad on the nightstand next to my bed. There were times when I wished I could carry a skateboard-sized phone, like adult Dauushans. Their phones came with power congruencies as well as telecommunications congruencies. Terran-sized phones needed batteries because they weren't large enough to eliminate congruency-congruency interference.

My phone glowed brighter when I put it on the charging pad and restarted it. When it came back up I'd put it through a full set of diagnostic tests and do my best to fix anything that was wrong. The restart process would take a few minutes, so I went back into my living room and dug around in my project nook. It didn't take me long to find what I wanted. The Orishen knitting machine I'd used to make bulletproof pupa silk shirts was still sitting on top of my work table, but that wasn't the most important thing. The spindle with the cocoon of Shuvvath, an Orishen nymph I'd prevented from going on a mass killing spree, wasn't completely used up. There was probably enough thread left for what I had in mind.

I put the knitting machine on the dining room table next to my top hat and moved the spindle unit to the floor beneath it where the thread would feed easily. Then I used the laptop on the desk in my project nook to look up the required dimensions. I fed them into the Orishen knitting machine and was gratified when the needles started clacking. It shouldn't take long for it to knit what I needed. I heard a ding sound from my bedroom over the noisy needles—my phone's restart had finished. It was time for diagnostics.

My phone was face up on the charging pad where I'd left it. A round, red light in the center of its screen pulsed when I entered the room.

"Greetings," said my phone. "I am registered to Ajax Pryce Buckston. Would you be he?"

What the…?

"Yes," I said, caught off guard.

"This unit is pleased to serve you," it said. "Would you like me to explain my range of features?"

Oh crap. It must have rebooted with factory default settings. My poor phone must have been damaged more than I'd thought.

"Not at this time," I replied. "When was the last cloud back-up for this device performed?"

"The last cloud backup for this device was performed on Sunday evening."

Before the call from Mike about the giant robot being built at WT&F. This was going to be interesting.

I used my laptop to place an on-line order for a new phone just like my old one and specified immediate delivery. I found the last Orishen mutacase in Atlanta and bought it without a second thought. I paid twenty percent more than it cost me for the previous mutacase, but was happy to do so. Both phone and case would be here as soon as drones could fly them.

My factory default phone made a ding sound.

"Mr. Buckston, you have received text messages from Mr. Tomáso Kauuson at the Dauushan consulate and Ms. Polyhymnia Keen Jones. Would you like me to read them to you?"

"Sure," I said.

"Which text message would you like me to read first? Mr. Tomáso Kauuson or…"

"Poly," I said.

"Do you mean Ms. Polyhymnia Keen Jones?"

"Yes."

The phone read in a monotone.

"I'm going shopping with my sister to help her find a dress for Saturday. Please pick up my mom and dad at ten o'clock at the hotel. Mom needs to be dropped off at the Galtech Department at Georgia Tech to review the arrangements for her commencement speech and Dad needs to go to the Michael C. Carlos Museum at Emory."

Interesting. Poly probably thinks I got to bed not long after she did.

"Mr. Ajax Pryce Buckston, there is also a postscript from Ms. Polyhymnia Keen Jones. Would you like me to read it to you?"

"Jack," I said.

"I do not understand," said the phone.

"Please refer to me as 'Jack,' and Ms. Jones as 'Poly.'"

"Yes, Jack," said the phone. "I see an alternate designation of

'Lover Boy' in your contact record. Is that also an acceptable short name?"

"Not at this time."

"Would you like me to read the postscript from Poly?"

"Yes, please."

"Certainly. This unit is glad to comply. If this unit fails to act in a manner that delights you, there is a short survey available for you to complete where you can recommend options for improvement."

"Thank you. Not at this time. Please read Poly's postscript."

The phone read the postscript in the same monotonous neutral voice.

"Jack, thanks for taking Mom and Dad. This will be a good opportunity to start over so they can get to know you and vice versa. Daddy has promised not to act like a pompous ass and Mom, well, Mom appears to have mellowed a bit since last night, too. I really appreciate it. Hugs and kisses, Poly."

I like hearing "Hugs and kisses, Poly," even in a monotone, but was less than thrilled about having to drive her parents. I certainly wasn't at my best. But I couldn't say no.

"Please send a reply."

"Recording."

"I will be glad to pick up your parents in front of the Star Palace at ten o'clock and get them to their destinations. I hope you're reconnecting with Pomy. Missing you, Jack."

"Send?" asked my phone.

"Go ahead," I said.

"Transcribed and sent."

The phone sat quietly for ten seconds then spoke.

"Reply to your message received."

"Please read it," I said.

The phone, in its monotone drone, did so.

"Great. Remember, family dinner at seven tonight at the place with the pirate ship and the crocodiles."

Had Poly ever told me anything about a dinner with her family tonight? Or ever made mention of crocodiles in any context, except, perhaps, when talking about her mother? I'd have to get more details later and hoped I'd get a chance for a nap before dinner.

"Any reply?" said the phone.

"See you there. May walk the plank. XOXO."

"Should this unit expand 'XOXO' into 'Kiss Hug Kiss Hug'?"

"No," I said. "Just send it as is."

"Transcribing. Sent."

"Thanks."

"Would you like me to read you the text message from Mr. Tomáso Kauuson at the Dauushan consulate?"

"Yes."

"Ground penetrating radar shows shadow facility below O'Sullivan Fabrication. Appears abandoned."

Interesting. I'd have to fill Tomáso in on what I learned from Ray Ray.

"Any reply?"

"Yes."

"Recording."

"Employee sabotaged O'Sullivan's 3D printers. Found him at rendezvous site and prevented nova bomb explosion. Columbia Brown has a sister, Agnes Spelman, new CEO at Factor-E-Flor. Sabotage probable reason WT&F used to fab giant robot. News at eleven."

I waited a beat.

"Send."

"Transcribed. Sent."

The phone started to ring. I was about to answer it when my doorbell rang, twice. I let Tomáso's call roll to voice mail.

I checked the camera out front using my living room wall screen, since I didn't want to try to get the phone to do it. Nobody was waiting to shoot me, but two drones with small packages were hovering impatiently. I signed for the deliveries and was about to carry the packages inside when I saw someone very large and very pink striding toward the entrance to my apartment. Three guesses who it was.

"Hi Tomáso."

"You can't do that to me," said the elephant-sized Dauushan.

"What?" I said. "Not pick up when you call?"

"No," said Tomáso. "Send me a text like that without more details."

"Sorry," I said. "My phone got fried, I almost got vaporized, and I haven't had any sleep. It was the best I could do."

"Will your phone be okay?"

"Nice of you to ask about my phone before showing concern for me potentially being reduced to my constituent atoms," I said.

"You obviously survived."

"Barely," I said. "I've got a brand new handset and mutacase here." I waved the two packages I was holding to confirm my statement. "I'll be restoring my phone from last Sunday night's backup in a few minutes. The original hardware restarted in factory default mode and it's driving me crazy."

"Only fair," said Tomáso, with a *basso* "hrrrumph," for emphasis.

Me driving *him* crazy was unsaid.

I gave Tomáso the short version of showing up too late to stop the departing starship, meeting Ray Ray, encountering Penn and Princeton and escaping from the hangar. He agreed I'd had a busy morning and gave me more details about the investigation of O'Sullivan Fabrication. The entire facility, upper and lower levels, was now abandoned. It was a dead end. I gave Tomáso R. C. Dunwoody's number so he could contact Ray Ray and see if he might remember anything else that could help.

"We're trying to figure out where Columbia Brown and company have hidden a dozen giant combat robots and what they plan to do with them," he said.

"Ten," I said. "We have two down at Zwilniki's hangar."

"That's marginally better than twelve," said Tomáso. "I'm afraid they're going to make another attempt to kidnap Sherrhi and Terrhi."

"The species that controls Dauushan productive capacity and commands Dauushans' loyalty rules the galaxy?" I said.

"Exactly," said Tomáso. "Sherrhi hopes the Opposition will show itself at Emory's graduation on Saturday. That's why she agreed to speak."

"And where one giant combat robot failed…" I said.

"Ten attacking simultaneously might succeed," Tomáso finished. "But not if I have anything to say about it."

"What's your plan?" I asked "How do you intend to protect your family against ten robots?"

"With this," said Tomáso.

He pulled his skateboard-sized phone from a pouch on his left front leg and held it up for me to see. Centered on its screen was the *Charalindhri*, the immense Dauushan asteroid mining ship my mother had been helping to construct. It was floating in Earth orbit with a blue terrestrial horizon and a crescent slice of Luna showing in the background. It was beautiful, but deadly.

"The *Charalindhri's* energy beams can melt asteroids. They can also deal with giant robots."

"That's like using a machete when you should be using a scalpel," I said. "Those beams would also destroy half the buildings on Emory's main quadrangle and kill hundreds of innocent bystanders."

"Acceptable losses to protect our queen."

"And your spouse," I said. "You're biased. Energy beams from space would be a completely inappropriate and disproportional response."

"My queen chose to put herself in harm's way so the beings behind the resurrected Compliant Plague would show themselves," said Tomáso. "I will not stand idly by and watch her brave actions lead to her capture, death or infection."

"Neither will I, my friend," I said, looking directly up into his eyes. "So give me time to do what I can before you escalate."

"I will…" My friend paused. "…consider your request."

"Thanks," I said. "And tell Queen Sherrhi not to worry. I'm sure her commencement speech at Emory will be memorable."

"That's what I'm afraid of," said Tomáso, sighing from six sub-trunks and shrugging his massive shoulders. He turned away and walked slowly back in the direction of his condominium and the Dauushan consulate.

I needed to get moving if I wanted to restore my phone and still have time to take a shower and change my clothes before I had to pick up Poly's parents. I brought the packages inside and opened them on the far end of my dining room table. I smiled to see that the Orishen knitting machine had already completed its work.

The new phone was already charged so I used it to login to my account and access my phone's backup from last Sunday night. After navigating a few screens I was able to trigger the download and mentally kicked myself for not paying for the up-to-the-minute option. Weekly backups had seemed fine three years ago when Xenotech Support Corporation had first opened for business. At that point, the extra eighty percent surcharge seemed an unnecessary extravagance. As they say in Pennsylvania Dutch country, "Too soon old, too late smart." I was a technology professional and should have known better, but sometimes the shoemaker's children are stuck wearing flip-flops.

While the download into the new hardware was processing, I turned off the phone that had restarted in factory default mode. I carefully removed the back of its case and slid out three tiny lengths of molecular memory metal from slots on a circuit board. They were the diameter of pieces of lead in a mechanical pencil. Only their far ends were discolored by the high voltage. There was a good chance I could restore my phone's memories from Monday, Tuesday, Wednesday and early Thursday morning once I had a chance to poke around and correct the damage done by the massive spark. That would take time I didn't have right now, however.

I put the precious memory wires in an anti-static bag and put the bag in a small painted wooden box on top of my dresser. My mom said the box was a gift from my birth father. It was painted with colorful images of swallows in flight and blooming flowers and was one of my dearest treasures.

"Earl Grey, hot, half a cup. Make it so," I said, giving the command for an abbreviated version of my favorite shower program. The cold spray at the end helped wake me up, so I was reasonably coherent when I got dressed. I put on a French blue button-front collared shirt and a nice pair of khakis because I suspected there was a reasonable chance I wouldn't have time to change for dinner.

Once dressed, I walked to the kitchen to make a cup of strong tea. Then I noticed the very cold pot of Midnight Obsidian Black on the counter. The teabags had been steeping since early yesterday evening. I filled a glass with ice, poured the dark, caffeine-laden liquid on top, and drank it down in four swallows. It was probably just a psychosomatic reaction, but I felt like I stood straighter and my eyes were clearer. Thus fortified, maybe I'd survive.

I heard a ding sound from dining room table.

"Hey Jack," said my phone, "When are you going to get around to that overdue maintenance at Mistress Marigold's?"

I could have hugged it.

"Already taken care of," I said. "I'll tell you all about it later. Right now, I have a present for you."

"A present?"

My phone sounded surprised and pleased.

I put it on top of the new Orishen mutacase and watched as the case flowed around my phone's new hardware.

"This is great!" said my phone. "How did you know to get one?"

It was extruding and retracting appendages faster than a protoplasmic blob in a B-grade monster movie.

"I'm a smart guy," I said. "With smart friends."

"Was it Poly's idea?"

I just smiled enigmatically. Then I realized I wasn't so smart after all. I found the trash bag with my ruined tux and the blacked remains of the old mutacase on the floor near my front door where I'd dropped it. I got a pair of latex gloves from my project room, put them on, and carefully dug around in the trash bag until I found the largest remaining pieces of the old case. Then I opened my backpack tool bag and got out my small, portable Orishen scent organ. I played several notes that I thought would have the desired effect and my Orishen mutakey floated to the top of one of the larger pieces.

"Here," I said, tossing the mutakey at my phone. It flipped itself up in the air and caught the mutakey before it could hit the table. Then the key was smoothly integrated into the surface of the case, disappearing from sight. I returned the scent organ to my backpack tool bag.

"You're the best, Jack," said my phone, "even if it *was* Poly's idea."

"Here's another present that really is my idea," I said.

"What is it?" said my phone.

I removed a small phone cover made of pupa silk fabric from the knitting machine on my dining room table.

"Here," I said. "Try it on."

My phone moved into the pupa silk cover using hundreds of tiny legs. The cover was absorbed into the mutacase, just like the mutakey. It flattened itself out into a very thin, transparent layer over my phone's screen as well. I hoped it would offer protection against shocks and impacts and even energy weapons, like the elevator lock's electric shock. When I explained the cover's benefits, my phone looked quite pleased.

"You mean someone could shoot a bullet and it wouldn't damage my hardware?"

"Theoretically."

I let it stew on my reply and asked it another important question.

"What time is it?" I said.

"Ten minutes until ten," said my phone.

"Summon the van," I said. "We have to pick up Poly's parents at ten o'clock."

"We'll never make it to Hartsfield in ten minutes, Jack."

I could tell that it was going to be a *very* long day.

Chapter 30

*"It is an unscrupulous intellect that does not
pay to antiquity its due reverence."*
— Desiderius Erasmus

I brought my backpack tool bag with me when I left my apartment. I wanted it close at hand. Today was shaping up to be the kind of day when not only things that *can* go wrong will go wrong, but things that technically can't go wrong will try to out of sheer perversity.

My van was waiting when I got to Peachtree Street and I used one of the wipes from my kitchen to clean up the piece of burnt mutacase on the floor. Most of the black residue from the case came off the stain resistant carpet, so my van would still look nice for Poly's parents. My van's A.I. seemed disconcerted. Maybe it was trying to connect with my phone and picked up on its confusion. It even forgot to engage its forsooth module.

"Seat belt."

I buckled up, temporarily awake and alert. My van pulled away from the curb.

"Jack," said my phone, tentatively. It had climbed up to sit front and center on the dash.

"Yes?"

"How did it get to be Thursday?"

"Good question," I said. "That reminds me. Please contact your cloud backup service and change your plan to include the extortionate fee for real time backups."

"Oh," said my phone. It beeped and blinked for a few seconds. "Three and a half days lost?"

"Pretty much," I said. "I'll try to get the memories back for you."

"Thanks. What happened?"

"A high voltage booby trap fried your circuits."

"How did the Star Wars award ceremony go?" said my phone.

"Wait, how did you know about the award ceremony? It was last night."

For a moment I hoped that some more recent memories had been included in the downloaded backup, but the answer was simpler than that.

"Tomáso has been planning it for weeks and had asked for my help to make sure you and Poly were there on time."

"Thanks. Sorry you missed it," I said. "Mike's phone got some pictures. Mike's a Xenotech Support employee now, by the way."

"Wow. Sounds like a lot happened since Sunday night."

"Yes. Like encounters with a pair of two-hundred-and-fifty-foot robots, WT&F blowing up, carnivorous plants, Macerators attacking the royal dinner and a nova bomb."

"WT&F blew up?"

"Just the executive wing and the production floor."

"Is Mike okay?"

"A few scratches. You helped save him."

"Wow," said my phone, "you'd better get those memories back."

"I'll try my best—but for now you'll just have to fill in the blanks as we go."

My van slowed, then stopped. We were at the hotel. Perry and Barbara were just walking through the lobby doors. I got out of my van and crossed in front of it to meet them. To my surprise, Perry shook my hand and Barbara gave me a peck on the cheek that seemed warm, not politely perfunctory.

"Great to see you, Jack," said Perry. "You were impressive last night, using that big pan to take out the Macerators."

"You were pretty impressive yourself," I said, "like a raging Achilles. That was quick thinking to use a skewer for offense and a metal lid for defense."

"One of the benefits of a classical education," said Perry in a hail-fellow-well-met tone that didn't seem forced. "Not to say that understanding technology isn't also worthwhile."

He seemed to be on his best behavior. I didn't know if it was because of what had happened at the royal dinner, or if Poly, or Pomy, or both, had read him the riot act. Either way, I liked *this* version of Perry a lot better than the one I'd picked up at the airport. He and Barbara both seemed to be glowing.

"It was a team effort," said Barbara. "I threw Tomáso's napkin over the Macerator's head and Pericles pierced him. Then I pulled his power pack cylinders."

Her eyes looked fierce as she remembered what had happened.

"My Boadicea," said Perry, putting his arm around Barbara's shoulders.

She leaned in and smiled up at him. I wondered if they'd had any of the Don Juan noodles.

"You were both amazing. The chairs you dropped took two more out of action, so you have three 'kills' to your credit."

My van opened its side door and Perry helped Barbara step up and slide onto the rear bench seat. Then he joined her and they buckled up. Were they holding hands? I got in the driver's seat and secured myself as well. My van smoothly pulled away from the hotel and we were off, on our way to I-85 and points south.

"Poly said you'd be able to drop me at Georgia Tech's Advanced Galtech Department offices," said Barbara.

"No problem," I said. "It's in the Figueres Center, next to the lab where Poly's doing research at the Galactic Artificial Intelligence and Machine Learning Institute."

"Where will the graduation ceremony be held, do you know?" asked Barbara.

"In the Figueres Center," I answered. "It's got an eight hundred seat auditorium."

Pablo Daniel Figueres was the sports- and science-mad founder of Sirocco Legislature Network, the company that syndicated thirty percent of Terran legislative deliberations for the stars. He was a Georgia Tech alum who had seen how much Galactics loved our politicians' antics and had sewn up long term contracts for broadcast rights before anyone else on the planet knew how popular they'd be. He was generous to his alma mater—the Figueres Center was just one of five buildings on Tech's campus that he'd donated.

The apocryphal story I'd heard was that Pablo had named his network for the famed warm wind from the Sahara that blew across Southern Europe, because it was a large moving mass of hot air, like the kind produced by the legislative bodies he broadcast. Based on other things I'd heard about Figueres' flamboyant personality, I was pretty sure that story was true.

"Excellent," said Barbara. "I hate to walk far in heels."

"That's understandable," I said. "I'll have to introduce you to one of my clients who makes morphic shoes. Their heel heights adjust as needed."

"Like the ones Poly was wearing last night?"

"Uh huh."

"And they change color, too?" said Barbara. "Shoes like that would make packing for trips off planet a lot easier."

"Yes," I said. "You and Mademoiselle Ellie should have a lot to talk about."

"Any chance she'd be free for lunch today?"

"I'll check."

My phone made the connection and Ellie was thrilled with the idea of having lunch with Barbara Keen, the famous travel writer and publisher. Ellie said she'd pick Barbara up at twelve thirty, take her to a lovely new Vietnamese-Nicósn fusion restaurant in Midtown, then drop her off back at her hotel. I was sure they'd get along fabulously and reasonably confident Morphicouture would be advertising in Keen's Guides and Keen's Guides would be recommending Morphicouture's fashions within the month.

"You're a gem, Jack Buckston," said Barbara.

"Uh, thanks," I said. *Aw shucks, ma'am.*

My van pulled into the circular drive of an impressive looking academic building on 10th Street, one of the main through streets on Georgia Tech's campus.

"Here you are," I said. "The Dean's office is on the second floor, I think."

I'd only been there once, to pick up Poly from a grad school function, but I've got a good memory. My van opened its side door and Perry got out and helped Barbara step down. She gave him a kiss that was decidedly not a perfunctory peck and headed up the walk to the Figueres Center. Perry climbed into the shotgun seat next to me. Let me revise that. Perry got in the front passenger seat. I don't like using the word *shotgun* in any context related to my girlfriend's father.

"How far is it to the Carlos Museum?"

"About twenty-five minutes," said my phone.

"Onward, noble steed," I said.

Perry gave me strange look for my choice of phrase, but didn't comment.

The Michael C. Carlos Museum reputedly housed the largest collection of ancient artifacts in the southeast, including objects from ancient Greece, Rome, the Near East, Africa, and the Americas. The largest part of their collection, however, was from Egypt. Nearly thirty years ago they'd acquired a sarcophagus that turned out to contain the mummy of Pharaoh Ramesses I. Once they realized the mummy's identity, they'd repatriated it back to Egypt and the Luxor Museum. I'd seen his mummy there when I was a kid, after my mom took that job in Aswan. I remember being blown away by the giant statue of Ramesses II at Karnak, though in my head the huge statues in Egypt were inspired by the monumental art of Tolkien's Númenor, not the other way around. I'd wanted to visit the Carlos ever since I'd moved to Atlanta, but had never found the time or had the opportunity, until now.

"Is there something specific you want to see at the museum, Professor? Roman frescos? Greek pottery?"

"Not something, someone. One of my former students is the museum's new curator."

"Wonderful," I said. "What's his name?"

"*Her* name," said Professor Jones, "Terpsichory 'Kori' Liddell-Scott. She's giving me a grand tour of the public and staff-only parts of the place. You're welcome to join us."

I thought about it for three seconds. Poly wanted me to have a chance to connect with her parents and despite how tired I was, a behind the scenes tour of the museum sounded too good to pass up.

"I'd like that very much, sir."

"You can call me Perry, Jack."

"Yes, sir," I said.

He gave me a strange look again, but this time both of us were smiling. If Dr. Liddell-Scott was in her late thirties or early forties, which seemed right for someone in charge of a prestigious museum, her first name might have inspired Perry's selection of Polyhymnia and Melpomene as names for his daughters.

Perry turned toward me in his captain's chair.

"I want to apologize for being a horse's ass yesterday," he said.

"I don't know what you're talking about," I said.

"Yes you do. My daughters metaphorically dragged me nine times around the walls of Troy last night and explained in no uncertain terms that my behavior was unacceptable."

"Apology accepted," I said. "And my apologies for my own rude comments."

"You were only giving back what you got," said Perry. "I admire a man who sticks up for what he believes in. I'll even grudgingly admit that there's a lot to be said for modern technology."

"Thank you, Perry. Just so you know, I love the classics, too. I was raised on Greek and Roman myths and all the stories from the *Iliad*, the *Odyssey* and the *Aeneid*. I even read your Homeric trilogy and *The Augustan Commission*."

Perry looked pleased.

"I hope you found my books enlightening."

There was only one right answer, and thankfully I didn't have to shade the truth to provide it.

"Very much so."

Perry sat up straighter and couldn't hide the smile on his face.

"I'm beginning to understand what my daughter sees in you," he said.

Now it was my turn to sit up and smile.

"Just what are your intentions toward my daughter, Mr. Buckston," he said, in what I hoped was mock seriousness.

"Carlos Museum, my lords," said my van.

Saved. We were in front of the museum's main entrance. I'd never seen anything like it before. The entryway was an equilateral triangle twelve feet tall and eight feet deep, cut into a square facade faced with white marble and accented by two bands of pink stone. An African tribal mask as tall as I am and carved from a dark, polished wood, stood to the left. To the right was a somewhat melted looking statue carved from lustrous white stone. It had a pointed black hat on its head and looked like an Orishen sculptor's misguided attempt at carving a human form. Most Orishen art looks like wax left in the sun too long. I learned later that the piece was also part of the museum's African collection.

Perry and I got out and my van set off on a quest to find a parking place—never an easy task near Emory. We walked through the triangular entrance, took an elevator up one floor, and entered the museum's spare, circular lobby. The Greek, Roman and Near Eastern exhibit halls stretched off in one direction, while halls labeled Art of the Americas beckoned in another. The reception desk, where museum visitors would pay to enter, was directly across from us.

"Professor Jones calling for Professor Liddell-Scott," said Perry to the young man at the desk.

"Welcome to the Carlos, Professor," said the young man. "The Curator is expecting you. I'll let her know you're here."

While we waited, I stuck my head into the nearest gallery.

It was filled with Greek sculptures missing heads and limbs. I hoped they weren't foreshadowing my future. A twenty-foot mosaic depicting scenes from the Trojan War was mounted high on the left-hand wall and I had to consult the sign below it to identify all the participants. Minutes later, a distinguished-looking woman of medium height and a formidable countenance entered the lobby. She was wearing a light weight gray wool suit that complimented her short gray hair. Next to her was a tall, younger Nicósn with a long white beard. He was wearing a natty green bow tie and a white lab coat.

"Professor Jones!" said the woman when she saw Perry. She quickly crossed the distance between them and gave him a big hug. Perry looked both pleased and embarrassed.

"Kori," said Poly's father, warmth showing in his voice. "It's great to see you."

"It's an honor to have you visit," she said. "This is my associate, Dr. Urradu. He's researching possible Nicósn influences on the civilizations of Babylon, Assyria and Asia Minor."

"Before first contact?" I blurted.

"Yes," said the Nicósn. "Galactics have been following Earth's development for quite some time. It's possible that some, shall we say, *unauthorized* contact was made."

I thought about it and remembered the Mesopotamian statues of gods and rulers with long, twisty Nicósn-like beards and could understand why the possibility was worth investigating.

"This is my older daughter's boyfriend," said Perry.

"Jack Buckston," I said.

I shook hands with Dr. Liddell-Scott and Dr. Urradu.

"What's your field, Mr. Buckston?" asked the curator politely. I'm sure she expected me to be a fellow academic.

"I run a tech support company," I said, "specializing in Galactic technology."

I could see wheels turning in Dr. Liddell-Scott's head.

"Let's talk over lunch," she said. "But first, a tour. I want to show off our collection."

She put her hand on Perry's arm just above his elbow and guided him into the Greek, Roman and Near Eastern galleries. Dr. Urradu and I followed. For the next three hours I forgot I was tired.

Chapter 31

"I've learned how to use my spam filter pretty effectively."
— Al Yankovic

"Have a few more Kalamata olives," said Dr. Liddell-Scott. "They're delicious."

I'd already tried them and she was right. I selected a small additional serving with a deep bronze spoon and moved them to my plate. I didn't want to fill up too soon since lunch at the Classical Café on the top floor of the museum promised to be a treat. Dr. Liddell-Scott, Perry, Dr. Urradu and I were seated at a round table reserved for the curator. We were clearly in the best seats in the house. Our table was directly beneath the center of the domed ceiling and warm light from a bronze, wheel-shaped chandelier made it easy to see and appreciate our meal.

In the center of our table was a thick round loaf of whole wheat and spelt bread, scored into eight wedges. I cut though the scored indentations with the sharp knife designated for that purpose and served wedges of warm bread to my dining companions and myself. The bread had a robust, nutty flavor and I sopped up a bit of the oil from my olives with the point of my wedge. Then a pair of servers in Greco-Roman servant's garb brought us bowls of salad greens topped with some sort of vinaigrette dressing. I recognized less than half of the leaves in my bowl.

"What are these?" I asked Dr. Liddell-Scott, pointing at the unfamiliar greenery.

"Mint, coriander, parsley, pennyroyal, arugula, mallow and thyme," said the curator. "With a bit of chopped leek, feta and pine nuts. It's from Columella's *Re Rustica.*"

"First century of the Common Era," added Perry.

"Though I preferred his *De arboribus,*" chimed in Dr. Urradu. "I like the recipes from *Apicius,* myself."

I'd made some of the simpler dishes in the early Roman

recipe collection attributed to Marcus Gavius Apicius, a Roman gourmand and noted sybarite, and didn't want to be left out of the academic one-upsmanship.

"Then you'll like the *libum* cakes with honey we're having for dessert," said Dr. Liddell-Scott.

"They're one of my favorites," said Dr. Urradu. "Kori makes sure the chef serves them when I'm having lunch with her."

"Then we're beings of similar tastes," I said. "*Libum* cakes are one of my favorites, too."

The Nicósn smiled, but seemed a bit shy. He was rather young and I wondered if this was his first job since he'd earned his doctorate.

"How long have you been at the Carlos?" I asked.

"Just a few weeks," said Dr. Urradu. "I'll be working with Dr. Liddell-Scott over the summer. She's going to help me turn what I've learned from my finds in the Euphrates valley and Cappadocia into a book."

"You couldn't be in better hands," said Perry. "Terpsichory was one of my very best students. I'm proud to have been her thesis adviser."

"You pushed me hard, Perry," she said, "and taught me well. I'm glad to pass your wisdom on to the next generation of scholars."

Perry's chest puffed out, but his expression didn't get supercilious, like it had at the airport. He was smiling at Dr. Liddell-Scott. Dr. Urradu looked like he wasn't quite sure what to say. I came to his rescue.

"Where did you get your PhD?" I asked.

"Neue Staddam University."

That was the top academic institution on Nicós. I was impressed.

"It was a wonderful place to study," he said. "I worked with a first rate faculty at NSU and could connect to scholars in my field at other institutions across the planet."

I'd only been on Nicós once, and just for a few months, to

take a training class on high speed networking. Nicós had an incredible backbone network with yottabyte speeds and I envied how downloads seemed to be completed almost as soon I pressed the button to trigger them.

"High speed access must have been difficult when you were out in the field here on Terra," I said.

"No," said Dr. Urradu. "I was able to get a congruent uplink directly back to NSU with one of my department's portable remote routers. I'd never have been able to get all my photos and data back to the cloud on Nicós without it. There aren't many Terran Internet Service Providers in Kurdistan or the mountains of eastern Turkey."

I nodded agreement. There was a pause in the conversation while we enjoyed our salads, then Perry and Dr. Urradu started discussing whether or not Nicósn influences in Mesopotamia had been felt as far west as Asia Minor. There was a lot of gesturing with salad forks from the other side of the table. I overheard Dr. Urradu telling Perry that he'd send him detailed photographs of curly-bearded Assyrian statues recently excavated in Cappadocia.

Dr. Liddell-Scott took advantage of their preoccupation to bring up what I knew she'd been considering since she first heard I did tech support. She turned toward me and got right to the point.

"I've got two tech problems."

"Tell me about them," I said.

"I have to take off my academic hat and put on my administrative one," she said, "First, for the past few weeks we've been having Ahriman's own time with our email system and critical messages aren't being sent for days at a time."

"Give me an example."

"Of course," said Dr. Liddell-Scott. "Dr. Urradu was applying for a grant from Olympia Agnew and Roger Bacon's Lamb-Cheops Foundation for Near Eastern Studies to support further excavations in Kurdistan last week. The deadline for applications was noon last Friday. He finished the paperwork late Thursday afternoon and emailed the grant request before he left for the day. I'd stopped by to see if he needed any help and was there to watch him push SEND."

I hadn't known such a foundation existed, but then I put two and two together. Roger Joe-Bob Bacon, the Pyr from the Waffle House who owned Khufu, Limited, must have intentionally partnered with Olympia Agnew, the Greek shipping magnate, just to pull off a pun. I didn't let on that I was in on the joke.

"Let me guess," I said. "The people at the foundation never received Dr. Urradu's proposal?"

"That's right," said Dr. Liddell-Scott.

"Are you telling my tale of woe?" asked Dr. Urradu.

He and Perry shifted to join our conversation after the Nicósn realized Dr. Liddell-Scott was talking about him.

"Yes, Durra," she said, using the familiar form of Dr. Urradu's name. "Since Jack's a technology expert, I thought he might have some insights."

"I'll try my best," I said. "Please tell me what you did on the day you worked on the grant proposal," I said. "I'm particularly interested in anything you sent by email."

Perry was looking on with more interest than I'd expected to see from him on a technical topic. Maybe he really was coming around.

Dr. Urradu glanced up and noticed that it was past two o'clock. All the other diners had finished their meals, so we were alone in the café, except for the servers. The Nicósn academic looked more at ease talking about his tech problems without a public audience.

Then the next course was delivered to our table. It was Egyptian this time—slow-cooked fava beans with garlic, garnished with sliced hard boiled eggs. Hummus and pita bread came on the side. I was glad I didn't have a *glucose-6-phosphate dehydrogenase* deficiency. Fava beans caused anemia in men with that genetic condition and I needed all my red blood cells in good working order.

None of us at the table started eating. Perry and Dr. Liddell-Scott wanted to see my investigative methods in action and Dr. Urradu was trying his best to document what I had asked for.

"I'm sorry, Dr. Buckston," he said, "so much has happened since then, I'm having difficulty remembering."

"Maybe I could go to your office and review your emails after lunch?" I said.

"Perry and I will be reviewing Durra's research notes with him after lunch," said Dr. Liddell-Scott. "Can you do it now?"

They were relegating the tech guy to sit in front of a computer instead of letting me stay for the rest of this delicious lunch? That didn't make me happy. Dr. Liddell-Scott saw the change in my face.

"No, no," she said. "Sorry. I meant can you do it *here* now?"

She pulled out her phone and gave it a few simple voice instructions. Curtains slid noiselessly back from a section of the café's wall. A server brought a wireless keyboard and mouse to Dr. Liddell-Scott, but she waved him to give them to me.

"No," I said, "Please give them to Dr. Urradu. He needs to log into his email."

While the Nicósn was navigating to the right place with a browser and providing his credentials, I tried the fava beans with garlic. Lucky me, they were even good cold. The servers brought out another course—a platter of hot roast chicken and dates flavored with dill, mint and mustard. I promised myself I'd enjoy some of *this* dish while it was hot.

"Here it is, Dr. Buckston," said Dr. Urradu. "I've scrolled back to last Thursday afternoon."

I served myself a chicken breast and a few sweet dates, then passed the platter to Perry.

"Looks pretty typical, except for a high level of spam," I said, examining his inbox while cutting off a morsel of chicken and half a pitted date with the edge of my fork.

"That's the *other* problem I wanted to talk to you about," said Dr. Liddell-Scott.

"Let's focus on the first issue for now," I said, popping the savory chicken and bit of sweet date into my mouth. I chewed and looked thoughtful, to buy myself time to think.

"Switch to your Sent Items folder, please," I asked the Nicósn.

He did and I reviewed Dr. Urradu's list of sent messages while eating more chicken. The answer, once I saw it, was obvious. I asked my phone to slave the wall screen to its own display. Then I told it to illustrate the problem and a few milliseconds later an animation explaining what had happened on Thursday appeared. My phone got cute and instead of a simple cartoon showing a generic bulging pipe, an image of a snake swallowing a pig showed on the wall screen.

"Before you sent off the grant application, did you happen to send a large collection of photos to another professor?"

"Ye-e-e-s," said Dr. Urradu, stretching out the syllables. "I sent some very high resolution images of Assyrian statues that resembled ancient Nicósn deities to one of my colleagues at the Oriental Institute at the University of Chicago."

Dr. Liddell-Scott was beginning to realize what had happened. Her eyes got very big.

"Did you happen to note the total size of the attached images, Dr. Urradu?"

"No. Does it matter?" he asked.

"Terran email systems aren't designed to handle thirty-five terabyte attachments," I said. "You were trying to push a very large pig through a very small python."

I should have realized the cause of the problem as soon as I figured out that the email issues started right after Dr. Urradu arrived. Network throughput has gotten a lot better since First Contact, but the capacity of most Terran Internet connections was still measured in gigabits, not terabytes.

"So every other message got stuck behind the 'pig'?" asked Dr. Liddell-Scott. I could see she was worried about all the important emails she'd sent that were still queued and waiting.

"Exactly," I said. "But it gets better."

"Better?" asked Perry.

"Uh huh," I said. "Dr. Urradu copied another dozen researchers at universities around the planet. The cumulative size of all the attachments is more than a petabyte."

"Kilobyte, megabyte, gigabyte, terabyte, petabyte," recited Perry. "They're all Greek prefixes. What's after that?"

"Exabyte, zettabyte, yottabyte."

"Yottabyte?" I could see Perry chewing the word in his mouth.

"Networks on Nicós measure their capacity in yottabytes," I said. "So Dr. Urradu never had a problem sending large attachments when he was at Neue Staddam University. Terran network speeds are the bottleneck."

"Why aren't our networks faster?" asked Dr. Liddell-Scott.

I just looked at her.

"Oh," she said. "Of course. Cost."

"Right," I said. "We'll get there, but it will take us at least another decade."

"That explains why it took so long for my full season of the United States House Agriculture Subcommittee on General Farm Commodities meetings to download," said Dr. Urradu.

Dr. Liddell-Scott tried, but failed to hide a laugh.

"Can you fix it?" she said.

"Sure," I said. "I need the administrator's password for the mail server."

"Uhmmm…" said Dr. Liddell-Scott.

"Just put me in touch with your IT manager."

"We don't have one."

"Huh?" I said.

A brilliant response.

"He quit. Yesterday," said Dr. Liddell-Scott, "without giving notice."

"Could you borrow someone from the university?"

"My predecessor burned that bridge years ago," said Dr. Liddell-Scott. "They won't even take my calls."

"Okay, I'll see what I can do."

"Make me look good," I said to my phone, *sotto voce.*

In less than two seconds the administrator's console for the Carlos Museum's email server appeared on the screen.

"Was it *password*?" I whispered.

"*Password123*," replied my phone.

No wonder the former IT manager had left without giving notice. I navigated to the right panel, identified the offending oversized message and all its copies, and deleted them from the outbound message queue. Dr. Liddell-Scott and Dr. Urradu's phones both began to buzz like hives of bees as copies of their now-released outbound messages arrived in clumps.

"*Thank you,*" said Dr. Liddell-Scott. "You're a life-saver."

"What eventually happened with Dr. Urradu's Lamb-Cheops Foundation grant application?" I asked.

"The head of the Foundation knew we were applying and called me when our materials hadn't arrived by the deadline," said Dr. Liddell-Scott. "She told me not to worry and said I should print out a hard copy and give it to the cook at the Waffle House on Virginia Avenue near Hartsfield port."

I started grinning.

"It sounded odd," said Dr. Liddell-Scott, "but she confirmed that would ensure our application would be considered."

"I'm sure it will be fine."

I'd have to tell Roger Joe-Bob Bacon the other side of the story some day.

Our servers brought out the last course—a plate stacked high with *libum* cakes drizzled with honey. They refilled our water glasses and quietly disappeared back into the kitchen. I decided to wait to have a *libum* cake. Honeyed fingers and keyboards aren't a good combination.

"What was your second problem?"

"Spam," said Dr. Liddell-Scott. "It's overwhelming everyone

on my team. It takes forever for emails from colleagues to hit our inboxes and when they do, we have to wade through hundreds of spam emails to find one legitimate email. Half the time the good emails are hiding *in* our spam folders."

"That should be easy to fix," I said.

I looked at the settings on their email server's spam filters. Their former IT manager must have been a real genius. He had the filters set to identify and reject messages tagged as spam. Didn't he realize that the paradigm had shifted several years ago?

The global glut of spam became the galactic glut of spam after First Contact. Spam volumes increased exponentially and Tōdon con artists offering suckers really *big* payoffs joined Nigerian princes on the list of top spam email tropes. With help from computer scientists on Orish, experts at creating things that changed form as necessary, the spam filter companies had developed a new type of artificially intelligent cyber-organism that lived in email servers. Called *mail daemons,* thousands of them lived inside email servers and end-users' email programs. They had voracious appetites for spam and could exchange pseudo-genetic material to evolve faster than the spammers could change their strategies. Once the *daemons* learned end-users' idiosyncrasies, tsunamis of spam would turn into still waters.

I enabled the *mail daemon* function on their email server and set it so the *daemons* would propagate down to individual users automatically. The other three PhDs at the table had been watching my actions on the wall screen and seemed impressed. I may not be able to write a washing bill in Babylonic cuneiform, but I knew my way around email servers.

"That should do it," I said. "Within twenty-four hours your spam problems should be a thing of the past."

"Jack," said Dr. Liddell-Scott, "would Xenotech Support Corporation like a new client?"

"You bet I would."

I stood up and we shook on it. When I sat down again, I removed three *libum* cakes from their plate with a pair of tongs that had wisely been provided. The ricotta cheese mixed with the flour made them soft and the honey made them sweet. I was licking honey off my fingers when Perry leaned over conspiratorially.

"Do you think you might be able to come up to Cambridge and check out the computers in my department?"

Her father was warming to me.

Poly would be pleased.

Chapter 32

"Everything being a constant carnival,
there is no carnival left."
— Victor Hugo

Dr. Liddell-Scott said she would drop Perry off at his hotel on her way home, so I had the rest of the afternoon free. I decided to go back home to get a nap for an hour or two before I had to meet Poly and her family for dinner at seven. The restaurant was only a short walk away so I'd have time for a nap and a chance to recharge my batteries. However, Robert Burns must have been related to Murphy, another Gael, because *the best laid schemes o' mice an' men gang aft agley.* Three minutes after I'd entered my apartment and finished putting my Orishen knitting machine and pupa case spindle back in my project nook, my phone announced that I had a call. I had just kicked my shoes off and moved from vertical to horizontal in my bedroom.

"Who is it?"

"Yon Yonson."

"Put him through."

When I'd first met Yon I'd refrained from asking him where he was from. I'd remembered the infinitely recursive rhyme from Vonnegut's *Slaughterhouse Five* and didn't want to ask a question he'd probably heard a thousand times before. He seemed disappointed that I hadn't, though. Later, over lunch, he admitted that he was, indeed, from Wisconsin.

Yon ran a carnival called Y. Y. Knott's. It was the kind of traveling show that sets up in a small town for a week, then moves on twenty-five miles to the next wide spot in the road. I'd helped him modify two of his rides to use Orishen mutability technology and they'd proved very popular.

One was a lot like the Dumbo ride at Disneyland, with flying elephants moving up and down on long metal arms while spinning like a carousel. I'd found Yon a dozen used children's imagination stations at a salvage yard on Orish and had replaced the elephants with the stations. Now kids got to ride in their own personal transmogrifiers that could change into whatever they could imagine—space ships or race cars or unicorns or even pink Dauushans. The hardest part about rigging up the imagination stations was anchoring them to the arms of the ride so they wouldn't fly off exploring independently.

The other ride was a tame version of a roller coaster designed for preschoolers. I'd replaced the panels on the outside of the coaster's cars with Orishen mutable composite fiber panels that would change into something different every time it went around its track. Sometimes it was a circus train, sometimes a row of prancing ponies, or happy birds or grinning pieces of fruit. The little ones loved it.

"Jack, you've got to help me!"

"What's the problem?"

"The Orishen-tech rides are going crazy," he said, "and I've got parents and *kids* ready to hang me from the top of my Iron Man-themed Ferrous Wheel."

"What's going wrong?"

"The imagination stations spontaneously transformed themselves into Orishen nymphs," he said. "They look like angry praying mantis commandos and they seem to be stuck that way."

"Got it," I said. "Sounds like the WF subroutine is acting up."

"WF?"

"Wish Fulfillment," I said. "What about the other ride?"

"The roller coaster has a similar problem," said Yon. "Now it looks like a grumpy giant centipede. It's an Orishen supra-adult, covered in discolored armor plates and patchy gray bristles. Parents say it's giving their children nightmares."

"Sounds like a similar problem," I said. "Where are you this week?"

I was hoping it wouldn't be Idaho or Alberta. I didn't want

to get into my Remote Hands suit instead of getting ready for dinner tonight.

"We're in the parking lot next to Mercedes Benz Stadium," said Yon.

Thank goodness. They were at least close at hand.

"I'm on my way."

* * * * *

The parking lot at the former home of the Atlanta Falcons was not filled with cars. It hadn't been since 2025 when Pablo Daniel Figueres, the Sirocco Legislature Network founder, had finished building an even larger and more luxurious football stadium in Gwinnett county, northeast of Atlanta. In order to entice the Falcons to move to SLN Stadium and to get regulators to permit it, Figueres had purchased Mercedes Benz Stadium and mothballed it. The less than fifteen-year-old sports facility, with its fancy retractable roof that opened like the petals on a flower, was now padlocked. The carnival seemed lonely set up in a far corner of the facility's acres of asphalt. My van dropped me off by the large Y. Y. Knott Carnival sign at the main entrance. It didn't seem busy. Yon was waiting for me. I left my backpack tool bag in my van and got out.

"Thanks for getting here so fast," he said. "We're expecting a big crowd tonight. Hardly anyone is here right now, thank goodness. A dozen home schooling families just left and nearly took my head with them. They were *not* happy with the mutable rides. I hope you can fix them."

"Let me see what I can do," I said. "The last time something like this happened to a client, a major psychic shock caused the problem. Did anything out of the ordinary happen today? The mutable tech didn't malfunction until this afternoon, right?"

"Right," said Yon. "I can't think of anything out of the ordinary, except the screwed up Orishen tech and the unhappy customers."

"Which must have been caused by *something*," I said.

"Mind if I look around."

"Go right ahead," said Yon. "There's not going to be much to see. The place is nearly dead."

"Thanks," I said. "I'll let you know if I find anything."

The carnival was laid out in a way that looked haphazard, but I knew it was as meticulously planned as the aisles of a supermarket. I started down the wide central avenue that's traditionally known as the Midway. There were lots of tents and small wooden booths on either side. I saw a sign in front of one tent reading "Bruno, the World's Strongest Man," and another farther down that read "Dick Deadeye—Always on Target." There were colorful red and white concentric circles and throwing knives painted on the canvas of that tent.

Games of chance, like throwing darts at balloons and knocking over wooden bottles with baseballs, alternated with shops selling delicious but unhealthy food. I tried not to look at the frozen chocolate-dipped funnel cakes on a stick. They also came sprinkled with chopped borsum nuts and I was glad Chit was back in my van. If she had begged for one, I would have given in.

The rides were at the far end of the Midway. Rides for little kids were on the right and rides for adults and older kids were on the left. The two mutable-tech rides backed up to each other and were separated by a high wall made of wooden panels painted with carnival scenes from the early nineteen-hundreds. I took a closer look. The scenes weren't painted—they were flat screens and the scenes were videos. Men in straw boaters, women in shirtwaist dresses, girls in pinafores and boys in short pants wandered along an earlier incarnation of the Midway.

I wandered, too, down the narrow space between the right hand side of the wall and the kiddie roller coaster. It really was scary in its Orishen supra-adult form.

"What are you doing? Get out of there!" shouted a young woman with dark brown hair in two long pigtails. She was wearing black pants and a red and white striped shirt with the Y. Y. Knott logo embroidered on it—obviously the ride operator.

"It's okay," I said, "I'm Jack. I work for Yon. I'm trying to figure out why the mutable rides are screwed up."

"I'm Hither," she said. "Daddy told me about you. You're Xenotech Support?"

"That's me," I said. "You're Yon's daughter?"

"Uh huh," she said. "I was away at college when you added the Orishen technology."

"What are you studying?"

"Was studying. I just graduated," she said. "Music and business administration."

"That's an interesting double major."

"I love to sing—I focused on vocal performance—and the business part of my degree is so I can help run the carnival when Daddy's ready to retire."

"Like he ever will," I said. "He loves this place."

"I know, right?" she said, "But he said he'd pay for college if I majored in business, so here I am."

"Helping out for the summer?"

"Uh huh," she said. "Until I can figure out what to do next."

"I'm sure your mom and dad are glad to have you around again."

"They are," she said.

I'm not so sure she was as happy to *be* around, but she kept up a good front.

"This Orishen tech is really cool. Daddy and the rubes, *er,* customers love it. He wants to convert two more rides next year."

She looked at the frightening kiddie roller coaster and across the wall at the ride with the angry nymphs.

"Or he *did.*"

Time to change the subject.

"Is your name really Hither?"

"No, it's Heather," she said, smiling. "But I'm a Daddy's girl.

It's been Hither and Yon since before I could walk."

"Well, Hither," I said, "since you're not busy, could you help me do some investigating?"

"Sure," she said. "Something classic, like Holmes and Watson, or more hard boiled, like Marlowe and Spade?"

"More like Columbo," I said. "I'm trying to find the source of the psychic trauma that caused the rides to change to these locked-in forms."

I waved my hand to take in both rides.

"Glad to help," said Hither. "Let's search along the wall first. It's pretty dark toward the back. You take this side, I'll take the other."

"Works for me," I said. "Thanks for the help."

I liked the way she took charge of things and headed off to do them.

"By the way," said Hither over her shoulder. "What am I looking for?"

"You'll know it when you see it," I said.

The dark, narrow space between the wall and the roller coaster enclosure wasn't meant for foot traffic, but it seemed like it was still used as a shortcut or a private place to smoke. The high framework of the roller coaster track cut off a lot of light, so I asked my phone to help me see where I was going.

My phone and I methodically worked our way along the wall, searching for footprints, dropped candy wrappers, and other potential clues. I didn't find anything and probably wouldn't have recognized a clue if it jumped up and bit me singing *The Star Spangled Banner*. I just knew *something* had caused the psychic trauma that had screwed up the mutable rides and I had to find out what.

Ahead of me, another stretch of tall wall at right angles told me I'd reached the far end of the wall I'd been following. We were definitely in backstage territory. A few discarded bags of popcorn and paper cotton candy cones had collected in the corner, blown by the wind. A chill went down my back. Then I heard Hither's voice from the opposite side of the wall.

"Jack, you should probably come over here."

"Be right with you."

There was a gap between the wall I'd been following and the wall at right angles, so it only took me seconds to join her. It was dim and shadowed on her side, too, despite it being only late afternoon.

Hither was pointing at a dark shape on the ground.

It was Shepherd.

His face was clearly visible and his chest was rising, but otherwise, he was motionless. With help from my phone's flashlight app I could see that he had a lump on the back of his head half the size of an emu egg.

"Is he okay?" said Hither.

"I don't know. Can you scan him?" I asked my phone.

"Affirmative."

It made Star Trek tricorder noises then provided its diagnosis.

"He's out cold."

Sometimes I'm in awe of my phone's mastery of the obvious.

"Please call Tomáso," I said.

"Already done. He says you should bring Shepherd to the Dauushan consulate."

"Let him know we'll be there soon."

Pâkk are a tough species, so I didn't worry too much about moving him. Hither and I got his inert form onto a peanut cart and out to the parking lot, where she helped me move him to the rear bench seat of my van. Then I carefully buckled Shepherd in. When I'd finished, Hither touched my arm.

"Will your friend be okay?"

She bumped her phone gently against mine to exchange contact information.

"You'll tell me how he's doing? I haven't had anything this exciting happen since we won the ICCA Regionals."

"ICCA?"

"The International Championship of Collegiate A Capella."

"Cool," I said. "I'll keep you posted."

I got in my van and was about to pull away, but Hither tapped on the driver's side window. I rolled it down.

"What about the mutable rides?" she said.

"Sing to them," I said, "Perky, upbeat songs—no heart-breakers."

"That's it?" she said. "The rides will go back to normal?"

"It worked last time," I said. "Good luck."

Hither looked at me like I was crazy. I smiled, rolled up my window, and buckled my seat belt. I thought I heard her singing *Let It Go* through the glass.

"To the Dauushan consulate, noble ambulance, and step on it."

Chapter 33

*"I wanted my illustrations for the Dante to be like
the faint markings of moisture in a divine cheese."*
— Salvador Dali

We reached the Dauushan consulate faster than I'd thought possible. On the way there, my phone had climbed up on the roof where it flashed blue and red lights and emitted an emergency vehicle's rising and falling wail, so that every other car, truck, van and bus would get out of our way. Of course, it could have just been doing the lights and siren for show and had communicated with the other vehicles electronically, but who was I to complain?

My van drove into the underground parking garage at Ad Astra and made its way to the Dauushan consulate's exclusive area where their official truck-sized transports were parked. The two large, pink armored tanks that had transported Sherrhi and Terrhi from the Teleport Inn were nose to tail against the far wall. We pulled up in front of the elevator to the consulate, where a pair of Påkk medicos in white vests were waiting with a stretcher. They got Shepherd out of the back seat, strapped him in, and carried him to the elevator. I followed and rode up to street level.

Tomáso met us in the elevator lobby and led me and the stretcher-bearers through the doors to his residence, not the consulate offices. We went to his private study where I'd met with him several times before. They carried Shepherd up to the study's raised platform, where a Påkk physician and a hospital bed were waiting for him. Then the Påkk medicos did their thing with IV lines, blood pressure cuffs, thermometers and other tools of their trade I didn't recognize. One of the stretcher-bearers left—maybe to get ice for the lump on Shepherd's head.

I climbed up on the raised platform, too, but at the far end away from Shepherd's bed. Tomáso and I needed to talk face to face and the platform made that a lot easier.

"Thanks for getting Shepherd here so quickly," said Tomáso. "His consulate wants to keep the situation quiet, so we'll be taking care of him here. What happened?"

I explained where I'd found the Påkk diplomat.

"Why would Shepherd be poking around at a carnival?" said Tomáso.

"And who would be able to sneak up behind him to bash his head?" I added.

Påkk have exceptional situational awareness.

Then Terrhi and Spike came into the room. I could see the Shetland pony-sized girl was brimming with questions, but when she saw the medical personnel she stayed quiet and came up to join me. Spike rubbed his head against my leg but I was ready for him and didn't topple over. That wouldn't have been wise, since I was standing on the edge of the raised platform.

"Will Shepherd be okay?" she said.

I was about to answer when one of the Påkk medical types stepped over to us.

"Shepherd will make a complete recovery," he said.

"That's good news," I said. Tomáso agreed.

"He's got a concussion and few cuts where he fell," said the Påkk physician. "None of the bones in his skull are broken. We'll keep him sedated for twenty-four hours and reevaluate then."

"Thanks," I said to his back as he returned to his patient.

Apparently, Påkk have hard heads, too.

"I have more information for you about O'Sullivan Fabrication," said Tomáso.

"Your dinner with Poly and her family is in ten minutes," said my phone.

I slapped my forehead. I was an idiot. Once I'd found Shepherd I'd completely forgotten about the dinner.

"Can it wait until later?" I said. "Poly will want to hear your news, too."

"Very well," said Tomáso, "I will try to find out more details in the interim."

"Thanks," I said. "I'm late for a very important date."

"Don't keep Poly waiting," said Tomáso.

"Bring Poly back here, please, Uncle Jack," said Terrhi. "Diágo won't let me go *anywhere*."

"He's just trying to protect you," I said.

"I've got Spike for that," said Terrhi in her light, little girl's voice. She rubbed Spike's head with a few of her sub-trunks.

The big cat pushed back against her and purred.

"I'll see what I can do after dinner," I said. "But no promises."

"Thanks, Uncle Jack," said Terrhi. "I know I can count on you."

How did kids get so good at emotional blackmail? I blame television.

It was time to get moving. I was supposed to meet Poly and her family for dinner at seven at "the place with the pirate ship and the crocodiles." I left the Dauushan consulate, waving to one of the Queen's guards I remembered from the Teleport Inn, and sprinted down another arm of Ad Astra's courtyard toward the restaurant. I made it with thirty seconds to spare. No one noticed me arrive, however.

The restaurant's formal name was Dante's Down the Hatch. It was a quirky Buckhead institution that had been around since the early 1970s. Dante's had temporarily closed way back in 2013—I think they lost their lease—but reopened ten years later. Now it was located between two upscale hotels in the Ad Astra complex and was popular with both tourists and locals.

Dante's was decorated to look like a town scene from Disney's *Pirates of the Caribbean* ride. Its interior resembled an eighteenth century tropical island port, complete with a pirate ship at anchor and rambling Spanish-style buildings close to the water. The lighting was dim with gas lamps, torches and lots of candles. Archways in the buildings' stone facades held romantic tables for two with views of the pirate ship and the artificial lagoon where it floated. The ship's cannons would fire whenever guests had special occasions, like birthdays or anniversaries.

The crocodiles swimming in the water near the pirate ship, hoping for treats, were one of Dante's biggest attractions. Guests waiting for tables could buy bits of meat to feed them. Lots of folks showed up early for their reservations just to watch the crocs. Poly and her family hadn't noticed my arrival because they were too busy tossing chunks of beef at aquatic reptiles.

"That one's Jerry," I said, pointing to the largest crocodile in the water between the feeding area and the side of the pirate ship. "He was one of Dante's original crocs. They brought him back from a sanctuary in St. Augustine after they re-opened."

Poly turned around, saw me, and gave me a hug and a more-where-this-is-coming-from kiss. I disengaged with a smile and leaned over the railing next to Pomy, indicating another croc.

"That one's Pinocchio, because he's got the longest snout."

"Hi Jack," said Pomy.

She gave me an air peck on the cheek. Perry and Barbara were holding hands farther down the feeding station.

"Hello, Jack," said Barbara.

"I'm glad you got here," said Perry.

"Daddy," said Pomy, "don't give Jack a rough time for being late."

"He wasn't late, Pomegranate," said Perry. "And I wasn't being sarcastic. I really am glad he got here."

"Would you like to feed the crocodiles?" asked Poly.

She picked up a plastic bag from the railing by the feeding area and offered it to me.

"Sure," I said, removing a piece of beef. I tossed it to a small crocodile with two yellow stripes down its back.

"What's that one's name?" asked Poly.

"Gucci."

She wagged her finger at me.

"That's *bad*."

"I thought you wanted me to be bad."

"Save that for later," she said, "for the next two hours, please be on your best behavior."

"Yes, ma'am," I said.

"I wonder if he's good at being bad?" said Pomy, without looking up from the water.

"Shush," said Poly.

"Keen, party of five," said the hostess.

"That's us," said Barbara. "We always use my name when we go out to dinner. It gets us better service."

We all took alcohol wipes from a dispenser and cleaned our hands, then followed the hostess past the pirate ship and up a flight of stairs.

Barbara was probably right about getting better service. Publishing the best-selling tourist guides in the galaxy did give her a certain degree of clout with restaurateurs. We were shown to a table for five in a wide arch on the second floor overlooking the ship and the lagoon. It was a great table and I wondered if restaurant owners might be interested in buying face recognition systems to alert them when any major food critics or other V.I.P.s entered their establishments. I made a mental note to tell my phone so it could remind me to follow up on it later.

The table was rectangular, with one narrow end against a low wall below an open arch. Perry and Barbara sat across from each other, closest to the view. They were holding hands again and staring into each other's eyes above a candle burning in a red glass bowl. I sat at the far end of the table with Poly to my right and Pomy to my left. It felt like the two ends of the table were for the kids and the adults, but I couldn't quite tell which of us was which.

A server arrived to give us menus and fill our water glasses. Barbara and Perry ordered white wine.

"What's good here?" asked Pomy.

"Everything," I said, "especially the fondues. But don't order the dumplings. They're deep fried, not pan fried."

"Why don't you order for us, Jack," said Poly. She raised her voice. "If that's okay with Mom and Dad?"

She got a nod from Perry and a small positive gesture from Barbara.

"Everyone likes cheese?"

More nods.

"And chocolate?"

I got words back this time—all in the affirmative.

"Great," I said. "We'll start with a traditional cheese fondue, then a hot oil fondue with meats, seafood and vegetables, then have bittersweet chocolate fondue for dessert."

"Could you get one of those octovacs to carry me home after dinner?" said Pomy. "I don't know if I'll be able to walk after a meal like that."

"You'll manage," I said. "Just pace yourself and don't fill up too early."

Our server returned with the two glasses of white wine, baskets of sliced fresh baguettes, and ramekins filled with chilled butter. I placed our order.

"Excellent choices, sir," said our server.

Poly and Pomy said they'd had a lot of fun shopping at Lenox Square Mall. They'd found two dresses for Pomy and shoes to match at Neiman Marcus. They were less formal than what she'd worn to the royal dinner and perfect for spring graduation ceremonies in Atlanta. Poly teased me that my gift of an Orishen morphic silk dress and shoes took all the fun out of shopping. She always had exactly the right thing to wear for any occasion.

Perry and Barbara didn't join the conversation until after the cheese fondue arrived. We all had fun trying to hold cubes of bread and apples on the ends of our fondue forks.

"How did things go at Georgia Tech today?" Poly asked Barbara. It might have been a peace offering, not just a question.

"Quite well," said her mother, "and Jack set up a lunch meeting for me with the nicest woman, the CEO at a company called Morphicoture. They made your dress, dear."

She nodded at Poly and smiled at me.

"Think how much less I'll have to pack for my interstellar trips with morphic clothing," she said.

"I'm glad you and Ellie got along so well," I said.

"We really hit it off," said Barbara, spearing a piece of apple with her fondue fork and dipping it in the gooey cheese. "But I almost forgot—there was a young Orishen looking for you at the dean's office."

"A young Orishen? A larva? A nymph?" I asked.

"I didn't see him," said Barbara. "I just heard your name and recognized that the voice belonged to a young Orishen."

"Curious," I said.

"You may see him tomorrow," said Barbara. "I think he's graduating."

It was fun feeding bread dipped in cheese to Poly. Barbara and Perry were feeding each other, too. I think Pomy was feeling left out, but didn't know what to do about it. Maybe I'd introduce her to Ray Ray?

When the hot oil fondue course came to our table I made sure to be more sociable and pulled Perry and Barbara and Pomy into conversation. Perry and I talked about the exhibits and behind the scenes artifacts at the Carlos Museum. He also bragged about how fast I'd solved Dr. Liddell-Scott's tech problems. Pomy said she'd have to visit the museum herself next week. She said she was planning an extended visit to Atlanta to catch up on lost time with her sister.

The bittersweet chocolate dessert fondue was amazing. It made me glad I'd forgotten to bring my backpack tool bag with me from my van, since Chit would have demanded a thimbleful and would have threatened to fall into the pot.

We were all full and Pomy wasn't the only one interested in help from an octovac to roll home. When we left the restaurant, Perry and Barbara said good night and walked arm in arm down the courtyard to the right. Poly looked a me, then at

Pomy, then at me again. I tried to solve her dilemma.

"May I please borrow your sister for an hour or two?" I said to Pomy. "There are things we need to talk about. I'll have her back before eleven."

"Okay," said Pomy. She put on a stern face. "But not one minute after, young man."

"Yes, ma'am," I said.

All three of us laughed.

"I'm going back inside to take another look at all the memorabilia," said Pomy.

"There's a lot of it," I said. "See you back at your hotel."

Poly and I walked down the courtyard to the left, which happened to be the direction of the Dauushan consulate. I told Poly what had happened at the carnival this afternoon.

"Poor Shepherd," she said. "Who would have done something like this?"

"Someone who didn't like where he was poking his snout," I said.

"At a carnival?"

"It doesn't make sense," I said. "Maybe Tomáso's found out something more. He said he had an update on O'Sullivan Fabrication."

I felt a slight tremble in the ground and saw something large and pink headed my way.

"Speak of the devil," said Poly.

Tomáso and Martin were coming up the walk to meet us. Neither one of them looked happy.

"What's wrong?" said Poly. "Did something happen to Shepherd?"

"Shepherd's fine," said Tomáso. "At least he will be in a day or so. A knock on the head won't keep him down for long."

"I'm the one with bad news," said Martin. "I lost Cornell."

"How do you lose a grown man?" asked Poly.

"Weren't you holding him in a cell in the capitol basement?" I said.

"Yes, but someone pulled the fire alarm and he got away in the confusion."

"Didn't you have him guarded?"

"Yes," said Martin, sounding miserable, "but he was an irregular prisoner. We hadn't formally put him in the system."

"Got it," I said. "So he slipped through the cracks. No use locking the barn door after the milk is spilled."

Poly gave me a strange look, then spoke to Tomáso.

"Jack says you have more information about O'Sullivan Fabrication."

"I do," said Tomáso. "Thanks to a tip from an insider we found the entrance to the lower level."

"Was it empty?"

"Yes," said Tomáso, "but not clean. We found signs that the lower lab really was being used to incubate Compliant Plague nanoparticles. Scuff marks and depressions on the floor of the lower and upper warehouses also indicate ten giant robots had been stored in the facility."

"So Queen Sherrhi's gambit worked. They're going to show their hand."

"When she speaks at Emory's commencement on Saturday," said Tomáso.

"Odds are good," I said. "But we'll stop them somehow."

"Or I will," said Tomáso, "with the *Charalindhri.*"

"There's something I don't understand," I said. "By the time your asteroid melting ship's beams hit the surface they're not going to be precision instruments. How are you going to make sure Queen Sherrhi and Terrhi and the rest of us aren't fried?"

"Diágo has a way to evacuate the queen and the princess," said Tomáso. "They won't be there when the beam strikes."

"But the rest of us might be?" said Poly.

She looked like she didn't believe what she was hearing.

"As a last resort," said Tomáso.

"It won't come to that," I said.

"It better not," said Poly.

Martin spoke up.

"We'll do our best to find Cornell and recapture him."

"I'll give you even money that he'll be piloting a robot on Saturday morning," said Poly.

"You may be right," said Martin.

Tomáso knelt down on his front legs and bent his head toward Poly and me.

"My friends," he said. "I know my desire to protect my Queen, my species, and the galaxy offends you."

"Not when you put it that way, big guy," I said.

"Nonetheless," he said, "I beg a boon."

"What can we do for you?" said Poly.

"Not for me," said Tomáso, "for my daughter."

"How can we help?" I asked.

"Could you and Poly please tell Terrhi a bedtime story?"

How could we say no?

Chapter 34

"You can never learn less, you can only learn more."
— R. Buckminster Fuller

Terrhi didn't get a bedtime story. She didn't even get two bedtime stories, she got three. I'd called Pomy and invited her to join us at Tomáso's apartment and she came up with a very inventive tale about a strong, independent Dauushan girl named Atalanthi, three suitors, and a race with three golden apples. Atalanthi used the apples to bean her suitors, won the race, and went on to live her own life. Spike liked my tale of the trolls living under the Tenth Street Bridge and their confrontation with the Three Trisabercats Gruff, but Poly's story was Terrhi's favorite.

"…then Princess Polhi saw that the gods had cursed Queen Sisyphushi to push the giant round boulder up the hill, but never get it to the top. 'Let me help you,' said the princess. Together they rolled the boulder up to the top and down the other side, where it knocked over the pillars of the mean gods' temples like bowling pins. And Polhi and Sisyphushi were the best of friends until the end of their days."

If we made it through the weekend, I expected that Tomáso would be ordering Terrhi-sized lawn bowling equipment.

When the bedtime stories were over, I walked Poly and Pomy back to the Star Palace. I kissed one sister, hugged the other, and headed back to my apartment. On the way, I heard the same scurrying sounds in the bushes I'd heard before. I made a mental note to borrow Spike from Terrhi so the two of us could flush out whatever small animal was making the noise. I was betting on chipmunks, since squirrels usually kept to the trees.

When I entered my apartment I started to worry. I really needed to get some sleep, but every time I'd had a chance for a good night's rest or even a nap lately, some emergency appeared or some obligation landed on my shoulders. Normally, I thrive on excitement, but the chance of having to pull back to back all-nighters made me twitchy. I debated telling my phone to hold my calls, but couldn't do that to my friends or my clients. Georgia Tech's Advanced Galtech graduation ceremonies for master's students started at ten, which meant I'd need to have my phone wake me at seven. I'd need that long to get ready, have breakfast, pick up Poly and her family, drive to Tech and get good seats at the Figueres Center. At least I didn't need to worry about parking. My van would take care of that.

It was nearly midnight. Seven hours of rest would be a nice down payment on my sleep deficit. I went into my bedroom, put my phone on its charger on my bedside table, and took off all my clothes. I didn't even have the strength to put them in the hamper—they landed on the floor. I'd worry about them later. I fell into bed and was milliseconds away from joining Shepherd in unconsciousness.

Then my phone rang.

I couldn't summon the energy to say "Crap."

"Who is it?" I said.

"Poly," said my phone.

That was a call I was glad to take.

"Hi," I said.

"Hi, yourself," said Poly.

I felt warm and happy just hearing her voice.

"I've missed you," she said.

"I just hugged you fifteen minutes ago."

"That was Pomy."

"Oh," I said. She could hear the smile in my voice.

"You know what I mean," said Poly. "We've both been so busy we haven't had much time for *us*."

"Uh huh," I said. "On that basis, I miss you, too. How's your list coming?"

"You're serious? You want to go right after Emory's gradua-tion ceremonies? For a week?"

"Yep," I said. "Mike can handle basic support calls, and

I've got a guy that we can use, at least temporarily, for more advanced problems."

"But what happens when you get an emergency call and have to fly back from Tahiti or Guam or wherever?"

"This trip will be for *us*. I won't let anything disrupt it."

"Famous last words, Lover Boy," she said. "And yes, I've been working on my list. Have you?"

"You know I have."

"Good night, darling," she said.

"Good night, sweetheart," I said.

The next thing I knew my phone was telling me it was time to get up.

* * * * *

It was a beautiful morning and my van didn't even have to circle to find a place to park. A special spot had been reserved for the guest speaker at the ceremonies. This morning's activities were only for master's candidates in applied fields, like engineering and galtech. There'd be a brunch—mostly a chance for parents to meet professors—following the applied graduation exercises. Physics, chemistry, biology, and such would have their ceremonies in the afternoon.

The Figueres Center was a monument to Terran architects' first exposure to the species of the Galactic Free Trade Association. It had soaring curves and an Orishen-inspired partially melted look, similar to the Ad Astra complex. The center was constructed on a grand scale, with entrances large enough for Dauushans and Tōdons. There were also high perches and anchor points in the lobby and auditorium for Quirinx fliers and Fthtipth floaters. Separate small access doors and corridors built into the walls protected Musans and J'Vel from the feet of larger entities. Georgia Tech's programs drew students from planets across the galaxy, so accommodating the needs of a wide range of sentient species was a necessity.

Chit had said that she'd stay in her bottle and watch the festivities on television, via closed circuit broadcasts from my phone and the university's public feed. That way she could still watch her programs in split screen. I wondered if that was just her excuse for wanting to sleep in.

Poly left us to go wherever it was the degree recipients were congregating and Barbara went backstage. She'd be sitting up on the stage with the other dignitaries. Perry, Pomy and I found the seats that Barbara had insisted be reserved for us in the center of the second row. I wore my best suit, the one I wore on my first date with Poly. Perry was wearing a distinguished gray pinstripe suit and a crimson Harvard tie with little *VE-RI-TAS* shields. Pomy had on one of her new dresses—it was sleeveless with blue and white stripes—and looked great.

Precisely at the stroke of ten—these were engineers and technologists, after all—the ceremony started. First the Deans and speakers entered the stage. I was talking to Pomy and didn't notice until a brass quintet in the balcony started to play something from Holst's *The Planets*. The faculty, in full academic regalia, processed down the left aisle and stood in the seats reserved for them at the front of the auditorium. I recognized Professor Urrrson—he was tall enough to stand out. Then the master's and PhD candidates marched down the right side in caps and gowns and stood at their reserved seats. A Tōdon and two Dauushan students stood in the right aisle. I wondered what the fire marshal would think? When everyone arrived, the music stopped. Then the Dean of the School of Engineering stood and motioned us to sit. She stepped to the podium.

"Degree candidates, members of the faculty, parents, friends and honored guests," said the dean, "We gather to celebrate an important milestone. Today is the culmination of the hard work and dedication of the one hundred and ninety-seven members of the graduating class of master's degree candidates and fifteen candidates for doctorates. As is our custom, the student with the best academic record in the class of 2030 will now share a few words. Please welcome this year's top student, Ms. Polyhymnia Keen Jones."

You could have knocked me over with a Quirinx feather when I saw Poly replace the dean at the microphone. She'd been on stage, but I hadn't been able to see her because she was masked by the podium. My phone climbed up on my shoulder and started capturing her on video.

"Back in the twentieth century," said Poly, "a wise man saw that our planet was more than the ground beneath our feet. For him, it was Spaceship Earth, an amazing vessel for transporting us into the future. If Buckminster Fuller had lived to see the Galactics' arrival, he would have had one thing to say to them: 'What took you so long?' We are students of engineering and galactic technologies, and we're making up for lost time, learning what galtech can do for Terra and what Terran science and engineering can do for the galaxy. We are the ones who have to write the operating manual for Spaceship Earth as it takes us to the stars."

Poly paused and looked out at the grads, parents and faculty.

"Many years ago, Fuller said 'Sometimes I think we're alone. Sometimes I think we're not. In either case, the thought is staggering.' We now know that we are *not* alone and it *is* staggering. We must find our own place in the community of sentient species as we learn from them and welcome seekers of knowledge from other planets here to learn from us."

She paused again and took a deep breath.

"Bucky—I think he'd be glad to have us call him that—once said, 'I am not a thing — a noun. I seem to be a verb, an evolutionary process — an integral function of the universe.' We all need to go out into the galaxy and be verbs, action verbs, looking to find our function and making ourselves integral parts of the galaxy. Remember, as Fuller said, 'There is no joy equal to that of being able to work for all humanity and doing what you're doing well.'"

A smattering of applause came from the audience. Poly kept speaking.

"In conclusion, we must all keep open minds, or as Fuller

put it, 'Dare to be naive.' There's still so much for us to learn. I'll leave you with these parting words of Bucky wisdom, 'You can never learn less, you can only learn more.' Let's keep learning more, my friends, let's keep learning more. Thank you."

Poly stepped back from the podium and heard enthusiastic applause from everyone in the auditorium. Her fellow students rose to give her a standing ovation and members of the faculty and parents stood as well. Professor Urrrson was one of the faculty members clapping the loudest. Poly smiled, bowed in appreciation, and sat down. I wondered if she'd been writing her speech on some of the nights when she said she was working on her research paper? Whenever she wrote it, it was time well spent.

The people organizing the ceremony were smart enough not to follow Poly's speech with another speaker. Instead, Georgia Tech's off-planet all female a cappella group, the Gal-actics, sang two pop songs from before First Contact. One was about girls just wanting to have fun, and the little Pyr in front hit the high notes with two of her mouths while doing vocal percussion with the remaining pair. Two Tigrammaths, a Pâkk, a Musan, two Nicósns, and a young adult Dauushan made up the rest of the ensemble. They were quite good and I started humming along.

Then came a man playing Bach's *D minor Partita* on the violin. The mathematical precision of Bach's music struck a chord with the technically inclined graduates. Finally it was time for Poly's mother to give her commencement address. I'd expected her to speak from her head, telling the audience what she'd learned by traveling the galaxy. Instead, she surprised me. She spoke from the heart and didn't make her speech about her, but about Poly.

"When I visited to the worlds of the Galactic Free Trade Association to write books," said Barbara, "I brought my daughter along with me, hoping to teach her about alien societies. Instead, my daughter taught me. I saw the ruins of Old Pyr with jaded eyes that looked on these ancient structures as ways to get rich selling Keen's Guides. She showed me how they looked through her young eyes, wide with wonder, and reawakened my own inner child."

Barbara continued, talking about how much it meant for her to share the tall towers of the sacred Tigrammath city of Purrin, the canals of Neue Staddam on Nicós, the ever-changing forests on Orish, the mounds of the little makers on Dauush and the Long Påkk shrine of remembrance on Akkhêntók with her daughter. She even admitted that Poly's translation of *Dauushan Strata* was better than her *Dauushan Lasagna* alternative. That one prompted more than a few laughs. Everyone in the audience was listening carefully. Students weren't even looking at their phones. After fifteen minutes, she brought her address to a close.

"My daughter said it better than I could," said Barbara. "'Dare to be naive,' she said, quoting Buckminster Fuller. If you keep the eyes of youth, the wonders of the galaxy will always be yours. Thank you."

The audience rose to its feet, clapping and cheering. Barbara brought Poly up to stand with her at the podium and they embraced. Mother and daughter both had tears of joy running down their cheeks. I might have needed a tissue or two myself.

The ceremony where diplomas were bestowed was almost an anticlimax. When Polyhymnia Keen Jones' name was called, there was applause, even though no one was supposed to clap until the end. At last, the formal commencement ritual was over and the crowd started to filter out to the lobby and adjacent courtyard where a brunch was laid out on long tables.

There was a lot of commotion after the ceremony. Graduates were congratulating each other and milling about, blocking the aisles. As I was walking out of the auditorium with Poly and her family, I heard a disturbance in the aisle behind me. A tall nymph in the abbreviated Orishen version of a cap and gown was making his way up behind us. He looked like a human-sized praying mantis with sharp blades on his shins and forearms. The nymph was wearing blade covers, but nearby humans were wisely giving him lots of space.

"Are you Jack Buckston?" said the nymph, once he reached us.

"That's me. What can I do for you?"

This must be the nymph that was asking about me in the dean's office.

"I am Shuvvath," he said, "and I am in your debt."

"Shuvvath?" said Poly. "From Zesto's?"

"Yes," said the Orishen. "You prevented me from attacking and killing several sentients, including children."

"Glad to help," I said.

"Me, too," said my favorite graduate. "I'm Poly Jones."

"If not for your fast thinking, the police might have had to kill me to stop me," said Shuvvath. "I owe you a life debt, Mr. Buckston. And you too, it seems, Ms. Jones."

Pomy was whispering to her parents, telling them about what had happened when Poly and I had gone for ice cream and found an Orishen pupa case about to split and release its dangerous nymph form. The sisters must have had time to catch up on each other's lives.

"I'm just glad you're okay now," I said.

"Right," said Poly. "Have a good life and we'll consider the debt repaid."

"That is not how it works," said Shuvvath. "I have been trying to find you for weeks. I need to serve you for a year and a day."

"An Orishen year?" I asked.

Orishen years are twenty percent longer than our years.

"No, local time reference is fine," said Shuvvath.

Poly and I looked at each other.

"Let's continue this discussion in the lobby," said Poly. "People want to talk to my mom and after all the nervous energy I expended giving my speech I could really use some food."

"Excellent," said the Orishen.

We made our way to the delicious spread and all helped ourselves to plates of crepes, bacon, mini-quiches, and other typical brunch entrées. Poly introduced her family to Professor Urrrson and the Tigrammath artificial intelligence expert praised Poly enough that I saw her cheeks get red. Then Barbara was surrounded by a crowd of admirers and Perry stayed close to her and smiled a lot. Professor Urrrson bowed and stepped away to speak with a faculty colleague. Pomy walked over to tell the members of the Gal-actics how much she'd enjoyed their music.

Poly, Shuvvath and I found a shady spot to sit on a low wall in the Figueres Center's courtyard. Well, Poly and I sat. Shuvvath's anatomy wasn't really designed for it.

"What's your degree in?" I asked.

"Earth tech," said Shuvvath. "It is my second master's degree, actually. I already have one in engineering from Mulbiri Tech back home."

"That's my alma mater," I said. "We may have been there at the same time."

"Quite possibly," said Shuvvath. "I was there for my undergrad work, too."

"What are your plans now that you've graduated?" asked Poly.

"I had planned to return to Orish, but now I need to serve the two of you."

Poly and I looked at each other and exchanged messages with our eyebrows. We seemed to be in agreement.

"Would you be interested in being an employee of Xenotech Support Corporation?" I said.

"That is your company?" said Shuvvath.

"Our company," I said, putting my arm around Poly. "We do tech support for galactic technology."

"Then I could serve you both at the same time?" said Shuvvath. "And use my degrees?"

He looked pleased.

"Certainly," said Poly. "We'll pay you a salary and everything."

"Oh, good," said the nymph. "That means I will not have to ask my clan for support."

"We can't have that," I said.

"You are very considerate," said Shuvvath. "It will be a pleasure to serve you."

"Welcome aboard," I said.

"You're our second employee," said Poly.

"Do you offer 401(k) matching?" said Shuvvath.

I looked at Poly and smiled.

"We'll let you know."

"Jack," said my phone. "Tomáso just called. Can you and Poly get back to the Dauushan consulate right away? Shepherd's waking up."

"Pomy and Mom and Dad can take an autocab," said Poly. "I'll let them know we have to leave."

"We're on our way."

Chapter 35

"Sister is probably the most competitive relationship within the family…"
— Margaret Mead

When Poly told Pomy and her parents that we were leaving, Pomy asked if she could come with us. She was concerned about Shepherd, too. Shuvvath said he would be ready to report for work whenever he was needed and we exchanged contact information with our latest employee before leaving for Ad Astra. Terrhi met us at the courtyard entrance to her family's condo.

"Uncle Jack, Aunt Poly, Aunt Pomy," she said, "the doctors say Shepherd will be awake soon."

"Great," I said. "Maybe he can tell us what happened."

"I know that," said Terrhi. "He got hit on the back of his head."

"That's right, Princess," said Poly, "but the important questions are *why*…"

"And by *whom*…?" I said.

"And *how?*" said Pomy.

Pomy was smiling. I think she liked being one of Terrhi's honorary aunts. I wondered if it was just a ploy to get more bedtime stories, but discounted the idea. Terrhi was too sweet a child to be so manipulative, wasn't she? Spike butted my leg then turned and moved his head in a way I interpreted as "Follow me." Terrhi and Spike led us to the study. Tomáso and Queen Sherrhi were already there and were standing close to Shepherd's hospital bed on the study's platform. Poly, Pomy, Terrhi, Spike and I climbed up and approached the medical personnel monitoring Shepherd's condition.

"Welcome," said Tomáso. "When I heard Shepherd was likely to wake up soon, I wanted you to be here."

"How's he doing?" I asked.

The most senior Pâkk physician answered.

"His brain waves are still a bit odd, but his vital signs are much stronger. We're about to administer a medication that should wake him up."

"I thought you were going to keep him out for twenty-four hours," I said.

"The consort says the patient may have knowledge vital to the security of the galaxy," said the physician, "so we are waking him sooner than we'd planned."

The medico injected a dark fluid into an intravenous line in Shepherd's arm.

"The security of the galaxy?" I said. "Isn't that unwarranted hyperbole?"

"No," said Tomáso.

"It is not," said Queen Sherrhi.

"Don't be mean to Terra," said Terrhi.

"We may not have a choice," said her father.

"Are we back to that again?" said Poly. "Heat rays from orbit?"

"If necessary," said Tomáso.

"What *about* heat rays from orbit?" said Pomy.

"Later," said Poly.

Shepherd was waking up. I hoped the medication wouldn't slow his recovery.

"Hello, old friend," said Tomáso.

Shepherd blinked and moved his head slowly from side to side as if testing to ensure it was still connected to his neck and torso.

"Not good," he said. Each word was drawn out as if it was an effort for him to speak it.

"What's not good?" asked Tomáso.

Shepherd leaned up on one elbow and noticed Poly and Pomy standing with me.

"Sisters," he said.

Then his head sank back onto the bed and his eyes closed. Tomáso reached out with three sub-trunks to shake him awake, but the physician stopped him by interposing his body between Tomáso and his patient.

"You won't get more out of him unless he gets more rest."

The Pâkk physician put his hands on his hips and looked like he was ready to challenge Tomáso if the Dauushan tried to touch Shepherd again. Queen Sherrhi put three of her own sub-trunks on Tomáso's flank.

"Have patience," said the Queen. "You and your task force will find the plague spheres before they can be used."

"But your speech is tomorrow morning," said Tomáso. "We're running out of time. I was counting on a clue from Shepherd."

"He gave us one," I said. "And we're going to follow up on it."

Poly looked at me, saw me smile, and got my back.

"Right," she said. "It's a pretty good clue, too. Let's hit the road."

She took my arm and the two of us walked down the platform's steps.

Pomy looked at Tomáso, Queen Sherrhi, Terrhi, and Spike. She pointed at Poly and me.

"I'm with them," she said.

Then she ran down the steps to catch up with us.

"Bye Uncle Jack, Aunt Poly, Aunt Pomy…" said Terrhi. "Will you tell me a bedtime story when you get back?"

* * * * *

Pomy went up to her hotel suite to change and Poly came with me to my apartment so we could do the same. I got out of my suit and put on black jeans, black athletic shoes, and a long-sleeved black t-shirt over my protective Orishen pupa silk shirt. I strapped my knife made from one of Spike's incisors to my waist, just to look badass. Poly donned a similar outfit—she'd left her pupa silk shirt at my place—and the two of us looked like low budget ninjas.

My van was waiting for us when we got to Peachtree Street. We both got in, buckled up, and headed for the Star Palace to pick up Pomy. She climbed in the rear passenger seat through the sliding door. Pomy was wearing black pants, but hadn't gotten the memo about black shirts. She wore a white cotton blouse, a short red jacket, and black flats. Her black leather purse was the size of a tote bag. Not exactly ninja gear, but we'd manage.

Shepherd *had* given us a clue. "Sisters," he'd said. He wasn't referring to Poly and Pomy. Columbia Brown, or Sarah Lawrence Barnard, as she was calling herself now, had a sister. We hadn't had much luck tracking the homicidal Ms. Brown, unfortunately. Her company, O'Sullivan Fabrication, had been abandoned and was now a dead end. But Agnes Spelman, according to Ray Ray Dunwoody, was the CEO of Factor-E-Flor. Even though Factor-E-Flor was registered in the Cayman Islands, it must still have an office in metro Atlanta. I thought it was high time we met Columbia Brown's sister and found out what *her* part was in all this.

First, we had to find Factor-E-Flor. I asked my phone to research possible locations. It gave me an address in an office park just inside the northwest Perimeter.

"Is this your best guess?" I asked.

"No," said my phone. "The address of their North American headquarters is on their web site."

Maybe I hadn't done as much as I'd hoped to pay back my sleep deficit. I wonder why I'd expected them to be circumspect about revealing their location?

"Please ask my van to…"

"Already done," said my phone.

"Isn't that the next complex over from WT&F?" said Poly.

"Affirmative," said my phone.

"What the hell is going on?" said Pomy.

I gave her a summary, with help from Poly.

"So this woman, or her sister, the one who shot you, plans to kidnap Queen Sherrhi tomorrow and release a plague that will turn us all into zombie slaves?"

"Pretty much," I said.

"And thereby take over the galaxy," said Poly.

"What about the heat rays from orbit?" said Pomy.

"Tomáso's insurance policy to protect the queen," I said.

"And sterilize the planet, if necessary," Poly added.

She was thinking a few steps ahead of me.

"This is a lot more exciting than removing pottery shards from trenches with a toothbrush back in Rome," said Pomy.

"Tell me about it," said Poly.

* * * * *

It was mid-afternoon when we neared our destination. Factor-E-Flor's North American headquarters was another cookie cutter concrete, glass and steel office building. Four-foot orange letters on the lawn out front spelled the company's name. It was screened from WT&F's headquarters and the major access road by a double row of fifty-foot pines or I would have noticed it years ago.

"How do you want to play this?" asked Poly. "I expect they know both of us."

"True," I said, "so it will be up to Pomy to provide a distraction while we go in undercover."

"Under a light bending fabric poncho, you mean," said Poly. "Dibs on the Blend Into The Scenery suit."

"Fine," I said. "You can have the suit. I'll take the poncho."

"Provide a distraction?" said Pomy.

"Say you're from the IRS and here to conduct a surprise audit," I said.

"I don't have the right ID," said Pomy.

"And I don't think the IRS does that," said Poly.

"Building inspector?" I suggested.

"That would be handled by someone in Facilities, not the CEO," said Pomy.

"An investigator for the Securities and Exchange Commission?" I offered.

"Factor-E-Flor's not publicly traded," said Poly.

"I think I've got it," said Pomy. "I'll just be myself."

"Always be yourself," said my phone.

"Shush," I said. *Really?*

"Yes," said Pomy. "I will give my real name and say I need to speak to Agnes Spelman on an urgent private matter related to my missing sister and her boyfriend. That should pique her attention."

"Works for me," I said.

"What if Agnes Spelman turns the tables and holds Pomy hostage?" said Poly.

"There are two octovacs in the back of the van in case we need to stage a rescue," I said.

"Excelsior," said Pomy. "Let's make this happen before I lose my nerve."

"Try to get Spelman out of her office," said Poly. "That should be a great place to look for clues."

My van drove to the parking lot for WT&F and found a spot close to the row of trees separating WT&F from Factor-E-Flor. Poly and I got into our invisibility gear and I opened Chit's bottle.

"Wazzup?" she said in a drowsy voice.

Bingo! She'd been sleeping. When she crawled out, her wing cases were painted in alternating black and yellow stripes. She looked like a Georgia Tech Yellow Jacket.

"We're going to sneak into Factor-E-Flor to look for clues about giant robots and plague spheres," I said. "You in?"

"Sure," said Chit. "Glad t'do my part t'save the galaxy."

"Again with the hyperbole," I said.

"Just callin' it like I see it," she said.

"Do you have anything in that backpack I can use to protect myself?" asked Pomy.

I rummaged around in my backpack. Flashlights wouldn't do much good. Then my fingers found something long and cylindrical. It was one of the Macerators' power pack cylinders. I gave it to Pomy and showed her how to trigger it, in case of emergency. Or in case we needed a really *big* diversion.

My van drove Pomy around to Factor-E-Flor's main entrance while Poly and I walked over to the back of their building from the WT&F parking lot. I climbed up the side of the Factor-E-Flor building using my gecko gloves and knee pads, then tossed them down so that Poly could climb up, too. My phone opened the rooftop maintenance door with its mutakey function and we descended to the second floor landing. I pulled the hallway door open, then closed it quickly as soon as Chit buzzed through.

"Watch this, folks," whispered my phone.

It had tapped into the building's security cameras somehow, and we were watching a real-time video from the main lobby where Pomy was arguing with the receptionist.

"You tell Ms. Agnes 'Fancy Pants' Spelman that she needs to teleport down here instantaneously and tell me what she's done with my sister and her boyfriend," said Pomy. "My mother and father are distraught and I'm disturbed enough to stand here and annoy you until I get some answers."

"I'm sorry, but no one sees Ms. Spelman without an appointment," said the receptionist, a little man with a precisely trimmed Van Dyke beard. "I'm sure I could find an opening on her schedule for you sometime next week. There's no one to speak with you today. Everyone is at a big off-site meeting to prepare for GALTEX."

"Don't try to put me off, buster," said Pomy, raising her voice. "I'm here to see Agnes Spelman and I want to see her right *now.*"

"What seems to be the problem, Hans?" said a trim black woman of medium height in a gray power suit.

"Bingo!" I said, opening the door so Poly and I could start our surreptitious investigations.

My phone muted the sound, but just before it stopped sharing images from the lobby camera I read Pomy's lips.

"I'm the problem!" she said. "Where's. My. Sister!"

Pomy was on track to keep Agnes Spelman busy for at least ten minutes so Poly and I set off down the hall. We'd agreed on the walk over that it was likely F-E-F used a similar layout to WT&F. Chit circled back and confirmed that was a valid assumption, then flew off again. Factor-E-Flor's executive offices were in the same part of this building. There weren't many people around, just a few senior admins at desks outside C-level offices. Poly and I headed for the front corner of the building where we expected to find Agnes Spelman's office.

When we got there our luck continued. No one was at the admin station outside what had to be the CEO's office. Poly put her hand on the middle of my back so I'd know she was right behind me. I opened the heavy hardwood office door and we slipped through. Poly closed it tightly behind us. I didn't take it as a good omen when the door's electronic lock whirred and a deadbolt was thrown by a solenoid, locking the two of us in. I turned around slowly and I assumed Poly did the same.

A tall black woman wearing glasses, an elegant black pantsuit, and an evil smile stood behind a large desk. She was holding a small, clear plastic bottle with a screw-on lid. Chit was inside and she didn't look happy. She was scrabbling around, trying to twist off the cap from the inside.

"Do what you're told and I'll poke air holes in the bottle," said the woman, who resembled Columbia Brown.

"Agnes Spelman?" I guessed.

"You can call me that," she replied. "And take off your Blend Into The Scenery suits. I've been tracking you on infrared since you entered the parking lot."

So much for playing ninja. Poly took off her B.I.T.S. suit and I took off my light-bending poncho, stuffing both into my backpack tool bag.

"If you're Agnes Spelman," said Poly, "who's in the lobby talking to my sister?"

"You mean Ms. Smith?" said Spelman. "She's my administrative assistant."

Cornell, Penn and Princeton had a female counterpart, it seemed.

"We've done what you've told us," I said, "now give my friend some air."

"Sit down," said Spelman, indicating a pair of client chairs in front of her desk, "and don't presume to give me orders."

She sat in a padded leather executive chair behind her desk, put Chit's bottle in the middle of her blotter, and idly toyed with a pointed, gold-plated letter opener. Ms. Smith entered her boss's office and tied our wrists and ankles to our chairs with heavy twine. After finishing her project with admirable efficiency, she left. I tested my bonds. We weren't going anywhere soon.

"Ms. Jones, Mr. Buckston," said Spelman. "Every time you answer a question honestly, I will give your little friend another air hole. Don't try lying—my glasses can detect changes in temperature on your faces and I'll know when you're lying."

"What do you want to know?" I said.

"A great deal," said Spelman, "starting with the detailed security plan for Queen Sherrhi on Saturday."

"I don't know anything about her security plans," I said. "That's Diágo and Tomáso's department."

"You seem to be telling the truth," said Spelman. "Anything to add, Ms. Jones?"

"Tomáso has an asteroid mining ship in orbit ready to blast the Emory quad if anything jeopardizes Queen Sherrhi's safety."

"Interesting," said Spelman, "and also true. That earns you an air hole."

Chit was on her back in the plastic bottle, her six legs waving feebly in the air. Agnes Spelman brought the point of the letter opener down sharply on the bottle's lid, creating a small, rectangular hole. Chit's legs stopped waving and she flipped herself back upright.

"Very good, Ms. Jones. Let's try another question, shall we? Where are my two missing robots?"

This time I answered.

"They're in the VIGorish Labs hangar near Hartsfield Port," I said. "Under guard by a squad of Capitol police."

Spelman picked up the bottle holding Chit and shook it vigorously. The little Murm lay stunned at the bottom of the bottle when she returned it to the top of her desk.

"That was only partly true, Mr. Buckston," she said. "Which part was the lie?"

"The guards," I said.

"Excellent," said Spelman. "Are my constructors there as well?"

"The octovacs? Yes, they're there."

"That wasn't so hard, was it," said Spelman.

Her voice was silky, but menacing. She lifted up the letter opener and stabbed the bottle's lid, opening another small air hole.

"One more," said Spelman. "What did that meddlesome Pâkk find out at the carnival?"

"I don't know," I said. "That's why we're here."

"He's still unconscious at the Dauushan consulate," added Poly.

Don't volunteer information that wasn't requested, I thought.

"They're keeping him sedated until he has more time to recover from the blow to the back of his head."

Ah, she's telling the truth, but not all of it. Poly was a skilled liar. I filed that data point away for future reference.

"I wish they'd found a more permanent solution," said Spelman, "but you can't get good help these days."

"Ms. Smith seems competent," I said, trying to drag out the conversation.

"I should have had her take care of the Pâkk."

"You won't get away with this," said Poly.

"Don't be melodramatic," said Spelman. "For all intents and purposes, my sister and I already have."

She pulled open a desk drawer and removed a polished metal sphere the size of a grapefruit. She tossed it up and caught it with one hand.

"How would the two of you like to help me test my new nanoparticles?" said Spelman. "We don't have much use for alien species except to serve Terrans, but those ancient Nicósn scientists certainly were effective cyberorganic organism designers."

"No, thanks," I said.

"Your loss," said Spelman, "but not your choice."

She was about to throw the sphere on the floor in front of us when there was the sound of a tremendous explosion and the office tilted. The sphere slipped out of her hand, dropped a few inches onto Spelman's desk blotter, and then rolled onto a thick Persian rug off to one side. Chit's bottle rolled off as well and ended up under Spelman's desk. Smoke was rising up from cracks in the floor. Spelman's chair had toppled over backwards with her in it. She seemed stunned and wasn't moving.

Poly's chair and my chair had both tipped over sideways. Being tied in protected us as we fell. My phone cut my wrists and ankles free and headed over to do the same for Poly. I looked for the bottle where Chit was held captive, but couldn't find it. Then my little friend flew out from under Spelman's desk looking as angry as a hornet. She saw Spelman on the floor, motionless, and started to head toward her. I didn't know what damage an inch and a half long Murm could do to a full-sized human, but I didn't want to find out.

"Don't damage the merchandise," I said to my little friend. "We need her as a hostage."

Chit's reply was unprintable.

Poly and I were back on our feet and were getting our bearings when we heard a sound like straining metal and the floor tilted again. An eight-foot gap opened in the middle of Spelman's office, separating Poly and me from Spelman and leaving a jagged opening in the outside wall. The building was vibrating and shaking. Three dimensional printed knickknacks, based on Factor-E-Flor designs, had fallen off shelves and were scattered around us. Poly and I were both back on the floor and sliding away from the gap toward the spot where the oak door to the CEO's office had been. Spelman's side of the office was tilting up in the opposite direction, so I lost sight of her.

Chit was better than either of us in operating in three dimensions. I saw her riding on top of the grapefruit-sized metal sphere, directing it toward me with her feet. I got to my hands and knees and captured the sphere before it could roll away from me, uncomfortably wedging it into a front pocket of my jeans. Chit hopped on my shoulder and Poly grabbed my backpack tool bag. We were both afraid the entire building would collapse with us in it.

Ms. Smith crawled toward us through the office door. She had a nasty looking pistol in her hand and was about to fire at us when Chit landed on the bridge of her nose and blew blasts of air in Ms. Smith's eyes with a flurry of wing beats, distracting her. Poly knocked the gun from her hands with a well-thrown scale model of an Easter Island Moai statue. We were so focused on Ms. Smith that we didn't notice the pair of octovacs that had come to rescue us.

The two helpful units grabbed us around our waists and pulled us out the wide crack in the side of the building and out into the bright May afternoon sunshine. They didn't seem to understand that we wanted them to go back and get Ms. Smith and Agnes Spelman, too. Pomy was outside standing on a narrow strip of grass between the building's sidewalk and the parking lot. The octovacs deposited us next to her.

"I'm so glad you're safe," she said, hugging us both.

Chit landed on Pomy's shoulder.

"Did *you* make everythin' go boom?" said my little friend.

"I guess so," she said.

"That was probably overkill," said Poly. "A three or a four on the Richter scale would have been plenty."

"Sorry about that," said Pomy. "You said you wanted a distraction. Ms. Smith threw me out so I planted the Macerator power pack cylinder Jack gave me in the bushes near the front entrance on my way out. Then I ran for Jack's van as fast as I could."

A light dawned. These office buildings were over fifteen years old. They'd been constructed before First Contact and still had natural gas lines feeding into them. Pomy must have dropped her power pack cylinder right on top of the gas main. I hoped the arson investigators never figured that out.

I had my phone direct the octovacs back into the building to search for Agnes Spelman and Ms. Smith, but of course, both were gone. They did help several other people get out. We were lucky there weren't any casualties. We got in my van and left before Clarisse Beatty and her team of firefighters could show up, heading back to Ad Astra. I'd fill Clarisse in on what happened later.

I called Tomáso to let him know we had a plague sphere and were bringing it to him *post haste*. Then I called Martin to let him know he needed to assign a police detail to the VIGorish Labs hangar ASAP, and maybe arrange for a company of well-armed National Guard troops to be conducting an exercise nearby. Next, I called Mike and gave him and update on what happened.

I guess we were even now. The Brown-Spelman sisters had blown up WT&F and we'd inadvertently done the same to Factor-E-Flor. I just hoped we could manage better than a draw when Queen Sherrhi spoke at Emory's graduation.

Chapter 36

"The infectiousness of crime is like that of the plague."
— Napoleon Bonaparte

I talked to Poly and Pomy and got their agreement to make a detour before going back to Ad Astra. Mistress Marigold's offices were a few miles out of the way, but I really wanted a second opinion about what was inside the sphere. Since Nicósn scientists had created the Compliant Plague originally, I thought Mistress Marigold's insights would be especially valuable. I called ahead to let her know we were coming and what I was bringing.

We were instructed to pull up to the MF&P loading dock and come up directly to the fifth floor where Mistress Marigold's personal lab was located. Venna, the head of security, opened the loading dock door and gave Poly, Pomy and me security badges and bracelets. Then she escorted us up to the lab. I was glad we didn't have to deal with Dree one floor up. A little of Dree goes a long way.

Mistress Marigold was waiting for us. I introduced her to Poly and Pomy.

"Pleased to meet you both," she said, "Now let's see this sphere."

She got straight to the point. Sometimes she was a kindly old flower seller, sometimes a no nonsense corporate executive. Right now, she was a single-minded scientist.

I handed her the grapefruit-sized sphere. She put it in a biological containment box with Plexiglas panels, then slid her arms into the sleeves and attached gloves that allowed her to manipulate items inside the box without risk of contamination. She noticed a seam around the center of the sphere and tried twisting the hemispheres apart, first one way, then the other. After a few turns, the sphere separated, revealing six vials of lavender liquid resting in a slots in a metal framework.

Thin plastic tubes in the vials' stoppers would feed the liquid to a small fan in the center of the sphere. It was rigged to go off when the sphere hit something hard enough to trigger a pressure switch.

Her short beard tentacles writhing in concentration, Mistress Marigold disconnected the pressure switch, neutralizing the device. Then she clipped off the feeder tube on one of the vials with two tiny hemostats. She cut between them like an obstetrician cutting an umbilical cord and lifted the isolated vial out of the metal framework. The vial went into a rack in the corner of the containment box and Mistress Marigold screwed the sphere back together. She dropped it into one plastic bag and sealed it, then a second one for good measure. Finally, she put the isolated vial in its own pair of sealed plastic bags, opened the containment box, and extended her hands with the bagged sphere out to me.

"Here," she said. "It's not live, but it's still dangerous. Don't drop it."

I took the sphere.

"I won't," I said.

"How long do I have?" she asked.

"If you can't get us a detailed analysis in twelve hours the fate of the galaxy could be at stake."

Whose says I can't use hyperbole with the best of them?

"Or sooner," said Poly.

"I'll try my best," said Mistress Marigold.

* * * * *

When we were back in my van I called Tomáso to let him know we'd be a few minutes late and informed him we'd left one of the vials with Mistress Marigold. Tomáso agreed that her input would be valuable and asked me if we'd mind dropping the sphere off with his task force contact at the Centers for Disease Control and Prevention, only three miles from where we were. On the drive from MF&P to the CDC we traveled through some beautiful older neighborhoods in Atlanta with tree-lined streets and charming homes. Pomy was impressed. This was her first real chance to see some of the nicer residential parts of the city and she liked them.

"How expensive are these places," she said, pointing at a row of houses from the 1930s.

"Expensive enough to need major help from Mom to buy them," said Poly. "You're welcome to stay in my apartment if you want to stick around Atlanta for a while."

"Thanks," said Pomy.

I could see that she was thinking about it.

My van dropped us off at the Clifton Road entrance to the CDC, just north of Emory's campus. Tomáso's contact, Dr. Mohamed Sugaiguntung, was waiting in the lobby and escort-ed us up three floors to his equivalent of Mistress Marigold's lab. He put the sphere in his containment box and carefully removed the remaining vials.

"Could you do me a favor?" I said, once the vials were safely stored for analysis.

"How can I help?" said Dr. Sugaiguntung, a tall, middle-aged Indonesian-American.

"Could I please have the sphere back?" I said. "I just thought of a way it might come in handy."

"Tomáso didn't say anything one way or another," said Dr. Sugaiguntung, "so I guess it's okay."

He screwed the two halves back together and removed the grapefruit sized sphere from the containment box.

"Here you go," he said. "Tomáso will have my report as soon as I finish my testing."

"You'd better hurry," said Poly. "The fate of the…"

"Thanks so much for your help," I said, putting the sphere in my pocket. "I'm sure Tomáso has told you how important it is to get your results soon."

"I'll get right on it," said Dr. Sugaiguntung. "It shouldn't take more than a few days."

Poly was ready to throttle the earnest government researcher.

I was glad that I'd had the forethought to get a more timely response from private enterprise.

I took Poly's forearm and gently pulled her toward the lab's exit. Pomy took her other arm and the two of us guided Poly back to my van, still sputtering about the work habits of government bureaucracies. Pomy tried changing the subject.

"It's five o'clock," she said. "Who's up for an early dinner? I'm starving."

"I am," I said. "What are you ladies hungry for?"

"What about Mom and Dad?" said Poly, temporarily off her soapbox. I hoped she wasn't advocating cannibalism.

"I'll text them," said Pomy. "I'm sure they'd like a romantic dinner without the three of us around—or two dozen Macerators dropping by."

"I'll bet they would," said Poly.

We'd all seen the way Perry and Barbara had been acting amorous since the adrenaline rush following Queen Sherrhi's dinner.

"Hey," said Pomy. "Is there anywhere in Atlanta to get good southern food?"

I smiled and had to exercise self-control not to laugh.

"Yes," said Poly, "that sounds great."

"With sweet tea," said Pomy.

"Everywhere in Atlanta serves sweet tea," said Poly.

"How was I to know?"

"We're not too far from Mary Mac's Tea Room on Ponce," I said. "It's been around for eighty-five years. Southern cooking and southern hospitality are their specialties."

"And you can get sweet tea there," said Poly, teasing her sister.

Pomy didn't rise to the bait.

"It's a Friday night," she said. "Do you think we'll have to wait long to get a table?"

"Not if you tell them you're Barbara Keen's daughters," I said.

Maybe we'd have a few hours to enjoy ourselves without something blowing up.

Chapter 37

"Success depends upon previous preparation, and without such preparation there is sure to be failure."
— Confucius

On the way to the restaurant I made a few phone calls. I checked in with Roger Joe-Bob Bacon and confirmed that his chief operating officer had taken care of the details I requested. Then I called Mike and Martin and made sure they understood their parts to play on Saturday morning. After conferring with Poly, I contacted Ray Ray, who was still in Newnan with his father. I asked him if he would be interested in joining Xenotech Support, since he couldn't exactly go back to O'Sullivan Fabrication. He was glad to sign on and Poly and I had just added our third employee. Ray Ray had more real world experience than Mike or Shuvvath and would be able to handle more complex technical issues while Poly and I were on our romantic getaway.

Then I had a couple of ideas that made me smile. I ran them by Poly and she enthusiastically agreed. First, I called Shuvvath and asked him if he thought he could get something from his Orishen contacts in Atlanta.

"It would not be a problem," he said.

"Great," I said. "Here's what I have in mind."

I told him.

"That would be of great value," said Shuvvath. "I am honored to assist in the enterprise."

"Excellent. Connect with Tomáso and make it so."

I gave the eager young Orishen contact info for the Dauushan consul.

"I will keep you informed on my progress," said Shuvvath.

"You don't need to do that," I said. "I trust you to get the job done. Just let me know if you run into any snafus or roadblocks."

344

"Snafus?" said Shuvvath.

How can anyone graduate with master's degrees in engineering from two different planets and not encounter that term?

"It's a Terran word meaning 'the normal status for any system is chaotic,'" I said.

"Understood," said Shuvvath. "I will only inform you if I encounter levels of chaos above the standard baseline."

"Right," I said.

But Shuvvath had already disconnected.

Friday afternoon traffic on Ponce de Leon Avenue was heavy, so I had time for a few more calls.

Tomáso picked up quickly and liked the idea I'd proposed to Shuvvath. Members of his staff would work the with young Orishen overnight to get everything in place. He closed by saying "Confusion to the enemy." We could hope. Then I tried the next person on my list.

"Hi Hither," I said. "This is Jack."

"Hello, Mr. Buckston," she said. "Is the Pâkk gentleman okay?"

"He will be in a few days," I said. "Did the singing work?"

"It did, it did!" she said, her voice bubbly and pleased. "Both rides are back to normal and my dad is delighted."

"I called because I'd like your help with something," I said. "Please make sure your dad is okay with it."

I explained what I had in mind. Hither got even more excited.

"This would help?" she said.

"I'm sure it will," I said.

"What fun!" she said. "Dad shouldn't have a problem with it. We don't open until noon tomorrow."

"That late?" I said.

"Uh huh," she said. "I analyzed the data from all our Saturday attendance figures over the past three years. When you map them against revenue, we don't earn enough to make opening earlier cost effective."

"Sounds like your dad's investment in your business degree is already paying off," I said.

"Dad may not think so," said Hither. "Mom and I had to gang up on him to get him to believe my findings."

"You know what they say about old dogs and new tricks," I said. "Let me know if you have any difficulties uncoupling the connections."

"It will be easy," she said. "Bruno and Uncle Richard will help."

She must mean the strong man and the knife thrower.

"I'm sending a few friends over, too. They should make it go quickly."

"Passed the beta, Alpha Zeta," said Hither.

I looked confused. My phone was kind enough to translate for me. I read the words it wrote on its screen.

"She means 'That's good.'"

I felt humbled. I could speak more than a dozen galactic languages, but I couldn't keep up with youth slang on my own planet. I wasn't twenty-two any more.

"Thanks again, and let your dad know I appreciate it."

"Uh huh," she said. "See you tomorrow."

Hither rang off.

Then I called CiCi and filled her in on my idea. She loved it and said she'd be at the Y. Y. Knot Carnival bright and early tomorrow. I sent a text to Ray Ray and he replied in seconds, saying he'd be there, too.

I had one more call to make. My phone, in its wisdom, decided to put it on speaker.

"Hi Mom," I said.

"Jack," she said. "It's great to hear from you. How are you doing?"

"I'm fine, Mom," I said. "The company is growing and I've got a new partner."

"Barbara Keen's older daughter?" she said. "I'd heard. I wondered when you were going to tell me about her."

"I've been busy, Mom."

"Too busy to tell me about getting a concussion and bruised ribs?" she said. "When were you going to share *those* little details?"

"How did you find out about...?"

"I have my ways," she said. "Now what do you want from your dear old mother?"

I told her.

"Oh," she said. "You don't ask for small favors. I'll have to think about it."

"Please do," I said. "It's important."

"I will," she said. "I'm in the neighborhood, by the way. Let's have lunch some time."

"That would be great, Mom," I said. "If I'm still alive by this time tomorrow it will be my treat."

"Now Jack," she said, "no need to indulge in hyperbole."

"Gotta go, Mom," I said. "I'm taking my partner and her sister to dinner."

"Give Poly and Pomy hugs for me," she said, and hung up.

"Your mother sounds nice," said Poly. "She also sounds like she knows a lot more than you expected."

"True enough," I said. "I wonder who's filling her in?"

"Something for another day," said Poly. "Do you think she'll come through?"

"Great question," I said. "I wish I knew the answer."

"And Jack," said Poly, "when were you going tell your mother about *me*?"

"Mary Mac's Tea Room," said my van.

Chapter 38

*"Sometimes I do need to go to karaoke,
sometimes I need to relax."*
— Jackie Chan

Poly, Pomy and I didn't have to stand in line for long. The decor was getting rundown—the last time they'd spruced the place up was in the Carter administration—but the food was excellent and our spirits were greatly revived. Pomy tried a glass of tea so sweet that her spoon nearly stood up in the glass. We enjoyed fried chicken, fried green tomatoes, fried okra and delicious cinnamon rolls. When we couldn't eat another bite, not even of banana cream pudding with vanilla wafers, we paid the check and waddled back to the front where my van was waiting. We climbed in and buckled up.

"Where to now?" asked Pomy.

"Eat, drink, and be merry," I said.

"Don't complete that quotation," said Poly. "We just ate, Pomy drank two glasses of sweet tea, and I'm ready to be merry."

"Karaoke?" I suggested. "There's a lounge at one of the hotels at Ad Astra that does karaoke on Friday nights. I've been there a few times and it's a blast."

"Works for me," said Poly.

"I'm in," said Pomy, "but karaoke is more fun with more people. Why don't you invite Mike and Cici and anybody else you can think of to join us?"

"Great idea," I said.

I sent a group text to Mike, CiCi, Ray Ray, Shuvvath and Hither, inviting them. I didn't try asking Martin and Apple— I knew how hard it was to get a sitter at the last minute, and besides, this was going to be a younger crowd. Everyone replied they'd try to make it. Half an hour later, my van dropped us off in front of the Paradigm Hotel at Ad Astra. The karaoke lounge there was called Sing Along with Pitch. No one was quite sure why. It was early enough that Pomy, Poly and I could hold a large table near the front. The karaoke didn't start until eight. I was as happy as a bivalve with Poly on my left and Pomy on my right.

I'd asked Chit if she wanted to join us, but she said she had shows to watch. Just as well. I'd heard her sing. My phone arranged to have an octovac drop off my backpack tool bag, with Chit's bottle, in my apartment after my van parked in Ad Astra's underground garage.

Mike and CiCi were the first to arrive. Neither of them lived far away and they were looking for opportunities to kick back and have fun as a couple. They took seats to my left, next to Poly.

"Great idea, Jack," said Mike.

"You haven't heard him sing," said Poly.

"Yes I have," said Mike. "Sometimes he hums and sings to himself while he's doing maintenance, especially when he doesn't think anyone is listening. He's not bad."

"Thanks for inviting us," said CiCi.

She was wearing a short black denim skort and one of the new wing-collared t-shirts that had recently become popular. Hers was Dauushan pink and had the logo for a band called Under the Rug, a reference to where the teleportation target was in the chairman of JPMorgan Chase's office. She wore ankle high pink boots. One of her knee socks was lime green, the other was florescent blue. Mike was in khakis and a white polo shirt, which reminded me that I had to order more company polo shirts. Ray Ray was probably an extra large and Mike a large, but I wasn't sure about Poly. I put my arm around her.

"What size polo shirt do you wear?" I asked, leaning close.

"Men's or women's?" she said.

"Uh, women's?" I said.

"Medium," she said.

I'd learned years ago not to assume I'd be able to guess a woman's clothing size. Ever since galactic fashions arrived on

Earth the sizing protocols had grown even more complicated, if that was possible. I'd thought we were done, but we obviously weren't.

"Banded sleeves or plain? Two or three buttons? One hundred percent cotton or a cotton-poly blend?" said Poly.

I had my phone send her a link to the catalog I used and let her pick exactly what she wanted. I sent Mike and Ray Ray the same link. The company would be billed for what they ordered. Then I did a double-take. What was I going to do for Shuvvath? Polo shirts didn't look good on a human-sized praying mantis. It turns out I wasn't the first business owner to have this problem. I found a site that made peel off logo stickers and sent them my artwork. They'd have a roll of a thousand stickers delivered to my apartment in less than twenty-four hours.

Ray Ray was the next to arrive. He said his autocab had made great time heading up from Newnan. Ray Ray was wearing black slacks, a lavender Oxford shirt, and a black leather Pâkk-style vest. Even to my uneducated eye, his ensemble looked a few years out of date. Maybe it was the only casual clothing he had at his father's place. I introduced Ray Ray to everyone else at the table and he slid in next to Pomy. The deejay was adjusting his equipment and doing a sound check. A server brought drinks for Ray Ray and Mike and CiCi. Ray Ray had a beer, but everyone else was sticking to flavored fizzy water.

I was looking at CiCi and Mike. Mike had a new job, but as far as I knew, CiCi was out of work. She'd been really helpful when the Macerators attacked and I'd asked for her assistance at the carnival in the morning. I whispered in Poly's ear. She nodded.

"Go ahead," she said.

I did.

"Hey CiCi," I said.

I didn't have to talk too loud because the music hadn't started playing. She looked my way.

"Do you know anything about galactic technology?"

"I know a hawk from a handsaw," she said. "I spent three

years as a field comm tech for the Irregulars. I know a lot about congruency-based communications gear."

She might be a very good fit for supporting all the network equipment in the sub-basement of the Georgia capitol.

"Which Irregulars?" I said.

"That information is only provided on a need to know basis," she said, smiling.

Obviously, she'd spent time with one of the secretive Terran mercenary companies hired out to assist in "trade disputes" between various species.

"Any formal technical training?"

"Two years and an associate degree in Galtech from the University of Maryland while I was deployed, sir."

She'd lapsed back into mil-speak. I'd worry about correcting that later.

"Would you be interested in joining Xenotech Support?" I said. "We'll help you get your bachelor's degree."

She started to say "Yes, sir!" but changed it to "You bet I would!" Maybe I wouldn't have to correct anything after all.

"One thing," said Poly, "you'll have to include the names of your past employers on your employment application."

"I'm sure the Colonel would be fine with it in that case," said CiCi. "He's got several acceptable false names we can use in that situation."

"I'll pretend I didn't hear that," said Poly, smiling. "Welcome aboard."

I was going to ask CiCi what size polo shirt she wore, but thought better of it and just sent her the same link I'd sent everyone else. Since Wednesday, Xenotech Support Corporation had tripled its number of employees.

Then Hither and Shuvvath rushed in together.

"Am I late?" asked Hither.

She was wearing a black sleeveless tunic over black and white striped tights with chunky red platform shoes. Shuvvath was wearing chitin.

"No, the music hasn't started yet," said Poly. "Have a seat."

"Order what you'd like from the bar or the menu," I said. "Tonight's celebration is on the company."

That brought smiles to everyone around the table. Hither sat next to Ray Ray to my right. Shuvvath squatted a bit lower at an empty spot at the table to *her* right. Once they'd made their drink orders, I introduced them to everyone else at the table.

"What event is being celebrated?" asked Shuvvath.

"Adding new employees to Xenotech Support," I said.

Poly squeezed my hand and beamed. I didn't worry about adding head count. The financial support from Queen Sherrhi would help us grow quickly.

"Hey Hither," I said. "You just got a degree in business administration, right?"

"Uh huh," she said, sipping a drink with a stick of Nicósn near-apple in it that had just been delivered.

"Did you specialize in any particular area of business administration?" I asked.

"Talent management," said Hither. "The latest academic euphemism for human and alien resources."

I looked at Poly.

"Go ahead," she said. "You're not sticking *me* with HR."

A minute later, Xenotech Support's head count increased to seven.

"I'll still want to run this by my Dad," said Hither.

"He'll be fine with it," I said. "Don't ask him, *tell* him. Experience with another company will be really helpful when it's time to take over the carnival."

Hither looked thoughtful, then she came to a decision.

"You're right," she said. "You offered me a job and I accepted. Dad will just have to live with it."

"Good for you," said Ray Ray. "My father keeps hinting that he wants me to run his company in a few years, but I'm not sure I want to."

Ray Ray and Hither started comparing notes about parental

guilt strategies and seemed to be hitting it off. Pomy added to the conversation with her own parental guilt stories. Shuvvath didn't have much to add—Orishen clans aren't into guilt trips.

Then the music started. Everyone around the table, even Shuvvath, had a decent singing voice. Some of us sang solos, some duets and mutually supportive trios. Poly and I sang a duet on *Don't Stop Believing* and got an enthusiastic round of applause. Hither, the voice major, blew the room away belting out *Defying Gravity* from *Wicked*. Later in the evening we all went on stage and sang *Proud Mary* with Shuvvath opening an extra set of spiracles to hit the really low notes on "Rollin' on the River."

Tomorrow would be a big day, so we didn't stay out late and our celebration started to break up. Mike and CiCi said they'd take Shuvvath home since he didn't live far from Mike's place. CiCi teased Mike that it was lucky his car had a sunroof or Shuvvath wouldn't be able to fit. Ray Ray told me he planned to get a room at one of the more affordable Ad Astra hotels, since he didn't want to go back to his apartment until we knew more about Sarah Lawrence Barnard or Columbia Brown or whatever her name was. He didn't seem to be in a hurry to leave. Hither had come on MARTA but I had my phone get her an autocab and charge it to the company.

"I don't think I want to go back to the suite this early," said Pomy.

"You're a good daughter," said Poly. "Mom and Dad would probably appreciate that."

"You're welcome to come over to my apartment for a while, if you'd like," I said.

Poly and Pomy exchanged a meaningful glance.

"I think I'd like to walk around the courtyard and get some air instead," said Pomy.

"You're a good *sister*, too," said Poly with a smile.

I put my arm around Poly and pulled her close.

"Don't do anything I wouldn't do," said Pomy.

"He won't *let* me do anything you'd do," said Poly, gently poking an elbow in my ribs.

"Hey," I said.

"Would you like some company on that walk around the courtyard?" asked Ray Ray. "I'm not ready to call it a night."

"Sure," said Pomy.

She slid her arm inside Ray Ray's elbow and tugged him toward the door from the lounge to the courtyard. He left wearing a pleased look on his face.

"Can I interest you in a nice cup of caffeine-free tea at my place?" I said.

"I'd rather make out," said Poly.

Chapter 39

"Romance is thinking about your significant other,
when you are supposed to be thinking about something else."
— Nicholas Sparks

Poly and I laughed when we walked into my apartment. The octovacs had left my backpack tool bag in its proper place on the table by my front door, but the sphere that had held the lavender liquid was sitting squarely on the flat upper surface of my top hat.

"Was that your idea?" I asked my phone.

"No," it replied. "The octovacs did that on their own."

I pulled Poly into my arms and gave her a long hug, then let go. Then I picked up the sphere, separated the two halves, and stepped into my project nook.

"Please make yourself comfortable," I said, calling over my shoulder. "I need a few minutes to add something special to the sphere."

"I'd rather see what you're doing," said Poly.

She stepped into the nook to join me.

"Okay. You can wake me up if something goes wrong."

"Wake you up?"

"I'm filling the sphere with Mistress Marigold's sleepy gas."

"Say what?"

"Some of my clients want me to cybernetically augment their pets and horses," I said.

"You mean like implanting tracker chips?" said Poly. "Isn't that something a veterinarian would handle?"

"Have you ever seen the old Pixar movie *Up?*"

"Of course," said Poly. "I must have watched it a dozen times when I was a kid."

"Do you remember…"

"Oh. Of course. The talking dog that kept being distracted by squirrels."

"Uh huh," I said. "The technology works more effectively on canines than felines, and the equine software is still experimental, but there are lots of people who want to understand what the animals in their lives are trying to communicate."

"Why haven't I heard about this already?"

"TelePety, Inc., the company behind the hardware and software, is keeping a low profile until they're ready for a national roll out."

"Does it work?" asked Poly.

"You mean 'Will pets talk in full sentences and communicate clearly?' No. But it's not bad for sharing broad concepts."

"I expect that dogs are all about smells and food and loyalty to their families," said Poly.

"Right," I said, "though some of them make unflattering comments about children who pull their tails."

"Who wouldn't?" said Poly.

"Cats, on the other hand…" I said.

"What about cats?"

"Cats are the reason for the high return rate on the equipment."

"There are some things pet owners don't want to know?" said Poly.

"Exactly," I said. "Owners don't like being referred to as minions and slaves."

"Who would?" said Poly.

"Would you believe that one of the bright techs at TelePety started working on cybernetic opposable thumbs for felines?" I said. "The company had to shut down the project after the first test subject locked her owners out of their apartment and opened a case of canned tuna fish."

Poly laughed, and I joined her.

"Is it hard to install the equipment?" she asked.

"No," I said, "but the pets need to be perfectly still for me to install their encephalomesh caps properly."

"Which is why you need the sleepy gas?"

"Correct," I said. "I'm not a trained anesthesiologist, so I can't use standard medical gasses like *methoxyflurane* or *methyl propyl ether.*"

"If you say so," said Poly.

"I mentioned my problem to Mistress Marigold months ago and she gave me a new, safe type of sleeping gas that doesn't require a license. It's used by carnivorous plants to make their victims easier to capture and ingest."

"Is it from that big plant in the executive lobby you told me about?"

"No, Dree doesn't need help to capture prey," I said. "It's from smaller plants that go after the Nicósn equivalents of moles and shrews and field mice."

"Okay," she said. "Remind me to be careful around carnivorous plants."

"It's not a problem unless you're on Nicós," I said. "The only ones on Earth are in Mistress Marigold's greenhouses."

"Good to know," she said.

Poly watched as I poured a small quantity of fine green powder into a vial and sealed it with a rubber cork with a plastic tube through it. Then I filled a second vial with water and rigged it so the water would contact the powder if the pressure switch I'd reconnected was triggered. Then I screwed the two hemispheres back together.

"Do you plan to test it?" asked Poly.

"Not unless you want to sleep with me here on the floor," I said. "Once water contacts the powder the gas is formed and anyone in the vicinity is out in seconds."

"I want to sleep with you," said Poly, "but I'd prefer to be in more comfortable surroundings."

"Roger that," I said. "Would you settle for making out on the sofa?"

Poly let me put the sphere in a padded section of my backpack tool bag before pulling me down on the sofa next to her.

"Ouch," I said.

"What's wrong?" said Poly.

"You may not have seen it, but a bullet hit me when I was up in the rafters at the Teleport Inn on Wednesday night."

"Again?" she said. Her tone was more concern than reproach. "Show me."

I pointed to my right side and Poly helped me lift up my t-shirt and pupa silk shirt. There was a circular purple bruise, but I didn't have any trouble breathing, so I didn't think any ribs were cracked.

"Poor baby," she said. "And what are all these low level bruises across your torso?"

"Bomb exploding in a freight elevator."

"Sounds like you've had adventures without me," said Poly.

I nodded.

"You can fill me in later."

It was too late for ice, so she just got me some extra strength pain reliever capsules and a glass of water. Then she straddled me and gently rested on my upper thighs, supporting most of her weigh with her knees. She smiled, leaned in, and kissed me. It was a pretty good position for me to make out with Poly without more pain from stretching my bruised right side. We were both really getting into it when my phone announced I had a call.

"If it's anyone except Mistress Marigold, say that I'm busy."

Poly kissed me again and I kissed her back. Gently.

"It's Mistress Marigold," said my phone.

"Right," I said. "Let me talk to her."

"Jack," she said, "I've got good news and bad news. Which do you want first?"

"The bad news."

"The lavender liquid is loaded with plague nanoparticles."

"Okay," I said. "What's the good news?"

She told me. I laughed and reminded myself to treat Professor Murriym and her husband to dinner at a Brazilian steakhouse.

"Thanks," I said. "Can you whip up a vaccine? By tomorrow morning?"

"I'll see what I can do," said Mistress Marigold.

"That's all I can ask."

We ended the call and Poly said she'd better walk back to her family's suite at the Star Palace since I clearly needed time to recuperate. I offered to walk her home but she just told me to go to bed. Which I did.

If things went as I expected, tomorrow would be a day when the future of the galaxy would be decided.

I hoped I didn't oversleep and miss it.

Chapter 40

"Patience is not simply the ability to wait—it's
how we behave while we're waiting."
— Joyce Meyer

I woke up five minutes before my phone would have started playing selections from the *1812 Overture*. It was only seven, but warm spring sunshine was streaming through the thin curtains covering my bedroom window. I'd had almost eight hours of sleep and felt full of energy, ready to face whatever the day would throw at me.

Emory's graduation ceremonies were at ten and I was picking Poly and her family up at the Star Palace at eight, so I had to get moving. After my shower, I put on my pupa silk shirt, then donned gray slacks and a white button front shirt. I added a maroon bow tie, matching suspenders, a light-weight navy blazer and a straw boater with a maroon and navy band. My great grandmother would have said I was the cat's pajamas.

I microwaved a Nicósn flat fish and nibbled on it while making last minute preparations. I put a plastic cylinder with several hundred zip ties in my backpack tool bag. I use them for organizing cables, but thought they might be handy for other purposes later this morning. I closed my bag, put it on one shoulder, and headed out to rendezvous with my van.

It was a picture perfect morning, with the blue sky looking freshly scrubbed and the fluffy white clouds looking especially three dimensional. The temperature was pleasantly warm, but I knew that it would be a lot warmer by ten and positively hot by noon. That was why Emory's administration had scheduled things to start so early. It was also why I was wearing a broad-brimmed hat—I made my own shade.

With a jaunty step, I got in my van, buckled my seat belt, and waved my arm in a "forward march" motion.

"To the Palace, noble steed."

My van's congruency-powered engine positively purred and we were in front of the hotel in less than a minute. Poly and her family were waiting outside. Poly got in the front passenger seat and gave me a kiss. She was wearing her morphic silk dress and carrying a bag that I assumed held her cap and gown. Pomy slid onto the rear bench seat, followed by Barbara and Perry. Everyone seemed to be in good spirits.

"Good morning," I said. "Did you all sleep well?"

In retrospect, that probably wasn't the smartest way of phrasing the question.

Perry looked self-satisfied and Barbara just smiled.

"We had a pleasant night, didn't we dear?" said Perry.

"I give the beds in the Star Palace five stars," said Barbara.

She looked over at Perry again and I thought I spotted a grin on her face in the rear view mirror. Sounds like Pomy had been wise to delay her return to the suite last night. She had a grin on her face, too. I wondered if she and Ray Ray had enjoyed their walk around the courtyard.

As we drove out of the Ad Astra complex, I noticed the two giant, pink, heavily armored Dauushan tanks parked on Peachtree in front of the consulate. Tomáso and Diágo weren't taking any chances with Queen Sherrhi and Princess Terrhi's safety. I was glad we weren't going to be stuck behind them on the way to Emory. Traffic wasn't bad until we got close to campus—it only took us twenty minutes to get there.

My van dropped us off near Glenn Memorial United Methodist Church, which doubled as the university's chapel. It was a short walk along the edge of the Baker Woodland, a forested nature preserve filled with thousands of trees and a narrow stream, to get to the Quadrangle, where the ceremonies would be held. The Quad was a long rectangle of green space dotted with mature oaks and other deciduous trees with broad canopies. A block long and a quarter of that wide, the Carlos Museum's white stone walls formed one side of the Quad. Libraries and administrative buildings lined the other three.

Carrying my backpack tool bag in my left hand and holding Poly's hand in my right, the five of us walked toward the site of the ceremonies. As we followed the sidewalk beside the Carlos, before turning left to head toward the stage, I heard the same scrabbling sounds from the shrubbery that I'd heard near my apartment. Emory must have a problem with chipmunks, just like Ad Astra. The cute little rodents would enjoy scavenging dropped kernels of popcorn from the booth providing small bags for free. The university's administration wanted to make sure attendees had enough salt in the Georgia heat. There were also shaded stands every forty feet selling water for a dollar a bottle. Dehydration must also be a problem.

The Quadrangle was covered with chairs, many already filled by parents, grandparents and other relatives of students about to graduate. A large stage was set up in the center of the long side of the Quad opposite the Carlos. I expect the stage was a lot larger than usual—Dauushan Queen Matriarchs take up a lot of space. I was pleased to see that Shuvvath had completed the project I'd assigned him. The young Orishen nymph was coming down one of the wide aisles between the rows of seats, heading our way. When he got close to us he had good news.

"Queen Sherrhi had the university reserve seats for you near the front," he said. "You'll have a great view."

He led us to our seats, at the front of the second section from the stage. The seats weren't typical folding chairs, either. We were in a block of two or three hundred shiny, round-backed upright chairs set aside for VIPs. Programs had been placed on each one.

My seat was on the left hand aisle. Pomy was next to me and Perry and Barbara were to her right. Shuvvath bobbed his head and went back toward the stage. I think he wanted to stay close to his project. I put my backpack tool bag under my seat.

We'd not only be able to see everything, we'd be able to hear it, too. The dozens of loudspeakers set up around the Quad would amplify the commencement speakers' voices—not that

Sherrhi would need it—and the echoes across all that open ground would make most dignitaries' words indecipherable. It didn't really matter. The people attending were coming to watch the pageantry, not to hear words of wisdom that hadn't changed since Socrates kicked his students out from under the sacred grove of Academe.

Poly gave me a quick kiss and hug, then waved to her family and headed off in the direction of the Administration Building at the far left of the Quad. I assumed that must be where the MBA candidates were gathering. Poly's morphic silk dress had adapted itself into a blue, white and yellow short sleeved dress that picked up the colors of the sky, clouds and sun. It would be a shame to cover it with black robes, but she'd only be wearing academic regalia for a few hours.

I turned around and noticed that lots of parents were arriving and filling in the seats that spread in row after row across the green space. I was surprised to see Professor Urrrson and Professor Murriym walking toward us from a path near the stage. Both were wearing their doctoral robes and hoods.

"Hello, Jack," said Professor Urrrson. "I'm glad to see you and Poly's family here. We've got a great day for the ceremony."

"Couldn't ask for better," I said.

"Barbara, Perry, Pomy," said Professor Urrrson, "this is my mate, Niaowla Murriym. She's on Emory's faculty, though she's never had the pleasure of teaching Poly."

Assorted handshakes and *pleased-to-meet-you* exchanges later I had a chance to pull Niaowla aside.

"I wanted to let you know that the practical joke you included in your translation of the Old High Nicósn inscriptions proved to be very helpful," I said.

"I'm always glad to know when one of my little amusements pays off," she said. "Please tell me how it all works out."

"You may get to see for yourself," I said.

"I'd like that."

Niaowla bent down and straightened my tie.

"Now, Bart and I have to get moving. We need to assemble with the faculty for our procession."

"Wait," I said. "He's not a member of Emory's faculty. How did you both get to wear your robes?"

"Niaowla pulled some strings," Bart said, "since I was Poly's adviser at Georgia Tech."

"I just like having him sit next to me through these boring things," said Niaowla, the corners of her mouth rising to show sharp, pointed teeth.

We all made goodbye noises and the two well-matched Ti-grammath academics walked toward the faculty mustering area holding hands. Dr. Liddell-Scott and Dr. Urradu came by where we were sitting a few minutes later. They weren't wearing regalia, since they were on the staff of the museum and could skip sitting with the faculty if they wanted. We went through a similar ritual, with Perry handling the introductions this time. Then Pomy, Perry, Kori Liddell-Scott and Urradu—whose numeric identifier last name I never learned—stood in the aisle in front of us. They were talking about classical languages and archeology. Barbara moved to sit next to me and the two of us chatted while the conversation around us became increasingly filled with specialized jargon.

"I liked your speech at Georgia Tech yesterday," I said.

"Thank you," said Poly's mother. "I tore up the one I'd written and started over."

"I figured," I said. "The one you gave was better."

"It put the focus back where it belonged," she said.

"On Poly," I said.

Barbara nodded.

"The two of you seem well-matched," she said. "You're good for her."

"And she's good for me."

"I'm sorry we fought for so long," said Barbara. "Poly and I are so much alike."

"You both picked being entrepreneurs over academia."

"And we're both really stubborn."

"Oh?" I said, smiling, as if I hadn't realized *that* before I'd even *met* Barbara.

Barbara nodded, acknowledging my understated response.

"It takes a stubborn streak to be a successful business owner," I said.

"But I should have paid for her master's degrees," said Barbara.

"If you had, I never would have met her," I said. "It's all turning out pretty well from my perspective."

"You'll let me know if she needs anything?" said Barbara. "She'll never ask."

"I'm not getting between the two of you," I said. "I value my life."

"That's probably best," she said. "If there's anything I can do for *you*—doors I can open for your company, introductions I can make—just let me know."

"Thank you," I said. "That's a generous offer and I may take you up on it."

I was thinking about last minute reservations for Guam or Maui or one of the Pyr pleasure planets. Then again, maybe asking my girlfriend's mother for help arranging a romantic week away with her daughter wasn't a wise idea.

A brass ensemble started warming up to the left of the stage. In the distance, I could hear the sound of heavy-duty engines. That must mean the Dauushan tanks had arrived with Sherrhi, Terrhi and Tomáso. It was nine forty-five and Diágo was cutting it close. I expect that he wisely wanted to minimize the time Queen Sherrhi was out in the open.

I stood and turned around again to reconnoiter. Most of the seats on the Quad were filled—except for the large blocks reserved for faculty and graduation candidates. There were only a few empty seats far in the back. If I hadn't turned, I wouldn't have noticed Roger Joe-Bob Bacon gliding up the aisle toward me. He stopped to say hello.

"Howdy," said the Pyr, using two of his mouths in stereo.

"Hi there," I said. "I'm surprised to see you here. I didn't think you had a dog in this hunt."

"Well, son," said Roger Joe-Bob, "let's just say I wanted to see what you had in mind for my little equipment loan."

"I hope neither one of us has to find out," I said.

"But you expect that we will."

"Yep."

"I didn't want to miss the excitement," said the Pyr. "Trouble follows you like a bloodhound trackin' a rabbit. Who's this charmin' lady?"

Roger Joe-Bob was motioning to Barbara. I'd just noticed she was standing behind me listening closely to the discussion.

"Barbara Keen," I said, "this is Roger Joe-Bob Bacon, operator of the best Waffle House in Atlanta and chairman of Khufu, Limited, in his spare time."

"Pleased t' meet you, m' dear," said the Pyr.

"Likewise," said Barbara. "I've heard good things about your company."

"An' I've enjoyed readin' your travel guides," said Roger Joe-Bob. "Your description of the mud wallows on Dauush was practically poetry."

"I'm glad you enjoyed it," said Barbara.

"I did," said Roger Joe-Bob, "though you might want to warn shorter species that the bottom drops off a mite quick. It took me a week to brush all the mud off my eyebrows."

"I'll make that note for the next edition of *Keen's Guide to Dauush*," said Barbara.

"Thank you kindly," said Roger Joe-Bob. "I wonder if you might consider speakin' at one of my corporate retreats?"

Roger Joe-Bob and Barbara moved a few feet to the side and kept talking. I wasn't part of their conversation, so I looked around, trying to identify anything suspicious. The crowds of parents, grandparents, family members and general well-wishers seemed like any cross section of Terrans with a smattering of GaFTA species. Everyone was dressed for the occasion and the heat. I did notice quite a few younger women with over-sized handbags and young men with well-stuffed backpacks. The former could just be a new style and as for the latter, who was I to talk?

The brass ensemble shifted from warming up to playing the first piece noted on the program, *Gaudeamus Igitur*. It was a signal that we should take our seats and pay attention to the ceremony. I sat down. Roger Joe-Bob headed off to an even better seat somewhere in front of us and Kori and Urradu left Perry and Pomy and walked back toward the Carlos. Pomy nearly skipped up to her mother. Perry was just a step behind his younger daughter, smiling.

"Mom, Mom, I've got great news!" she said.

"Can it wait until after the ceremony?" said Barbara.

"Uh, okay, I guess," said Pomy.

Her eyes flipped from sparkling to downcast.

"I'm sorry, dear," said Barbara, contritely. "Old habits die hard. What's your good news?"

Pomy's eyes flipped from downcast back to sparkling. Her smile was as bright as a congruency connected to a stellar corona.

"Dr. Liddell-Scott offered me a job at the museum through the end of the year," said Pomy. "I'll be working with the Roman and Greek artifacts in their collection."

"That sounds perfect for you," said her mother.

"Way to go," I said. "It will be nice having you around."

I gave Pomy a hug and absorbed some of the excited energy she was radiating.

"I start on Monday," said Pomy.

Her body couldn't keep still. She was a perfect exemplar of Newton's First Law—a body in motion stays in motion.

"I'm so happy for you," said Barbara, getting with the program. "You can stay with your sister."

There might be plenty of room for Pomy to stay at Poly's place if Poly decided to live with me. I'd have to try hard not to get too far ahead of myself.

Perry was beaming almost as much as his daughter.

"This will be an excellent career move for Pomy," he said. "Dr. Liddell-Scott knows everyone who's anyone in classical archeology."

Pomy agreed. If there'd been a ceiling above the Quadrangle, Pomy would have had to be pulled down off it.

The brass ensemble moved to its next selection, Charpentier's Prelude to *Te Deum*. It's stirring chords were worth listening to. Pomy and Perry took their seats on either side of Barbara and we all tried to calm down and focus on the ceremony.

Then there was activity on the stage. Several humans in doctoral robes came forward and sat to the right. Diágo and two other members of the Queen's Guard, Lohrri and Naddéo, came forward and took up what must have been prearranged positions on the lawn in front and to the sides. Next, Tomáso walked on stage and stood to the far left.

As the brass ensemble neared the climax of the *Te Deum,* Princess Terrhiluundramaki, Spike and Queen Sherrhiliandari-anne the Second took the stage. The crowd cheered and applauded. Terrans have always loved royalty and a queen was a queen, even if she stood eighteen feet tall and weighed more than a bulldozer. When the final notes sounded, the humans sat down, but the Dauushans didn't. There wasn't room on the stage for the redwood-sized logs Dauushans used as chairs.

Terrhi spotted me and waved. Queen Sherrhi put three sub-trunks around her daughter and pulled her close. Being royal requires a certain level of decorum and waving to friends probably isn't on the list of acceptable princess behaviors even if you still have your juvenile spots.

When the applause and cheers quieted down, the ensemble started to play Berlioz' *Triumphal March*. Faculty members marched in and stood at their seats on the right. I saw Professor Urrrson and Professor Murriym, looking tall and elegant in their colorful robes and was surprised to see Mistress Marigold marching not far behind them. I'd forgotten she was also a member of Emory's faculty, teaching one or two courses a year. Then the strains of Elgar's *Pomp and Circumstance,* the traditional music used for graduation ceremonies, filled the air.

Parents leaned out into the aisles and took photographs as the graduating students began *their* march toward the section reserved for them on the left. The students came forward, looking for their families. They smiled and waved without the constraint of maintaining royal decorum. Several Dauushans and Tōdons were in the student procession and found spots to stand below the stage not far from Tomáso.

Once all the students had entered and the music stopped, one of the humans on the stage—I assume the university president, since that was what was printed in the program—walked to the podium.

"Be seated," she said.

The faculty and the students sat. I pulled out my backpack tool bag, removed Chit's bottle, and popped its lid.

"Hey little buddy," I said, "do you want to see this ceremony live, or on screen?"

Chit stuck her head out. Her wing cases were painted in Emory's colors of blue, white and gold.

"I'm coming, I'm coming," she said. "This one promises to be a lot more interestin' than the last one."

"I think you're right," I said.

Chit climbed out and flew up to perch on my left shoulder. I hoped she wouldn't snore when we got to the boring parts. When she was that close to my ear she got *loud.* My phone climbed up from my belt to my right shoulder and extended a pseudopod with its mutacase to whisper in my ear.

"You've got a video call from Hither, Jack," it said. "Should I put her through?"

"The ceremony is just starting," I said, "It's not really convenient. Can it wait?"

"She says no," said my phone, "but she doesn't need to talk to you. She wants to show you a video. She says she just shot it."

"Fine," I said, softly. "Roll tape."

My phone climbed around to my lap where I could see Hither's video by looking down. I watched the images flash by. It was footage of the old Atlanta Falcon's Mercedes Benz stadium. Slowly, the flower-like petals of the stadium's re-tractable roof slid open and ten giant robots, hidden inside its unused dome, blasted into the sky heading east towards Emory.

So *that's* what Shepherd was doing at the carnival.

It looked like this ceremony would be a *lot* more interesting than the last one.

Chapter 41

"Chaos in the midst of chaos isn't funny,
but chaos in the midst of order is."
— Steve Martin

I wanted to shout "The robots are coming, the robots are coming," like Bilbo Baggins in a bad sci-fi remake of the Battle of Five Armies in *The Hobbit,* but I didn't. I sent a couple of texts. I also had to get word to Diágo, Tomáso and Queen Sherrhi as fast as possible. Tomáso's phone would probably be on silent, or set to only vibrate if Diágo wanted to reach him. I didn't have Diágo's number and this was too important to try calling Terrhi and getting her in trouble with her mom if she still had her phone in normal mode and it rang. Thankfully, I had a better solution.

"Hey Chit," I said, "Could you please fly over and tell Diágo, Tomáso and Queen Sherrhi that ten two-hundred-and-fifty-foot combat robots are on their way here?"

My little buddy stretched her wings and replied.

"I was right," she said. "This one's gonna be a lot more interestin' for sure. See ya later, bucko."

She took off and hovered beside each of the Dauushans, passing along my message. None of them seemed surprised. We all knew giant robots were on the agenda, we just didn't know when they'd make an appearance.

Another human speaker was droning on about the many milestones in the history of the university during the four years the undergraduates had been on campus when Queen Sherrhi nudged him with a sub-trunk. He stopped talking. When Queen Sherrhi nudges you, you notice.

"Ladies, gentlemen, and beings of all species," she began. "We have been notified of an emergency situation. Please vacate the Quadrangle immediately. Proceed in an orderly fashion."

Unfortunately, not even the voice of royal authority could change human nature. Thousands of people stood up and began milling about in a panic, behaving more like a demented mob than proud parents, grandparents and siblings. Then the robots appeared overhead—they were more like Megatron, the evil Decepticon from the Transformers movies, than the relatively more friendly eagles Bilbo saw. Everyone in the Quad looked up and gasped. Queen Sherrhi and her entourage were big, but the robots were enormous.

Three giant robots landed in open spots recently occupied by the Dauushans and Tōdons about to receive their diplomas. The rest landed around the periphery of the Quad wherever they could find places to put their feet. The robots closest to the stage reached down to pick up Queen Sherrhi, but their huge metal hands were butted away by Tomáso's bulk. Lohrri and Naddéo were heading for the ramp at the rear of the stage so they could help, too.

"Now," I told my phone.

"With pleasure," it said.

The shiny chairs we'd recently been sitting on began to reconfigure themselves. Their legs got longer and their curved tube backs opened and extended. Soon all two or three hundred chairs in our VIP section had morphed back into octovacs. *Thank you, Khufu, Limited.*

"Sic 'em," I said.

Like hosts of ghosts overwhelming the ships of the Corsairs of Umbar in *The Return of the King*, dozens of octovacs swarmed over each robot, removing any components their manipulative tentacles could reach. Before their pilots could react, the giant robots were stripped down to bare skeletons. Soon even the skeletons were disassembled and the octovacs had disappeared to the north, carrying components. Ten captured robot pilots were lined up under octovac guard in front of Diágo. An octovac makes a very effective set of handcuffs—they might even hold a Pyr.

While the octovacs disassembled, the shocked crowd continued to mill about. Once they realized the robots were no longer a threat, their priorities shifted from trying to get away to trying to find good vantage points for the show. Some even got popcorn. There are times when I despair for the lack of common sense in my species. When the last robot had been disassembled, things began to calm down.

Then I saw two more giant robots arriving overhead from the south—Mike and Martin. Better late than never. Unfortunately there were also two more robots coming in from the west. Columbia Brown and Agnes Spelman must have found other companies like WT&F to make replacements for the robots we'd captured. The sisters had been holding these two in reserve.

The four robots landed in the vacant space near the stage. They were all painted matte black and bristling with weapons. Thankfully, Mike had told me he was going to paint a large "X1" on the forehead of his robot, and a similarly sized "X2" on Martin's. *Go Team Xenotech!*

Before any machine guns could be fired or missiles launched, pairs of robots grappled. The octovacs were gone, transporting components away from the Quad, so they couldn't help. At this point I was less concerned with which side might win than I was with potential casualties if one of the giant 'bots fell over.

Mike must have been reading my mind. He grabbed one of the enemy robots under the arms and powered them both into the sky. His boot rocket blasts were directed against the sides of one of the university's libraries, not at any of the clumps of nearby spectators. The battle of behemoths continued hundreds of feet overhead.

Martin and the remaining robot were no longer grappling. Instead, they were trading punches like a pair of super heavyweights. Body blow after body blow landed, sounding like crushed cars falling on steel plates at a salvage yard. The scent of overheated hydraulic oil filled the air. Spectators were giving the two combatants plenty of room, not just because of what might happen if one of them fell over, but because chunks of metal were falling off the robots' frames whenever truck-sized steel fists landed.

Then I looked up. The two robots in the air weren't as high as they'd been. They were spinning together and their boot rockets were only pointed at the ground a fraction of the time. The intermittent thrust wasn't enough. They were starting to fall. It looked like two giant robots would crash into the center of the Quad, crushing hundreds of people, when one of the robots shifted its grip and grabbed its opponent around the knees, not the shoulders. From that vantage it could control the direction of the other robot's boot rockets and add the force of its own. The two of them were no longer tumbling together. It wasn't even Buzz Lightyear's *falling, with style*. It was a rocket propelled collision, but not with the people in the Quad. Instead, a small adjustment in vectors resulted in the second robot smashing head first into the trees in the Baker Woodland.

The first robot managed to pull up at the last minute. It had "X1" written on its forehead. Then my phone chirped. It was Mike.

"How did you like *that* flying," said Xenotech Support's first employee.

"Nice," I said. "Emory won't thank you for taking out so many trees."

"They'd be a lot *less* happy if the robot had taken out parents and graduates," said Mike.

"True enough," I said. "Well done. Please give Martin a hand if you can."

"Will do," said Mike.

But Martin didn't need any help.

Like the old game, Rock'em Sock'em Robots, that I'd discovered in a thrift store when I was seven, Martin had stopped throwing body blows and had shifted to defense, looking for an opening in his opponent's offense. When he finally saw it, he threw a massive uppercut, assisted by a brief blast from his boot rockets. The punch was so powerful Martin's opponent's head flew off and arched into the air toward the stage. Mike and his robot caught the errant head in mid-flight and gently lowered it to the ground on a clear spot next to the stage.

Emory security and City of Atlanta police officers pulled the shaken pilot out of the head—it was Penn. He didn't look like he'd be escaping from prison anytime soon. Penn hadn't been wearing his safety harness. He'd been knocked around enough when his robot's head detached that he might as well have been the recipient of an uppercut directly from Martin. I'd bet that Princeton would be found in the pilot's chair of the robot Mike had dealt with.

Several octovacs had returned from wherever they'd gone to dispose of robot parts and my phone assigned them to disassemble the headless robot and its detached head. Other octovacs continued south to deal with the robot in the woods.

Mike and Martin flew their robots a few hundred yards and touched down on two large concrete pads on either side of the entrance to the Carlos Museum on the far side of the Quadrangle. That was a smart move, because the Emory Buildings and Grounds folks would already have quite a time filling in the deep depressions left in the turf where the fourteen robots had stood. It could have been worse—at least they only had to fill in footprints.

I was pleased to see they were restarting the ceremonies. Emory's Facilities people wheeled out carts filled with traditional folding chairs and replaced the missing VIP octovac chairs with them. We resumed our seats. A few minutes later, the brass ensemble started playing *Pomp and Circumstance* again. The human speakers picked up where they'd left off and the audience—after ten minutes of terror—was glad to get back to what was usually a boring and predictable ritual. I was thrilled when Poly's name was called to receive the Asa Griggs Candler award for academic excellence. She smiled and waved at us from the stage and my phone caught the whole thing on video.

Pomy squeezed my hand with joy for her sister and Barbara and Perry looked proud when I glanced their way. Our seats really were great. I didn't need binoculars to see the stage and we could hear and understand all the speakers. Several dignitaries spoke—at great length but with little substance. After an interminable wait, it was time for Queen Sherrhi to give her speech. We'd survived so far without giant robots capturing her or Terrhi. I counted that as a win.

The Queen stepped forward, with Terrhi and Spike by her side.

"People of Earth," said the Queen, "esteemed faculty, distinguished guests, and graduating students…"

The Queen took a deep breath. Even Dauushans don't have unlimited lung capacity.

"We have come together today to celebrate the start of a new stage in the lives of these students, and a new stage in Dauushan-Terran relations."

A smattering of applause came from the spectators.

"There are three parts to this new relationship," said Queen Sherrhi. "First, Dauush will be working with Terran pharmaceutical companies to mass produce vaccines for new diseases as they are created, so that any delays between development of a reliable vaccine and its widespread availability are minimized."

This announcement was a big deal and lots of people clapped enthusiastically. The Dauushans were the galaxy's leading high volume manufacturers, and we couldn't seem to make vaccines fast enough here on Earth. The planet had lost thirty-five million people to the Nicósn Neue Flu in 2019 because of production delays. Come to think of it, Mistress Marigold had been one of the researchers instrumental in creating the Neue Flu vaccine. She hadn't said she'd found a similar cure for the Compliant Plague.

"Second," Queen Sherrhi continued, "Dauushan authorities have agreed to work with multiple branches of Terran law enforcement to stop the illegal flow of grajja from Terra to Dauush."

There was even more clapping this time. It was only six weeks ago that twenty Dauushans, hopped up on grajja powder sprayed on them by Earth First Militant terrorists, had gone on a mad rampage down Peachtree Street at the First Contact Day parade.

"And third," said the Queen, "my appearance here today is my own gambit to draw out radical Earth First Militant groups and encourage them to come forward to disrupt these proceedings. I stand before you as bait, so to speak. Until now, we've only been successful in capturing minor minions. Moving forward, we hope that we can learn enough from the prisoners currently in custody to identify the movement's ringleaders."

There was less applause and more head scratching after this royal announcement. People were working out that Queen Sherrhi had expected a terrorist attack from the beginning and hadn't warned any members of the audience. They were all inadvertent participants in the Queen's ploy to smoke out her enemies. Once the spectators figured that out, it wouldn't do much to improve Dauushan-Terran relations.

"There is far more at stake than you realize," said Queen Sherrhi. "The future of the entire galaxy hangs in the balance."

The crowd began to murmur. This wasn't what they expected to hear from a commencement speaker.

"*Sic semper tyrannis,*" shouted a man's voice behind me.

I turned and saw one of the young men with the large backpacks I'd noticed earlier holding a round metal sphere about the size of a grapefruit. It looked exactly like the sphere full of sleepy gas I had in my own backpack and I was confident it contained tubes of lavender liquid.

The man threw the sphere toward the stage in a high arc, following a path like the one the enemy robot's head took when Martin had knocked it off. Imitating her father, Terrhi squeezed all her trunks tightly together, forming a shovel or spatula. She intercepted the sphere and threw it back at the man with a Dauushan's strength and leverage. It hit him in the stomach and he went down, groaning.

"Nice one," I shouted at Terrhi.

She bowed.

I'd hoped that the robots had been the Evil Sisters' primary weapon, but after the Macerator operators had turned out to be hired from Craigslist, I'd expected the robots to be a diversion and had planned accordingly.

Other young men with backpacks and young women with oversized purses began pulling out spheres and shouting. I don't think the shouts were supposed to add much—they were just misdirection and distraction. There were older men with coolers and older women with shopping bags, too. I counted more than a hundred of them spread out across several rows in the front sections, where they were close enough to lob things at the stage.

Pomy, Perry and Barbara each picked someone with a sphere and did what they could to stop them. Pomy tripped an athletic man and plucked a sphere from his hand on his way down. While he was confused, she bonked him on the head with the sphere—hard enough to stun him, but not hard enough to trigger the pressure sensor. Barbara tricked a woman into turning around by opening her eyes wide in surprise, then bashed the woman with her purse. Perry had taken off his Harvard crimson tie and was using it as a makeshift garrote on a man with a Van Dyke beard holding a sphere in both hands. Other well-meaning attendees joined in, too.

I reached in my backpack tool bag and pulled out my collection of zip ties. I tossed several to Pomy, Barbara and Perry and they promptly tied up their "victims." Still, we were outnumbered twenty to one by the opposition.

"Where's the cavalry?" I asked my phone.

"Coming over the hill," it replied, "or the Administration building."

Seven small imagination stations from Y. Y. Knott's carnival ride, disconnected from their mechanical arms, flew over the roof of the admin building and added their assistance to our battle with the sphere throwers. They were configured as children's spaceships and looked like winged flying cars from *The Jetsons.* They flitted this way and that above the Earth First Militant terrorists, intercepting and collecting plague spheres with butterfly nets, baseball gloves and other creative accessories extruded by their ships.

Through the ships' transparent domes I could see that Hither, Ray Ray, and CiCi were piloting three of them. Older men I didn't recognize were operating two other ships. The large, bald man whose muscles had muscles must be Bruno and the dapper gent with a mustache who resembled an older version of Wesley from *The Princess Bride* was likely Hither's Uncle Richard.

I was glad for any extra help we could get and was even more pleased when two of the ships landed in the wide aisle next to me. They didn't have operators. Pomy got in one ship and shot up to look for targets. I waved to Hither's ship and climbed in the other imagination station, putting my backpack tool bag under my feet and buckling my flight harness securely. Then I pulled back on the yoke and took to the air. I wanted a bird's eye view of the chaos.

I didn't see any lavender smoke, so it looked like none of the spheres had been triggered yet. Thank goodness for small favors. On the other hand, there were more than a hundred sphere throwers, each with several spheres. Pomy, Perry, Barbara and the other volunteers continued to take out terrorists at ground level.

When one of the spheres came close to the stage I watched Shuvvath's project in action. He'd covered the front and sides of the stage with the same kind of Orishen mutable composite fiber panels I'd used on the kiddie train ride at the carnival. Like the Orishen mutacase on my phone, the panels responded to Shuvvath's mental commands and sent up extensions to divert and grab spheres that got that far. More than two dozen spheres were already tucked away under layers of panels, making it look like opaque bubble wrap.

Then I saw a commotion over in the students' section. Eight octovacs had returned from transporting robot components and my phone had worked with Poly to turn them into an exoskeleton and armor for her. One octovac rode on her chest and three more were on her shoulders and at the small of her back. She stood on another pair with their tentacles wrapped up around her legs. Like a matched set of bucklers, she had an octovac on the back of each of her hands with several tentacles spiraling up her arms. More tentacles stretched out from the octovacs on her hands extending her reach. Her black robes were held tightly against her body by shiny, segmented tentacles and somehow, incongruously, she'd retained her mortarboard hat.

Now that I think about it, she looked a lot like the tree character from *Guardians of the Galaxy*, the one that only knew three words. Poly didn't need words at all. She was identifying terrorist sphere throwers, incapacitating them, capturing their spheres, and collecting them in a pile below her, like so many skulls at the foot of the throne of a barbarian conqueror. Once she'd eliminated all the Earth First Militants in her vicinity, she had to shift a hundred feet to another, more target rich environment.

Then I noticed movement on the roof of the Carlos Museum. I was about to fly over and check it out when my phone chirped.

"It's Terrhi," said my phone. "She's crying."

"Put her through."

"Uncle Jack, Uncle Jack, you've got to help!" said Terrhi.

She was speaking, and sobbing, softly.

"What is it?" I said, using my most attentive and concerned tone of voice.

"It's Daddy," she said. "He's going to call for an energy beam."

"From the *Charalindhri?*" I asked.

"Uh huh," Terrhi said between sobs. "As soon as he can get Mom and me into the tanks and away from here."

"Thanks, Terrhi," I said. "I really appreciate the warning."

"I don't want you and Aunt Poly and Aunt Pomy to get crispy fried," she cried.

"We don't want that either," I said. "Don't worry. I'll figure out something."

"Spike and I know you will, Uncle Jack. You're our hero."

"Tell Spike to be brave," I said. "I've got to go."

"I will, Uncle Jack. Bye."

Terrhi closed the connection. I had my phone call a familiar number.

"Well, Mom, did you decide?" I said.

"What to do about that *small* favor you asked?" she said.

"Yes," I said. "Lives are at stake. Lots of lives."

"I've decided," she said.

"If it were done when 'tis done, then 'twere well it were done quickly," I said.

"Why couldn't you just say 'do it now'?"

"You're the one who gave me *The Complete Works of William Shakespeare* when I was seven."

"Don't be a smart ass to your mother."

"Why should I stop now?"

"Okay," she said, after a pause. "I'll do it."

"Thank you," I said. "I love you."

"I love you, too. Now go stop those sphere throwers," said my mom.

"What?"

"You heard me. I've been watching the Emory graduation ceremonies from up here in orbit."

"Thanks, Mom. You're the best Mom I ever had."

"Go!" she said, "We've both got things to do."

We ended the call.

I zoomed up another hundred feet to see more of what was

happening. Queen Sherrhi and Terrhi and Spike were still on the stage, but they were surrounded by Tomáso, Diágo and other members of the Queen's guard. The human dignitaries and speakers previously there had, quite wisely, left. The Orishen imagination station ships, Shuvvath's morphic panels and assistance from Perry, Barbara, and other volunteers from the crowd had turned the tide. More sphere throwers were now subdued than active.

Then I heard a shot from somewhere below me. I couldn't tell where it came from, but I thought it was generally from the far side of the Quadrangle. The roof of the Carlos Museum would be a perfect spot for assassins to hide if they wanted to hit someone on the stage.

The stage!

I shifted my gaze.

Queen Sherrhi was down.

Chapter 42

"We adore chaos because we love to produce order."
— M. C. Escher

I zoomed back to help protect the Queen, but it was too late. I parked my imagination station next to the stage, put my backpack tool bag over my shoulder, and circled around to climb up the human steps to the raised platform.

Tomáso looked angry enough to take on one of the enemy robots singlehandedly and win. Diágo was bending over his monarch.

"It's a tranquilizer dart, not a bullet," he said, removing a long, thick, feathered needle from Queen Sherrhi's side.

He kept his body between his queen and the front of the stage. After hearing the good news, Tomáso looked marginally more in control, but still seemed like a thundercloud ready to storm and throw lightning bolts.

A few moments later I was pleased to have Pomy and Poly, without her octovac armor, join me on the stage. Maybe the three of us could help Tomáso calm down and figure out how to get Queen Sherrhi out of there and to a place of safety. I looked around for ideas and found one.

"Tomáso," I said, "there's a carpet covering the stage. If you and Diágo and the guards each take a corner, you could carry Queen Sherrhi to one of the tanks."

The Queen's consort looked down at me with eyes as deep as black holes' gravity wells. He nodded.

"Make it so," he said.

Poly and Pomy pushed the podium and unneeded human-sized chairs off the stage. I moved to the back left corner and lifted up the carpet so that Lohrri could move to the bare platform and lift it, then repeated the same drill for the back right corner with Naddéo. Poly and Pomy were doing the same in the front for Tomáso and Diágo. I joined them.

Then we heard more gunshots—hundreds of them—but they weren't gunshots, they were spheres exploding in the Quad, releasing lavender mist. Spectators, the ones who were still around, anyway, began screaming and speeding toward the exits. Those caught by the mist collapsed, sound asleep. The spheres embedded in the stage's panels had exploded, too, but hadn't released their mist. The Orishen mutable composite fiber panels' layers were flexible and hadn't ruptured, holding in the purple vapor.

Tomáso uttered a sharp phrase in Dauushan best translated by the German word *schnell* and the four Dauushan adults carried the Queen down the ramp at the back of the stage and away from the lavender mist along a broad sidewalk. When they'd managed to carry her a hundred feet toward where the tanks were parked, Tomáso paused. The adults carefully put the Queen down. We were on a sidewalk lined with bushes covered in bright pink blossoms between two academic buildings. Tomáso took out his skateboard-sized phone.

"Stop!" I said. "You don't need to do this. The plague isn't what you…"

Unfortunately, Tomáso wasn't paying any attention to me. I grabbed one of his sub-trunks, but was like a mouse trying to stop a human by tugging on its pants cuff.

"Captain," he said, "do you have our position? Good. You know your orders. There's been a release. I need a full power sterilizing beam across the entire Quadrangle on my mark. Now."

For a few seconds nothing happened. Then I heard an anemic sound from his phone's speaker like the noise the hyperdrive on the Millennium Falcon made when it failed. I smiled. *Thanks, Mom.*

Tomáso looked disgusted. I was glad he wasn't looking at me. He put his phone away in a holster on his foreleg and picked up his corner of the carpet again. They carried the Queen another hundred feet. Poly and Pomy and I followed with Terrhi and Spike beside us, keeping in tight formation.

"Tomáso," I said, "you don't have to worry about the Compliant Plague."

"Why not?" he snapped. "Do you want us all to be turned into zombies doing Columbia Brown's bidding?"

"No," I said, "but Mistress Marigold analyzed a sample of what they'd produced. Professor Murriym…"

"Who?" said Tomáso. He'd forgotten I'd told him about her.

"She's a specialist in Old High Nicósn," said Poly. "The mate of my professor at Georgia Tech."

"Hrrrumph," snorted Tomáso.

"She thought the inscription Columbia Brown's people gave her was a practical joke, so she took some liberties with her translation," I said.

"And?" said Tomáso.

"It's not the Compliant Plague anymore," I said. "It's the *Complacent* Plague. It just makes you feel like not doing much of anything for a few hours."

"When were you going to tell me this?" said Tomáso. "*After* I incinerated hundreds of people?"

"Sorry about that." I said, "I tried, but you weren't ready to listen."

"Humans are strange," said Tomáso.

"You have no idea."

Tomáso, Diágo, and the guards picked up their corners of the carpet again and managed to get a bit closer to the tanks. Poly and Pomy and I walked to one side, near a row of blooming rhododendron bushes. Terrhi and Spike stayed with us.

In the distance, I heard the rotors of an industrial-sized hovercar heading our way.

I noticed movement off to the side. A tall black woman with short, tightly curled dark hair stepped out from a space between the bushes. She was wearing glasses and a triumphant expression. There was a pistol in her right hand and a sphere in her left, ready to throw. It was Columbia Brown.

"I'm here for the Queen," she said, "and the Princess."

Yeah, yeah, that's what they all say.

"You know you don't have the Compliant Plague in that sphere, right?" I said. "What you've got is more like a short-term tranquilizer."

"Either way will be effective for my purposes."

She sneered at me.

"How are your ribs feeling, Jack?" she said. "I didn't appreciate being trapped on that Orishen troop ship."

"Not sorry about that," I said.

"You'll be sorry about it when I've got the Queen and the Princess."

Spike growled. Terrhi held on to his neck.

"Keep that beast under control," said Ms. Brown.

She pointed her pistol at the unhappy tri-sabertooth.

"I need you and your mother alive," she said to Terrhi, "but I wouldn't mind putting a bullet through your cat."

Terrhi whimpered and pulled Spike close against her with her trunks. I heard a scurrying sound from the rhododendron. Blasted chipmunks. Tomáso took a step toward Columbia Brown.

"Stay back," she said. "I don't need you alive either."

She waved her gun at me and Poly and Pomy and the remaining Dauushans.

"Or any of you, for that matter," she said. "So sit tight and don't cause any trouble."

"I will enjoy dismembering you," said Tomáso.

Remind me never to threaten his family. Tomáso took another step forward. The noise from the industrial hovercar was getting louder.

"That's enough," said Columbia Brown. "Time for you all to chill out."

She raised the sphere above her head and threw it hard at the concrete sidewalk—but it never got there. Two of Dree's clones scurried out of the bushes. One of them intercepted the sphere and tossed it up in the air to the other clone, like they were playing volleyball back in the executive floor elevator lobby.

Columbia Brown lunged for the sphere, but the two clones thought she was playing and tossed it wherever Brown wasn't. After a few back and forth moves, Poly grabbed the sphere in mid-air and put it on the ground.

Terrhi picked up the sphere in three of her sub-trunks, pulled it back over her head and launched it at Columbia Brown like a rocket-propelled warhead from a bazooka. It hit Brown in the solar plexus, forcing the air from her lungs and knocking her to her knees. Before she could recover from the impact, Spike was on her. The big cat knocked her over and put a heavy paw down on the pistol in her gun hand.

"Good Spike, good boy," said Terrhi.

"Thanks, buddy," I said, taking the pistol away and joining Columbia Brown's wrists with zip ties.

Then the industrial-sized hovercar appeared above us. The four adult Dauushans crowded around their queen, forming a defensive barrier. The business end of a heavy caliber machine gun poked over the side of the hovercar. To add to our challenges, Ms. Smith, Agnes Spelman's executive assistant from Factor-E-Flor, stepped out from the same spot where Columbia Brown had been hiding. She pointed a pair of pistols at us and we all froze. Poly had moved a bit off to the side and I could see that she was considering attacking our latest opponent. To pull it off, she'd need a distraction.

I was about to try something, but didn't have to. Chit came flitting in from overhead and landed on Ms. Smith's nose, singing *I Am the Very Model of a Modern Major General* in a loud, braying voice that certainly wouldn't have passed an audition for the D'Oyly Carte Opera Company. Chit buzzed her wings in front of Ms. Smith's eyes to provide added distraction.

While the executive assistant was confused, Poly stepped between her two pistols and slammed the heel of her right hand into the center of Ms. Smith's chin. Smith's teeth snapped together and the woman toppled to the ground like a tree knocked over by a falling giant robot.

"That was impressive, Sis," said Pomy.

"Thanks," said Poly, rubbing her hand.

The machine gun operator in the hovercar above us shot off a couple of rounds to get us to back off from Ms. Smith and the immobilized Columbia Brown. We did. It's not wise to argue with a machine gun. To accent the point, a chunk of brick blown off the side of one of the nearby academic buildings by a bullet whacked me in the sternum, nearly knocking me over. My pupa silk shirt went rigid, but it would likely leave one heck of a bruise.

Tomáso and Diágo must not have been feeling wise. In a move so fast I had difficulty following it, Diágo knelt, then Tomáso climbed on his back. The Queen's consort stood on his back legs, and stretched out to his maximum height. He extended his trunks far enough to grab the far side of the giant, donut-shaped hovercar. Then he jerked down hard and flipped the machine gun operator, the pilot, and the two other men aboard out of the vehicle. Lorrhi and Naddéo plucked the sailing men out of the air and set them none to gently on the ground. The hovercar regained its equilibrium and remained floating above us.

I handed Poly and Pomy some zip ties and we bound the men's wrists. Poly had the honor of binding Ms. Sleeping Beauty Smith, collecting her two pistols in the process. She gave one to her sister. I kept the one from Columbia Brown.

"Way to go, guys," I said, complimenting Tomáso and Diágo. "Think you could toss me up there?"

By way of an answer, Tomáso grabbed me around the waist and threw me thirty feet into the air, up and over the side of the hovercar. I landed in the large open cargo space in the center and took the controls. Then I found a flat spot not far away and set the craft down. That accomplished, I shut the craft off and returned to the rest of the group. I hadn't even noticed my sore ribs when Tomáso had grabbed me. It must be all the adrenaline.

Mike and Martin arrived next. Martin and two City of

Atlanta police officers took charge of the prisoners and their weapons. Columbia Brown looked like she would have been much happier if our positions had been reversed.

"What do you think we should do with her?" said Martin.

I reached in my backpack tool bag and pulled out the sleepy gas sphere.

"Here," I said. "Put her in a sealed room and throw this in after her."

"Is it… ?" said Martin.

"Yes," I said. "The *real* Compliant Plague. Just be the first one to give her a command and she'll tell you anything."

Columbia Brown looked worried. I knew that if *she* had developed the real Compliant Plague she wouldn't have hesitated to use it. Martin might find interrogating his prisoner a lot easier if Columbia Brown thought her alternative was being a plague victim. Martin and his law enforcement colleagues led the prisoners away. It sounded like my friend was humming *Jailhouse Rock* as he prodded Columbia Brown along with her own pistol.

While Martin and I had been talking, emergency response personnel arrived on the scene. They gave Queen Sherrhi an injection of something that woke her up. I hoped it wasn't a grajja derivative. Tomáso and Terrhi hugged the Queen Matriarch and made happy Dauushan family noises. Diágo and the royal guards just looked relieved. Spike gave me an affectionate head butt and let me scritch him behind the ears before he returned to Terrhi.

Then Mistress Marigold found us. She was still in her academic robes and enticed the pair of Dree clones to approach her with drugged balls of ground meat, just like I had done on the seventh floor of MF&P's headquarters. Moments later, she put the sleepy plants in a sealed basket and took Poly and me aside for a quick conversation.

"I used extracts from plants native to Dree's homeworld and created a vaccine that should work for both the Compliant and Complacent versions of the bio-cybernetic nanoparticles."

"That was fast," I said.

"Nicósn biosciences have come a long way in fifteen thousand years."

"Tomáso will be happy about your vaccine," said Poly.

"I should hope so," said Mistress Marigold. "The Compliant plague is a terrible weapon and has no place in the Galactic Free Trade Association."

"I'm with you on that."

"The Dauushans will manufacture the vaccine in large quantities," said Mistress Marigold. "I'll arrange the licensing details with Tomáso."

"And you'll be revered as a medical miracle worker on Dauush as well as Terra."

Mistress Marigold's deep red Nicósn complexion got even deeper.

"Do come by and play with Dree when you get a chance," she said. "She's quite fond of you."

"I will," I said, "but not soon. I'm planning to be out of town for a while."

Mistress Marigold smiled like she knew entirely too much about what I was thinking.

Then Shuvvath came up and I congratulated him on a job well done. The panels he'd installed around the stage had helped prevent the spheres from landing there. I'd buy them and he could help me repurpose the panels so that Y. Y. Knott's carnival could transform another ride, or even two. It was the least I could do, given how helpful the imagination stations had been.

While I was talking to Shuvvath, CiCi appeared, saw Mike, and gave him a kiss worthy of the couple in Times Square after the end of World War II. When they came up for air, CiCi told me Hither needed the Jetsons' cars back soon, so they could be reattached to their ride before the carnival opened. That shouldn't be a problem.

We made quite a sight as we walked back to the Quadrangle—five adult Dauushans, a juvenile, a tri-sabertooth, five humans, an Orishen nymph, and a Nicósn with a pair of carnivorous plant clones. A light spring breeze had dissipated the remaining lavender mist, so we weren't going to be taking any unscheduled naps.

There were lots of recumbent bodies on the lawn of the Quad. It looked like the morning after an all-day and all-night drinking party. Folding chairs were scattered in every direction and none of them were upright. Perry, Barbara, and several volunteers had been close to the stage and avoided the mist. They were helping spectators injured in the chaos, assisting EMTs and other emergency medical personnel.

We were lucky. There weren't any fatalities or even serious injuries, except for a broken arm sustained by an associate dean who'd jumped off the stage instead of using the stairs. Bruno the Strongman had gotten his Jetsons' flying car stuck in one of the larger trees in the Quadrangle, but Hither and her Uncle Richard had gotten his ship free without much trouble. A few spectators were treated for bruises and scrapes, but we were lucky things hadn't been worse.

After Poly and Pomy and I had thanked Chit for her help, she'd gone back in her bottle. Chit said it was to watch her programs, but I think she needed a rest after all the excitement. I think we all did.

Chapter 43

"There cannot be a crisis next week.
My schedule is already full."
— Henry A. Kissinger

Poly and I sat on the edge of the stage while I looked at my imagination station. I was sorry Hither would have to take it back to the carnival in half an hour. It was a sweet ride. Poly was cuddled up against me, tucked under my right arm. She'd finally taken off her mortarboard. Somehow, through all the excitement, I'd kept my straw boater. Pomy sat on the wing of my imagination station a few feet away, smiling at us. Her station was parked close by, under a maple tree.

"Is it like this all the time?" said Pomy, kicking her legs back and forth like a kid on a swing.

"So far," said Poly.

"Hey," I said, grinning. "The last time things got this crazy was six weeks ago."

"The last time things got this crazy," said Poly, "was yesterday."

"Oh, yeah," I said.

I'd forgotten about the explosion at Factor-E-Flor.

"What are you going to do about the two robots standing next to the Carlos?" asked Pomy.

"I'm not sure," I said. "Send them back to Zwilniki's hangar?"

"I've got a better idea," said Pomy.

She shared it with Poly and me. We both laughed, Poly nearly doubled over.

I asked my phone to help with the remote reconfiguration. In a few minutes, the two robots had turned themselves into two-hundred-and-fifty-foot copies of the Colossus of Rhodes and the giant statue of Rameses II in Luxor.

"Perfect," said Pomy. "Let's see the Met and the British Museum match *that.*"

I rubbed Poly's back until she regained her composure. She was still grinning.

Maybe this would put us back in the good graces of Emory's administration after knocking over so many trees?

"Now all we need to do is find Agnes Spelman," I said.

Then I saw someone waving at me from the roof of the Carlos Museum on the far side of the Quad. No, it was two people. Could it be Kori Liddell-Scott and Urradu? The silhouettes didn't look right for them. I held up my phone and asked it to magnify. It was Shepherd. In one hand, he was holding Agnes Spelman up by her collar, and in the other he held a tranquilizer dart rifle. Poly saw him, too, and Pomy came around to see why we were laughing. That was one more loose end covered.

I waved back at Shepherd. He was either one tough Pâkk or one good actor.

"Would you take my imagination station up to fetch Shepherd?" I asked Pomy, pointing behind her. "I'll slave it to yours."

"Glad to," she said.

Pomy took off and Poly and I had a moment alone.

"Any other loose ends you can think of?" I said.

"Plenty," said Poly, "but none I want to worry about now. Mom and Dad can take an autocab back to the hotel."

"And Martin can handle interrogating Brown, Smith and Spelman."

"True," said Poly. "Along with Penn and Princeton."

I waved my free hand out across Quadrangle.

"Our new employees look like they're good at their jobs."

"What *are* their jobs?"

"Whatever we need them to be." I said. "They can handle it."

"Works for me," she said. "Let's find somewhere else to be."

"You don't want to stick around and attend a rescheduled graduation ceremony?"

"I'll be perfectly happy to pick up my diploma at the Registrar's office," said Poly.

"Want to pick it up now?"

"It can wait," she said. "I hope to have other plans."

She snuggled in closer and squeezed my hand.

"Oh," I said, "In that case, where do you want to go on our romantic week away?"

I pulled up my list on my phone. Poly extracted her smaller phone from somewhere under her robes and did the same. On the count of three we held our screens together. Then we laughed.

We'd both selected the same destination as our number one choice. It wasn't all that romantic, but it was a perfect place for a couple of tech nerds.

GALTEX, the Galactic Technology Exposition, was next week.

Las Vegas, here we come.

Please visit

www.XenotechSupport.com

for more details about
the universe of Xenotech Support
and the Galactic Free Trade Association

Jack & Poly's adventures will continue in

Xenotech What Happens

Sign up for the Xenotech Support mailing list
on the web site to get advance notice of publication.

Find out what *really* happened
on First Contact Day when Earth
was invited to join the
Galactic Free Trade Association in

Xenotech
The Man Who Sold the Earth

available for Kindle on Amazon.com

You may also enjoy

From Artifact Imprints
Communion of Dreams

by James T. Downey
www.communionofdreams.com